No Good Deed

THE CHRONICLES OF BREED: BOOK FIVE

K.T. DAVIES

SCIMITAR MEDIA

Published by Scimitar Media

www.scimitar-media.co.uk

ISBN-13: 978-1999747480

Cover design by Scimitar Media

Original cover art by Michael Gauss

To Raven and Gabe,

the best rum crew a cove could wish for

Chapter One

There are times in life when you cannot retreat or advance. Like a fly in amber, you are trapped in a moment, unable to do anything but observe just how deep the pot of arsepickle is in which you are drowning.

Sharp fangs fastened on my neck. Pain flared, the fire in me died, and the world spun into frozen darkness and dragged me down…

It wasn't the first time I had been bitten by something, but it was the first time a blood drinker had got their fangs into me. Having been on both ends of a good bite, I could say with certainty that it wasn't like being gnawed by a wild animal or a pel-addicted gutterling. Like the bite of a mosquito, the strike was precise. There was a loud crunch as skin and scale were pierced, followed by a nerve searing pain that drilled down into neck tendons and left me paralyzed in the iron grip of my attacker. My fury vanished, and consciousness slipped from my grasp like a handful of water. So, this was how I ended, not as I had expected, with a bang, but a whimper.

Despite the hot suns beating down, the courtyard was airy. Draped across the shuttered houses, magenta bougainvillea flowers glowed in the fierce light. In the center of the deserted square, a fountain in the shape of a dragon spewed a stream of diamond-bright water. Thirsty, I closed my eyes, dipped my head in the shimmering bowl, and drank. Rather than quench my thirst, the water burned. I opened my eyes, saw red. Blood dripped from the dragon's mouth, filled the bowl, stained the polished cobbles. Drenched in scarlet, I gagged.

As cold as death, a bony hand clamped over my mouth. "Don't fight," someone whispered as visions of memories that were not mine tumbled through my mind. It felt like I was drowning in a stranger's dreams as people and places died and fell to ruin over and over again.

"Rest," someone commanded. "Be calm, forget."

My racing heart slowed. The hard edge of the waking world crashed through the walls of my dreaming mind, and the strange memories faded like mist in suns' light. I opened my eyes and saw Effie and Swann. They were wrapped in each other's arms and although they looked pensive, they seemed less terrified than when I was about to burn their house down, something which, on reflection, was a little rude of me. Beside me, resting on his slender haunches was someone I had not seen in a lifetime.

I licked my parched lips, tasted iron. "Leo?"

He canted his head, an expression of amusement and surprise writ upon his rattish visage. His obsidian eyes reflected my blood-splattered physog.

"That's Duke Leo to you," he said. His tail whipped around his slender, silk-clad body as he gracefully climbed to his feet. The prehensile tip tucked itself into the pocket of his black taffeta coat. "Have we met?" He peered harder, as though attempting to read my thoughts in my face. I wished him luck in that, for I wasn't thinking much of anything. I had gone from burning hot to ice cold and was stunned by the transformation. I wondered if, like a quenched blade I would be tempered by the experience of almost succumbing to the Paradox of Power or be shattered by it.

"I don't know," I answered honestly.

He snorted dismissively. "No, of course, you don't. You're drunk." A sly smile played upon his ruby lips. "On me."

I looked at my hand. The skin was already scabbing over, and a couple of fingers that I was sure had been broken appeared whole. I tested my injured leg. It didn't hurt. I wiggled my toes and found that they performed the task most admirably. "That's odd."

"I have healed you," said Leo. "Now get up. You are coming with me."

I did as I was bid without questioning my compliance. Swann put his arm around Effie, squeezed her shoulder reassuringly. Leo turned to him. "You too."

The talismancer's face dropped. "Hey, now, Jimma. I've done my part—" he began.

"You're done when I say you're done." Leo's tone of voice remained icily calm, but his tail twitched warningly.

"Just a minute…" Effie began. Leo fixed her with his cold, black stare. She swallowed and took an involuntary step back. "If you hurt him…"

"It'll be all right, love," said Swann without conviction.

Leo politely inclined his head to Effie. "You have my word, madam. As long as your beloved does as I tell him, all will be well."

"I think you'd better leave, Duke," said Swann, shielding Effie with his skinny body. Runes inscribed upon the wall, which had lain dormant and unseen until now, began to glow with a lurid, green light.

Leo smiled, displaying his pearly white fangs. "A show of strength? How delightful. Of course, you are aware that if you invite me into your demesne, you render yourself powerless?"

Swann blushed. "Er…"

He looked at me. I shrugged.

Leo chuckled. "We learn something new every day, eh?"

The light of the runes faded.

Leo nodded. "Congratulations. You passed the idiot test. Now, say farewell to your wench."

Swann almost dragged a furious Effie from the room. I didn't catch what they said to each other, but the tone of their whispered words was sharp.

Leo chuckled. "Lovers' tiffs are so amusing, don't you think?"

A carriage drawn by a team of night-black horses was waiting outside of the talismancer's abode. The hulking driver was wearing a heavy coat with the collar turned up and a wide-brimmed hat pulled down over his face. He looked up as we left the house, red eyes shining from beneath the brim. He didn't speak but acknowledged the duke with a nod.

Hooded and with his face averted from the encroaching light of dawn, Leo climbed aboard. "Get in," he commanded. Still shivering and disorientated, I nonetheless meekly complied. Swann was more hesitant and cast a longing glance towards his lover standing by the door, her tear-streaked face a mask of rage and sorrow.

I sat beside Swann. A thin trickle of blood ran down my neck, hot against my cold skin. It was hard to reconcile that my attacker was the dollish fellow sitting opposite with his dainty daddles folded on his lap, looking for all the world like butter wouldn't melt. The driver's whip cracked, and the horses set off at a brisk canter. The road was rough, and we jounced from side to side as they raced the light to our unknown destination. More than once during the wild ride, Swann and I were thrown together.

Notwithstanding my current condition, I had it in mind to beat the tar out of the pel-addled prick as soon as the chance presented itself. Upon seeing my unconcealed antipathy, he took every opportunity to try to mend our friendship with reassuring and comradely smiles. I replied with hard-eyed stares to let him know that we were no longer friends. That I bore no malice towards the duke was a puzzle which, as soon as I turned my attention to it, seemed to be of so little import that I quickly forgot all about it.

"Do you mind if I smoke, jimma…Your Grace?" Swann enquired.

"Yes, I do," said Leo. "It's bad for your health."

Silence descended. After about half an hour, the duke hammered on the roof and raised the window blind. The carriage slewed to a halt. Curious, I peered out of the window and saw that we were on a rise, which afforded an excellent view of the wounded city.

North of the river, a sizable portion of Valen was aflame. On the slopes below, looters were running through the streets, chased by the vengeful cries of the recently dispossessed. There was no sign of the city guards. I imagined it was because they were all swarming over the rubble of the royal palace and were too busy to protect the common citizens. In the distance, an ominous pall of smoke marked the location of the gilded ziggurat that should have been Ludo's tomb.

"Behold; the destruction you have wrought," Leo intoned from the shadow of his hood.

"Sh…shame on you, Swann," I said, my teeth chattering and sweat pouring off me like I was running a fever.

Swann looked aghast. "Oh, no, jimma. This is all yours."

"It wasn't my fault," I said with as much indignation as I could muster. Neither of them looked convinced.

The tip of Leo's tail twitched. He laced his fingers, fire dancing in his black eyes. "If not yours, then whose fault is it?"

"Ludo's," I said without a moment's hesitation, for I believed it to be true.

His lordship nodded slowly, although I didn't think it was because he believed me. It felt more like my words had confirmed his own thoughts with regards to the small matter of why the city was afire. "We will speak more of him when we reach my demesne."

"Could we talk now? Only, I've got somewhere to be." I offered in the vain hope he might let me go so I could finish what I'd started. "People to kill, you know how it is."

He looked at me like I was a turd in a jar before hammering his bony fist on the roof. The carriage lurched forward, and the horses charged through the smoke. Part of me considered that I should make a run for it before we reached any fucking 'demesne', but something stronger than hate kept my arse on the seat. I noted in passing that my reluctance to do a runner was far less concerning than it should have been. While I continued to ponder my uncharacteristic lack of gumption, the carriage drew to a halt. The air tasted of salt and corruption.

I had expected Leo's lair to be beneath the city, where the other Leo had resided. But we were above ground, under the covered carriageway of an aged mansion. Elegant and decrepit, old cracks crawled through the walls like frozen lightning. A short flight of submerged steps led to a black and white tiled entrance, shielded from the wan suns' light by an intricate, coffered ceiling. An inch of water lent a shimmering luster to the floor. We were in the marshes; the dying land where freshwater bog met the incoming sea. A roiling fog surrounded the mansion, but to the north, I spied the maudlin spires of tombs poking above the ancient cemetery walls.

The duke did not disembark with Swann and me. He stayed in the carriage, which was driven away without explanation. A cold wind sighed like a dying breath as a pair of verdigrised copper-clad doors swung open, inviting us to enter.

"Well, isn't this lovely?" I said as I admired the sepulchral entrance, which was wreathed in an unnatural darkness. "What do you think, Swann? Do you like the demesne of your—sorry, *our* benefactor?"

The talismancer rose to the bait and rounded on me. "You left me little choice, jimma. If it is any consolation, he offered to help you. I didn't ask."

"Funnily enough, it isn't." I made a point of wiping the blood from my neck. "Pray tell, how did that conversation go? 'Excuse me, Mr. Talismancer, could I bite your friend on the neck, suck out their blood, and give them some of mine to drink?' 'Why certainly, Mr. Infernal, be my guest.'"

"Was that supposed to be an impression of me?"

"The second one? Yes."

"I don't sound like that."

"Yes, you do."

"That sounded like a rat with its bollocks in a knot."

"I was going for weasel, but close enough."

"Listen, Chas. You broke the Paradox of Power." He ran his hand through his straggly hair like he was searching for something in his mousy thatch. "You were going to die, and gods only knew who else you would have taken with you."

I hated it when people confronted me with the truth when I was trying to be angry. It really threw me off my stride. "You could have…scribed something, or made a charm, or talisman. You could have done something other than give me to a fucking blood drinker. They wield powerful magic, you know?"

"That you almost took my fucking head off was a bit of a clue, aye. There just wasn't time to do anything save accept his offer of help, and he did save you."

"He saved *you,* don't you mean?"

He fumbled his pipe from his pocket, flicked his fingers and conjured a light. "I didn't know he was going to do what he did. He just said he could help." He lit the pipe, took a long pull, and closed his eyes. "I saved you from the ziggurat, don't forget that."

I couldn't dispute that, but damn it, part of me wished he'd just left me. "Next time someone offers to help you, maybe find out how before you accept."

"I'm sorry, jimma."

The doors creaked like they were laughing. "After you." I smiled tightly and stepped aside.

Swann paused on the threshold, closed his eyes, and grasped one of the many charms hanging around his neck before entering. I followed him into the entrance hall, which immediately lit up with fools' fire that burned eerily blue in obsidian sconces. A marble staircase with an iron balustrade sculpted to look like wild briars climbed to a shadow-wreathed landing. Living creepers had been left to run wild and grew in thick profusion up the walls, desperate to reach the faint rays of light that bled through cracks in the ceiling. Once we were inside, the door closed behind us of their own volition. "What do you think we should do?" said Swann between puffs of his pipe.

"Wait until the Dimber-Damber's had his beauty sleep, I suppose." Exhausted, I sat on the steps.

"How are you feeling?" Swann asked.

"Bit late to ask now, isn't it?"

"Let us not go over that again, jimma. You seem unnaturally…You don't seem yourself." I could only assume he was hedging because he was afraid of Leo.

"In what way?"

He looked around nervously before lowering his voice and continuing. "You seem unusually compliant."

Ludo's face appeared briefly in my mind's eye, and part of me knew that I should be hunting the bastard down, not sitting in a derelict mansion with this pricklet. An agile rat scuttled up the vine.

"Chas?"

"What?" Swann was looking at me with a concerned expression on his face. "What were we talking about?"

"Never mind."

While we waited, Swann paced and did his damnedest to smoke himself into a stupor. After the exertions of the previous few days, I fell asleep and woke when the door opposite the stair swung open.

"Enter," called Leo.

Muttering under his breath, Swann stumbled across the hall. I stood up, yawned, and stretched stiff limbs before following him. Like the captain of a haunted ship, Leo was standing on a raised walkway that ran around the perimeter of a once grand chamber. He was framed by what had been a gracefully arched window. The glass had long gone. The carved, marble fretwork had cracked and crumbled. Although the room was open to the elements, it was elegant in its decrepitude, lit as it was by foxfire lanterns and the bloodred afterglow of suns' set.

Swann sketched an awkward bow. "No offence, your grace, but I need to go home. My partner will be worried sick, you know?" He gripped a handful of charms.

Leo gave a thin-lipped smile. "Ah, yes, the beautiful Effie. I like her." He yawned, his tail swishing lazily. "She has fire. I like that in a person; much like a moth to a flame, warmth draws me." It was a subtle threat but not lost on Swann who, despite being a cunt, wasn't stupid. His shoulders dropped.

I confess, I was grateful to the talismancer. For once, the sharp edge of Saint Fuckery's eye wasn't entirely fixed on me. Leo locked his hands behind his back, his eyes narrowed against the fatal bleed of sunlight dying on the marshes. As the day died, the children of the night came out to play. Rats, big and small, old, and young came to join us. Those not bent on chasing roaches or each other sat back on their haunches, whiskers twitching, bright eyes regarding Swann and me with idle curiosity.

A sleek, white rat scampered up to Leo and pawed at his ankle. He picked it up. "I suppose you're wondering why I've brought you here."

"I was more wondering why you sucked my blood and then force fed me yours," I said. Swann groaned and gave me a warning look which I ignored.

Leo smiled at the rat, kissed its tiny noggin like a doting father. "You bled on the book."

"I don't understand. Is that a metaphor?" I looked to Swann, but he just shrugged.

With his attention still on the rat, Leo reached inside his coat and pulled out the little poetry book I'd taken from the tomb.

"I fucking knew it. What did I say? Never rob tombs in ancient cemeteries. Never. I should have known."

"Yes, you really should," said Leo, clearly enjoying himself. "Your blood was familiar to me. It reminded me of an old friend. Alas, one who is no longer with us."

My heart quickened. "Mother Blake?"

He nodded, tucked the book back inside his coat. "It is not my custom to speak of the dead." The white rat clambered onto his shoulder, burrowed into his dark curls, and wrapped its tail around his bloodless neck.

"She was my mother."

Jaw tight, he nodded again. "I was very fond of her."

I wanted to say 'so was I' but that would have been a lie. It's not that thoasa don't have feelings, it's just that they're deeper than those humans seem to experience, not portioned out and sliced so thin that every utterance has a different meaning depending on length and pitch. She was my mother, and I felt like I had been eviscerated when she was murdered. The void she left in my life could never be filled, but I was not *fond* of her. She was as mean as a snake with its tail on fire— and that was on a good day. "Listen, Duke. I don't mean to push the point, but as I've already done you a solid by retrieving your book, and as dear old mama was your mucker, we should part as friends who've done each other a good deed, what say you?"

"What about me?" Swann looked aghast.

"You can boil in your own piss for all I care," I side-mouthed while keeping my peepers on the blood drinker.

Leo sighed heavily. "Ludorius has destroyed the Midnight Court. He has brought about the deaths of dozens of my fellow princes. He has turned friend against friend." He dropped his unwavering gaze on me. "There is anarchy, disarray."

"'Tis beyond dispute that he is without doubt the king of cunts. You have my word; I will end him forthwith."

His tail twitched. "A laudable sentiment."

I bowed. "Glad we agree. It was a delight, but I cannot tarry for as the saying goes, 'vengeance waits for no thoasa'."

"I have need of your services," he said before I had chance to leg it.

Now it was my turn to sigh. "There has to be a hundred enforcers who will gladly help you become King of the Court. You don't need me, your Dukeness."

He laughed softly, displaying the little needlers he'd stuck me with. "You misunderstand me. I do not wish to rule. I wish to retire."

"Do you need help packing your..." Do not say coffin. "...Things?"

"Thank you for the offer, but no. I have other minions better suited to such mundane tasks. I am immortal. Retirement from the Court for me does not mean sliding into decrepitude. Eternity lies ahead."

"You want to end it all?" I asked a touch too eagerly.

He fixed me with a baleful stare. "No. I simply do not wish to spend the whole of time alone."

A familiar feeling of dread rolled around in my gut as I waited for the hammer to fall.

"I would have my lover restored to me." He tapped his chest. "She who owned the book, owns my heart. Without her, it is but an empty vessel. Without her, life has no meaning."

I nodded in the manner of a thoughtful cove. "I see. I used to have some skill at sorcery; alas no more. And I was never any good at necromancy." I clapped Swann on the back hard enough to make him stumble. "Here's your man."

Leo shook his head. "I have skill enough of my own in that regard. I need you to find and retrieve something for me. It is an object that will restore my lover. What I need are your light-fingered talents."

"Of course you do."

"This object is called the Vascellum, although its name may have changed many times. It will bring her back. You will find it."

"I would love to help, but I've a prior arrangement with that fucker Ludorius." I turned to see that the floor was covered in rats.

So many rats.

"I wasn't asking," said Leo.

Swann cleared his throat. "I have prior claim to Breed's services, Duke. We made a deal."

I rounded on Swann. "Oh, you can go fuck yourself. We made that deal before you handed me over to this biting cove." I took a half step towards the door. "Look, you're both clever coves and well-versed in the magical arts. Why don't you help each other find whatever magical bollocks you're hankering after, and I'll go and put Ludo down for the betterment of all." I thought it a solid and worthy argument.

Alas for me, Leo did not agree. "Come here, Breed."

"No." I walked towards him. "I will not, sirrah," I said as I came to stand before the duke.

"You are my creature now. To do with as I wish. The deal *we* made is running through your veins." He didn't raise his voice; if anything, he sounded bored, which was a little hurtful. "Kneel."

"Go fuck yourself." I dropped to my knees.

"Draw your blades."

I drew my blades.

Leo stroked the white rat. "Put them to your throat."

I tried to fight the command with all my will and wits but nevertheless held my blades against my neck like a pair of shears, ready to cut my head off should he but say the word. *No. I will not. I will not, I—*

There was a crackle of energy behind me, and lightning crawled across the ceiling. "That's enough," said Swann.

Leo glanced over my shoulder and smiled. "I revoke my invitation, Mr. Swann." His gaze fell on me. "Breed, kill Swann."

Eager to obey, I flipped backward off the step and kicked the talismancer in the face as I landed. He sprawled on the floor. I dropped onto his chest and pinned his arms with my knees. White fire flew harmlessly from his fingers as the breath rushed from his lungs. You do not fuck around when you're out to kill a sorcerer, so before he could recover, I brought my blades down with the intention of splitting his skull.

"Stop," the duke commanded.

I pulled the blades an inch from Swann's waxen mug.

"You too, Swann, or I promise, the lovely Effie will not live to see the dawn."

I could see the conflict in Swann's eyes, and a desperate part of me wanted him to unleash all hell upon me and the malevolent puppeteer, but the lightning died and with it all hope of release.

"I own you both," Leo intoned.

For once, I couldn't argue.

Chapter Two

"This is awkward," I said to Swann, who was wheezing beneath me, splashing like a dying fish in the flood water that covered the floor.

"Get off," the talismancer gasped.

"It's not up to me, jimma," I said and gave what I hoped was a wry smile even though I felt sick to my stomach. "I wish it was."

"Let him up," said Leo. I got up and sheathed my swords. Swann clambered to his feet.

"Listen carefully," said Leo. "Because I will not repeat myself." He looked to the door just before there was a timid knock. "Enter."

An amphibane hopped in. She was young and unusually for her species, her skin was dead white instead of green or brown. She carried an ax slung over her muscular shoulders.

The duke's jaw tightened. "This better be important, Mayereen."

"It's a matter of some urgency, sire," she said, her eyes swiveling towards me and Swann. She was breathing heavily, smelled of smoke, and had a few bruises and cuts that I guessed had been earned in a fight.

"Can't it wait?" Leo's gaze flicked to me and Swann.

There was a rumbling as of something collapsing in another part of the mansion. Shouting was followed by a loud shriek which ended abruptly. "I don't think so, sire."

For the first time since meeting him, the duke looked momentarily flustered. The mask of serenity returned quickly, but the line of his jaw was a little harder when he turned to me and Swann. "Wait here, this won't take long." He swept from the chamber, followed by the amphibane.

Swann immediately lit his pel pipe and took a long pull. "I can't believe you were going to fucking kill me," he said while pacing and furiously. "You were going to do me in, jimma. That is not right. It's so…dark."

"Don't blame me, blame the syphilitic pig pizzle who sold me to a blood drinker." I sat on the marble steps. A thick pall of smoke was slowly turning the sky over Valen a lurid orange as the city continued to burn. I put my head in my hands. "What has he done to me?"

"It's always all about you isn't it, *Breed*?"

"No, it isn't. It has until recently been about saving your fucking city, nay the whole, damn Empire from the clutches of a madman."

He coughed, slapped his chest. "I thought you were trying to kill the one who murdered your mother."

"That too."

"Sweet Salvation. What am I going to tell Effie?" He wrapped his arms around his head.

"Do that a bit harder, you might squeeze out the stupid," I snarled. "Damn it! He has me, Swann. He fucking owns me."

"Didn't you hear him? He owns *both* of us. This is why I've avoided entanglement with the Court."

"You're telling me you've never worked for a noble of the Midnight Court?"

"Not directly, and what work I've done has been for cold, hard currency, not threats or favors. Before your friend Ludo came along no one would have threatened my family. It wasn't how business was done."

"It is now, and he's not my 'friend' Ludo."

"This isn't good, jimma. This is seriously affecting my equilibrium, which is never a good thing."

"Fuck your equilibrium. He's done something to me. It's not like a compulsion spell. It's deeper. It…it's in my blood."

Swann stopped pacing and looked at me with an expression mixed two parts revulsion and one part pity, like I was a sick animal you should hit with a rock and put out of its misery.

His expression hardened. "Blood magic is death magic. It is not for the living," he said, and I thought I caught a glimpse of the sorcerer who had pushed the Paradox of Power almost as far as I had. It was but a fleeting glance, and the glassy, unfocused gaze quickly returned.

"I assure you, I'm not dead."

He leaned in. "I meant the duke, not you. You are just his imp, a familiar."

"Like a bonded servant?"

"Aye, more or less." He ran his hand through his hair. "This kind of blood magic—the kind known only to the infernal, is beyond me, jimma." He looked towards the window. "She's going to be wondering where I am."

"She might not." I offered. "She might think you're already dead. She could be planning your funeral wake as we speak." They say you shouldn't kick a man when he's down, but if you ask me, that's the best time to hurt someone who has offended you.

"Why would you say something like that?" He shook his head in disbelief. "I'm here because I tried to help you."

I laughed. "No good deed goes unpunished, Swann. You want my advice?"

"No."

"Get the fuck out of here."

"What a wonderful plan. I don't know why I didn't think of it myself."

"I'm serious. Take your woman and get the fuck out of town, out of the Empire."

He shook his head. "There's no running from people like him."

"Not true. You can run away from anyone except yourself, gang lords, demons, even dragons. Sure, they may catch you, but you can always run."

Something outside caught my attention. If it hadn't moved, I wouldn't have noticed its mottled brown-green hide, perfectly camouflaged in the fecund swamp. A cloudy eye swiveled towards me, met my gaze. It ruffled its gills, slowly unfurled a pair of tentacles, and slipped silently under the water.

Another scream rang out and was abruptly silenced. Shortly thereafter, the door swung open, and Leo breezed in. There was color in his cheeks, and although he seemed otherwise composed, he stank of death.

"Please, forgive the interruption. Now, where were we? Ah, yes. I was about to tell you about the quest." He seemed to be in a better mood than when he'd left.

"The quest?" I enquired, dread gathering around me like the gloom over Valen.

"Yes."

"Bit dramatic, isn't it? You're supposed to send knights on quests not thieves and drugged-up sorcerers."

He chuckled. The white rat stuck its face through his curly locks and wrinkled its nose disapprovingly. "Would you prefer I call it a mission, or would, 'job' be more to your liking?"

"I'm just saying 'quest' sounds a bit pretentious."

"But that is what it is. It is a quest for an object that will restore my love to me. Should I call it something else, something less accurate just to satisfy your prosaic sensibilities?"

I raised my hands in surrender. "I'm not wedded to it, call it what you want, fuck's sake."

"That's fuck's sake, *sire*."

"Sire."

"Better."

I still thought it sounded pretentious, but you have to pick your battles.

"So, you want me to cast a divination?" Swann enquired hopefully. "Or make you some charms? I can do that."

Leo shook his head. "No, no. You're going on the *quest* with Breed."

Swann gave a nervous laugh. "No jimma, I can't do that." He ran his hands through his hair. "Honestly, you wouldn't want me in the field. I'm a city boy. I'm old."

"You don't look old." He sniffed. "You don't smell old."

"Oh, I am. I've got bad knees, a bad back, not to mention a weak chest."

Leo blinked slowly a slight smile played on his lips. "Are you finished?"

"You offered to help control Chas's paradox. That was it."

Leo's eyes flashed and he flourished his tail. "And I did. Like a metaphysical surgeon, I excised the madness of sorcery, drew the poison and in so doing, saved your life, Breed's life—the life of the beautiful Effie, and the lives of every soul within a mile of that shack you call a home. You owe me."

I cleared my throat. "If we're leveraging good turns, I retrieved your book."

He gave me a hard look. "You think picking up a small book of poetry from an unguarded tomb is akin to saving hundreds of lives?"

"Is it good poetry?"

He laughed. "Ah, the arrogance of youth, although you should know better."

"How's that, Your Gracefulness?"

"I am older than I look'. Isn't that what you're fond of saying and isn't it the truth?"

I shrugged. I hated that he knew more about me than I did about him.

"Please." Swann begged. "Effie needs me."

Leo snorted. "I doubt that very much." Changing tack, he softened his tone. "You have my word, Swann. I will take care of her. These are dangerous, lawless times. I will make it known that she is under my protection and rest assured, my name carries weight in Valen. Neither of you need look so glum. I don't want you to fight. I just want you to find something precious only to me. To that end, I will send the White Rat with you.

"Something tells me you don't mean that." I pointed at the rat on his shoulder.

"*That* is a she, and no." Leo looked beyond me as footsteps approached.

I turned. The fellow was still garbed in the heavy coat and broadbrimmed hat. "The coach driver? With a name like 'the White Rat' I'd expected someone more… ratlike." As I'd previously clocked, he was tall and broad in the back. His eyes had changed color and were now warm brown and very human. His jaw was square and framed by a thick mane of glossy, dark hair, and he moved with an effortless grace bespeaking a measure of agility that belied his size. In short, he was the kind of man who set the hearts of human dames aflutter and by the way he carried himself, knew it very well.

He bowed to Leo before turning to me and Swann. "My name is Nicodemus, but my friends call me Nic."

I waited for him to say, 'but you may call me' but he didn't, and I didn't like it. I preferred lumpen warrior types to be nice and thick and predictable in every way – all the better to fox and bamboozle should the need arise.

"I'm Swann." Swann waved.

All eyes turned to me. "I'm screwed, pleased to meet you."

"Sorry?"

"Breed. People call me Breed."

Leo stroked his pet rat. "An enforcer, a sorcerer, and a thief. We have our crew."

I was an excellent fighter and had until recently been a rather brilliant sorcerer. To be known merely as 'a thief' did not sit well with me.

Swann raised his hand. "Items that can restore the dead aren't my thing, jimma. Wouldn't a necromancer be more use than me?"

"Have you ever met a necromancer you can trust, or indeed, who was sane?" said Leo. All agreed it was a fair point.

"So where are we going on this quest?" I asked and hoped that Fate would throw me a bone and it wouldn't be far. Alas, it seemed that Fate was all out of bones this night.

"The Vascellum was last reported as being seen in Voskva," Leo replied. "Nicodemus has all documents I have gathered pertaining to its last known location. Funds for the journey will be provided. But don't take advantage. Whoring, drinking, and drug use do not count as expenses. If you want to fornicate, and or render yourselves witless with narcotics, you do so out of your own pocket, and on your own time." His gaze fell on the White Rat.

'Call me Nic' grinned wolfishly and slapped his hand on his chest. "I swear, I'll live like a monk, brother."

Leo raised an eyebrow. "A first time for everything I suppose."

Looking at the pair of them, it was hard to imagine they were spawned by the same sire and dam. Leo resembled a skinny rat in a wig and even though he smelled like a wet dog, Nicodemus looked like the muscular hero from a tawdry novel.

"I'm sure you'll all become firm friends and share many exciting adventures on your quest." Leo gave me a pointed look. "I cannot stress to you how important this mission is to me. Succeed and you will be well rewarded."

"Out of curiosity, what happens if we fail to find this thing?" I asked because someone had to.

Instead of answering, Leo turned his gaze to the window and stared silently at the smoke-laden sky.

"The ship sets sail on the early tide," said Nicodemus. "Which is four hours from now, give or take." He turned to leave.

"Hold a moment." I raised my hand. "Is that it? 'The Whateverthefuck is in Voskva, now off you trot'?" Leo turned; his rat leaped from his shoulder onto a nearby vine and scurried out of sight. He showed no emotion in his face, but his tail thrashed angrily. Sensing I was on thin ice I added, "I'm not trying to be awkward, Your Grace. But we need more information than that. Voskva's a big country."

"And cold," Swann added glumly. "And gloomy."

The White Rat hid laughter behind a cough and leaned nonchalantly against the door. Leo gave him a hard look, and the air between them turned decidedly chilly.

"I have provided all the information you will need to hunt down the Vascellum, complete with translations. You can familiarize yourselves with every book, scroll, and diary account while you are at sea."

Swann raised his hand. "I also don't mean to be difficult."

"No, indeed. It is clearly a talent you share," Leo muttered.

Swann ignored the comment and took a steadying breath. "If I am to be of any use, I need my equipment. I also *need* to say goodbye to my wife."

Leo held all the cards, but if he was smart, he wouldn't hold them too tightly. Knowing Swann was also dangling over the precipice of the Paradox, he'd be wise to throw him a bone. Having little faith in the wisdom of others, I took a step back and hoped to the gods the fang-faced bastard didn't make me attack Swann again because I doubted that I'd get the drop on him a second time.

Tense silence curdled the air, but at last, Leo looked to his brother. "Go with him," he said and then fixed his gaze on Swann. "Get what you need, say your farewells, and for the sake of all, do not try to cross me."

Swann bowed. I could see he was still angry but also relieved that he had won this minor victory. "That's great, jimma, er, Duke Leopold," he said and then legged it like his arse was on fire. The White Rat followed at a leisurely pace.

I took a few exploratory steps towards the door. "I've also got some equipment to pick up, lockpicks and knives and…stuff."

Leo raised an eyebrow. "I'm guessing that sounded better in your head."

"Not really, but I'm having a bad day."

"Wait here for Nicodemus and Swann to return. I have to go and kill some people before the sunrise."

"I could come with you. You might need a hand." I offered, keen to leave the waterlogged manor.

His claws lengthened, his eyes glowed red, and his mouth split into an unpleasantly toothsome grin.

"I'll take that as a no."

Chapter Three

"**D**arkness has a home in me."

"That's a bit deep," I said.

Swann leaned against the rail. "It's the first line of a poem."

"How lovely. Don't recite the rest, eh?"

He laughed until he coughed, phlegm rattling in his bony chest. "Not sure that I can. My memory isn't what it was." He steadied himself against the rail as the ship rolled in the waves.

I was leaning over the quarter-deck. For want of anything else to do, I was seeing how long it took for gobs of spit to vanish in the choppy wake. Valen had stopped burning and was vanishing over the horizon, which was a relief. Leaving cities on fire was becoming a bad habit of mine. Not that what happened was entirely my fault; cities burn down *a lot* even without angry sorcerers rampaging through the streets. Grand palaces and temples rendered in marble aside, most buildings in a city from squalid slums to solid merchant houses, are made from wood, straw, and muddy dung render. Lit and heated by candles, oil lanterns, and fires of every stripe, I'd bet my wotnots that Valen would be on fire again within the week just because some clumsy cunt had knocked a candle over.

"Darkness has a home in me," Swann said again and took a long pull on his pipe. "Something, something and never shall the linnet weep. Something, something." Swann sighed mournfully. "I miss her so much."

"It's been three hours."

"It feels like a lifetime. If I thought I might never see her again, I would throw myself overboard."

"You're so high, you'd just float."

While we idled, the crew worked around us, hauling ropes, furling, and unfurling canvas, and climbing up and down the rigging. There weren't any arrachids in the crew but one of the officers was a thoasa. There were also a handful of ogren and a similar number of amphibane. The captain, a dour cove by the name of Kasov, was mostly human but had enormous eyes and a soft, featureless face reminiscent of an amphibane. He didn't mix with the likes of me and Swann, but he did pass the time of day with Nicodemus, who despite paying well for our passage, kept himself in the good books by helping to haul and furl.

"Have you ever crossed the Great Ocean?" Swann asked.

Like a bloated corpse, an image of the kraken flipping *the Widow of Ching* onto her side floated from the depth of my memory. I gazed into the gloomy waters and wondered what might be lurking in the darkness, watching the shadow of the ship, considering if it should reach up and take it. "Aye. It was a long time ago though." *A long time ago, in another life.* "Wasn't the best of journeys to be honest."

"Ah. Seasick?" He nodded as he climbed the rail and dangled his bare feet over the side as the ship tacked to catch the wind. "I have a charm against that."

"Not sure that a charm would work against..." I stopped myself short of mentioning krakens and fighting brachuri within earshot of the sailors. "Why don't we make a start on those documents?"

He scratched his head. "Documents?"

"The ones Duke Leopold sent."

He smiled blankly, took a pull on his pipe, and then sniffed his shirt. "I can smell her perfume."

"Fuck's sake." I put my fingers in my mouth and whistled to Nicodemus, who was staring moodily across the ocean, dark locks flying in the wind. When he looked over, I mimed a key going into a lock. It took him a moment but then he gestured to below decks. "Come on, Swann."

"Yeah, sure, jimma…I'll be down in a minute."

"Now, because I don't trust that you won't fall overboard."

He grinned stupidly but climbed down and we headed to our cabin. *The Cloud* was an old, wide-bellied cargo ship, but the cabins were pokey, fit only to accommodate malnourished humans. The amusingly named 'state room' the three of us shared was the second largest after the captain's cabin. There was room for three narrow bunks. Two were on the bulkhead side and one against the hull beneath the porthole. There was space beneath the single bunk for the two trunks belonging to Nicodemus and Swann and the chest Leopold had sent with the documents about whatever the fuck he wanted us to find.

I owned the clothes I was in; an old doublet and breeches donated by Swann. I had a pouch with two half-crowns, some copper and tin pennies, and a Voskvan drosh which was worth two mugs of ale and a pie, or so Nic told me when he generously gave it to me. I also had my swords and that was it. From what I could tell, Swann had packed some entirely ridiculous and impractical clothes, a brick of pel, a half-dozen pipes, and little else. What Nicodemus had in his trunk he kept to himself. Knowing his pedigree, my bet was on either grave dirt or body parts.

"Here." Nic threw me the key to the chest and took a small, steel mirror from his pocket. A wooden lid over the single bunk allowed it to double as a table when the bed wasn't in use. I unlocked the chest while Swann made a meal of clambering onto the top bunk. Nic began primping in the mirror. First, he examined his pearly whites to see if there was any food caught between his fangs and then, more amusingly, he teased his hair for, I assumed, aesthetic appeal.

Curiosity got the better of me. "D'you have somewhere to go?" I asked.

"Mayhap, aye. I've got my eyes on the bosun, you know, that little half-ogren with the big dugs. I'll bestow my favor on her or the cook," he said as he plucked a hair from his nose. "Or both, if they're lucky."

"What about all this?" I tapped the chest. "We need to plan, to narrow down the search area."

He frowned, had a last, appraising look at himself before tucking the mirror back in his pocket. "You and Swann can read 'em. That's what you're here for. Enjoy, and don't wait up." He slapped me on the back and swept from the cabin.

Swann began to snore. I kicked his arse through the bunk, not hard, but enough to wake him. He flailed, sat up, hit his head on the deck beam. "We were going to go through these, remember?"

"Damn, jimma," he said, clutching his head. "That hurt. I'm not warded against attacks from friends."

I had to laugh. "You need to redouble your efforts in that case, for we are not friends."

He rubbed the red mark on his forehead. "Don't start this again. I have done my best for you."

I flicked my hair spines over my shoulder and turned my head to better display the bite mark on my neck. "This is your best, eh?"

He took out his pipe and crumbled a silver-wrapped ball into the bowl. "You're going to have to let this go, jimma. I told you a million times. He came to me, said you were in trouble, said you were kin to his friend, and he wanted to help you. I know you don't want to admit it because I didn't when it happened to me, but you were close to breaking the Paradox." He drew deeply on the pipe. "I did what I thought best at the time. I've got other people to look out for, people who rely on me. You don't understand."

He was right, and that stung. I tipped the contents of the chest onto the makeshift table. "Let's see what we have here, shall we?"

"Later." He lay back in a sulk and drew the curtain across his bunk.

To prove I was the better person, I refrained from dragging him from his pit and smashing his brains in against the bulkhead. Instead, I just dragged him from his pit and shoved him onto the lower bunk.

"How dare you!" He batted at me ineffectually, only stopping when he dropped his pipe.

"Aye, that's it, set the fucking ship on fire. At least you'll die stoned."

"You are like a fucking child. A violent, angry child."

I mimicked his tone. "And you're a grubby little pel head. What's your point?"

Fury lit in his eyes as he retrieved his pipe. It didn't bother me; I preferred angry to sulky. I began sorting through the pile of documents.

"Do not lay hands on me again," he said, with just the slightest tremor of emotion in his voice.

I had to laugh. "Don't piss me off and I won't." Although literate, I am no scholar, and it wasn't long before my mind began to wander. Looking at the pile of parchment and notebooks caused a little piece of me to die. I picked something up, sniffed it. "Is this...is this ogren skin?" I thrust it towards Swann, who shied away before his sorcerer's curiosity got the better of him.

He took it and held it up to the light. "It's definitely skin. Not sure if it's ogren. Very inharmonious. We should get a padandra to bless this. Or burn it on a sacred pyre."

"Can we read it first? And what's a padandra?"

"A holy teacher of Obruna, you know, the Celestial Light of the Universe? I've been getting into it."

"It's passed me by I'm afraid." I should have just nodded.

His eyes lit up. "Oh, jimma, you should totally align yourself to Obruna's energy, everyone's doing it back in the city."

I smiled and nodded. "I bet they are. Why don't you tell me all about it when we've had a look at these and worked out where the hell we're supposed to be going, and what the hell we're looking for." It occurred to me then that my new lord and master might be insane. History was littered with the blood-splattered accounts of crazed kings and insane empresses. He wouldn't be the first lunatic to send a set of idiots on a pointless quest.

Magical flames lit on Swann's stained fingers as he sparked up his pipe. "You seem keen."

"I wish to expedite this 'quest'. I've a killer to find."

"And kill."

"It's different. Anyway, before that I need Leo to release me. For that to happen I need to find his shiny for him."

His sloppy grin faded. "What if he doesn't let us go, even if we find it? What then?"

"Let's deal with one problem at a time, eh?"

Hours passed in studious silence as we bent our heads to the task of cyphering the multitude of accounts. The grey eye of the porthole blazed gold then deepened through bronze, to purple, to indigo as day shifted to night. Swann lit the lantern. It swayed in time with the gentle roll of the ship as it pushed through the waves lapping at the hull like hungry kits.

Swann yawned and closed the book he was reading. "If I have it right, we will arrive in the port of Sevast. If we follow the route detailed in the Professor Unaskil notes, we should travel from there to Muzansti Lensk which is on the border of Knyev. The Vascellum itself might be…" He drew a weary breath and pinched the bridge of his nose. "A book. A ship. A relic of Saint Dero the Bloody, an ancient spirit, or a pungent mist."

I could feel my brain frying in its own juices. "Just…kill me now and do it quickly. I'm done with books and maps."

"Oh, no, jimma. You're not getting out of this that easy."

"Perhaps we could kill each other. A death pact?"

Before we could work out the details, the ship rocked violently. "Ware aft!" someone who sounded like Nicodemus shouted. The thunder of feet hammered through the deck. Visions of fighting brachuri and kraken scabs came to mind. "Not again." I grabbed my swords and ran for the stairs. I was not alone and had to wait my turn at the ladder with the rest of the off-duty crew. I was perhaps alone in considering how I might parley for my life should a swarm of fighting brachuri be attacking. When I got on deck, I saw that the focus, if not the cause of the commotion, was Nicodemus.

He was standing aft, a harpoon drawn back, sizing up something dark that was thrashing behind the ship. He planted his feet and cast the heavy weapon. Those closest to him raised a cheer as a bloody foam spread across the ocean. "Please, don't be a kraken," I said as more harpooners scrambled aft, some taking to the rigging to get a better angle on whatever had risen from the deep.

"Aren't you going to help? Swann asked when he finally made his way on deck.

"No," I answered, somewhat bemused by the question.

When the crowd at the stern parted, I could see that whatever had rammed the ship was much smaller than the vessel and posed no danger. To join in now would be for sport and I never killed for fun. Another ragged cheer went up, louder than the last. Nicodemus emerged from the knot of sailors and made his way across the main deck, modestly shrugging off congratulations while making lingering eye contact with the bosun. A cloud of gulls descended on the carcass of whatever had just been turned into a blubbery pin cushion. Excitement over, the sailors on watch got back to their duties, and the off-duty crew returned to the bunkroom. Nicodemus spent a few minutes talking quietly with the bosun. I headed back to the cabin. Not long after, the hero returned.

"There you are." Nic beamed. "Did you see me?"

"Er, no, when?" I craned to look out into the narrow passage. "What have you done with Swann? If you've chucked him overboard Leo won't be pleased."

His cocky grin became a frown. "That's Duke Leopold to you. And no, I haven't. He's on deck, enjoying the night air. Didn't you see me kill the sea serpent?"

"I saw some commotion." If he wanted his ego buffing, he'd have to go elsewhere.

He crept into the cabin and closed the door behind him. "I chummed the water and waited fucking hours for something to bite." He sounded gleefully proud of himself. "Shame it was only an old sea snake, but it did the job."

"We'll all sleep safer tonight thanks to you." That he'd deliberately tried to attract the attention of a sea monster was an act of stupidity too great for my limited grasp of mathematicals to calculate.

"The bosun thinks I'm a proper hero. Which reminds me…" He put his arm around my shoulder like we were bosom friends. "Would you mind fucking off for a few hours? Only I'm on with Carmella. That's the bosun."

"Doesn't Carmella have her own cabin?"

"No, she shares."

I stuffed the papers in the chest and locked it.

"Well?"

"All right. Just don't fuck on my bunk." I tapped on the table. "Or the table. Because it is over my bunk, and I do not wish to lie here for the remainder of the trip smelling your combined fuck unguents."

He grinned. "You have my word. We'll fuck on my bunk, Swann's bunk, the floor, against the door, the wall, but not on your bunk or the table." He gave my shoulder an over-friendly squeeze making me instantly regret my decision.

Chapter Four

The southern coast of Voskva thrust out into the black waters of the Great Ocean like the head of a spear. To the east, jagged cliffs towered three hundred feet above the thundering breakers. To the west were a series of scalloped bays and the port city of Sevast.

It was late in the year to be traveling north across the ocean to a land that did not slide into a majestic russet autumn. In Voskva, autumn had teeth. Rather than turn gold and scarlet, foliage blackened and withered under the lash of cruel winds and bitter, unpredictable snowfalls. Autumn's cruelty was but a prelude to the murderous cold of winter when ice showers and snow swept down from unnamed mountains like wolves and devoured the weak and unprepared. In all the descriptions I had read or heard of the land of Voskva, the word 'gentle' was never used.

It was a wild day when we sailed into the protective arms of the harbor. The ragged sky and churning sea became as one, tumbled together in shades of grey, black, and silver. The howling wind plucked the salt-hardened rigging like harp strings. Every plank and board of the ship flexed under the strain of prisoning the wind in taut sails while glass-toothed waves shattered upon the hull.

Swann came to join me on deck. "Did you sleep well?" he asked more cheerfully than I would have expected with the ship being tossed around like a toy. He was bundled up in a long, patchwork coat.

"Like a babe."

He grinned knowingly. "Same. It's the energy. Did you notice it's mellowed since Nic started bunking with the bosun?"

"If by 'mellowed' you mean we're not choking on his fuck stink then yes, it has."

He nodded to himself and began to turn away when he remembered something and stopped. "Oh, would you mind punching me?"

"Is that a trick question?"

He chuckled. "No. Just give me a jab, not too hard, but you know, a little bit hard. Not the face, or the stomach, I'll puke." He turned side-on. "Here, just in the arm." He closed his eyes and braced like he was about to receive the headman's ax.

"That is tempting, Swann, it really is, but no, I'm not going to punch you." I smelled a rat, and it wasn't the one fucking the bosun.

"I give you leave. Please, I'm testing something." He swayed, but somehow his inebriation countered the roll of the ship, and he was able to maintain his balance.

I tapped the nearest sailor on the shoulder. "Punch him, would you?"

The sailor put down his mop, spat on his knuckles, and wound up a punch. A ray of sense must have broken through the pel fog shrouding Swann's brain, and he raised his hands in surrender.

"Ah. No, thank you, jimma. I just remembered that I've got to pack some things." He gesticulated airily and scurried back below deck.

Bemused but not surprised, I stayed where I was, and the sailor returned to swabbing. As invigorating as it was standing there, holding onto the rail as the prow smashed through the waves, I was bored of being on a ship and sick of being cooped up with a sex-obsessed narcissist and a pipe-shot talismancer.

Due to confinement with a pair of pricks, I had distracted myself from thoughts of murder by studying Leo's eclectic collection of papers on the Vascellum. I didn't enjoy study; I was more of a doer than a reader of other's deeds, but that didn't mean I couldn't when I had to. When I'd been Malin's advisor, I'd burned the midnight oil many a night poring over maps and weighty tomes as we worked to forge a new kingdom from the ashes of the old. Thinking about those days made my head spin. I had lived a long life there, in that other world, spent decades by Malin's side. And now where was I? I was 'a 'thief' in thrall to an infernal prince of the Midnight Court. I had to laugh.

The sight of the port of Sevast brightened my mood. The city was situated on Sevast Bay, on the western side of the Bergo peninsula. It straddled the River Graska, which cut through the peninsula from the forest-shadowed heartland of Bergo. According to one of the sailors from elsewhere in Voskva, the province was once ruled by cannibalistic beetle people who were vanquished by the Mage Lords or some such bollocks. I stopped listening when she started telling me about the famous and extremely strong, 'better-than-any-you-have-in-the-soft-southern-Empire' type of stone that was mined in Bergo and that it was also renowned for a unique kind of sour cheese.

"Ah, Breed," said Nic.

"Ah, someone else I've been trying to avoid." I smiled.

He chuckled, tucked his shirt into his too-tight leather trousers. "You're very funny. So anyway, where are we headed from Sevast?"

"Again? Really? I've heard of fucking one's brains out but always thought it was just a saying. I told you yesterday."

"I was distracted."

"I gave you a map."

"You did." He raised a clawed finger as though to say, 'one moment' as he rummaged through his many coat pockets. Eventually, he pulled out the crumpled map, upon which I had marked an area of Voskva, near Muzansti Lensk, which was the last known location of the Vascellum. "Right, got it. So, we'll need about three weeks supplies and a wagon and…Very well."

"So, you're still coming with us?"

He looked askance. "What else would I do?"

I shrugged. "I thought you were planning on signing on with the crew and marrying the bosun."

He chuckled but there was a bittersweet edge to his smile. "That was just silly lovers' talk. And besides, Leopold would not approve."

"Ah. Does he have his fangs in you too?"

"No." He scowled like a child. "He's my brother, I serve him willingly, and with love."

I nodded. "Aye, me too."

Only Nic received acknowledgment from the crew when we disembarked. Several of the sea dogs slapped him on the back. He swore oaths to see them again, and after exchanging promises of eternal love and fealty, the bosun gave him a long, passionate kiss before the White Rat sauntered down the gangplank like a cat who'd had all the cream.

Because he was incapable of doing so himself, I was left to carry Swann's trunk along the dock. Much like any port, the area was busy, loud, dangerous, and grim. On account of the cold weather, the smell of fish guts wasn't overpowering, and the bodies of recently deceased derelicts and unlucky sailors were in a better state of preservation than they would have been back home at this time of year.

Off in the distance, I could see what looked like gallows set up in one of the market squares. Standing in the middle of the platform with a sign around his neck instead of a noose was a sorry-looking cove being pelted with fish heads. I tapped a fellow on the shoulder who was mending a squid pot and pointed to the square.

He unclamped the chewed stem of his pipe from his lips and pointed with it. "Samizort," he said and then realized he was talking to a foreigner. "Bad citizen, a liar."

"You get pelted with fish heads for telling lies?" That was worth knowing in my line of work.

The old salt nodded and jabbed his pipe towards the square. "Sign say, 'I lie about size of Great Voskvan Fishing Fleet to foreigner. I am fool'." The old fellow shrugged, then laughed, and then nudged me as though we were both in on a joke. "I know him. He is a fool!" I nodded and hurried after Swann and Nic, leaving the old barnacle giggling into his pots.

When we reached the outskirts of the docks on the edge of the city proper, Nic ducked into one of the many inns that catered to sailors and travelers and gestured for us to follow. I didn't read Voskvan, but the sign hanging over the door depicted a kraken.

"This'll do," said Nic, who was obviously not as fastidious as the creatures he was named for because the inn was a dump.

"For what?" I asked.

"For you to wait while I secure a wagon and supplies."

"We'll come with you," I said, as he seemed keen to leave without us.

"Aye, I could do with a walk," said Swann, still swaying to the rhythm of the ship.

"No, no. I'll be quicker on my own. Stay here with the luggage." Nic insisted. His glance flicked to Swann, who was already drawing the attention of a few crusty sailors who were enjoying their mugs of breakfast rum. When Nic left, I shoved the trunks under a table in a snug booth along with my swords. I'd wrapped them in a nondescript bundle because the sailors on *The Cloud* had mentioned permits were required to carry weapons in Sevast. Swann slid in beside them and I went to the bar. Unlike the talismancer, I had no actual desire to drink alcohol, but one should never trust the water near a dock, so beer it was. I spent my single drosh on two mugs of what looked like runny treacle and a bowl of pickled plums, which I hadn't asked for.

"Oh, yummy, beer." Swann clapped and put the pipe down before picking up his mug with both hands like a child afraid of spilling. "Look at them." He pointed out of the window at a group of rum coves in scarlet tabards. "What the hell do they have in the wagon?"

I leaned over and peered through the tiny, grubby windowpane. "Some kind of beast. Not sure what." The thing in the wagon had six limbs, horns, and black scales. The crew escorting the wagon were carrying an assortment of unusual weapons. "They look like mercs."

"How can you tell?"

"They've got the swagger, the bad outfits, and the stupid weapons. Also, they've left their kill uncovered for everyone to see. It's attention seeking. Clearly, none of them were hugged enough as children."

He chuckled. "And you were?"

"Drink your beer before it sets." The oblique mention of childhood got me thinking about Mother, which in turn got me thinking about Ludo. Before I could get down to some serious brooding, a cove in the next booth raised his mug to catch my eye.

He smiled behind a thick, full beard and tipped back his fur cap. "Empire, yes?"

I nodded and hunched over my beer, which wasn't unfriendly enough to stop him coming over and sitting down opposite me and Swann. "I have been to Empire. Is very beautiful."

I nodded again. "I don't speak much Voskvan," I said in halting Voskvan. He laughed.

"No, you don't, but I speak good Imperial, yes?"

"Very good," said Swann smiling.

I didn't like this cove; he was too friendly, too full of himself. And he looked out of place here, being neither sailor nor traveler as far as I could tell.

"I am Ferdul Myra. You are here with friends?"

"No," I said.

"Yes," said Swann, a beat behind me.

I smiled. "Sort of."

Ferdul laughed and slapped the table. "You are funny, lizard. I like you. You have a drink with me, yes? Good, Voskvan rum, warm up you cold scales."

"No, thanks," I said, gesturing to my mug.

"Lovely!" said Swann, encouraged by Ferdul's aggressive cheerfulness. Ferdul went to the bar to order the rum, which I noted the barkeep was reaching for before he asked. I also noticed that he didn't pay. This was a set-up. I blamed Swann for looking like an easy mark. The Voskvan sat down and immediately raised his tin cup of rum.

"To the glory of the Archonate!" he said in perfect Imperial.

Swann enthusiastically picked up his rum and joined the toast.

I raised my mug of beer. "The Archonate." Whatever the fuck that was.

Ferdul knocked back his drink and sucked a shuddering breath through clenched teeth before slamming the cup on the table. Swann downed his rum like it was water, because where there's no sense, there's no feeling. I waited for him to light his pipe on the off chance he might set his head on fire. Alas, he had the sense to refrain from sparking up.

"So, you are here for business?" said Ferdul.

Sure that Swann would make a liar out of me, I didn't answer.

"No, jimma," he said. "We're just here to see the beautiful country of Voskva, do some travelling, see some sights. Experience the rich culture."

I don't know what the Voskvan was expecting but I could tell Ferdul didn't believe a word of it, and who would? He looked questioningly at me.

I shrugged. "I just carry his bags."

"Yes, you are strong." He gave me an appraising look. "Lizard people are good workers, yes? You work like dog. That is what they say, no?" Don't scowl, my friend. "Hard work is very good thing in Voskva. Hard work leads to progress, to freedom." He guffawed.

I suppose it must have been that I was tired from the long journey, but I couldn't be bothered to mock the fellow. Indeed, I even lacked the wherewithal to tell him to go fuck himself, which was very unlike me. I smiled instead and sipped my horrible beer.

Ferdul swiped the extra rum and downed it. "Was nice to meet you, but I must go to work now. Enjoy your stay in our country."

"What a nice fellow," said Swann as Ferdul swaggered from the inn. "I've got to pee." The talismancer ambled out the back of the inn. The blessed relief of being alone to peacefully enjoy my pickled plums was short-lived. Scant minutes after he left, the door to the inn was thrown open and a couple of what had to be local catchpoles wandered in, quite spoiling my appetite. The senior of the two had a rust-colored beard that hung to his wide, steel-reinforced belt. As with many middle-aged humans, the belt was more of a girdle, engaged as it was in a heroic battle to hold back the dread forces of too much of a good thing. His subordinate's less impressive beard frizzled out at mid-chest over an unimpressive gut. However, the studded clubs they both carried were equally worthy of respect. The pair made deliberate, unhurried progress through the near-empty bar. I wasn't sure if they were expecting trouble or looking for it. Either way, they moved with purpose. I nursed my ale and kept my head down. Just when it looked like they were going to leave the inn, Rust-beard stopped and returned to my table. I didn't look up. He nudged Swann's pipe.

"Yasa nya?" he said. I played ignorant, stared at my ale. "Who's is?" he said in Imperial.

I looked up and shrugged. "Is something wrong, sir?"

He slammed the club down, bouncing the pipe across the table. All conversation in the bar stopped. Everyone averted their gaze.

Rusty grabbed me by my shirt and hauled me to my feet. Not content at that, he shoved me up against a wall." "Yasa nya!" It was like we were ghosts. No one so much as glanced in our direction.

"Papers!" Rusty spat in heavily accented Imperial.

"I don't have any papers yet. I—" I didn't get the chance to say anything else as he rammed his club against my throat.

"You bring drugs to Voskva. You need license!" He continued to berate me, and I continued to choke. "How dare you come to our country and bring this filth?"

Usually at this point in an altercation, someone is spitting teeth and it usually isn't me. This was far from usual. I didn't have any fight in me. True enough I was irked, nay furious that he was choking me while spitting the remains of his breakfast in my face. I just didn't have the desire to do anything about it save gasp for breath. A nagging little voice in the back of my mind rather rudely enquired what the fuck I thought I was doing letting this maggot-faced turdnip get the better of me. The answer was that I had no idea. My grasp of consciousness began to loosen. I feebly groped for the club pressed against my windpipe. The sound of blood hammering through my head grew deafening. I should have been fighting for my life, yet I couldn't muster the wherewithal to so much as slap the paunchy nothous. Before Death claimed me, Fate took pity. He let go. I gulped a mouthful of lovely, lovely air – which was when he slammed the butt of his club into my vulnerable gut. I began to sink to the ground, only to be met partway down by a knee to the face. Lights flared twice, once when the knee connected with my jaw and once when my head bounced off the wall.

"You think you can attack a Voskvan officer? You are not in the Empire now, dog. Yvan!" he shouted as the world darkened around me. "Put the buckles on this criminal."

Chapter Five

Astoundingly, I hadn't done anything to deserve a beating. I hadn't said anything provocative, stolen anything, or killed anyone, and yet here I was, crammed in the back of a prison wagon with another ten unfortunates.

"I shouldn't be here," I said. "I haven't done anything wrong." It felt so strange saying that and for it to be true.

Someone laughed as I would have done on any other day. What stung most was that I'd let the minge-faced gollumpus do me over without so much as offering a token resistance, let alone wiping the floor with the prick. I had never let myself take a beating like that, not even when I was a kinch, and couldn't fathom how I'd allowed it to happen today.

"I too have been unlawfully detained." The fellow who spoke was a nervous-looking cove garbed in priestly robes. He looked like an ogren, save he was only three-quarters the size. As most gods appear to hate hair on the head, his pate was shaved, which contrasted with his hairy everything else. "By the Holy Eye, I did nothing wrong, broke no laws…"

"No one cares…" someone muttered.

"…Shut your mouth…" snapped another and fixed the prattler with an angry stare.

"Leave him be," said a sailor with tattooed knuckles. "We be in the wrong place at the wrong time. Damned quota, innit? My bad luck to be ashore on a round-up day."

"What's that then?" I asked, although by inference I could already guess the broad shape of it.

"It's the Archonate." She spat between her feet. "Now they've smashed the old regime, they've got a hard-on for making Voskva 'modern'. As far as I can tell that means they write slogans, kill dissenters, and line their own pockets. They're like the last lot, only these clowns wear uniforms instead of crowns."

"For all our sakes keep your damn voice down, woman!" another of the prisoners hissed while casting fearful glances towards the door.

"What are they going to do? Send me to prison?" The sailor laughed bitterly. "Equality in poverty! Chains do not bind us, only ignorance! You'll see those slogans written everywhere. Meanwhile, farms are left to rot because all the young and strong have been forced to go work in factories, mills, and mines producing shit no one wants or can afford."

"No," said the Ogren shaking his head in disbelief. "I'm a priest of the Dawn Way. They wouldn't dare."

"Dare what? Make a lone, ogren runt vanish?" The sailor waved her shackled hands. "You think you're special because you wear a dress for god?"

"I have influential friends and good standing in the community. My brothers and sisters will come and look for me and this mistake shall be rectified," said the priestling, his words at odds with the panic writ upon his furry face.

The sailor snorted. "And where will they look for you, poppet? Who will they turn to for help when the law is the criminal?" Then, leaving the youth to digest the hopelessness of his situation, she turned back to me. "Every month they round up outsiders. They've got agents working the docks and the inns. They pick out strangers, those with strong backs and no connections, or drunks." She grinned at that. "They make up uruxshit charges—drunk and disorderly, insulting the Archonate, that kind of thing. Then you get sentenced to a 'correctional' spell in the mines. Which, no matter how long they give you is always a life sentence." Her jaw tightened. "Anyway, you'll see soon enough. Fucking Voskies."

"Propaganda and lies! Voskva is not like that," said a short, stocky human with meaty dabs. "We have an honest judiciary. All mistakes will be cleared up in the court." He rummaged in a leather satchel from which he pulled a sheaf of papers. "I'm Voskvan, a clerk from Tomansk." He brandished the documents like a talisman. "I have papers vouching for me, signed by the late Autcharch Smarn of Tomansk, may the light of the Archonate forever shine upon his memory." He chuckled. "Oh, no. I won't be going to any mines, you'll see. And do you know why? Because I really was arrested by mistake."

A humanish woman who also had something of the ogren about her sneered. "Smarn was executed by the Archonate for being 'unfaithful'. Trust me, you're holding arsewipe, not a ticket to freedom."

The clerk gave her a filthy look and thrust the papers back into his satchel. "When I am released, I'll raise a glass of procav to your stupidity."

A gloomy silence descended. I pressed my face to a hole in the wagon and tried to get my bearings. The road we were on was surprisingly straight and paved with warm, cream-colored stone. The buildings that lined the road were mostly log cabins built over two floors with ornate window frames and steeply pitched roofs.

Behind them were brightly painted three-story houses. Beyond the modest dwellings rose blue, red, and gold onion-domed towers and spiral turrets. Perhaps the colors were bright because otherwise they might be lost in the jaundiced yellow coal fire smoke belching out across the city.

By the time we finally stopped, bellies were rumbling, bladders were full, and the suns were dipping towards the horizon. We passed through a spiked gate set in a forbidding, stone wall beneath the unwavering gaze of tarred heads which adorned rusting spears mortared into the parapet. The clerk from Tomansk clutched his satchel, and fretful whispers were cut short when the wagon came to a juddering halt. The crunch of boots on gravel was followed by the sound of bolts being drawn. Mastered by fear, some of my fellow occupants cowered, tried to make themselves as small as possible. It availed them nothing. The door was thrown open and the nearest prisoner was dragged from the wagon. The fellow stumbled and fell, which was a misstep that earned him a vicious kick in the ribs from the fire-eyed thoasan guard.

"Everyone out!" the guard demanded. After his demonstration of casual brutality, the carriage occupants were only too keen to comply, and the wagon emptied quickly. We were harried towards a log hut while guards casually swiped at anyone who came within range of their clubs as they joked amongst themselves and commented on our various shortcomings. When the clerk from Tomansk dropped his satchel and tried to retrieve it, one of the guards cracked his skull with his club. There was a sickening crunch, and he went down shaking and twitching. I glanced over my shoulder and saw the guard standing over him, watching dispassionately as he choked to death on his tongue.

Encouraged by whips and boots, the rest of us were split off like tuskers being herded to the slaughterhouse; only instead of sows, boars, and squeakers, we were separated into Voskvans, foreigners, and ogren. It struck me that they hadn't pulled any pure thoasa or arrachids. I suspected because they couldn't parley obedience from even the weakest of those kinds of warspawn, which didn't say much for me. Me, the sailor, and another couple of Imperial humans were shoved into a hut, which was already full to bursting. The floor and walls were reinforced with steel plates. I would have casually tested the bars on the solitary window, but a furious half-ogren who had apparently not eaten in five days beat me to it. Driven by privation to blind fury, he rived at the bars while shouting for food and water and his rights under the law. Given what I'd seen and how I'd been treated, I considered he was either the greatest optimist I'd ever met or as mad as a sack of shaken snakes. Whatever ailed the poor cove, the cure came in the form of a single, well-aimed shot through the window.

When no guards appeared and the screaming died down, I carefully crawled through the spatter of brain jam and bone shards to the body, whereupon I made a most pious show of covering the remains while robbing what I could find. Pickings were thin, and all I managed to lift were a couple of tarnished silver buttons and a small gold earring. Needs being what they were, I stashed the meager chink in the last place anyone would want to search and then wedged myself in the corner of the hut. The space was a luxury bequeathed by the grace of the mostly headless corpse who I'd dragged aside with all due solemnity. I stayed there for the rest of the night and due to the presence of my headless friend, managed to avoid being stood on when my fellow detainees began to fight like rats in a trap over what scraps of food they could steal from each other.

I woke to a chill dawn and the sound of hobnail boots crunching on frozen ground. All eyes turned to the door as it was unbolted and flung open to reveal a thicket of polearms. With such a show of strength, all that was required to empty the hut in double-quick time were shouts and threats. As no cause came to mind for which I was prepared to bleed, I allowed myself to be swept along on the outflowing tide. Wagons were waiting at the end of the long row of huts where pale faces pressed against the barred windows watched as we ran past. People called out when they saw someone they knew, but with the encouragement of whips and clubs, no one stopped to claver. Even casting a sideways glance earned me a stroke of a split cane across the back, which to my surprise, I took with nary a growl of complaint.

I'd expected them to herd us into the wagons, but instead we were lined up before a gallows tree, its branches laden with three twitching fruit. Standing to the front of the scaffold, like an actor upon a stage, was a cove as round as he was tall with small, dark eyes peering from beneath a tall, fur hat. As was the fashion, his black beard hung to his armored belt and waved like cotton floss in the stiff, morning breeze. He rocked on his booted heels and watched as the guards bullied us into two ranks.

"I am Autcharch Sayev," he announced with all the self-importance you might expect of such a charming fellow. "You are here today to face judgement." He slammed his little fist into his palm. "You have broken the laws of the Archonate, the laws of the people." It's never a good sign when someone standing before a gallows tells you you're about to be judged. I wondered if I should perhaps make a break for the skull spiked wall or grab the little prick on the scaffold and barter him for my freedom. Alas, all I did was lower my gaze. "As punishment for your crimes, you will work off your debt to the people in the Kazalstas Coal Mines. You will serve Voskva and her citizens for five years. That is the judgement of the people of Voskva. So say I, Autcharch Sayev of the 4th district Correctional Facility of Sevast Province." He raised his hand and couldn't resist smiling as his words were met with gasps, sobs, and curses. "Before you embark on your journey of rehabilitation, any who wish to appeal the sentence step forward now."

I'm not what you might consider shy or retiring, but even I knew to stay where the fuck I was and keep my tongue behind my teeth. Although distraught, all but one of the other prisoners were of a like mind. The walking cautionary who stood forward was a thickset human, still in his prime and no worse for a few minor cuts and bruises. I watched with morbid curiosity as he went to stand in the shadow of the gallows.

"Brother Autcharch Sayev," he said and bowed. "Sir, I am an honest merchant from Tlini. I was kidnapped in broad daylight by thugs purporting to be Sevast City Watch. There were witnesses. I have been wronged, sir. I appeal—"

"Come closer. That's it." The Autcharch cut in, a wicked gleam in his eye. The knot in my gut tightened on behalf of the feckless cull. "That's far enough," said Sayev.

It was then that a cannoneer, probably the one who had taken off the ogren's head, made their presence known for a second time. Having seen the muzzle flash, I wasn't surprised when the shot from the roof of the building behind the gallows was fired. It was a sharp angle, but the aim was true and made a ruin of the merchant from Tlini.

"Appeal denied." The Autcharch could hardly contain his glee. Indeed, he was so keen to deliver the line that in my opinion, as someone versed in the theatrical arts, he threw it away. "Anyone else?" The Autcharch didn't wait for an answer as it was obvious that no one in their right mind would speak up after being showered in burning flesh. "Wise decision." I got the feeling that the Autcharch was a failed actor and therefore all would be wise to be wary. A failed anything is most often a bitter thing, and bitter things can be vicious. He clapped. "Acceptance is the first step on the road to salvation. Go now, with hope in your miscreant hearts. Rejoice! Rejoice that you are on the road to redemption. All hail Voskva! All hail the Archonate!" He turned his back as we were herded towards the wagons.

"Have no fear, scum. Nothing goes to waste! They'll work you to death then make pies of you and feed you to your comrades in chains," said a laughing guard as he kicked a skinny cove.

"Won't get many pies out of that little puke," said a thoasa who was throwing people into the wagons.

When we were loaded— too many into too small a space, the teams of woolly urux pulling the wagons lurched into motion. There was no room to sit, and those few quivering wrecks who had lost strength in their limbs had to rely on the kindness of their more robust neighbors to support them. I forced my way to the door, where a small grill allowed air and a limited view. I'd expected that we would travel in convoy, but soon after leaving the compound, the wagons went their separate ways. My wagon headed east, towards the interior. The steady clop of hooves was accompanied by crying, cursing, and beseeching of gods and saints. The mantra 'this can't be happening' was repeated like a prayer. I could have told them to save their breath, but who was I to disavow anyone of their beliefs? For my part, I felt strangely detached from the situation, untouched by their fear as though I was watching all that transpired from a distance. The old urgency I used to feel in such straits, the passionate desire to unfuck my situation with all haste was entirely absent. It felt like I was trapped in a dream that was on the verge of becoming a nightmare and all I could do was watch.

Chapter Six

It took almost three days for us to reach our destination. The wagon had pulled over both nights and our guards had set camp for themselves, but that was a luxury denied to me and my unfortunate fellows. No food was provided and drinking water was passed out but once a day. No doubt the cruel treatment was designed to winnow the weak and crush the spirits of those who survived.

Scared and angry, the prisoners grew fractious, and the denial of a ladle of brackish water led to savage fights. But there were also moments of kindness. On the second night, an ogrenish cove supported a stick-thin, insectoid woman and gently held her until she died. Still in the grip of an uncharacteristic malaise, I kept my own counsel throughout.

On the third night, the wagons pulled into a torchlit compound surrounded by a high, wooden stockade. The spear topped walls were patrolled by bored-looking guards and slavering tuskers with iron-tipped spines. A Voskvan in the wagon said the sign over the gate read, 'Magnificent Heartbeat of the Nation: Kazalstas Coal Mine (Number 2)'. It was a ridiculous name for what I would soon discover was a horrible place.

"I shouldn't be here..." came the familiar refrain from somewhere in the wagon. It was greeted by the equally predictable admonishments to shut the fuck up. I didn't add to the chorus, but I couldn't help thinking that I really shouldn't be here either.

The air tasted strongly of coal dust, and beyond the glare of torches, the rust brushed skeletons of winch towers imprisoned the indigo night in their steel bones. We were unloaded outside of a hut where I could see prisoners being shaved like livestock. When their dignity had been cast to the wind, the sorry crew were herded inside and then harried to the forges where the sound of irons being fitted rang like temple bells. When my turn came in the shearing shed, the cutting cove advanced upon me with a dead-eyed stare. I raised my hands as he came on. A kick in the back threw me forwards. The shearer grabbed a handful of hair spines and hauled me to my knees.

I didn't fight back. For the first time in my life, I was frozen with fear and unable to act. I felt sick; my guts trembled and fluttered. "Wait!" I pleaded. "It's not hair! It's skin and blood. If you cut my spines, I'll bleed out." It was an exaggeration, but I would bleed, and it would hurt like hell.

He grunted as though my words were gnats buzzing in his ears and wrapped a handful of spines around his fist. A couple of the other prisoners working in the shed grabbed my arms. Again, for reasons beyond my grasp, I didn't resist. "Don't, I pray you!" I begged in halting Voskvan.

"Niu! Stop that, you fucking idiot."

The fucking idiot with the shears turned to a woman who was forking piles of hair and fur into burlap sacks.

"It's a fucking lizard. It'll bleed to death if you cut the spines," she said, punctuating her speech with stabs of the fork into the bales of hair. "And if you kill it, you'll have to take its place, and then I have to take yours and I don't want to cut fucking hair. Do you want to work in the mines?"

Just to be sure, Niu snipped the end of one of my spines. It was small consolation that blood squirted in his face. I yelled. Niu slammed the butt of the shears into the side of my head, somehow managing to ram them into my earhole. I saw stars and would have fallen were I not being held by the barber's assistants. They released me, and the fucking idiot Niu dragged me to my feet and thrust me in the direction of the forge while cursing at me for bleeding on him.

"Dirty, fucking tert blood. It's poisonous, you know," he complained to the woman.

"Shut up, you fucking idiot," the woman repeated without looking at either of us.

Bleeding, disorientated, and with a sore ear, I stumbled into the forge where some of the others from my wagon were being measured for their jewelry. As panic murmurated in my gut like a flock of starlings, an errant part of my mind noted the ancient quality of the ironmongery. It was an odd thing to focus upon. Even more peculiar was that the sight of the shackles took me back to my childhood. *'Pick up the pace, you little louse, or you'll be wearing dead men's chains!'* Nix had said when I fell behind on a run across the rooftops of Appleton. I'd mistakenly thought she meant gibbet irons. Several lifetimes later I was experiencing a revelation. Why waste perfectly good irons and bury them with the dead when, according to the mountain of chains, so many were required for the glory of Voskva?

A shove from a fellow prisoner encouraged me into the forge. I did not resist when my turn came for leg irons to be hammered in place. Three feet of filth-encrusted chain linked them allowing enough play to walk but not enough to run or stride. I noted with a twinge of sadness that they weren't warded. Pride aside, all that would be required to remove them would be to smash the bolt or, if the tools came my way, cut the chain. Strangely lacking the will to do anything about my predicament, I stumbled through the stages of processing until I fetched up by a low roofed hut.

Men and women milled outside. Some of those who had clearly been here longer lounged within on long rows of wooden pallets. Their feet dangled over the end above rivers of water which ran freely through the sod roofed hut. No expense had been spent save that there were bad paintings on the walls of grim-faced men and women who I guessed must be the Archon Council. The leaders of Voskva stared unwaveringly from the moss and rag-lagged walls above signs written in Voskvan that I couldn't fathom. There were no fires or lamps, but the smell of coal was thoroughly enmeshed with the blue-glazed air.

"Hey, Red. Over here," someone called in halting Imperial.

I turned and saw a cove sitting with her back to the side of the hut beckoning me to join her. At first, I thought she was a venerable creature, but as I got closer, I realized she was just particularly wrinkly. When she stood to greet me, that assessment was partially confounded. The wrinkles ironed out as they stretched to accommodate her seven-and-a-half-foot frame. The skin of her face remained lax and hung in soft folds around her small nose and mouth. Her eyes were tiny pinpricks of light, bright within the shadow of her sagging brow.

"You are lost, yes? Don't worry, we all were once. See this?" She pointed to a daub of red paint on her patched coat. "It means I'm a New Prisoner Liaison. Only they don't call us prisoners, they call us 'the Indebted'." She winked. Her hands were huge and gnarled, each finger twice the length and thickness of mine. What passed for her hair was closer to a tangle of briars, with long sharp thorns twined in a tumbling crown around her gourd-shaped skull. "There are others. If you need to know something, don't ask a guard, ask someone with a red patch." She pointed to a half dozen others who were herding my fellow disorientated newcomers. "When the guards ask you if you have any skills. Try to think of something useful, yes? Painter, surgeon, smith…what do you do?"

"Er…" Admitting to being light-fingered was probably not a sound strategy in a prison. I had to think quickly, which was harder than it should have been. "Surgeon's assistant," I blurted. I could have said mortician, but I didn't fancy disposing of corpses from dawn to dusk.

"Oh, that's useful, yes? They like to get the most they can out of us." She patted me on the shoulder. The weight of her hand almost buckled me. "Can you pull teeth?"

"I have removed a few, aye."

"Even better. Your skills will keep you from the coal face, which is the last place in the world you want to be, yes?" She shuddered. "It is hell down there. There's gas, floods and...unnamed horrors that hunt in the darkness. Also, there are the guards. The ones they send down there are worse than the monsters, yes? Yes." Her habit of saying yes after almost every sentence was not as reassuring as she probably thought it was. "Keep your head down and your mouth shut, and you never know, you might end up like me. Up here all the time, yes?" Her thick stumpy fingers uncurled and reached for the sky like branches hungry for the suns to set sweetness within them and bring forth bud and leaf.

"What do I call you?"

She canted her head quizzically as though the question was perplexing, but then enlightenment dawned, and she nodded. "Ah. Yes. We don't use names here. I am Red Patch Seven, or 'Sevs' if you wish, but don't let the guards hear you say that. Diminutives are decadent and frowned upon by the Archonate. Silly I know, but they don't need much of an excuse to beat people. The guards here enjoy their work, yes."

I shrugged my bruised shoulders. "I noticed."

"They do not recruit beings with empathy to work here. Or perhaps they do, and they lose it over time." She rubbed her nose and glanced nervously into a distance I couldn't see from my lower vantage. "The most brutal are the Tasklisk…er…Thoasa, yes?"

I felt a sudden attack of borrowed afront, which was queer as all I had in common with thoasa were physical characteristics. Culturally, I had nothing in common with Voskvans of any stripe, including thoasa, and yet I felt the prickle of having somehow been slighted. "Are you sure?"

She nodded. "Oh, yes, child. Others with more stomach for such things will regale you with tales of their nasty habits. Don't believe everything you hear, just most of it. It's best to avoid them when you can." Her hand drifted without thought to an old burn on her side. "Bind your hair, rub dirt on your skin. You look new, so the Indebted will try to take advantage, and the guards will beat you more to teach you your place. Keep your head down, blend in."

I looked around. Me and my fellow new arrivals did indeed stand out like cocks in a henhouse. Although my comrades had a modicum of safety in numbers on their side. Shaved and powdered they looked like a flock of ghosts. Aside of patches of human skin, I was the only cove who happened to be bright red and orange. Sev's advice was sound if a touch hopeful.

Before my new friend could continue her welcome speech, the ground began to rumble beneath us. It was followed by the muffled boom of buried thunder. Shortly thereafter, a gout of oily smoke burst from one of the mine shafts beyond the huts. The cage winch screamed, and the smell of burning ropes and hot steel added to the gassy stench of coal dust filling the air. Some ran towards the mine head, more ran away from it.

Sevs nodded. "Don't worry, it happens a lot. There's plenty of coal here but it is a dangerous land. We're close to the river, and the rotten marshes, and ancestors-know-what monsters. Voskva is blessed with an abundance of monsters. You can hear them sometimes, howling in the darkness."

"Thanks for the warning."

"Do you have anything of value?"

"In exchange for your advice?" I needed to know; the answer would determine if she got a piece of leather thong or a silver button.

"For a token, yes?" She smiled. "I've been here a while. My token has value with some."

It might be urux shit, but it was the best offer I'd had of late. "Just a minute."

I nipped around the side of the hut and retrieved a button. After giving it a rinse in a puddle, I slipped it into her hand.

She nodded as she took the silver button. "A nice piece, and still warm. Not your first time enjoying the hospitality of the state, yes?"

"First time in Voskva."

She reached up and snapped a thorn from her hair and handed it to me. "Display it somewhere. Wear it in your clothes, a string around your neck. It has no magic…not here, but it has some small influence with some, a silver button's worth at least."

"Out of interest, what would a gold button have bought me?"

She gave a laugh that sounded like the spatter of rain on young leaves. "This is not the kind of place for such fanciful speculation. Go, join the others, and remember what I said."

Before heading over to the knot of newcomers milling outside of the hut, I anointed those bits of me that clothes didn't cover with mud and then waited with the others as work details brought the bodies out of the mine. A guard not supervising the corpse retrieval shouted for newcomers to form up. We shuffled into three ranks, where I made sure to put myself in the second and hunch down behind the cove in front. Even with the savage encouragement of the guards' boots and whips, it took a couple of minutes for the ragged crew to assemble. I wondered idly if Swann and Nic were looking for me. Something told me they weren't.

"Any skills?" A tert guard bellowed in my face.

"Surgeon," I said confidently and hoped I'd got the right word and hadn't accidentally called him a cunt in Voskvan.

The guard rubbed his jaw. "Surgeon, eh?" he laughed. "Tasklisk surgeon," he said again, obviously amused. "What fucking use is that? Tasklisk don't get sick."

Either his laughter or his words were enough to draw the attention of a nearby thoasan guard. I wondered if I might have found a friend in the green-gold female, but when I saw her snort and smelled the stink of her ire bloom in the air, I realized I had not. She marched over, tail swishing, and I thought she said, "What you say, Dogface?"

Dogface gestured to me and said something along the lines of "This tasklisk is a surgeon."

She snorted. "So?"

"Never seen a tasklisk surgeon before."

The thoasa spoke too rapidly for me to catch much other than her declaring that I wasn't a thoasa, I was a tert.

"Half thoasa," I said, which it turned out was a mistake. The thoasa narrowed her eyes and took two steps towards me. I could see the backhand coming and swayed aside out of reflex. Had I been sensible, I would have taken the hit.

Dogface chuckled and said something that included, "You have a friend." Whatever the whole content, it did not go down well. Like water, the thoasa's anger followed the path of least resistance. Furious, she spun and lashed out at me with her tail. I realized that losing was the only option. I braced but even so, catching the full force of the powerful strike in my gut knocked me off my feet. I hoped that would be it, but no one ever said thoasa were easy to placate once their anger was stoked. She grabbed me by the shirt and snarled something in Voskvan that I didn't understand. Under normal circumstances, I would have raked her with my claws or tried to gouge her eyes out, but these were far from normal circumstances. My usually reliable survival instincts had gone on an unauthorized leave of absence. I was bereft and bewildered, although with hindsight, the lack of a will to fight probably saved my life, if not my pride.

"Say it!" she said. She put her hands around my throat and began to squeeze, which was at odds with her request, but I was in no position to tell her that.

"I…don't know what…" I gasped.

"She said, 'Say you're not a thoasa'," someone I couldn't see offered helpfully.

"Not tasklisk," I said in halting Voskvan.

She snarled in my face and gave me a parting squeeze before slamming me into the dirt and storming off with her tail thrashing angrily.

Having had his fun at my expense, a chuckling Dogface turned his back and continued questioning the other new prisoners, leaving me curled in the dirt practicing breathing. As I lay there, I watched someone wearing a pair of mismatched boots held together with string wander over and stand before me.

"Surgeon, eh?" It was my helpful translator who was, again, speaking excellent Imperial.

I groaned in an affirmative manner. A moment's pause was followed by a filthy, half-gloved hand reaching down. The nails were dirty, human, short, and chewed.

"I'm the doctor here," he said with an embarrassed laugh. "Well, more, 'barber surgeon'. More barber – well, more tooth-puller actually."

I looked up and saw a surprisingly plump fellow with curly, mousy hair looking down at me. His pale blue eyes look small, imprisoned as they were behind the scratched lenses of a pair of mangled, wire-frame spectacles. He was wearing a patched overcoat that was tied around the waist with string. Here, let me help you," he said with a genuinely friendly smile.

I warily took his hand. Despite the kindness of his offer, I had to help myself up as he couldn't support my weight and began to topple. "Let's get to the infirmary before they change their mind." He pointed to the winch house. "Our chariot to hell awaits. I'm only joking, it's not that bad below once you get used to it." He pointed to the thorn pinned through my shirt. "Ah, I see you've met Sevs. She's a strange one. Alas, she lacks even the slightest grasp of politics, progressive or otherwise, but she has a good heart that I think is in the right place for her species. Cheer up, this is your lucky day."

Having just been rolled without so much as attempting to defend myself, I could not agree with his optimistic assessment.

Chapter Seven

As I liked being underground, I wasn't gripped with the same terror that was carved on the faces of the other new prisoners in the rattling winch cage. But I didn't descend unscathed. The horror that consumed me, that gnawed at my guts, was that I'd let myself take a beating. I had naively thought that not being able to use magic had made me 'ordinary', by which I really meant, 'weak'.

It wasn't.

Being unable to fight back made me weak, made me ordinary. It wasn't a humbling revelation that struck a chord with me. I wasn't going to start my own religion, sit on a mountain verbally wanking on about 'real strength is in the heart' or some such bollocks. I was terrified. For the first time I understood why 'ordinary' mortals were so petty and gave a fuck about everything. It was because like me right now, they were scared shitless. I didn't hold with it, didn't accept it, or respect it, but for the first time in my existence, I understood it. It was high upon the list of lessons I never wanted to learn. Of course, for every rule there is an exception. My savior was a soft-bodied cove, peering at the world through cracked spectacles, and yet he exuded a kind of confidence I would not expect of a fellow like him in a place like this.

"All out who's getting out!" the cage master barked.

"That's us." My rescuer gave my arm a reassuring squeeze as he helped me alight. The gate slammed down behind us. I saw the pale faces of the prisoners still in the cage yearn towards the light before they were swallowed by the stifling darkness.

"This is Level One. You will also hear it called 'Heaven's Gate' by the guards. We prisoners refer to it as, *adu odbyt.*" He giggled. *"*Which translates to 'hell's anus' in Imperial, I think. Just don't repeat that one in earshot of the guards."

"How many levels are there?"

"Currently four, ground water and rain allowing. Come, we don't want to be caught loitering." We headed west along the main tunnel, following cart tracks that shone like polished pewter in the faint light of cracked glow stones bolted to the walls. Voices echoed, and the sound of picks reverberated. The rattle of the chain pump drawing water from the face was accompanied by a constant spatter of rain that rang the pulley chains.

"Be it ever so humble," said the surgeon as he gestured expansively to a walled-off side tunnel. Above the doorway was a water-stained sign that I guessed said 'Infirmary'. The door was leaning against the frame secured neither by latch nor hinge. With some difficulty he shoved it aside and beckoned for me to enter. It was hot inside; the cooling blast of air from the lift shaft slid past the door and did little to dilute the fetid stink within. By the sound of our echoing footsteps, the chamber went back some way beyond a ragged curtain partition. As I'd expected, the smell of death hung in the air, along with a strong smell of piss.

He took a stub of candle from his coat pocket and stuck it in a tin cup on what looked like an operating table complete with an adjustable head rest at one end. Judging by the age of the bloodstains and the relative freshness of the breadcrumbs, I guessed that the table was used more for dining than operating. There was a chair which was held together by rope and the memory of sound carpentry. A sideboard was propped on bricks against one wall, and an unlit stove, water butt, and mortuary slab lay against the other. The rest of the tunnel was hidden behind the curtain. Mismatched pallets had been laid on the floor in a vain attempt to keep feet above the slurry. "If you smell gas, doff any flames immediately," he said.

"This isn't my first time underground."

"Is it your first time in a mine though?" He shoved the wonky spectacles from the tip of his snub nose. Like a sleek bodied creature that might live in a hedgerow or nest in a riverbank he regarded me with large, sad eyes. "Who are you by the way, what is your name?"

"Chas Amberley." I wanted to sketch a bow, but it didn't seem appropriate in a place like this. "I'm a physiker's assistant and I have no idea why I'm here."

He nodded approvingly. "If I believed in gods, I would thank them. As it is, I thank luck and happy coincidence for bringing you here while I am a prisoner."

"I was kidnapped. Dragged here on a lie."

Aghast, he shoved past me and listened at the excuse for a door, his shoulders tight as a hangman's knot. Eventually, he relaxed and returned to the table. "You must keep your voice down. Do you want to die?"

"Not right now, no."

He ran a hand through his greasy curls. "Forgive my abruptness and lack of manners. It has been a while since I've had company and much longer since I've spoken your bastard tongue."

"Excuse me?"

"Don't worry, it's just what we call Imperial, it's a term of endearment."

"Ah, right. I see." I didn't.

"I, am Ockzar Donvyr Millmets." He did a funny little heel click and then, more disconcertingly, grabbed me by the shoulders and kissed me on both cheeks before giving me a hug. When he looked at me again there were tears in his eyes. "You have come to the right place."

"I have?" I own, I was somewhat skeptical.

"Yes! I will teach you about the true glory of our liberation from the moribund and decadent past." He leaned in. "The real glory, not the *guwna prevdu* that the traitors who stole our revolution try to pass off as 'doctrine'." He snorted. "I will enlighten you, poor, downtrodden pawn of a corrupt, hierarchical system. And just so you know, I count your kind as *kin,* equal to humans in almost every way."

I gently but firmly unpeeled his hands and took a half step back. "I…er. Thanks."

He laughed and ledged his arse on the edge of the table. "I see you're curious." He smiled with a confidence born of a misunderstanding. I was confused, not curious. "I was part of the Glorious Uprising." He slapped his chest with a dimple-knuckled fist. "We failed but, oh, we failed *gloriously*, as I am sure you know."

"Sorry, I wasn't here long before I was done up by the law."

"Ah. A pity on both counts. Many true revolutionaries were also, as you so charmingly say, 'done up' and sent here to rot, myself amongst them. But we will not be silenced, and the real revolution will not be stopped," he whispered.

It seemed that I had misjudged the mousy fellow. It was possible that I had found a useful ally, someone who perhaps had contacts. I leaned in. "What did you do in the uprising?"

His face lit up. "I wrote pamphlets. Hundreds of them. Amongst the many causes I championed was the fair treatment of beings like you. Kresps in particular have a terrible time in Voskva. The People's Party refuse to admit them, can you believe it?"

Hope of a useful alliance faded. "Have you asked them?"

"The Peoples Party?"

"Kresps. Did you ask them if they wanted to be in the People's Party?"

He chuckled. "No, of course not, why wouldn't they want to join? But I digress. In short, because of my mission to denounce the doctrine of the Archon Council I was denied martyrdom. You see, my unbelievably valuable but utterly thankless work precluded me from joining the Day of Uprising on the Glorious 10th." He sighed heavily. "I console myself that I was there in spirit with my brothers and sisters as they died trying to storm the People's Palace."

Bored of the history lesson, I made a bid to change the subject. "It smells strongly of piss in here. Is there a leaky privy nearby?"

"Ah." He picked up a sloshing bucket and plonked it on the table. "I wasn't expecting company. Very few surgeons or indeed, surgeon's assistants are pressed into service. They tend to pick those with strong backs to work in the mines."

"If only I'd known when I was grabbed, I could have told them my trade. Any reason you keep your piss under the table?"

Before he could answer someone shouted from behind the ragged curtain. "Ockzar, you fucking weevil, where are you?" Whoever it was coughed. "Ockzar!"

"I'm coming! Damn it. Just hush, I'll be there anon." He took a tray of wires and teeth from under the table and put it down as though displaying a tray of the finest diamonds. "I make dentures. They are in high demand amongst the guards on account of how white I can make even old, brown nubs appear on account of my 'method'." He patted the bucket of piss.

"You clean dead coves' teeth with your piss?"

"Not always dead people, some donate while alive and yes, my piss and coal dust formula is excellent for removing grime. Behold." He held up a row of wired teeth and a loose molar, which in comparison was browner than those that had been wired. "See the difference?"

"I do." I did. "It's ingenious. Disgusting, but ingenious." A good set of false gnashers wasn't cheap. This little side-line would explain why he managed to stay hog round when even the rats in this shithole were skinny.

"Ockzar!" the angry invalid shouted again. "If you make me come find you…"

He slammed the teeth back onto the tray. "I'm coming!" he shouted and then muttered under his breath. "Ungrateful prick. Pass me that knife, would you?" He took note of the surprise that had leaked onto my face and laughed. "Don't worry, I'm not going to kill him. I'm just going to bleed him for his own good, he has bilious humors you see. Come with me and hold the candle."

"Got a nice pair of molars here," I said in my much-improved Voskvan as I sorted teeth into piles.

"Put them to one side," Ockzar mumbled absently as he carefully drilled a hole in a tooth. We had reaped a bumper harvest on account of a flood that had killed a dozen on the coal face earlier that week. In the month

I'd been here, assisting the industrious, if delusional revolutionary-cum-barber surgeon, I'd learned that floods and fevers were good for business. Collapses and explosions were far less lucrative because the 'mouth pearls' were often ruined by being crushed, burned or blown apart.

As there was currently only one patient in the infirmary; an old, petty thief called Stav, we had all the time in the world to work on Ockzar's profitable little business. Stav was doing his part and dying quietly of stomach cancer, drugged beyond pain's reach with a concoction of jail-brewed rum and some pel. It was interesting to note that, although happy to rip the teeth from still warm corpses, Ockzar was thoughtful enough to spend some of his hard-earned coin buying drugs to ease an old man's pain. While Stav drifted off to the void, we worked in the 'waiting room' as we called the curtained-off, first third of the infirmary tunnel. It was also where we lived, ate, and performed rudimentary surgery when the need arose, which was usually a couple of times a week. "So, what did you do to get the shiv?" The broken sliver of steel was Ockzar's most prized possession.

He gave a wry smile and then giggled like a child. "I sang the Heroic Litany — all twenty verses while Guard Ruslik, how would you say it? 'spunked his muck' over a painting of the Archon Council." He laughed harder. "I mean, at the time I was terrified, but in hindsight it's very funny. Indeed, whenever I look at that…" He glanced at the painting of the Archon

Council, which was hanging on the wall above the door, "I can't help but smile. The funniest thing is Ruslik didn't spill his seed over them as an insult. When he stands up during Denouncements and Affirmations and says he *loves* the Archon Council, he really means it."

"Is that the same picture? Did you keep it as a memento?"

The crunch of boots outside put an end to the discussion. Given they were trying to sneak, it was most likely a guard. I gestured to Ockzar, who put the tray of half-made dentures under the table while I swept the loose teeth into a can of cold piss and put it on the floor. We then set about scrubbing blood from our operating dining table.

Moments later, the door plank was shoved aside. It was an Autcharch, one of the official representatives of the People's Party. They were sent to the mines to root out counter-counter revolutionaries and royalist sympathizers while at the same time indoctrinating everyone else into the one and only way of the Archon Council. Autcharch Shez was a nasty, sour-faced creature. She wandered alone in the mines with impunity on account of the warded sigils of protection woven into the party insignia emblazoned on her coat and cap. Given her predilection for beating people across the face with the urux whip she carried, we both jumped to attention and kept our eyes down as she stepped inside.

"Praise be to the Archons of the People," she intoned.

"Long live Voskva, joyful and glorious nation!" we chanted in unison. Shez nodded and tipped my chin with the end of her whip. I was taller than the grey-haired viper, but still just about managed to keep my gaze lower than hers. It was a little game we played. I'd lost the last time she came for a visit but the cut on my jaw was almost healed.

"Has Millmets continued with your instruction, decadent, Imperial swine?"

"Yes, Autcharch Shez." She smiled tightly and feigned turning away. I saw what was coming and braced as the whip came back at me and caught me in almost the exact same place that she had struck me on her last visit. My head snapped back; my hands flew reflexively to my jaw.

"That's *Sister* Autcharch Shez, for we are all brothers and sisters in Glorious Voskva. See that you remember." Having satisfied her perverse desire to inflict pain, she left without another word. Ockzar remained rooted to the spot. Bleeding, I leaned on the table, undoing the work I'd just done. When the terror left him, Ockzar came over and helped me into the chair.

"You could have dodged that blow," he said as he began dabbing at the blood with an almost clean rag.

"She was in a good mood; I didn't want to spoil it by thwarting her."

"A person like you could snap her in twain, even with the wards."

"That's debatable. But why don't *you* ever fight back? When the guards push you around or make you recite poetry when they want to knock one out, why do you just take it?"

Ockzar focused on the wound rather than look me in the eye. "Nature has been uneven in her gifts. She gave me a fairly serviceable brain, but not much by way of brawn."

"So, what you're saying is, you're too smart to fight back?"

"Let's say I think I'm bright enough to know when I'm outmatched."

"But you asked why I don't fight back?"

He blushed. "We're very different people, you and I."

"Are you saying you're surprised I don't fight back because I'm too thick to forbear?"

"No, it's not that." He laughed nervously, betraying the lie. "Hold that there until it stops bleeding." He pressed my hand to the rag. "I've seen the way you look when someone roughs you up. Ferocity lights in your eye. If I might be poetic, it is like a flash of lightning, sharp but gone as quickly as it comes. It's like you're holding something back."

"Trust me, I'm not," I replied glumly. "I just…" It struck me then that I didn't know what was wrong with me. "I just need to get out of here."

"Even if your friends are looking for you it could take years. Why, my family have been petitioning for…eighteen months now, and they are no further in securing a re-trial than they were when I was first sentenced."

"I don't know how you stand it."

He shrugged and gestured to the teeth under the table. "I keep busy with my work and do my best to ease suffering where I can. I also write my manifesto, in my head of course, but it will be a great work running to many volumes."

"Many volumes? No one's that interesting."

"I am not, no. But my ideas? They will change the world."

Dreams. Ockzar lived in his dreams of revolution and hid from the horror of his existence in the stories he told himself about himself. There was a time I would have laughed at such a brain-bound cove, but right now I very much envied his gift for self-delusion. "My friends better pull their fucking fingers out, or I'm going to throw myself at the fucking fence," I said knowing that I didn't have the guts to do it.

"Don't do that." He looked horrified. "Don't even say such a thing."

"Why, would you miss me?"

"Well, yes, I've enjoyed your company, decadent Imperial swine though you are." He smiled with real warmth. "Also, if you throw yourself at the fence, you'll be reduced to a shriveled husk and your teeth will be useless, and that would be a waste of such nice, white fangs."

Painful though it was, I laughed. "Oh, speaking of which." I reached under the table and took out the tray of teeth and a set of dentures I'd been working on. "What do you think?"

Ockzar peered over the rim of his spectacles. "In a word? Nightmarish."

I was hurt. "What do you mean?"

"It's all fangs."

"And? You need to cater to all markets. Some of us have fangs."

"But not *all* fangs, surely? And besides…" He pushed his spectacles up his nose, as was his habit. "…My oppressed fanged brethren don't often have the money— due to being oppressed— to buy false teeth. Or indeed, due to your remarkable natural gifts, rarely the need for them." He smiled. "It was a useful practice for you, but best to disassemble them. I need the wire."

Perhaps thinking he'd offended me; he patted my arm. "It was a good effort, Chas, really. I am convinced that had you been given a proper education, you would have made an excellent dentationist."

"That means a lot to me." A lot of bollocks, but as I knew he meant well, I didn't elaborate.

Chapter Eight

Not counting guards, (but there were four), nine terts, twelve humans, fifteen ogren, and three amphibane Indebted, including me and Ockzar had been rounded up for the weekly Denouncement and Affirmation session. It was torture of a kind, administered in what had been a chapel excavated by miners in the bad old days before the Glorious Revolution.

In one of his many monologues, which ranged from the nature of the universe to soup, Ockzar had informed me that it had been built a century earlier by the miners. In those unenlightened times, it was dedicated to gods whose images had been destroyed and replaced with pictures of the Archon Council. Today, the brave leaders gazed upon us, haloed by the rays of the suns, surrounded by the adoring citizens they had freed from the tyranny of faith. As I stood there, chanting meaningless phrases in terrible Voskvan, something soft brushed my foot. I looked down and saw an uncommonly bold rat peering up at me, its slender tail tapping my foot. "Fuck off." I hissed. Evidently slighted by what I thought was a perfectly reasonable comment, the rat squeaked indignantly and bared its long, yellow incisors before running through my legs and up the stairs to the main drift passage.

Beside me, Ockzar was showing off by loudly chanting the Heroic Litany, which he knew by heart, a smug grin on his cherubic face. Almost everyone else was mumbling their way through it. Like me, many were hampered by not knowing much Voskvan, which made for an interesting range of interpretations. When the gaze of Autcharch Shez fell like a blade upon a portion of the congregation, greater effort was made in that area. To the relief of all, she couldn't watch everyone at once from the pulpit where she presided over the weekly shaming of transgressors.

While we butchered the pompous litany, a bloodied and bound cove was dragged before the ranks by a thoasan guard. I was always disappointed when it was a thoasa. Call me an old romantic, but I just wanted them to be better. Of course, they weren't. They were like any other race, comprising angels, demons, and every shade of cove in between. I don't know if he caught me staring or if I was just lucky; either way, our eyes met, and the guard bared his fangs, and the scent signature of bones and blood bloomed in the air. I looked away, the dread of an impending beating knotting my guts. Shez raised her whip, and the recitation of the litany ended abruptly.

"Brothers and sisters, we have a dissenter in our midst." She waited for the obligatory jeers before continuing. "Brother Kydor was once a loyal soldier of the Glorious Revolution and beloved of the Archon Council. But he has fallen!" She paused to allow for more booing. "Yes, my indebted brothers and sisters, he has fallen to the twin evils of egotism and self-Indulgence." Everyone knew the drill and heaped curses upon the insensate prisoner. Unlike Ockzar, real revolutionaries like Kydor had been sent to the mines to die. If the lack of food combined with hazardous working conditions didn't finish them off, then the beatings that followed the Denouncements and Affirmation meetings did for them sooner rather than later. "He has stolen food from his brothers and sisters! What do we say to the selfish and the greedy?"

"Shame! Shame on you! Shame, shame…" The mass response echoed around the chamber. It was so loud, so desperately fervent, that it almost masked the sound of the bones of the earth beginning to grind. The rats heard it though and began to flee the chamber in their droves. The chant died. A shout went up from somewhere in the main drift tunnel, and a fine mist of stone dust began to fall. When the ground started to shake, I grabbed hold of Ockzar, braced, and waited for the thunder. As quickly as it had begun, the rumbling subsided.

Ockzar sagged, visibly relieved. "Just a small one."

Although that seemed to be the case, the tremor was enough to alarm Autcharch Shez. She gestured to the guard who, likewise keen to leave, picked up the barely conscious dissident and carried him from the chapel. "Finish the Litany, Guard Brother Ruslik," she said before rushing from the chapel, no doubt heading directly to the winch cage. Ruslik and the remaining guards looked longingly after her before rushing us through the remaining verses. When we were done, we were encouraged to disperse quickly by a well-placed boot or two. I put Ockzar between me and the bulls as we hurried from the chapel, the aftershocks of whatever disturbance had just occurred still shivering the ground.

"Did you get it?" I asked Ockzar.

"Yes, here." He made to pass me the chisel he'd just bought from Ruslik, but I stopped him.

"Not here, you fool."

"I don't want it a moment longer," he hissed. "It's a hanging offence to be caught with something like this. No trial, just a straight drop."

"I know! Just wait until we're around the corner, for fuck's sake."

The second we rounded the corner, he thrust the chisel into my hand.

"It's a bit small," I said as I stuffed it down the leg of my breeches and into the pocket I'd sown for that very purpose.

"It's a silver button and two sets of dentures worth of chisel. Be thankful he didn't just take our stuff and give us nothing."

"He wouldn't do that."

"You're sure, are you?

"Aye. Who else would he get to recite the Litany while he has a tug?"

Ockzar grinned. "You still owe me."

Up ahead, I spotted a family of rats; mother, father, and four kittens plopped from a hole in the passage and ran off down a side tunnel. "What was that, Ockzar?"

He huffed. "I said I don't think you listen to me sometimes."

"Probably less than you think." I grinned.

"You see? You don't care. If you're caught with a chisel, it's execution. If you're caught with broken shackles, execution. And even if you break your chains, you still have to get out of here. How do you plan on doing that?

"Up the chain pump. Easy."

"And then you have to get out of the camp, over warded fences, and past thoasan guards with keener senses than you."

"Fear not. I used to do this kind of thing for a living, and I was very good at it."

He rolled his eyes. "And when you're outside, what then? To the trackless marshes or—" Another tremor caused him to pause. "Or the freezing river? Trying to escape is a terrible idea."

I leaned in. "Don't worry, I've got everything in hand."

A sudden cry went up from somewhere behind us. It was followed by another and then a whole chorus of shouts and screams. A moment later I knew why. The ground of the main passage began to rise beneath us like bread in the oven, buckling the cart tracks as it swelled. Ahead of us, I could see more rats dropping from their bolt holes and running down the same tunnel the rodent family had taken.

My gut said we should do the same. "Come on." I grabbed Ockzar by the arm and tried to hurry him along. My ears popped as the air was forced through the tunnel. The wave of pressure was followed by the roar of water growing louder by the second.

"Where are we going?" Ockzar shouted. By now water was pooling around our ankles, and miners were charging from tunnels, discarding picks as they ran for the winch cage. "We need to get to the winch!"

"We won't reach it. This way," I said.

"Where the hell are we going?" He was already panting.

"Follow the rats," I shouted over the din.

 Fearful and disorientated, Ockzar tried to pull away. "Are you insane?" he squealed.

Bored of the debate, I dragged him behind me and ran as quickly as he and the shackles would allow. As he was a foot shorter than me and by his own admission disinclined to physical exertion, that wasn't very fast. To add to my unending joy, as we headed down the tunnel more rats with the same idea swarmed after us. They weren't particularly aggressive; they just didn't want to drown in the flood they'd sensed was coming. In a blind panic, they leaped and clawed and nipped at whatever was in their way, which happened to be us.

"We're going to die!" Ockzar yelled. "Let me go!"

He was panicking and therefore not thinking straight, so I ignored him. Having grown up with rats for playmates, I knew they could sense fires, floods, and earthquakes before they happened and were wise enough to flee from danger while lesser beings flapped and fardelled. Being one of the aforementioned lesser beings, Ockzar looked like he might just drop dead from the effort of putting one foot in front of the other. To underscore his ineptitude, he fell and almost dragged me down with him. I hauled him to his feet as the water rose swiftly around us and pit props began to creak and crack. By the time we'd gone another six feet, the water was over my waist and up to Ockzar's chest. Behind us, I could hear miners fighting to get to the cage lift.

Shaking with cold and fear, Ockzar fell silent and clung to my arm like his life depended on it, which it did. It would have been the easiest thing in the world to scrape him off and leave him to his fate. Indeed, I wasn't sure why I was wasting time and energy bringing him with me.

"Oi!"

I turned to see a particularly unpleasant thoasan guard who insisted on calling me 'runt'. He was standing near a side passage and covered in fresh blood, although he didn't look injured. Something that looked like a half-eaten body floated from behind him and bobbed against his knees in the swirling water. "Where the fuck do you think you're going?" he shouted at us.

I ignored him and pressed on.

Ockzar slowed his pace. "We should stop."

"The fuck," I hissed, incredulous.

"We can't outrun him."

"Don't ignore me, runt." The thoasa bellowed.

Above the shouting and screaming and roar of rushing water, I could hear a little voice in my head telling me to let Ockzar go. I was sorely tempted, but as we'd come this far together it seemed a shame to give up on him now. The thoasa wasn't giving up either, and shortly thereafter he caught up, yanked Ockzar from my grasp and tossed him aside like a wet rag. I was fast, but the thoasa was faster. He grabbed me by the shirt and pinned me against the wall.

"I said, where do you think you're going, runt?" He snarled in my face.

"Rats." I squeaked. "Follow…rats."

He thought about it for a moment and then cast me aside and dived after the rats. Something big and soft brushed against me under the water. "Shit. Ockzar!" I grabbed him before he could float away and hauled him to the surface. He gasped. The ground buckled. Whatever pumps had been slowing, the steadily rising waters finally gave out. Ockzar screamed and threw his arms around my neck as a wall of white water boiled towards us, carrying miners, carts, and other assorted debris. Out of time, I slung Ockzar onto my back like a sack of coal and took a last, deep breath before it hit.

I'd expected that I would allow myself to be carried with the flow, that I would skillfully guide myself along the walls and avoid being knocked senseless by a mining cart or indeed a miner. I also promised myself that if Ockzar didn't stop choking me, I would scrape him off my back like a barnacle off a rock. What I didn't expect was that something I couldn't see would wrap thick, sinuous coils around me and drag me and my passenger through the flood. My first instinct was to freeze when it grabbed me. My second was to struggle – until I noticed that whatever it was wasn't trying to crush me, eat me, or smash my brains in, whereupon I relaxed and let it take us.

As we powered effortlessly through the water, Ockzar's grip tightened. I knew it to be the last, fearful spasm of a creature aware that it was dying. Soon after, his arms loosened. I grabbed his wrist, felt the pulse slow. I'd failed. I'd tried to save him, but he was dying anyway, the fucker. It was vexing to be so thwarted. To satisfy my ego, I felt compelled to commit an ignoble sacrifice. Keeping a firm grip on his arm, I tilted my head back, pinched his nose, and breathed some precious breath into his mouth. His pulse quickened. While I was focused on extending the slender thread of his life, our serpentine savior maneuvered us deftly through the black water.

Warily grateful though I was, time was the enemy. Ockzar was floundering, and due to an uncharacteristic attack of generosity, my lungs were beginning to yearn for a gulp of air. Perhaps sensing my discomfort, whatever the thing was increased its speed. We caught up with the rats and swept through their sleek forms. The pressure of the water bore down upon me, my ears popped again. Just as I felt my head was about to burst, we shot out into the frigid night like a cork from a bottle of Voskvan fizz. The benevolent 'serpent' of water exploded in a shower of star-lit droplets. Distant lights blurred on the dark horizon. My hungry lungs gulped cold, crisp air like wine. I released Ockzar and was relieved to hear a howl just before I landed in a scummy bog pool. My relief was short-lived, for not a minute later the thoasa burst from the hole. Yellow eyes blazing, he rose from the mud. I struggled to my feet, the simple task hindered by the fucking leg irons.

"Indebted scum!" the thoasa snarled.

"Scum? That's nice." I flicked filth from my hands. "I didn't cause the fucking flood, you know."

He thrashed his tail. Took a step towards me. "Who do you think you're talking to, runt?"

"Oh, do fuck off. I just saved your life." I turned to help Ockzar, who was struggling to stand. I didn't expect the thoasa to be reasonable, but I didn't consider just how petty he was going to be. I could only apologize to myself for being so wrong-headed when the bastard leaped upon me and grabbed a handful of my hair spines.

Before I had chance to take a breath, he thrust me underwater and despite my best efforts, held me there. Not content to wait for me to drown, he kneed me in the gut. Air exploded from me, but by some miracle of self-preservation I resisted the reflex to gasp. Consummate actor that I was, I estimated a reasonable length of time that a prick like him would think a *runt* like me could hold their breath. I then had a last, desperate flail before falling limp. As I'd hoped, he released me. Breath held, I drifted, partially submerged while he turned his attention to Ockzar.

"The punishment for attempting to escape is death," the Thoasa said. Sudden movement sent me bobbing into a reed bed. Once I was amongst the weeds, I took the opportunity to breathe again.

"I implore you to be reasonable," Ockzar begged. "It wasn't an attempted escape; I was just carried along." He laughed nervously. "Unlike you, I'm only human. I lack the strength to fight against a flood."

"Don't arse kiss, it demeans you and insults me."

"You're absolutely right. Please, forgive me. I wasn't thinking."

"Shut up, scum."

"I am a prisoner of ideology, not a criminal. I am a philosopher."

"A thinking type, eh?"

"That is a more complicated question than you'd imagine, but yes, in essence." Ockzar sounded relieved, which was somewhat premature in my estimation.

"I'm going to fuck you, and then I'm going to eat you. Not all of you, just a few delicacies. What do you think about that, philosopher?"

"Is that a trick question?" Ockzar squeaked. "Please, just take me back."

"Take you back? Oh no, my fat, little friend. You've made your bed, now it's time to get fucked on it…And then drowned and eaten."

The thoasa advanced. Rooted by fear, Ockzar didn't attempt to flee or defend himself. When I was a sorcerer, I could have taken the thoasa without breaking a sweat. However, as much as I hated to admit it even to myself, sorcery or not, I lacked the stomach to fight. All I could hope to do was distract the prick, and to that end I began quietly hunting for something to throw, like a rock or a stick.

"Please, don't do this…" said Ockzar, who began to kneel in supplication before realizing that would put him under the water and so hovered awkwardly.

The thoasa burst out laughing. "Get up, physik. I'm not going to fuck you or eat you."

"You're not?"

"No, fool. I'm not a monster."

"You killed Chas."

"That? It's a freak of nature, and trouble. You, are a good Indebted. You keep your head down, you show respect, and you're going to get me a promotion when you tell the Commandant how I saved you." He canted his head, sniffed. "What the fuck is that?"

Whatever he'd sensed had moved quietly and stayed downwind until the last second, when I also heard and smelled it. With a roar, a huge, pale beast launched itself at the thoasa.

"Wait, Jimma!" Swann shouted. "I'm sure we can-"

An explosion of motion drowned out whatever Swann said as the water churned around the thoasa and the pale beast, sending waves crashing into the muddy banks. As the thoasa was now busy, I gave up any pretence of being dead and untangled myself from the reeds. The thoasa's adversary was as tall as he was and as powerfully built. Like the lizard, it had a tail and claws, and its long incisors gleamed yellow in the scatter of starlight. Feral orange eyes stared into furious yellow. Unlike the warspawn, the newcomer was covered in shaggy fur.

"Breed!" Swann shouted. He was standing on a narrow spit of ground. "You're alive. Nic, look, Breed's alive."

Nic, the aptly named White Rat, did not look. He slipped behind the thoasa, grabbed the warspawn's jaw in both paws, and in a savage display of strength and brutality, tore his head apart.

"Oh, jimma." Swann took a step back. Ockzar screamed. The thing— *Nic*, I reminded myself, brandished the bloody remains, and shrieked in triumph. "That was totally unnecessary." Swann coughed.

I dragged myself towards the nearest bank.

"Breed?" Swann was sweating pale but looked honestly pleased to see me. "I wasn't sure the message had got through. You know what rats are like, they can be so belligerent, but here you are. It worked!" He opened his arms to embrace me. I did not oblige.

"Yes. Here I am. And there I was, in prison. For over a month."

"Hey now, jimma." He lowered his arms. "There was nothing I could do to spring you any sooner."

Nic flung the pieces of head into the water and bounded away.

"Where's he going?" I said as his pale form disappeared into the night.

"To change and get dressed I imagine. Who's your friend?" Swann gestured to Ockzar.

"Get it away from me," Ockzar pleaded as he tried to paddle away from the guard's headless corpse while inadvertently drawing it towards him with his frantic sculling.

As amusing as it was to watch the Voskvan being chased around a stagnant pool by a headless corpse, I returned my attention to Swann. "That's Ockzar, and never mind him. You've got some serious fucking explaining to do, *jimma*."

Chapter Nine

"And I'm telling you, I want to go back. It is for the best," Ockzar stammered, his teeth chattering.

"Unbelievable," said Swann. "Do you need a hand with those shackles, Breed?"

"No. I have a chisel down my breeches." I turned to Ockzar. "And you are a proper, fucking ingrate."

"I didn't ask you to save me or kill the guard." Ockzar sniffed. He was wet and shivering and stank of bog and blood.

In comparison, Swann looked snug in a long, russet fur coat, a pair of fur-trimmed boots, and what looked like a sleeping cat on his head but was apparently a hat. I balanced the shackle on the flat stone and hit the chisel with a rock. The bolt rang as it cracked, and the cuff snapped open. I got to work on the other.

"You don't understand." Ockzar continued in the same, whiny tone. "I have friends working to free me. I was going to have my day in court."

"No, you weren't." I hit the chisel with the rock. "If I hadn't brought you with me, you would have died in that flood, or the next gas leak, or a collapse, or you'd have caught a fever. You were never getting out of there, Ockzar."

"You don't know that. You have no right to stop me returning. You're…you're oppressing me." He hopped from foot to foot to stave off the biting cold.

"Go then. Explain to your jailors —the same who will kill someone for not saying 'sir' fast enough— explain to them how it isn't your fault you escaped. It'll give 'em a laugh while they string you up by your bollocks."

Hot tears coursed down his cheeks, and he spat a string of near unintelligible curses until he ran out of breath, whereupon he sank into a sullen silence.

"So, what kept you, Swann?" I asked. He smiled weakly. "Where did you say Nic had gone?" He shrugged. "What is the plan? You do have a plan beyond 'shapeshifter murders guard', don't you?"

"Er, we need to head east, Nic said. He has a plan, sort of... I think." He waved his hands like he was trying to ward away wasps. "We'll work it out. Hey, it's just great to have you back."

"Nic has a plan? Nic the homicidal shapeshifter who thinks with his cock— that Nic?"

He let the mask of idiocy slip for a second and gave a wry smile. "I don't know what to say, jimma. I only found out that he was a shapeshifter when he tracked you from Sevast. He has quite amazing senses, and he can control rodents. I hardly needed to scry at all."

I snorted.

"Those rats were very helpful."

"They weren't that fucking helpful. I've been in prison for over a month."

"We searched for you night and day, honestly."

"You couldn't lie straight in bed, but do go on, I like a good story."

"That's so negative, jimma."

"Oh, I'm sorry, Swann. Please, do go on." I swept a bow.

He rolled his eyes. "We got nowhere in Sevast. Nobody would talk to us. Apparently, the city guard kidnap people all the time to work in the mines. We had to hunt you ourselves, and that was no mean feat because Voskva is huge."

"Apparently." I folded my arms. "So, you and your rodent friends found out where I'd been taken and then what? Did you cause the flood?"

He shrugged and smiled. "It seemed the easiest way. I have an affinity for water, and you carry my talisman."

I reached inside my shirt and felt the small tentacle pendant. "I forgot about this."

He inclined his head. "I didn't. Nic sent the rats to find you and I caused the waters to rise and sent a sprite to bring you to us."

"A lot of prisoners died in your flood."

"It couldn't be helped." He shrugged.

I was surprised by Swann's callous disregard for the lives of the other prisoners, though it was a side of him I'd suspected existed because you don't get far in his game by being nice. I unfastened the cord on which the pendant hung and tossed it to him. "This is yours."

He didn't look at me as he tucked it in his shirt. I threw the shackles into the bog. "Ockzar?" Ockzar looked up. His eyes were red-rimmed and staring from the effort to keep them open. "Your turn."

"For what?"

"The bracelets. It's time to break off your engagement to Kazalstas Mine." I gestured for him to put his foot on the stone.

He hesitated. "If we're caught, it's death."

"You've got to die of something, Ockzar. What are you saving yourself for? cancer? senility? Being run over by a gong cart? Or perhaps the pox is more to your liking?" Trapped in a fugue of impotent rage and cowardice, he balled his fists. "Aw, come on. If you're caught trying to escape, it's death. If you look askance at a guard, it's death. You've already crossed the line."

"This is your fault!" Another tear ran down his cheek. "I was a prisoner of conscience and you have made me a common fugitive."

"Yes, I see now that saving you from a slow death or drowning in the mines was a mistake." And as penance, I would have to carry the useless idiot until I could dump him somewhere. "Live and learn, eh? Now put your hoof on the fucking stone."

"Oh, fat jokes from you too now, eh?"

"What are you talking about?"

"'Hoof.' Like a tusker. Why not say, 'trotter' and have done?"

"It's just a turn of phrase. If I was going to insult you, trust me, it would be more overt. Humans look nothing like tuskers. Fat, thin, short, or tall. You're all made almost entirely of bitterness and raw nerves. Tuskers are much thicker-skinned."

He paced a little longer before putting his foot on the stone. His shackles were more worn than mine and the rusting bolts sheared cleanly. He rubbed at the calloused, puckered flesh of his ankles before picking up the shackles and hurling them in the nearest pool. Just another offering to that capricious cunt, Fate, whose chains it seemed I would never be able to break.

"Some people, eh?" said Swann, rolling his eyes as he sparked up his pipe, warm and dry in his furs while we dripped with cold mud in our prison rags.

Skeptical and perturbed, I followed the talismancer who hopped from grassy islet to grassy islet waving his pendulum. As the night wore on, the temperature plummeted. I was a resilient cove, but as ice spread like cataracts across moonlit pools, even I felt the cold bite. Ockzar was blue.

"Swann!" My voice carried further than I expected on the crystalline air. I cursed and cast a glance towards the distant lights of the mine, but there was no reason that anyone would be looking for us. The only witness to our escape was the thoasa, and he didn't have a head, let alone a mouth, with which to shout for assistance. "Wait up," I called again. "Ockzar's freezing to death."

Swann kept going, but I noticed his shoulders tense, so I knew he'd heard me. "Swann!"

He stopped; breathed a heavy, billowing sigh into the darkness. "We don't have time for this," he hissed as he retraced his steps back to us. "We need to keep moving."

"Give him your coat."

"What?"

"Give. Him. Your. Coat." Incomprehension. I pointed to Ockzar. "He's freezing to death."

Swann's lips thinned to an angry line as he tore off his coat and threw it at Ockzar.

Rather than exploding in an effusion of gratitude, Ockzar looked askance at the coat. "Red Kilicj fur?" He held it out like it was covered in puke. "This is the garb of the plijus."

"Oh, I know that word, don't tell me. No, it's gone. What is it, and why does it matter?" I asked.

"The plijus, the purse proud class. The wealthy." He sniffed. "Such luxury exemplifies all that is wrong with this country," he said through chattering teeth.

"Oh, Kilicj aren't rare, are they?" Swann asked, lending credence to Ockzar's foolishness. Ockzar nodded sadly. "I wouldn't have bought it if I'd known it was made from a rare beast."

"For fuck's…Just put it on." I snapped. Torn between morality, fear, and survival, Ockzar hugged the coat to him, but he did not put it on.

It was time to try a different tack. "You won't be able to write another pamphlet if you're dead, so just put it on, would you? We'll sell it when we reach civilization and give the coin to poor orphans, I promise."

"It is the principle of the thing, you understand," he replied weakly.

"And you are a man of principle who will soon be dead in a ditch if you don't wear it."

He took a deep, shuddering breath. "What I do now, I do for Voskva," he said, and solemnly put on the coat. When the great sacrifice was done, he turned to Swann. "I don't suppose you have any spare boots, do you?"

"Only the ones I'm wearing, but I don't think they'll fit you, jimma."

Ockzar looked affronted. "I wouldn't dream of taking your shoes, but I'll have you know, I have slender feet."

Swann raised his hands. "I just have big feet, is all I meant."

"Forgive me, Imperial. I made an assumption."

"Not at all, it's probably a matter of translation."

I wanted to put as much distance between me and the mine as I could and had little patience for their faux niceties. "Just dangle your thing, Swann and let's get going."

"I have to take it slowly here; the magical energies are confused."

"Ah, well, that's because many battles were fought here during the War of the Mages," Ockzar offered. "It was a decadent war, obviously, caused by greed and Imperial lust for power."

A shivering Swann nodded, and he uncoiled the string from his divining pendant. "I guessed as much. About the battles that is. Not sure I agree about it being a purely Imperial lust for power. I think it had more to do with demons."

"Imperial demons, yes," said Ockzar.

It was funny, listening to them discuss the events I'd lived through as though it was book-bound history. The smell of wood smoke put paid to my musings on the Schism War. Swann picked up on something too and bounded across the fractured ground. What I had taken to be an ancient tumulus through the drifting mist was the backside of a derelict hut. Abandoned on a half-drowned islet, the hut's sod roof had caved in on one side and curled over the tumbled, cobblestone wall. Nicodemus was there in his human form, hunched beside a smoking fire.

"Swann!" The shapeshifter leaped to his feet. His eyes were bright, not feverish, just clear and shining. His skin was pink and looked freshly scrubbed, as if he'd spent the eve in a bathhouse not dismembering thoasa in a bog. He was garbed in furs and leathers, his flowing locks neatly combed. An entirely unnecessary sword hung on his belt. He gestured to the fire where the bubbling contents of a tin kettle rattled the lid. "Chai's ready." He grinned at me. "You look well, Breed. Prison life suits you."

I squatted by the fire and let the heat plane some of the cold from my hands. "Nic. You look…less furry."

He ignored my comment and instead chinned towards Ockzar. "Who's this?"

Ockzar stepped forward, saving me the breath I had no wish to spend. "I am Ockzar Donvyr Millmets." He clicked his heels. "Philosopher, activist, and author."

Nic chuckled. "I don't know what half of that means. You came from the mine?"

Ockzar straightened. "Yes. I was a prisoner of conscience," he declared.

Nic laughed. "There you go again, talking nonsense. You're funny, like Breed. It must have been all right in there, eh? I mean, I thought our lost comrade would be starved, whipped and beaten dawn to dusk, and ridden like a bitch by some big, old ogren gang boss. Didn't I say, Swann? I said, 'Come on Swann, you lazy fucker, stop getting hammered, we've got to save poor Breed from a fate worse than death.' But looking at you, I see it can't have been that bad, eh?" He slapped Ockzar's gut in what I imagine he thought was a playful manner. Ockzar winced and smiled tightly.

Now I had seen what Nic was; the toothsome grin and bright-eyed enthusiasm took on a more sinister cast. There had been nothing of the man in the beast, but there was certainly something of the beast in the man, despite the show of affability.

"It was hell," Ockzar stammered, welling up again. "It was a nightmarish place with death lurking around every corner."

Nic laughed. "But look at you. You're like a suckling tusker with spectacles."

"It was terrible." Ockzar insisted, his lip aquiver.

Nic laughed dismissively and mussed the Voskvan's hair as if he was a pet. Obviously embarrassed, Ockzar pulled away.

"Come over here, Ockzar," I said. "Have some chai, it'll warm you up."

Ockzar hunkered down beside me, his pale cheeks flushed crimson.

"Did you bring any spare clothes?" I asked the others.

Nicodemus snorted as he poured three cups of chai. "Well, there's gratitude."

"Excuse me?" I said. Something like anger twitched within me. "Pray, for what should I be grateful?"

Swann took out his pipe and dropped a pinch of pel into the bowl, which he lit from a twig. "We don't need to do this."

"Oh, yes we do," I insisted. "For what should I be grateful, *Nic*?"

He looked at me like I was a puzzle he couldn't solve. "Er, we rescued you?"

"If it wasn't for Swann and his fucking pel, I wouldn't have needed rescuing."

Nic looked at Swann, who pulled hard on his pipe. "It wasn't my fault," he said as he puffed. "The pel was just a pretext."

"I should be going…" Ockzar made to rise.

"Sit down!" Swann, Nic, and me chorused. Ockzar sat as though struck. The fog thickened, deadened the air until the only sound that pierced the sullen silence was the crackle and spit of the fire.

Chapter Ten

"Feel better?" I asked Ockzar, who had drunk four cups of brandy-laced chai before falling asleep.

He yawned. "I'm not sure, but the chai was most welcome." He huddled into his new coat. Despite his very reasonable misgivings, he looked better than I had seen him in all the time I'd known him. Thanks to the fire, the liquor, and hot food, the graveyard pallor was already being replaced by a healthy, pink glow. At my urging, Swann and Nicodemus had grudgingly found enough clothes to stop him freezing to death. While thanking them profusely, in much the same obsequious way he spoke to guards at the mine, he complained quietly to me about the fit and bemoaned the fact that there wasn't any spare footwear or dry stockings.

"You'll just have to put up with it for now," I replied.

"I don't wish to be speciesist," he said, warning me that was exactly what he was going to be, "but that is easy for you to say. You don't wear shoes."

"Only because there aren't any to hand that will fit me. Trust me, I very much enjoy wearing shoes on those rare occasions they are available to me." I wiggled my toes in the warm ashes of the fire.

Pouting, Ockzar thrust his odd-booted feet into the ash beside mine. "It's different for us."

"Which 'us' is that? Philosophers or barber surgeons?"

"Humans. We have different needs. When out and about in inclement weather or hiking through rough terrain, a stout pair of boots is a requisite."

I smiled. "And a gang of serfs to carry your luggage, no doubt."

"Absolutely not. Although, if I did employ a brother or sister Voskvan I would pay them a fair sum for their labor. Serfdom was outlawed by the Archonate." He snorted. "It's one of the few things they've got right."

We settled into an easy silence and enjoyed a moment's respite before heading towards wherever the fuck we were going to find whatever the fuck we were looking for. After over a month in a penal mine, I was already done with this little adventure. I wanted to get back with the item and be discharged from Leo's service as soon as possible, so I could find Ludo before his trail grew too cold. That wasn't too much to ask, was it? Although, and much to my shame, when I thought about actually killing Ludo, the fire of anticipation that had previously burned so hot within me refused to kindle. I felt nothing, not the desire for vengeance or hatred towards him. It was like I was a stranger in my own mind.

While the suns struggled to shape a morning from the dreary mist, Ockzar dozed off again. Nic was busy grooming, and the talismancer gazed moodily at the miniature of Effie. I should have cleaned my swords but felt no impetus to do so.

"Why so glum, Breed?" said Nicodemus. I looked up, irritated by the intrusion. "You're free, and we're back on the trail." His face split in a toothsome grin.

I shrugged. "I'm not glum."

"You look glum."

"It's just the way my face falls, pay it no heed."

He leaned in closer. For a moment, I thought he might put his hand on my knee or something equally disturbing. "Was it prison? It can affect a person, so I'm told. I've never been caught for anything myself, so I wouldn't know, but I've heard from those unfortunates who have fallen foul of the law that it's a proper kick in the pridefuls." Although his tone said otherwise, the mirth in his eyes told me he was mocking me, trying to get a rise.

I did not wish to engage. "Aye, well it wasn't my fault that I got pinched. I told you, it was a setup."

"Absolutely, aye. It was a setup, I believe you." He paused a moment, and I thought that might be an end of it, but I was wrong, for he sparked up again. "But still." He gave a wry smile as he packed bowls and cups. "I just can't fathom how a Guild Blade, a deadly assassin, got pinched without so much as throwing a punch. It's curious, you know?" He wrinkled his nose.

I smiled tightly and tried to shrug off his question. "Just one of life's mysteries, I suppose. Try not to lose sleep over it."

"Prison is a trial even for those of the strongest character." said a suddenly awake Ockzar. "As I know only too well."

Nicodemus slapped him on the back so hard he almost knocked him into the fire. "I can imagine it must have been hard for you, professor." He once again turned to me. "But you being taken so easily. Were you drunk?"

"No."

"Had you been smoking Swann's pel?"

"No." I stabbed at the fire with a smoldering brand. It hissed, spat embers like venom.

Swann sighed miserably, tucked the miniature inside his coat, and got up from the fire.

"Where are you going?" Nic called after him.

"Over here. Is that all right with you?" he said before flouncing to the edge of the islet, whereupon he gazed moodily at the water.

"What's wrong with him?" Nic mused.

"Don't know," I said. "Aside of 'east', where are we going again?"

Nic took out a crumpled packet of papers from his bag and selected a map. "We're heading through somewhere called Kleminsko Forest, which is just over there. He pointed east. "After that, we continue on for a day or so, possibly longer." He glanced at Ockzar. "Depending on pace. There are villages on the way, so we can pick up supplies as we go. Well, that is if they're still there. This map looks about a hundred years old."

"Wait, you're going through the Dancing Forest?" Ockzar asked, a note of fear in his voice. "You can't go through there. It is a dangerous place, populated by strange creatures and ne'er do wells." He folded his arms. "If you are going through there then we must part ways, we simply must."

Nicodemus looked at me like it was my responsibility to remind the Voskvan that we'd already been over this.

"We've already been over this," I said, fulfilling my duty.

"That was before you mentioned you were going through an eldritch, doom-haunted forest."

"Doom-haunted?" I raised an eyebrow. "Bit dramatic, no?"

"Yes, deliberately so. It is doom-haunted. The Leshie lives there, and dreadful rusalkas and vukodlaks." He glanced nervously at Nic. "No offence."

"Huh?"

"Vukodlaks are er, how you would say, werewolves?" He swallowed hard, flushed scarlet.

"And?" said Nic, not seeing the connection between vukodlaks and him. "Simple fact is, you either come with us, or you're staying here."

"Stay here?" Uncomprehending, Ockzar laughed. "It's a bog. What? Do you expect me to live on frogs?" He shook his head. "Forgive me, but no, I've no desire to reduce my circumstances any lower than those I endured in prison. I will go south. That will be for the best." He pointed to the west. "I have friends in

Glavdaroc. Of course, I will refrain from mentioning any of you."

"You're either coming with us or..." Nic made a neck-ringing gesture.

"You'll kill me?" Ockzar laughed and looked at me. The truth dawned on him when he saw that I wasn't laughing. He swallowed, and the color drained from his face. "Gasvoy's ghost," he muttered. "You would kill me?"

Nic shrugged. "Blame Breed for bringing you along," he said dryly. Like a cat toying with a mouse, he was enjoying scaring the Voskvan and in so doing, annoying me. "We can't let you go, can we? I promise, as soon as we have done what we came here to do, you can be on your way."

Breathless with pent-up fury, Ockzar turned his ire upon me. "What have you got me involved with, Chas? Are you, are you spies?" I may be a counter-revolutionary, but I am a true son of Voskva." He slapped his chest. "I will not stand by while foreigners undermine my homeland."

Nic cracked his knuckles. "That's a pity."

I elbowed Ockzar in the ribs. "Fuck's sake, shut it, will you? You've a mouth on you like a brick through a window. I can see how you got thrown in the mines."

He stuck his stupid little nose in the air. "I have my limits."

"We're just looking for something that nobody else wants," I said, trying to shut him up before he got himself killed. "It's just a bit of old tat."

"An old relic," Nic added unhelpfully.

Ockzar's eyes grew wide.

"Not a *good* relic," I said quickly. "It's not a saint's big toe that performs miracles or anything. He means a bit of old junk; he just doesn't speak good Imperial."

Ockzar frowned. "I thought I was the one speaking a foreign language. Surely he understands what he's trying to say in his mother tongue?"

I leaned in close. "You'd be surprised how few born and raised in the Empire speak Imperial as well as you do. Most folk are ignorant pricks like him." I smiled at Nic.

Ockzar sniffed. "No, I can imagine. I have heard your country lacks good, basic education." He thumped his fist into his palm. "All great societies are founded on the principles of—"

"–Nobody cares," Nic interrupted.

Before the conversation could slide any closer to Ockzar actually being killed, the bog beside Swann erupted like a geyser. Something big and dark launched itself at Swann, triggering a ward of glass and lightning to spring up around the startled talismancer. Cursing, Nic tore off his coat and shirt and bounded over, while whatever was trying to attack Swann furiously lashed at the protective shield with wicked claws and a barbed tail. Quickly over the shock of the sudden attack, the talismancer coolly assessed his attacker from within the safety of the warding sphere.

The beast looked like a giant crayfish, save that it possessed a whip tail and a tiny head that did not look like it belonged to the body. It didn't appear to have eyes, but pinpricks of soft light pulsed on its smooth, featureless head set upon a body encased in a chitinous shell. It had four pairs of legs and two vicious claws. That it was attacking Swann didn't particularly move me. What bothered me was that its giant chelae reminded me of Ludo, and for that reason alone I disliked it.

Very sensibly, the talismancer was in no rush to engage the beast and seemed content to keep it at bay behind his ward. Nic appeared to have other ideas. Somewhere between man and beast, he leaped and landed on the creature's back. Nimbly avoiding the snapping claws, he dug his talons into the thing's head. It thrashed wildly and tried to whip him with its tail. With a roar, the White Rat performed his party trick and tore its head off. Nic held his trophy aloft as the giant body collapsed beneath him. However, the writhing thing in his hands was very much alive. It looked like a fat maggot with dozens of wormy, barbed tentacles which quested towards the shape changer and wrapped around his arms. Blood flowed as serrated suckers tore into his flesh.

Ockzar grabbed me by the shirt. "Kill it! Kill it with fire," he shouted in my face.

"You kill it with fire." I was horrified at the idea of going near the thing, which at that moment looked like it was trying to drag its maggot body into Nic's mouth. Enraged, the White Rat tore it from him, leaving several of the tentacles still attached to his arms. It hit the ground, thrashing and squirming. Swann dropped his ward. The brightly pulsing head of the maggot twisted towards him. Swann extended his hand, and flames engulfed the writhing creature. Its flailing tentacles shriveled, its body blistered and burst, spilling miniature versions of itself onto the muddy ground before the whole mess was immolated, and the air filled with the ghastly reek of burning fat.

"Bastarding, fucking fucker," a recognizably human Nic snarled as he ripped the remaining squirming suckers from his bloody arms and stamped them into the ground. Swann sank to his knees, and one of the amulets he was wearing around his wrist glowed briefly before turning to ashes. With shaking hands, he rummaged in his coat pockets and dug out a tiny ball of pel, which he stuffed into his pipe before returning to the fire. I noted that rather than use magic to light his pipe, he again used a burning twig.

"What the hell was that?" he said after taking a long hard pull. "I've never seen the like. Hey, Voskie, any idea?"

Ockzar pushed his spectacles up his nose. "I believe it was a Zocamasur, or 'brain maggot' as they are more commonly known. I have never seen a live specimen, but there is a preserved example in the University of Gramms. They are very nasty parasites that usually only attack wildlife."

"You could have warned us," Nic snapped. He was his usual self now, and the cuts on his arms where the suckers had attached were already beginning to heal.

"It was in a jar in a university!" Ockzar exclaimed. Nic glowered at him. Ockzar cleared his throat and continued in a more moderated tone. "I didn't expect to ever encounter a living creature. I am not a country mouse."

Nic narrowed his eyes and stomped over to the fire. "Country mouse? Are you trying to be funny?"

"No. Never. I'm the least humorous person I know."

"Leave him be," I said. Clearly Nic's blood was still up from the fight, for the next thing I knew he was looming over me, fists clenched.

"You've no room to talk. Why didn't you help?"

"You had it in hand, and Swann was in a ward."

He shoved me in the back. "Next time, pull your fucking weight," he said before collecting his scattered belongings.

I was momentarily torn between wanting to curl up in a ball or punch him in the face. It was such an acute split that I felt a pain in my head like someone had just stabbed me.

"Are you all right, Chas?" Ockzar asked. "Breed?"

"What? Yes, I'm fine."

"Your nose."

I wiped my nose and saw it was bleeding. "It's nothing." Puzzled and embarrassed that I hadn't even noticed, I looked away and saw that Swann was staring at me like he was a breath away from saying something. I waited, he stared, mouth slightly agape, breath held like it was his last and therefore too precious to let go.

"What's up?" I enquired. "Maggot got your tongue?"

He closed his mouth and said nothing. Despite having been saved from a grisly fate, he turned his unhappy gaze to the fire.

Chapter Eleven

"**W**ell?" Ockzar asked in a barely audible whisper. "It's disturbing, isn't it?" His myopic gaze darted nervously from tree to twisted tree.

"What?" Still preoccupied with how odd I'd been behaving of late, I hadn't listened to what he'd been prattling on about for the last hour or so, if not longer.

"The Dancing Forest. It is eerie, is it not? I confess, this is the first time I've actually been here, but I've read all about it and it is certainly living up to my expectations." He was like a child, excited and afraid all in one.

"It's obvious that some poetical cove had given it the flowery nickname, but I wouldn't say it was eerie." Pine was the predominant species of tree in Kleminsko Forest but by some quirk of nature, they were all stunted with twisted limbs and trunks as though frozen mid-movement. I had to smile. Humans were such peculiar creatures, as exemplified by Ockzar, who was both subdued and delighted by the thrill of knowing that there was probably nothing to fear. And even if there were fiends lurking in the stunted groves, they'd be wise to avoid a mage and a shapeshifter who had a fondness for tearing the heads off those things that got in his way.

It was mid-afternoon before the suns finally penetrated the heavy cloud cover that had greyed out the best part of the day and set a somber mood upon our party. Almost as soon as the temperature began to rise, the suns set sail for the horizon, whereupon feathery snow started to fall in sporadic, silver-beaded flurries.

"We need to watch our tracks," I offered, embarrassed by the plowed mess we were leaving behind us. "Where are we headed after here?"

"Still east," said an unhelpfully taciturn Swann. "And why bother about tracks. There's nobody out here let alone anyone eager to hunt us."

"It's good practice is all. And where's 'still east'? just in case something happens to you and Nic, and I have to continue on my own." I smiled warmly.

As though to align his fractured thoughts, the mage ran his hands through his hair. "There's a tower. It's about three days *due east*." He waved his hands as though trying to conjure words from the air. "It's called Vorgasty Vash."

"Forgasty Vash," Nic corrected. "Not Vorgasty."

"Close enough," Swann snapped.

"No, it isn't." Nic sniped back.

"I've never heard of it," said Ockzar. "Are you sure that's the right name?"

"Yes," said Nic, increasing his pace so that Ockzar had to trot to keep up.

"Only, it doesn't sound very Voskvan," he said, panting. "If I saw it written down, I'd know for sure."

"Does it fucking matter?" Swann muttered with uncharacteristic venom.

"Well, yes. You could end up in the wrong place."

Swann glared at Ockzar. "Who are you again?"

"Dinner, if he doesn't shut it," Nic answered, a wicked gleam in his eye.

Ockzar shot me a worried look. With feigned confidence, I dismissed the threat with a shake of the head.

Garbed in grey, dawn was breaking serenely by the time our company stumbled to the edge of the forest. We crept through the gloam as silent as thieves, our footsteps deadened by soft snow, which lay on a deep matt of pine needles. Unused to walking long distances, Swann and Ockzar were lagging behind. Preferring to be alone with my thoughts, I paced myself to stay equally in front of them and behind Nic. Perhaps out of habit from my time in the mines, I kept my head down as I trudged. Even so, I should have noticed the huge spider web before I walked into it. For possibly the second time in my life, I shrieked out of fright.

Nic spun around, his red eyes piercing in the grey mist. "What the fuck?"

I tore at the web. "It's nothing, just a spiderweb."

Clearly unamused, he put his hands on his hips. "What?"

Ockzar came running over. "What is it, what's wrong?"

"Nothing, just a spiderweb."

"Is that all?" Even he gave me a questioning look.

"It caught me off guard," I said, feeling more foolish by the second.

He chuckled. "It's a web, it doesn't move."

Swann came to my rescue. "Can we just get going?" he said before brusquely marching past Nic.

"You know, my brother employed you—" the shapeshifter began.

"—pressed me into service but do go on."

"*Employed you* because you had skills, because you were bold, daring, cunning."

"And defenseless at the time, let's not forget that."

"All I'm saying is something ain't right with you. You're distracted."

"I'm fine."

Nic shook his head. "You're not fine. You've lost your bottle."

"Bollocks." I tried to laugh it off.

A look of terror on his face, he pointed to something above me. "Look out!" he cried.

I yelped, covered my head, and cowered.

He smirked. "You see? You ain't right."

"I just walked into a giant spiderweb. If there's a giant web, it follows that there's a giant spider knocking around. Was I supposed to stand there and be bitten just to prove how brave I am?"

Nic marched over, put his hand on my chest, and shoved me. "I said, you ain't right."

I backed up. A sharp pain lit behind my eyes. "Knock it off, Nicodemus."

He shoved me again, harder this time. I stumbled. "Why, what are you going to do?" I did nothing, and I didn't know why. "You've lost it. You've turned as yellow as a field of ripe corn. Prison's broken you."

"All right, that's enough! I can't stand it anymore." It was Swann. He had a pained expression on his gaunt face. "It's not Breed; it's not prison. It's me. It's my fault. It's all my fault."

"What the fuck are you talking about?" I asked. A question echoed in Nic's expression.

Now that he had our attention, Swann didn't seem to want it. He toyed with his empty pipe and laughed nervously. "Well, when I say, 'it's my fault', not Breed's, it sort of is Breed's fault, after a fashion."

"What are you blathering about, mage?" Nic asked.

"I don't mean to pry, but what's going on?" Ockzar asked me.

I laughed. "I have no idea, but I bet it's something stupid. Eh, Swann?"

Swann frowned. "Breed threatened me a lot after Leopold stepped in to help after the incident at the ziggurat. It totally messed with my head; you know? It unbalanced my equilibrium, and trust me, that is not something you want to mess with." His gaze shifted to each of us in turn. "It might have been a bit of an overreaction on my part. Although, in my defense it wasn't supposed to have had such a profound effect."

"What wasn't, Swann? what 'it' are you talking about?" I asked, keen to find out what fuckery the talismancer had been up to at my expense.

Swann took a step back. "I haven't done much enchanting at sea before. Don't get me wrong, I have an affinity for water, but mostly rivers and lakes and the like— they're tamer, you know? Weaving spells at sea is hard, jimma. There's a lot of wild energy out there. Talismancy isn't just a science, it's an art, you know?"

"No." The three of us chorused.

"I put a geas on Breed not to attack me and it was too successful," he gabbled before turning to me. "And I'm sorry."

I folded my arms. "Aren't you, though?"

"I knew it," said Nic. "That's why Breed's been acting like a vaporing coward. You jeopardized our mission just because Breed was mean to you? Have I got that right?"

Swann threw his arms in the air. "I said, I'm sorry. Spells go awry sometimes. And it wasn't just 'Breed was mean'. Breed was very threatening. The same Breed who levelled a ziggurat."

"You levelled a ziggurat?" Ockzar asked, a look of surprised admiration on his face.

"It's a long story."

Nicodemus bared his fangs, clenched his fists. "You drug-addled dolt."

Swann stepped back; blue fire wreathed his hands. "Trust me, jimma. You don't want to do this."

I backed up. "I don't want either of you to do this."

"Neither do I," Ockzar muttered. "Not that anyone cares."

I tried to get between the two of them, but Nic shoved me aside. "You're a fucking moron, Swann."

"I've apologized, haven't I?" The talismancer spat, his angular features thrown into sharp relief by the glow of the witch light burning in his hands. "And who are you calling a moron? You overgrown, fucking rodent!"

"Take that back!" Nic roared. Ironically growing more feral and rodentlike.

"I'M SORRY!" Swann screamed. The ground shook, the trees shivered.

"Undo the spell," said Nic through gritted teeth.

"I will. I've wanted to do it for days, I just…" Swann hung his head. "I just didn't have the opportunity. The time never seemed right."

"Do it now," said Nic.

Swann shot him a venomous look before turning to me. "Before I undo the spell, give me your word that you will not seek vengeance for what I accidentally did."

"Why would I promise that, and why would you believe me even if I did?"

He sighed, put his hands on my shoulders, and took a long moment to compose himself. He was trembling, and when he looked up his eyes were brimming. "Meet me halfway, will you? I wasn't supposed to be here. I was supposed to spend the rest of my days making charms and baking bread with Effie. I got too close to the Paradox, and it burned me, jimma. I don't always think straight."

"This I have noticed."

"I am truly sorry, Breed, but it takes much of my strength just to keep control, you know?"

I knew. I knew what that raging tempest within felt like when the magic you had relied upon, that you had wielded with ease and deft assurance turned on you. That was the Paradox of Power. The more you used, the more powerful you became, and the closer it came to destroying you. You can never really control the power of the universe; you just think you can until the day it tries to kill you. "Very well. No vengeance." I raised my hands.

"Promise?"

"Sure, why not?" I said with a smile. "I promise."

Nic snorted. "The word of a Guild Blade under a geas. Yeah, right."

"I'm doing my best," Swann snapped. For a moment, I thought they might go at it again, but he turned back to me. "Are you ready, jimma?"

"Just get on with it. Hey, where do you think you're going?" I called to Ockzar, who was trying to sneak off.

"Nature calls," he shouted.

"Can't nature wait?"

"No. Nature needs to take a shit now. Or would you prefer I do it here?" He began fumbling with his breeches.

Nic snarled at him before turning his furious gaze back to Swann. "Undo the spell," he said with icy calm.

Swann did not give ground and smiled tightly. "I would, if you stopped interrupting me, jimma. May I, Breed?"

"Seeing as you ask so nicely."

He swallowed and tentatively gathered my hair spines in his hands. Unlike a full-blood thoasa, I had neither horns nor head plates, but neither did I have the tangle-prone lice straw common to humans. I had what

I considered to be the best of both worlds in a head of long, smooth, leathery spines. When Swann held them up, I saw that around one of them, there was a carved bone ring that I hadn't put there. The talismancer muttered an incantation, and the ring dropped from the spine.

"Is that it?" I asked because I didn't feel any different.

"Not quite. This is the foci, but I need to revoke the spell."

"How did you get that on the spine without me noticing?"

His cheeks reddened, and he looked at his feet. "A little incantation that encouraged you to sleep more deeply one night back on the ship."

Nic folded his arms. "You waited until I was out of the way, then?"

"I'm not sure if you were there or not, jimma."

They glared at each other like two halves of a shit sandwich, which I own, doesn't say much for me. I clicked my fingers before Swann's face. "If you wouldn't mind?"

He closed his eyes and began mumbling again.

Nic leaned against a tree. To emphasize how bored he was, he picked his teeth.

"There. Done." Swann smiled and wiped his brow with his coat sleeve. "It'll take a little time for the energies in your essence to realign."

"Eh?"

"It'll take a wee while to wear off."

"A 'wee while'? Prithee, how long is that?"

His gaze drifted to an open patch of sky where I assumed his mind's eye was sketching extremely complicated magical formulae upon the clouds. "Couple of days at most." He shrugged.

"That's the best you can do? It seems I have perhaps overestimated the complexity of the art of Talismancy," I said, unnaturally relaxed about the situation, which I now knew was thanks to his blasted spell. "Where's Ockzar? He should have been back by now."

Nic sniffed the air. "This way."

As we jogged out of the forest, I had visions of brain maggots feasting on the Voskvan cruelly murdered mid-way through taking a shit which would be an awful way to go. Before us, hundreds of grave mounds dotted a plain which stretched as far as I could see in all directions. That Ockzar had thought the Dancing Forest to be the scariest place on earth, but a valley full of burial mounds wasn't worth mentioning made me laugh.

"Over here," said Nic. We didn't have to break a sweat to catch up to Ockzar, who it turned out had not gone for a shit. He had run as far as his weak legs and poor sense of direction would take him, which was into a clearing ringed by large burial mounds. Rather than retrace his steps, he was trying and failing to climb up the side of one of the mounds. When he saw us, he redoubled his efforts but only succeeded in sliding down the side like a sack of turnips. When he landed, he jumped up and dusted himself down like nothing had happened.

"Bit far to go for a shit," I said.

"It was a ruse." He stuck his chin in the air. "I went for a piss but then decided to escape. If I am to die now, so be it." He did his best to sound defiant, but his lip was all aquiver beneath his stringy whiskers.

"All mortals die," said Nicodemus. "Some sooner than others, if you catch my meaning."

"Like a rock in the face," Ockzar muttered. Old bones and broken urns littered the ground. The huge stones that had once sealed the tomb entrances had long ago been smashed, and the black eyes of the tumuli glared from the depths of an unknown past.

"I'm curious, where the fuck did you think you were running?" Nic asked him.

"Anywhere away from you." He sighed, exhausted, and clearly resigned to his fate. "Chas and I struck up a friendship, that is true, but I am loyal to my homeland. I will not be party to dastardly foreign schemes."

A breathless Swann jogged into the clearing. "You could have waited for me."

"You could have stayed where you were," said Nic.

Swann smiled tightly. "But you didn't tell me you were coming back, jimma. It's just a matter of communication, you know?"

"Swann?" I enquired while he and Nicodemus threw knife eyes at each other.

He waved off my inquiry with a flick of his hand. "Are you listening, Nicodemus?"

Nicodemus sighed. "Yes, Swann, I am listening." He cupped his ear. "Behold! See me listening."

While they stared each other down, I helped Ockzar dust himself down. He was pale and sweaty and looked like he was going to puke. "Nobody's going to kill you. Well, we're not. Gods only know what fiends haunt these mounds."

"You don't think these mounds are haunted, do you?" He sounded surprised.

I laughed. "You don't? This necropolis is probably home to ghouls, demons, families of revenants, and half-mad old blood drinkers."

"You're joking?" he asked, more hopeful than confident. "This is your gallows humor, yes?"

"Don't push me, Nic," said Swann, interrupting me as I was trying to scare Ockzar into never running away again.

"What are you going to do, eh? Cast a geas on me? Just fucking try it, you skinny cunny."

I didn't expect to see them actually pushing each other when I looked around. Obviously, I needed to rethink my expectations. "Do you believe this?"

Ockzar nodded. "Why do you think I wanted to get away."

I whistled to get their attention. "Oi, Nic, let go of Swann before he melts your face off. Swann, let go of Nic before he rips off your sweetmeats."

"If you ask me, you should leave them to it," Ockzar side-mouthed as Nic and Swann continued to posture.

"It's tempting, but we need them to kill the monsters."

"Monsters? What monsters?"

Chapter Twelve

Because this little adventure just wasn't fun enough, it began to snow in earnest. Flurries driven by a wolfish wind whited out the mound-pocked plain and made me nostalgic for the maggot-haunted bog.

"How are you feeling now?" Swann asked me for the tenth time, his teeth chattering as he hunched against the gale.

"Irritated."

"Violently?"

"Ask me again in another five minutes."

"My feet are frozen, if anyone cares," said Ockzar. No one answered. When he stumbled and fell, I offered him my hand. He shook his head and rolled onto his back. "No, I'm done. Go on without me. I'll…I'll be fine."

"No, you won't." I called to Nic, who was out in front. "We need to stop."

"Not here, surely?" asked Swann.

Nicodemus kept walking. "On that we agree. We can make the foothills by nightfall if we push on. Then we'll camp."

"You can. We're stopping here." I helped Ockzar to his feet. He hung on my arm.

Nic squared up in what I imagined he thought was an intimidating stance. "I said, we go on."

Ockzar patted me on the shoulder. "He's right, you should go on, the weather's getting worse."

I felt a sudden flash of anger. "We'll see you there," I said.

"Are you all right?" Ockzar asked.

"No. People keep asking me annoying, fucking questions."

"At least they aren't threatening to kill you."

"Fair point." I drew a breath, calmed down. It wasn't fair to get annoyed with Ockzar when Swann and Nicodemus were more deserving of my ire. "We'll rest up in one of the mounds; get a fire going, eat something."

Ockzar raised his hand. "Would you mind if we take shelter *near* one of the tombs rather than *in* one?"

We were in the middle of the vast plain that rolled between the forest and some foothills. Either by design or erosion, the tumuli here were larger than those closer to the trees. Ancient paths wound around them; pale scars carved into the weather-blasted land. High above, hawks called as they hastened to their roosts as snow clouds flowered in the bleached bone sky.

"These are incredibly old," Ockzar said in hushed tones as he pointed at one of the black granite monoliths that flanked the path we had taken.

"Do you know what it says?" I asked.

He pondered the florid inscriptions incised into the stones. "It says, 'Keep out, here be monsters.'"

"Really?" I was impressed until his face split in a grin.

"I have no idea. I'm a futurist, not a classical scholar. The past is dead, my friend. The people who made this place are gone and forgotten." Disturbed by the wind or some critter, a trickle of loose stones rolled down one of the mounds, causing Ockzar to almost jump into my arms. Up ahead, Swann had slowed his pace and was glancing from us to Nic, torn between who to follow.

"What about we rest up in there?" I pointed to the mouth of an open tomb. "Get out of the weather for a bit?"

The futurist shook his head. "I am not ready to abide with the dead just yet, but you may do as you wish."

"I don't need to get out of the weather, you do," I argued. He folded his arms. "Very well." I looked around. A rogue knot of twisted pines had found a home on the leeward side of a robbed-out mound. Sheltering under trees wasn't as comfortable as in a nice, old tomb, but the trees would provide some protection from the inclement weather. "How about those trees? I trust you have no issue with trees?"

"They make me sneeze terribly in spring, but other than that, no."

"You clear us a firepit; I'll fetch some kindling."

A sheepish Swann trudged back and dumped his pack beside Ockzar before helping him clear a scrape for a fire. Nicodemus did not join us. He slowed up, and when he saw we weren't following him, loitered on the path. Rather than concede he had lost this fight, he took himself to the crest of a monolith-crowned mound, which was far enough away to demonstrate how much he disdained our company but close enough for us to see him doing so.

The tumulus under the trees had been stripped to the foundations, leaving only a narrow rind of the crumbling outer wall. By the time I got a fire going, Ockzar was already snoring fitfully on a bed of pine branches. As the only living adult within a mile, I covered him with the blanket from his pack, raked some ashes, and put a pan of water on to boil.

"D'you have the chai?" I asked Swann, who was hunched over the fire like a constipated gargoyle. He shook his head. "What have you got?"

He sulkily searched his pack. "Some watered wine, hard tack, and a piece of furry cheese." He tossed the cheese.

"Tsk, wasteful." I retrieved it, broke off the bit that had gone moldy, which on a whim, I bounced off Swann's head. He sighed but otherwise did not react.

"Who has the chai. Does Nic have it?"

"I suppose so, unless you or your prison wife has it."

"He isn't my 'prison wife' and he doesn't have the chai."

"As you say, jimma."

"I'll ask Nic. Don't let Ockzar fall in the fire." It might seem a trivial matter, but small things like hot chai on a cold day are important. It's not all fighting dragons and stealing rare artifacts.

The ring of stones on the crown of the mound on which Nic was brooding was painfully reminiscent of an angle gate. Wind, rain, and frost had worked them over and several of the stones had split. The White Rat was stretched out on a monolith that had fallen onto its side. His eyes were closed, and his hands were folded on his breast. He looked like an effigy on a tomb, a noble hero in death's sweet repose, which was undoubtedly his intention. I didn't like or trust Nicodemus, but as I was much older and a touch wiser than I looked, I understood something about what had made him the prick he was. I cleared my throat.

"What do you want?" he said without opening his eyes to show how little he respected me. As I was on a mission to find chai, I resisted the temptation to throw a rock at him.

"To be a thousand miles from here, but I'll make do with some chai."

He exhaled heavily as though the act of listening was tiresome but then leaped dramatically to his feet. This part of the performance was to show how unpredictable he was, as well as demonstrate his physical prowess. I leaned against one of the stones while he took the packet of chai and the kettle from his pack. "We're running low on supplies." He glanced pointedly towards our camp.

"I'm sorry about Ockzar. I didn't plan on bringing him, but I wasn't going to leave him to die when he was right there with me. Anyway, he's here now." As was my intention, my candid admission seemed to drain some of his ire.

"Aye. Well. As you say, he's here now."

"And he's a local, which might be useful."

He handed me the chai, the kettle, and some cups. "Perhaps. There isn't any sugar. Well, there is, but the bag split, and it spilled in my pack. Everything's fucking sticky now."

I took the supplies from him. "Thank you." He grunted his acknowledgment. I pressed my case. "Why don't you come and join us?"

"I prefer my own company."

"We need to work together."

"Don't tell me, tell that fucking idiot talismancer."

"I have." It was a small and useful lie; the oil with which to lubricate diplomacy's wheels.

"Good for you. I am not known for my forgiving nature."

"I'm the one he wronged, and I've let it go. As a professional with a job to do, and as a member of the Midnight Court, so should you." I was impressed with how reasonable I sounded.

He kicked at the dirt. "The Midnight Court is no more."

"Your brother's counting on you."

He looked surprisingly pained at that and stared hard at the ground. "My brother is retiring. What dreams we—" He gave a little, bitter smile. "What dreams he had regarding the Court are dead."

A bit like Leo. "I'm sorry, but we still have a job to do."

He sighed. "I know my duty."

"Do you want a cup of chai?"

"I'll make it."

I'd spent long enough in Malin's court that I could turn diplomancer when the situation required and counted the small capitulation to be a success.

And I was pleased with myself for the length of time it took me to turn around. Swann was rummaging in his pack beside Ockzar's slumbering form. Nothing of that piece of the picture was incongruous. What did not fit were the ragged, skeletal forms crawling towards them.

"Do ghouls come out at night?" I asked.

"Mostly, but not exclusively." Nic came over and saw what I was looking at. "Oh, shit."

"Quite."

While my heart was sinking into my feet, a blur of pale fur tore down the mound. Shortly thereafter, Nic and dozens of the creatures were fighting. "Beware the Dancing Forest he said," I said to no one, as a brilliant array of Swann's various wards flared into being. The talismancer generously stayed beside Ockzar, affording the now awake and screaming Voskvan some protection. Nicodemus let out an ear-splitting shriek. Moments later, dozens of dog rats appeared from the surrounding mounds and joined the fray.

Swann waved frantically. "Breed, get over here!" Dozens of pairs of luminous eyes swiveled in my direction.

"Thanks for that." I was unsure if I should run or hold my ground. While I wrestled with indecision, Nicodemus ripped into the dark mass of creatures that moved with the stiffness of puppets.

Thanks to Swann's shout, a knot of the bestial creatures came for the idiot alone on a hill. Unearthly light shone in their colorless eyes and shreds of skin flapped like tattered shrouds against their greening bones. Their noses were shriveled flat against their livid faces, and their lips had drawn back, revealing mouths full of wicked fangs not conceived by nature. With trembling hands, I drew my blades. I was so nervous that I dropped one and almost cut my fucking toe off. Blood flowed; anger flared. Cursing, I snatched the blade up just as the foremost glowing-eyed goblin lunged for me. Purely by reflex, I managed to interpose the steel between me and the ghoul. With little effort on my part, the keen edge of Volund's blade severed a handful of clawed fingers.

The injured creature fell back, yowling and biting at its mangled hand. Another took its place and swiped at me. From what I could tell, they were communicating with each other in a rudimentary language which was unusual for restless dead, which were for the most part, mindless. It struck me that if they could work together, they would have the advantage in this fight. While I pondered the embarrassing possibility that we might be outwitted by creatures that literally had empty heads, I parried and blocked a flurry of savage blows. Defending myself was a welcome improvement from cowering and cringing, but the residue of Swann's accursed geas still prohibited me from attacking.

Step by step, I was driven back across the mound. It was not the first time I'd been outmatched, but it was the first time I was afraid, and I didn't like it. I was the cunning thief that kept the locksmiths' families fed. I was the hunter in the darkness, the monster, the assassin feared by kings and princes. Months of pent-up fury began to strain against the crumbling wall of Swann's spell. One of the ghoulish creatures leaped upon its companion's backs and sprang at me. It was quick, but I was quicker and cut the damn thing in twain. One piece flew east, the other west.

The dam broke. "You think you're scary?" I bared my fangs and slashed another across its desiccated chops. Howling, it spun away. "You think you're the monsters?" I scissored my blades through the chest of another and kicked its twitching remains from my swords. "You don't know the meaning of the word."

However. It turns out they did know the meaning of the word 'distraction.' The first I knew about it was when one of the sneaky bastards came up behind me and sank its rotten fangs into the meat of my calf and dragged me to the ground.

"Swaaaaaaaann! You cock!" I raged as I stabbed down and severed the bud of its head from the stem of its neck. At the same time, I used Volund's blade to hack the hands from the first ghoul to try and take advantage of my soon-to-be prone position.

I swore that if I survived, I was going to choke the talismancer to death on his own bollocks, which was still a kinder death than he deserved. Heartening though the thought was, my revenge would have to wait. I hit the ground and rolled, mindful not to trap my blades. I came up on my knee and scythed my swords in an arc, taking the leg from the foremost fucker. With the preternatural strength of the unliving, it threw itself at me.

I kicked it and sent it sprawling down the side of the mound. Ignoring the pain in my calf, I put my back against a monolith for support and stood up. My legs were leaden, but I managed to pirouette to the left and take the head off another with a backhanded slice. One rushed me from the side. Claws scored my ribs. I sheathed my blade in its chest, but it still managed to fasten its fangs on my shoulder. Aside from the usual corruption of mold and dust, it smelled of licorice and stale wine. I cleaved it from chest to groin. It fell apart. I wondered briefly if it had any recollection of the life it had once lived as I gasped for breath. My lungs were working like bellows, but the air was thin and failed to satisfy my need. I looked down, saw my blood dripping onto the frozen ground. My limbs turned to water. I put my back to the monolith and slid down the stone as my strength left me.

I just needed a minute to catch my breath.

Just a minute to rest.

I let my head fall forward onto my chest.

Just a minute.

I closed my eyes.

Just a...

Chapter Thirteen

The podium was in the drawing room, which wasn't where it should be, but when he looked out upon the sea of faces in the Square of the People it didn't matter. All eyes were on him. Every face was filled with expectation and hope, if not outright adoration, as they waited for him to speak and deliver them from ignorance.

He would not let them down. He didn't understand why the guard Ruslik was there, pleasuring himself before a painting of the now-defunct Archon Council. No matter, the glorious rebirth of Voskva couldn't wait while he pondered such prurient incongruities. He must strike now, give the speech of his life while the iron was hot, forged in the fire of his heroic struggle to save Voskva.

Ockzar put the handcannon down and gripped the edge of the lectern like it was the helm of a ship and he was the captain. It was the perfect metaphor, for who if not him had led the fight against tyranny? With his heart, his spirit, and inspirational oration, he had steered the people of Voskva to victory. Today that victory would be acknowledged by the nation, nay, the world.

"My friends! Brothers, sisters—"

"Ocky?" It was Aunt Galitza. She was pushing the chai tray into the drawing room. Delicate Shen cups rattled on their saucers. Glazed cakes and pastries piled with candied fruit rocked on the three-tiered, silver cake stand. "Do you want some knuffle with your chai, dear?"

"Not now, aunty. Can't you see I'm addressing the nation?"

As was her way, she nodded indulgently but didn't really listen to him. "Yes, yes, Ocky. Now come and have some chai before it goes cold, you know you hate it when it's cold." She put the cake stand on the table, which but a moment before, had been the wheel of his ship...or had it been a lectern?

The crowd drifted into the music room, the soft suns' light shining upon their careworn backs. To see the great unwashed masses in his home brought a tear to his eye, even though they were leaving. "You are the heroes of the revolution!" he called after them. One of them turned around. His rough, peasant face split into an impossibly wide grin, his skin darkened to the color of slate, and his eyes began to glow with a malevolent light. The smile grew wider, the teeth longer and longer...

Ockzar woke with a start, his legs cramping from the nightmare. "Gasvoy's Ghost!" he exclaimed as a blinding light exploded before him and coalesced into a wall that seemed to be made of ice and lightning. Sparks flew as a grotesque creature threw itself at the wall and rebounded screaming into a mass of other nightmarish creatures. "What the hell? What are they?"

"Ghouls," said Swann calmly and dragged Ockzar towards him by his coat while keeping his eyes fixed on the monsters before them. "Stay close, jimma."

Ockzar crawled as close to Swann as he could without climbing on him. He wanted to; hugging someone always made him feel less afraid, but he settled for grabbing hold of his leg. Swann didn't pull away, presumably because he was concentrating on casting spells. Ockzar couldn't make out what he was saying, but he was sure Swann was muttering some kind of incantation. Terrified, Ockzar watched him tear one of the many colorful pendants from his wrist and throw it into the fire, which was also inside the magical dome. The flames blazed. Dozens of the ghouls leaped at them from all directions, hit the barrier, and burned.

He was more grateful than he could ever express that the barrier was keeping the ghouls out, but the smell of burning monsters was worse than the stench of the grave pits. He couldn't breathe. The harder he tried to draw a breath, the more difficult it became. *Calm down, Ocky! Remember what the physik taught you. Think of cold icebergs floating in the deep, blue ocean, cold icebergs.*

"Cold icebergs," he said.

Swann gave him a funny look. "What?"

"Nothing." The tightness in his chest loosened, and he was able to draw a shuddering breath. Huge and white and still utterly terrifying, Nicodemus bounded out of the darkness. The vukodlak let out an unearthly roar, grabbed one of the ghouls, and tore it in half. Black oily guts splattered across the barrier and sizzled. Ockzar wasn't sure what scared him more, the ghouls or the shapeshifter. He wondered if he would be less afraid if he couldn't see what was going on around him and shut his eyes. It was worse. He could now clearly hear claws scratching the shield, old, dry flesh burning, and the squelch of feet trampling in gods' only knew what. How could he be in a worse situation than a penal mine where he was forced to make dentures from the teeth of the dead? He opened his eyes, and his heart lurched in his chest.

Swann was standing beside him, arms outstretched. The talismancer's face was a mask of concentration, his fingers lit with white fire as he wove symbols in the churning air. Bile burned in Ockzar's throat as more body parts hit the magical shield and, bubbling and spitting, slid down the crackling surface.

"Breed, get over here!" Swann shouted.

Ockzar followed the track of his gaze to the stone-crowned mound. Ghouls were crawling over it, their ragged forms silhouetted against the grey sky. His friend was alone up there. "Come down. Please, Chas, come down."

Ockzar watched another ghoul throw itself at the barrier. With a single-minded determination that was as horrifying as it was impressive, it forced its hand through the ward. Its flesh burned; the bones blackened, but the claws kept reaching towards an oblivious Swann. Finding his voice, Ockzar screamed. "Behind you!"

Swann glanced over his shoulder. "Oh, I don't think so, jimma," he growled and made a fist. A charm dangling from his wrist glowed, the shield glowed, and the ghoul's blackened and burned hand landed beside him, still twitching. Ockzar kicked it away and wrapped his arms around his legs to stop them from shaking. The endless tide kept coming; the ghouls kept clawing at the barrier, kept hurling themselves at the embattled Vukodlak. He didn't want to die here. He wanted to die in his bed, a very old man with his many children and weeping wife by his side, but he couldn't see a way out. As he had done on more than one occasion in the last year, he hoped that when death came, it would be quick.

A bony hand grabbed his shoulder. He had intended to be stoic, but in the heat of the moment, he screamed.

"Steady on, jimma," said Swann. The sorcerer was breathing hard and looked like he'd aged ten years. "Are you hurt?"

He looked around; the fighting had stopped. "I'm not sure." He patted himself. "I'm fine, I think." Relieved, he laughed through tears. "Is it over?"

Nic rose like a bloody specter from behind a pile of mangled bodies. He was naked and covered in ichorous, ghoul blood. "Aye. It's over."

The golden shield flew apart like burned parchment. The cold air rushed in, followed by the stench of death and burned meat. Ockzar felt instantly vulnerable. The mage sank down by the fire. He was joined by the shapeshifter who settled on his haunches. Miraculously, other than ghoul blood, there didn't appear to be a scratch on him.

"What?" Nic growled at him, which was when he realized he was staring at a naked man.

"Where's Breed?" he asked. Nicodemus shook his head before lying down and closing his eyes. Swann looked to the hill before climbing to his feet. Picking his way through the bodies, he headed over to the mound. Ockzar felt sick as he noted there was no urgency in

Swann as though he was already assured of Breed's fate. As much as he didn't wish to leave the relative safety of the trees and the fire, Ockzar had to know what had befallen his friend. "Wait for me," he called as loud as he dared and followed the sorcerer.

By the time he'd clambered up the steep side of the mound, he was out of breath and feeling light-headed. He took a moment to regain his composure and wipe the fog from his spectacles. A half dozen ghouls lay within the ring of stones, their ragged robes flapping in the savage gale like broken crow wings. Breed was slumped against one of the stones, head on chest, and swords in hand. It was odd to see Breed armed, even stranger to think his acerbic assistant had killed all the monsters scattered across the mound. If he could ignore the bloodstained shirt, he could almost convince himself that Breed was resting. Almost. Ockzar had seen too many bodies not to know what he was looking at. Swann was kneeling with his hand against his friend's neck, his face set in a grimace.

"Is Chas...?" Ockzar asked. The talismancer sat back on his heels and took out his pipe.

"I never realized how long your hair was," said Ockzar as he straightened Breed's hair spines. "It's because you were never still and I never caught you sleeping, although I'm sure you must have." It had been worrying at first. Indeed, the first night Breed had spent in the infirmary, Ockzar had tried to stay awake lest he be murdered or raped while he slept. He managed a few hours but eventually succumbed to the arms of oblivion.

Hours later, he woke with a start to find that he was still alive, still a virgin, and that a pot of chai was bubbling on the stove. Relief swiftly turned to gratitude when Breed proceeded to repair some of the worst leaks and with a combination of brute strength and cunning, divert the stream that had been running through the infirmary for weeks.

"I'll never forget that first morning," said Ockzar as he folded Breed's stiff fingers around the hilt of a sword. "You had your feet up on the table. You were sitting in my chair, and had it rocked back on two legs. You had your hands locked behind your head like you were lounging in a garden." He chuckled. "I remember you said, 'What's the matter? Did you think I was going to murder you in your sleep or something?'" Ockzar smiled at the recollection of the best memory he'd made in many months. "Naturally, I said 'no', even though that was precisely what I'd considered might happen. You knew I was lying because you laughed then. You have quite the most annoying, yet infectious laugh of any being I've ever met, by the way." He fell silent as a wave of grief washed over him. He knew from experience that, like hunger, the feeling would pass, and he just had to ride it out, but it wasn't easy. When it did, he wiped his tears away. "Of course, your laughter was most annoying when I was the butt of the joke." He took a deep, shuddering breath. "Joking aside, I always felt that you respected me and that was more important than you will ever know." He covered the corpse with his blanket. "We didn't know each other long, but I will miss you, my friend, and I will miss your laughter."

While Nic slept, with Swann's help, Ockzar had laid Breed out on the recumbent stone on the mound. As it was fiercely windy up here, he pinned the blanket down with rocks. It would hold for the time being. Animals and decomposition would have their way, but for now it afforded a modicum of dignity.

After the initial shock had worn off and he'd smoked most of his remaining pel, Swann took one of Breed's swords. When he saw Ockzar watching him, he hurriedly explained that it was his and he had only loaned it to Breed. He was in no position to judge the Imperial. He had not only robbed the dead of their belongings but also their teeth, and when he'd tossed the bodies in the grave pits followed by a shovel of lime, their dignity also.

Nicodemus slept like the dead for a good hour after the attack. When he woke, he insisted on eating before helping Swann pile the ghouls by the fire. Ockzar stayed out of the way on the mound, a sick feeling of dread churning his gut. Now that his protector was dead, there was nothing to stop them from killing him. No matter how much he tried, he couldn't put the thought from his mind. It made him sick with nerves, and every time they bent their heads together or glanced in his direction, his heart thundered. Come on Ockzar, you are a philosopher, a poet, an orator. You survived the mines for over a year. Treat the Imperial swine like you would if they were guards. He sighed. "Oh, Chas, Breed whatever you're called." He looked at the blanket-covered body. "Why did you save me and then leave me?"

Summoned by the smell of death, a flock of crows swooped across the moody plain and alighted on the trees. Ockzar admired their efficiency as much as he despised their presence. "We're all just meat to you, aren't we?" he said as he slipped the map to Forgasty Vash under Breed's body. "Not all the stirring rhetoric in the world can change that. Not sorcery, nor infernal power." Stealing the map was a small victory, a possibly meaningless act of sabotage given their abilities, but it was the best he could do, and he was proud of himself for doing it. He might be a coward, but he was also a loyal son of Voskva and would not help foreigners steal from her. "Ah, my friend," he said as he plucked a twig from the blanket covering Breed. "All succumb to corruption and are consumed; the cycle continues, the world turns."

"That's good," said Nic, who he hadn't heard approaching. "It has a proper ring to it. You should write it down." He picked up a severed ghoul head and hurled it towards the pile of bodies by the campfire. It hit one of the trees and smashed with a hollow crack, startling the crows to flight, and splattering rotten brains across the ground. "Ah, balls."

"That was close," said Ockzar, who was sweating nails, having almost been discovered committing his act of sabotage.

"Aye," said Nicodemus. "It was. Fucking wind took it."

Ockzar didn't like Nicodemus. It wasn't because he was a vukodlak; he believed every sentient being had a right to exist so long as it abided by the just laws of the land. It was who he was, not what he was, that Ockzar despised. Nic was the kind of man who, when he deigned to notice men like Ockzar, would acknowledge them with a smirk or an insult or quite often violence which he would then brush off as 'horse play'. Ockzar had been bullied by men like Nic all his life. But no longer. If by some miracle he survived this madness, he would never again allow himself to be cowed by bullies. Like his hero Donvyr Maxint Gasvoy, this trial would be his test, and he would return to the world all the stronger for it.

"Like a blade, I was tempered by privation."

"Eh?" said Nic as he kicked one of the bodies off the mound.

"Nothing. Just reciting poetry. It's traditional at funerals."

"Oh."

Ockzar smirked to himself. The stupid Imperial didn't have a clue that it was one of the many memorable lines from The Enlightenment of Gasvoy, possibly the greatest declaration ever written and known the world over. Resolutely ignorant, Nicodemus took a piss against one of the standing stones.

"Hey, jimma." Swann called as he clambered up the mound. "Nic, you up here?" His pel pipe was hanging from his mouth and his eyes were glassy. He didn't acknowledge Ockzar, who was more than happy to be ignored.

"What?" Nic finished pissing and put his business away.

"We need to talk about…" Swann made a face and turned his gaze to the blanket.

"What?"

"I don't know how to put this –, necromancy isn't my thing, you know?"

Nic snorted and folded his arms. "No. What are you trying to say? That we should bring Breed back?"

The sorcerer took a deep breath. "What? No. I was just wondering." He scratched his head. "Is Breed really dead?" His emphasis confused Ockzar.

Nic walked over and poked the body. "Looks that way."

Swann shook his head. "No, I mean – yes, right now Chas, er, Breed, is dead. But after what your brother did." He clawed two fingers and jabbed them into his neck. "You know?"

Nicodemus looked at Swann like he was an idiot. "Not a clue."

For the first time, Swann looked at Ockzar and smiled, perhaps seeking support. Ockzar shrugged apologetically. *Drugs will be banned in my new Voskva.*

Swann turned his attention back to Nic. "I thought when a...well when someone like your brother does what he does to a person then they have a certain immunity to, er, death." He laughed. "This is so much harder than it should be." He drew on the pipe. "Come on, jimma, you know what I mean, surely?"

Nic turned slightly and stroked his chin, perhaps to hide the fleeting smile Ockzar saw cross his face. "Nope, not a clue, but Breed looked pretty dead to me. What, do you think we should burn the body? Shove a stake through the heart? Remove the head? What?"

At this point, Swann gave up trying to make the point he had thus far failed to make. "Fine. Whatever. Burn the body." He shrugged, defeated. "I don't care."

This wouldn't do. Ockzar had intended on returning to retrieve the bloody map. To distract himself from grief, he had devised a rough plan to mount an expedition of his own and find the treasure they were after. He would then sell whatever it was and use the proceeds to help fund his revolution. He did not want to see that opportunity go up in smoke with his erstwhile comrade. But what could he do to stop them?

"Excuse me…" He raised his hand and immediately regretted it. Both men glared at him. *You're skating on thin ice, Ocky, as his nanna would say, very bloody thin indeed.* "Breed was half thoasa and thoasa prefer sky burials." He felt sure that neither one of them was in a position to gainsay his lie.

Swann nodded. "Yeah, I've heard that too. But Breed might become like those ghouls, so we should burn the body."

"Voskvan ghouls aren't made like that, I assure you. And even if they were, this hill is hallowed." He lied.

Swann put his hands on his hips. "What's that now?"

Quit while you're behind, Ockzar. "You see the writing on the stone? It's a very ancient magical incantation. The dead in this mound, or indeed on this mound, will stay dead."

Swann narrowed his eyes and scrutinized the ancient script. At the same time, it began to snow again.

Nicodemus looked at the sky like he wanted to kill it. "It's not even fucking winter yet. Come on Swann, we're going." With that, he bounded down the mound.

Swann took a drag on his pipe and coughed. For a moment he looked torn, but then the wind scythed across the mound. He pulled up his hood. "All right, jimma. Wait up." The magician made to head down the mound and then noticed Ockzar. He glanced towards the camp. "Don't worry about Nic, just – you know, stay out of his way, eh?" Ockzar nodded, curious as to why the sorcerer was being so pleasant. The answer soon became clear. "Also, when we find the next village, do you think you could help me acquire some pel?"

Relieved, Ockzar smiled. He knew how to be useful to those more powerful than him. He knew how to work the angle, as Breed might say. "I could indeed. And I'll make sure no one takes advantage of you, as is common out here in the more rural parts of our great nation. Suffice it to say, if not outright hostile, some are suspicious of strangers, particularly foreigners. Don't worry, I'll take care of things."

"Aye, that's great jimma, just great." Swann slapped him on the back and strode off after Nicodemus. Before attempting the arduous climb down, Ockzar glanced over his shoulder for the last time, half convinced, half hoping, that Breed would sit up and grin at him. A raven landed on the end of the stone by Breed's feet. It furled its wings, glared defiantly at Ockzar, and cawed as though declaring, 'this is mine now'. With a heavy heart, Ockzar began his unsteady descent. Behind him, the raven's kin spilled from the sky and fell upon the mound like broken shards of midnight.

Chapter Fourteen

I have died many times, but this wasn't one of them.

It was close, certainly; to the novice it might *seem* like death, but I was a veteran and knew better. I couldn't move, I couldn't see or feel anything, but I knew I was alive because I was aware. Dying is akin to snuffing out a candle. One minute you're a bright, burning consciousness with a headful of thoughts profound and inane. Then with a breath, or a pinch, or more commonly the insertion of a few feet of steel, you're gone. No thoughts, no desires, just a whole universe of shit-all. I was conscious; therefore, I knew I was alive.

Given I'd been fighting ghouls when whatever
happened had happened, it remained a distinct
possibility that death was close. Like a feline that was
enjoying playing with its food, death might very well be
waiting for what it considered the opportune moment to
pounce.

And because I'd been fighting nasty, ill-mannered
ghouls, death, if it deigned to visit, would probably be
of the bitey, eatey variety. Trapped in my head with
such delightful musings, I was relieved when I began to
hallucinate. I thought I could hear bees buzzing around
inside my skull, which was not as unpleasant as you
might imagine. After an indeterminate length of time,
the buzzing became a burr with the same cadence and
rhythm as human speech. As hallucinations went, this
one was not only obscure but also rather dull, and then
I realized that although the words were frustratingly
beyond my comprehension, it *was* human speech and
that I could almost hear.

Awareness, coupled with the maddening sensation
of almost being able to hear again, gave me hope that
whatever had happened to plunge me into a death-like
state had only been temporary. I reasoned that the
bastardly coffin goblins must have delivered a potent
venom with their pernicious bites. Perhaps it was so that
they might savor their prey at leisure, or worse, that the
venom transformed those they bit into creatures like
themselves. Perhaps I would change and join the pack.
Sweet Salvation, I hoped not. Indeed, given the choice,
I would prefer to be eaten. In another life, I had briefly

been the unliving slave of a necromancer. I could say with certainty that the condition had nothing to recommend it.

Minutes, hours, or perhaps even days after I'd been marooned somewhere between life and death, I was overwhelmed with unalloyed joy when I thought I perceived a change in the color of the inside of my eyelids. I feared to put much store in the shift from pink to black but felt sure I was seeing nightfall.

Of course, I hadn't forgotten what my dear old mother had said about hope and fools, but she'd had her head cut off by a so-called friend, so what did she know? Unmoving and silent, I allowed myself to hope and waited expectantly for the next change in my circumstances.

And I waited.

And then I waited some more.

Drowning in a sea of despair, an ache woke me to the fact that feeling was returning. It wasn't much, but I focused the whole of my sensation-starved attention on the discomfort. It felt like I was lying on a stone. I was elated. I tried to move everything but failed to move anything. More time passed without improvement, save that the unyielding pressure of the stone became unbearable. It wasn't painful, just relentless and unchanging. I tried to yell and failed, but I did blink, which was a fair compensation given the circumstances. I did it again, reveled in the power even though my eyes were so dry they squeaked. Eventually my vision cleared, and I gazed upon the plains and valleys of a woolen landscape that lay inches from my face. Having spent a month living with him, I knew it to be Ockzar's blanket due to the smell of farts trapped in the weave. I did not have long to drink in the olfactory delights of lanolin and poor digestion before a gust of wind tore the blanket from me. It was evening. The sky was somber; the clouds were low and heavy with snow yet to fall. Crow shadows crossed the narrow field of my vision. Pinions creaked, and black feather fingers traced the spine of the wind as the flock scissored dusk with the bladed edges of their wings.

"By Monya's wide smile, what is it?" It was a woman's voice; high but not youthful, fragile but not aged. "Yalta, come take a look." Sodden fabric dragged across the ground.

"It's always, 'Yalta come look'. Could be anything, could be a Vroki in disguise waiting to eat my soul and carry me off to hell and ravish me for all eternity, but never mind that. It's always, 'Yalta take a look'. Ack, and my knees. I'm too old for this." A crone who I assumed was Yalta hove into view above me and sniffed. "Something exotic from across the sea and beyond," she rasped as she peered at me. Her eyes were entirely bloodshot, set in a face as wrinkled as a rumpled sheet. A straggly web of dirty grey hair clung to her skull, and her swollen knuckles were as big and round as planished ship rivets. More peculiarly, she was dripping wet even though it wasn't raining. Like a curious physik, she poked at the wound on my shoulder, sniffed the congealing blood, and wrinkled her nose before plunging a finger into the ragged gash. Grim though it was, I couldn't feel anything as she rummaged around. She sniffed the fresh claret, rubbed it between thumb and forefinger. "It won't turn."

"What? Why not?" said the first speaker.

"Someone has a prior claim."

"Well, I've never seen the like," a third gurgled, again from beyond the bounds of my limited view. Whoever they were, it sounded like they were gargling a mouthful of water as they spoke.

The red-eyed dame stared hard at me, water dripping off the end of her bulbous nose. "We should finish it off."

"Should we burn it, Kolna?" the gurgler enquired.

"Aye, Kniza, we should," said the hag.

Desperate to dispute her, I tried to speak. All I managed to produce was a spit bubble, but it was a start.

"No. We should bury it with an iron spike through the heart." Yalta suggested and casually patted me on the chest like I was an old hound about to be put down. "Fire will draw attention."

"What if its maker comes looking for it?" Kolna mused.

I'm giving you the abridged version of their conversation, for it ranged wide and ran long. Do not mistake me; I was grateful, for while they were talking, they weren't stabbing, burying, or burning me.

Another of the soggy wenches came to peer at me. This one was young. Like her hair and her skin, her eyes were dead white as though all color had been bleached from her. Her hair was bundled into a red, cotton cap and her russet dress was dripping wet. "How about putting it in one of the tombs?" Water ran from her mouth as she spoke.

"It'll just dig its way out," rasped red-eyed Yalta. "Like a rat."

Kolna finally came over to join her sisters. "We have to do something." She put her hands on her broad hips. The skin of her wrists was livid, and rope burned. She was wearing a white blouse with faded embroidery. Her feet were bare, her skirt homespun and patched. From what I could see, it looked like all of them had recently been swimming – which was a puzzle as there wasn't a river or lake within sight of this place. "We should chop it up and bury the pieces." She looked at me as though the sheer intensity of her gaze might make me vanish.

"Spiked with iron?" Yalta asked. She was so keen on staking with iron I wondered if she had shares in a smithy.

"Furgin lovl…" I slurred. I intended to say, 'fucking lovely'. That I managed anything at all I deemed a triumph. They looked as surprised as I was. Thus encouraged, I tried again. "Furglovel…"

"This is awkward," said Kolna. Her companions agreed.

"Do you think it understands us?"

"Voskvan?" Yalta laughed. "I very much doubt it."

Ha! Crinkle quim, little do you know. I tried to say with my eyes.

"A word if you would, sisters." Kolna gestured for them to follow her and led them out of my sight but not beyond the range of my hearing. "It's not dying," she whispered.

"No, thank the spirits, or we'd have more on our hands than a ghoul," said Yalta.

"I don't understand," said Kniza confirming her position as the thickest member of the trio. "What are we going to do with it?"

"Let me go and check in the Book of All-Knowing, eh?" said Kolna.

Kniza sniffed. "Do we have such a thing?"

"No of course we don't, you stupid girl." Kolna snapped. "Just hush and let me think."

"We should kill it. I'll get the spikes," said Yalta.

"No, Yalta. No spikes," said Kolna.

"A cold, iron spike was good enough in my day. I'm just saying..." the eldest grumbled.

"It's not been your day for thirty years," Kolna muttered.

"Don't be rude. And it's not like killing a human."

"I don't care. I'm no murderer. *We* aren't murderers."

They talked over each other, muttered, snapped, and argued about my fate until Kolna clapped her hands, bringing the unruly assembly to order.

"Then it's decided. We'll roll the dice," she declared. "Evens, we chop it up, spike the pieces, and bury them deep. Odds, we take 'em home and... I don't know, keep it as a pet or something." She sighed. "Are we agreed, ladies?"

They grudgingly agreed.

Dice? Fucking Dice? I was incensed. I could almost hear Fate's mocking laughter as I listened to the clatter of bones being shaken in a cup, which was followed by the toss, and then an agonizing wait as they teasingly rolled around.

A moment's silence was broken by Yalta cursing. "Best of three?" She sounded aggrieved. Given her eagerness to do away with me, I deemed it a good sign.

Kolna dragged her dripping skirts back over to me. "No. Fate has decided. Now let's clean up here and go home."

From the back of a cart pulled by a pair of enormous stag beetles, I saw that home was a cottage in a forest on the far side of the plain. We trundled along a narrow path through a gently undulating woodland towards the southeast if I read the stars right.

The cottage was small, whitewashed, and had a sharply pitched, shingle roof. Two lower windows were warmed by the honey glow of firelight. The upper windows were black with sloping lintels, which gave the impression of drooping brows. There wasn't a garden, but hardy winter herbs and shrubs grew in abundance where the shyness of the canopy allowed light to fall upon the ground.

They carried me inside between them. Their sodden footsteps echoed on waxed floorboards. A cheery fire burned in the hearth; a pot of something bubbled on the fire. Every surface that would take a blade had been badly carved with ugly flowers and even uglier figures. The many cupboards and dung plastered walls had not escaped embellishment. They had been garishly painted, which rather than hide the imperfections of the rough plaster, enhanced them. I wasn't well-bred enough to think it 'quaint' or 'rustic'; it just looked a bit shit. Mother would have loved it.

What distinguished it from the average, peasant croft were the great, fluffy-headed, pink and scarlet fungi, which grew in pots on the deep windowsills. Indeed, even though a fire blazed in the hearth, the air was damp enough to drink, and I steamed gently in the peculiar warmth.

In no hurry at all, Yalta cleared the kitchen table where I was unceremoniously dumped by Kolna and Kniza like a corpse ready for a pre-funeral scrub. A steady trickle of water ran down Kniza's chin dripping on me and soaked her heavy gown. From time to time, she would pointlessly wring the hem of the sodden garment.

"Cursed?" I rasped. The sound surprised me.

Yalta had gone over to the hearth to stoke the fire. When she heard me speak, her head snapped around, and she set her furious gaze upon me; one eye narrowed, the other rounded like a crown piece. She clasped her hands and cracked her gnarled fingers. "Aye." Snowflakes began to swirl against the windows. "Wait, you speak Voskvai?"

"No," I said in Voskvan.

She chuckled. "Dice are a holy oracle, you understand. We did not decide your fate by trivial means."

"Of course." It was urux shit, but I was in no position to argue and pretended not to see Kolna elbow Kniza in the ribs as she opened her mouth, most likely to gainsay the old dame.

"Here, sit up," said Kolna, who looped a thick arm around my shoulders and propped my head on a pile of cushions. "What's your name? Who is your master? Your master? Do you understand?"

"Yes," I said; I wanted to add that I was foreign, not stupid but again thought better of vexing them when I was helpless. "Leo." I croaked. I was still as weak as a babe, but I was sure that I could feel a tingling sensation in my fingers and toes as my sluggish blood slowly resumed flowing at its usual rate.

She frowned. "'Leo'? Is that even a name?" she asked her companions.

Kniza shook her head as she ladled hot water into a bowl of herbs. "I don't think so."

"It's in Pharria. I'm sure of it," said Yalta. "I knew a Pharrian once. He was a funny fellow; wore a wig and a hat and painted his lips and cheeks like a common whore although, he was anything but common if you get my meaning." She cackled. "You should wear a better hat for the weather, I told him."

"What did he say?" Kniza asked.

"I'm not telling you!" Yalta answered snappily. "It's too funny to share."

A pained-looking Kolna turned to me. "Is Leo where you come from?" she said slowly.

Speaking was exhausting and I mispronounced words. Ockzar had been a patient and generous teacher and met me more than halfway when it came to interpreting what I was trying to say. The wet sisters were far less accommodating and stoically refused to unpick meaning from my mangled Voskvan. Too tired to continue trying to explain who I was and where I came from, I closed my eyes and feigned sleep. Kolna prodded me a couple of times but gave up when I didn't respond and settled for plumping my pillow, which was an unexpected kindness. As I lay there, pretending to sleep while willing strength to return to my limbs, I was sprinkled with herb water and wafted with strong-smelling incense. Unlike the precise mathematical and metaphysical calculations Swann employed when making his charms, the sodden women appeared to rely upon a pinch of this and a sprinkle of that. Even their chanting sounded more like they were singing folk songs than reciting incantations, but I could feel the magic build in the room, feel it seep into my bones. Whether through their arts or because their songs were soothing, I fell into a deep and restful sleep.

When I woke sometime later, I felt refreshed. It was snowing, and the windows were skinned with luminous, powdery snow. The sisters were sitting huddled together by the hearth. Kniza was stirring the bubbling pot, Yalta was chopping herbs, and Kolna was stoking the fire. It was a charming scene; the only fault I could find in the homely picture was that the fire was clearly visible through their translucent forms. Without thinking, I sat up and swung my heavy legs off the table. My shoulder burned. I winced, and the women immediately became opaque. Now that my sense of smell had fully returned, I noted then that they all smelled strongly of river water.

"Back in the land of the living, eh?" said Kolna, a wry smile playing on her lips. "Come, warm yourself." She patted a stool beside her, leaving a wet handprint on the wood. "You heal quickly." It was a leading comment.

"Aye," I replied, not wishing to elaborate on those things I did not fully comprehend. The other two shuffled deeper into the inglenook to make room for me. The thick, gloopy bubbles of whatever was boiling in the pot popped, releasing the smell of pungent herbs. It was only now that I noticed there wasn't any food lying around. There weren't any of the usual peasant staples, no bread on the sideboard, no crocks of ale, rounds of cheese, or hams hanging from the rafters over the fire. There were plenty of bundles of herbs, both magical and medicinal; elf leaf, sage, daughter's regret, sorrow bane, and many others I didn't recognize.

"I don't mean to be rude, but what the fuck are you?"

"Busy, that's what we are," said Yalta, as she chopped herbs on a board on her lap before scraping them into the pot. She wiped her hands on her sodden apron. "But that isn't what you want to know, is it?"

"No. Well, that depends. If knowing what you are means you must kill me then I absolutely don't want to know anything. If, however, knowing what you are has no bearing on my continued existence, then yes, you have the right of it. I am curious about what you are, not what you're doing."

Kniza giggled. "You talk funny."

"So I'm told."

"We are the Shepherds of the Dead," said Kolna, her tone grave and touched with sadness. "We have been cursed to roam the wilds by the monster who murdered us. His magic is not strong enough to destroy us as it has those poor creatures that attacked you."

"Poor creatures? You mean the ghouls?"

"Yes. They were sacrificed as we were sacrificed." Kniza dribbled quietly. "But they weren't blessed by the Crow Mother. They were just ordinary people, farmers, villagers, townsfolk and travelers like you."

Yalta folded her arms. "He was always a strange boy. Smelled funny from the minute he was born. I knew he was a wrong 'un because this nose never lies."

"You never thought to smother him then? Save us from all this?" Kolna snorted. "The nose might not lie, but the mouth surely does."

The comment sparked an argument. While they were busy bickering, I shook my heavy legs and took a tentative step towards the door. The sisters didn't notice, but I kept half an eye on them as I tried the handle. There was a key, but it wasn't locked. I opened it and would have run like the wind were it not for the pack of slavering ghouls crowded outside. They looked at me, and I looked at them. Very slowly and very gently I closed the door and turned the key. "Bollocks."

Chapter Fifteen

"**B**reed and butter?" The girl asked.

Ockzar's heart skipped a beat. "I beg your pardon?"

"Bread. And. Butter?" she asked again, only this time louder, slower, and more sarcastically.

He cleared his throat and tried to will the heat from his face, which only made it worse. "Yes, and fried eggs, bacon, ham, cheese dumplings, salted chai. Do you have pickled herrings?"

She pulled a face like he'd asked for a turd on a plate. "I don't know."

He waited until it was obvious that she wasn't going to elaborate. "Would you mind finding out, sister?"

She huffed to show that she did mind before slouching off. He watched her broad hips sway and wondered briefly about what lay beneath the heavy skirts and tight bodice. *Stop that!* He scolded himself. She was not an object of desire; although, Gasvoy's ghost, she smelled sweet as a peach. He wiped his brow. She was not a peach; she was a hero of Voskva; a noble laborer building a better country with the sweat of her lovely brow and the strength of her undoubtedly mighty, man-crushing thighs. That said, she should know her livelihood depended on being civil to paying customers. She had been nothing but surly since they'd arrived the night before. Tired and cold, his companions had won over the innkeeper and overcome his natural distrust of foreigners by throwing gold at the problem. The coin, combined with Ockzar's native charm, had bought them a suite of good rooms for the night, pel for Swann, and two biddable maids for Nicodemus.

Ockzar had entertained the thought that he might also get a tumble, but the wench, who was just then returning to the bar, had told him in no uncertain terms that she refused to dally with foreigners *or their friends*. Foreigners he could understand, especially these two, but he felt affronted that she wouldn't entertain a son of Voskva. Well, more fool her because she'd missed out on substantial remuneration for a few minutes' work. "And I'll have some game pie, with turnips and gravy."

He slapped more of Nic's coin on the counter. "You do have game pie?"

She gave him a dead-eyed stare before shouting over her shoulder. "Do we have any game pie?" Startled by the sudden noise, a dog that was sleeping by the fire jumped up and barked in alarm.

"What?" A voice floated back.

"Game pie," she bellowed.

"What?" whomever asked again.

"Just go and ask!" Ockzar snapped more forcefully than he'd intended, but he wasn't having a good morning. "Go on!" He shooed her towards the kitchen. The last time he'd visited a country inn it had been on the way to a distant cousin's wedding. Despite getting food poisoning, he'd enjoyed the short time he'd spent with them, observing their simple, country ways. Still, he had been happy to return to Sevast and civilization. Damn, but he missed the city. He missed his friends; he missed the bars, the theatre, the libraries. He missed it all.

The girl returned and swept up the coins. "Ain't got game pie."

"Do you have any gorbushka?"

She stared at him a moment before returning to the door from where she shouted. "Do we have any smoked salmon?"

"What?" someone bellowed.

She headed into the kitchen. "Do we have…"

The dog barked again and followed the wench. Ockzar paced quietly until she returned.

"Yes, sir, we have gorbushka."

"If you must call me anything, call me friend, brother, or traveler, for I am 'sir' to no one."

She narrowed her eyes. "Yes, *traveler*, we have gorbushka."

After ordering breakfast, Ockzar reluctantly returned to their rooms on the first floor. Upon entering, he was assaulted afresh by the stench and the mess the others had made during their debauching. If he wasn't convinced that they'd hunt him down, he would just close the door and leave them to it. No wonder the wench wanted nothing to do with him. His louche associates were enough to put any decent person off.

Clothes had been thrown everywhere, including the bathtub by the hearth— the site of much outrageous carousing the night before. The remains of supper had been thrown across the table and ground into the floorboards. Swann was snoring on an overstuffed couch by the window with a smoldering pel pipe hanging from his lip. His eyes were half-closed, but

Ockzar sensed some part of him was awake, if not entirely conscious. It was said that pel, or 'kra' as it was more commonly known in Voskva, made people soft; that it weakened not just the spirit but the flesh. If that was true, Swann must surely melt like wax in the sunlight, given how much he had smoked the night before. Ockzar rolled the small truckle bed he'd slept on back under the one Nic had claimed for him and the girls. 'After all, there are three of us,' he'd argued much to the wenches' delight. He glared at the six dirty feet that were sticking out from under the quilt. Two pairs were small, and one was huge with hairy, taloned toes. One of them rolled over and wafted the quilt, releasing the smell of fuck sweat and sour farts into the room. It was disgusting, and he was incredibly jealous.

"Animals," he muttered. "Beasts."

"I wouldn't let him hear you say that, if I were you," said Swann. Without opening his eyes, he felt for his pipe with one hand and a blanket that had fallen on the floor with the other. "He might take offence and tear you to pieces."

"I didn't mean in that way." Alarmed that what he said might have been heard, Ockzar glanced at the bed and was relieved to see that no one stirred.

"He's not one for nuance." The talismancer wrapped himself in the blanket.

Ockzar swallowed. "Only a halfwit would think I was impugning his nature rather than his habits."

Swann grinned triumphantly as he winkled a pea-sized lump of kra from behind the cushion on the couch. A moment later, it had been expertly crumbled, stuffed in the bowl, and lit with a candle taper. Swan took a deep pull on the pipe and sank back against the cushions haloed in smoke. "I sense your humors are not in harmony, jimma." He offered the pipe. "Have a pull, it'll balance you."

"My humors are balanced enough, thank you, Mr. Swann." He wasn't feeling balanced, not in the slightest. Being trapped with these foreign maniacs was worse than being back in the mines. Except that back in the mines had been bearable when Breed was there.

"No one calls me Mr. Swann. My name's Dalowin."

"Breed called you, Swann." Upon hearing the sharpness of his tone, Ockzar realized he was not only upset that Breed was dead but also with the seeming ease with which Swann and Nicodemus had accepted it.

Swann sucked on his pipe and spoke as he exhaled. "You're angry about something, I can tell."

A knock on the door gave Ockzar the excuse not to answer him. "Come in," he said and cleared the table. The barmaid shoved the door open with the tray she was carrying. An older man with a sweaty, red face followed her in with the other tray. Ockzar's stomach rumbled appreciatively, and he forgot how upset he was.

When they left, Swann stumbled over to the table and poured a cup of chai. "Dig in."

Ockzar did not stand on ceremony. He piled a plate high with cheese dumplings, fried eggs, and salmon. To take food when it was there was a habit he'd learned in prison. It was only when he saw the smile on Swann's face that he refrained from adding any more items from the wonderful spread. He sat at the table and forced himself to eat slowly using a knife and fork. The simple act of sitting at a breakfast table with clean plates and delicious food made him want to cry. Breed would have noticed, would have made a joke to lighten his mood. Swann took a cheese dumpling, sat opposite him, and began to idly pull it apart before nibbling on some crumbs as though food was his enemy.

A head appeared over the mountain of quilts. It was one of the tavern girls who had bartered her morals for gold. The hussy slipped from the bed and picked through the rumpled pile of clothes that had been hastily discarded the night before. When she saw that Ockzar was watching her, a slow, languid smile spread across her face. Flustered, he looked away and poured himself a cup of chai.

"What's wrong, Voskie?" Swann asked. "Don't be coy, we're all friends here."

"But not all our friends are here, are they?"

"Ah. Breed."

"Who wasn't even cold before you and Nic began…debauching. It's not right. You shouldn't have." There was so much more he wanted to say, but he was too upset to articulate his feelings without sounding like a fool.

"You think we don't care? That we're being disrespectful?"

Ockzar nodded.

Swann pinched the bridge of his nose. "I forget what it must be like for someone like you. You're ordinary—that's not your fault by the way. It's a good thing." He laughed, but there was a bitter edge to the sound. "Indeed, I envy you."

"I am not ordinary." Ockzar was affronted. Mindful of the women, he leaned in close and whispered. "I'm a philosopher, a revolutionary, a prisoner of conscience – or would be if Breed hadn't rescued me."

The Imperial smirked. "Forgive me, jimma, it was a poor choice of words. You're not ordinary, you're mundane. You don't live in the same world as people like Nicodemus and me. And for that you should be grateful." He shuddered like someone had walked over his grave. "We do things differently in our world."

There was no denying they did things differently, spitefully, cruelly. "I don't think it's unreasonable that one might expect at least a single day of mourning. Even if you weren't friends, you were comrades, or doesn't comradeship mean anything in the mighty Empire?"

Swann took a bite out of a dumpling before tossing the remains on the table. "These are so good. I must get the recipe for Effie," he said, wiping his mouth with his sleeve. "We mourn in our own way. *I* mourn in my own way. Nic is…" He chuckled. "He is a man of action rather than deep introspection or tender emotions. He finds release from grief in…" He smiled. "In release. Me? I find solace in a pipe of pel, or whatever the hell this stuff is."

He sounded sincere, but the slack smile undermined the sentiment. Ockzar was not assuaged. "How can you say you mourn when you caroused all night?"

"I don't mean to sound callous, jimma, but why does Breed's death matter to you so much? You hardly knew each other."

Ockzar felt his cheeks redden. "Have you ever been in prison, Mr. Swann?"

"Not as such." The smile faltered.

"In the brutal crucible of prison, the strength of a friendship is measured in commitment, rather than length of time."

"What the fuck are you blathering about?" Nic threw the quilt back. stumbled from the bed, Ockzar averted his eyes. "Did you and Breed fuck or something?" Nic picked up his shirt, sniffed it then held it up like it was a puzzle too complicated for him to fathom.

"I beg your pardon?" Ockzar felt himself blush, *again*.

"Did you fuck?" Nicodemus mimed thrusting. "I bet you were the wench, eh? That soft skin, those pretty curls. I might do you myself, in the dark, after a gallon of wine." He winked at Swann, who pretended not to notice.

Ockzar's cheeks burned with embarrassment and fury. *Don't let him see that he's got to you, Ocky. Don't give him that satisfaction.* Ockzar did his best to compose himself before speaking. "You are not my type, and Breed and I did not share that kind of intimacy."

Nicodemus snorted and picked at the food. "Then you can't have been that close. Unlike Swann, who well and truly screwed Breed with his shit geas. Although if he hadn't de-fanged Breed you wouldn't have been friends at all."

"Hey now, that's not fair," said Swann without conviction. "It was meant to be a little curb, nothing more."

Ockzar felt the temperature in the room suddenly turn decidedly cold. Swann tapped his pipe out on the table. Ockzar coughed to get the women's attention. "I think you'd better leave."

They ignored him and looked to Nicodemus. Hardly glancing at them, he gestured to the door. Slighted, they gathered what clothes they hadn't managed to put on and departed.

Swann put his head back against the chair and pressed the heels of his hands against his eyes. "I'm averse to conflict, specifically when it is with me."

"Slaughtering ghouls is fine, but no harsh language, eh? Right, got it." Nicodemus shook his head as he peered at the map on the table. Aside from crumbs and wine rings, what looked like a ruined tower had been marked on the vellum. "Where's that other map?" he asked Swann.

Ockzar was sure if it beat any louder, they would be able to hear his heart pounding. He stuffed a dumpling in his mouth, chewed, swallowed, grabbed a second. Unused to rich food, his guts began to complain, but he needed to do something to calm his shredded nerves.

"You had it," said Swann.

"It's not in my pack."

"That's not my problem. Don't fret. I've dowsed this one. I'll find it. The pendulum never lies." He patted his chest. Trinkets jangled; polished beads sparkled.

Nicodemus narrowed his eyes. "It better not. Or I'll stuff it where the sun doesn't shine."

Swann sniggered. "Back to the prison sex, eh? You're fixated."

Ockzar finished his chai and stood up. "I'll go and fetch those supplies while you breakfast."

"Supplies?" Nicodemus asked.

"For the journey? We discussed it last night, the extra food and clothes you wanted?" He lied, confident that they were both insensible for most of the previous evening.

Like the mine guards employed for their viciousness rather than intellect, Nic pretended to know what he was talking about. "Aye. Yes, you go do that. There's coin…" He looked around. "…Somewhere."

Ockzar found the coin where he'd hidden it the night before and headed for the door.

"Oh, and Ockzar?" Nicodemus called as he reached for the latch.

He composed a serene expression before turning around. "Yes, Nic?"

"If you're thinking about running off with my money, just don't."

He laughed. "With those ghouls prowling about? Fear not."

"I'm not afraid, little man. I'm just warning you that there isn't anywhere you can go where I can't find you. Understand?"

"I wouldn't dream of—"

"Do you understand?" Nic growled.

Ockzar painted on a smile. "I understand."

He was still shaking with impotent rage when he got outside, but at least he hadn't let his feelings show in front of those two bastards. He wanted to run screaming from the pair of them and the nightmare into which he had been thrust, but he was too afraid. And to think, he had once considered that the mine was hell. He drew a deep breath and composed a face he wished the world to see. It was still early; merchants were just opening the shutters and salting the icy cobbles outside their shops. He hurried past stalls selling mutton, dried slake beetles, and lake flatfish to the shop he'd made note of when they'd arrived in the town the previous evening. As with all the store fronts, the rising suns and clenched fist symbol of the Archonate was painted on the wall. A giant carving of a shoe hung on frozen chains above the closed door. Ockzar knocked and tried the handle. It was locked, but he could see a light through the window. He knocked again.

"I'm afraid Navyu Shevin is a dissolute, old man. He drinks too much and seldom rises early."

Ockzar jumped at the sound of the voice and turned to see a jorskal of the Glorious Suns standing behind him. The grey-clad clergyman touched the brim of his tall hat and held out the suns and fist symbol. Being an educated man, he wasn't religious, but like all good Voskvans, he was required to show due deference to representatives of the only state-sanctioned religion. Unlike the last time he'd been confronted by a priest and had balked at bowing to the symbol of ecclesiastical decadence, he made his obeisance without hesitation.

"Glory be unto you, my son," the jorskal intoned. "I know all of my flock and you are not one of them. Have you come far?"

"Yes, Brother, from Sevast."

He considered Ockzar's words more thoughtfully than they deserved. "Sevast? That's a long way to come on your own."

"I'm not on my own." He spoke without thinking and instantly regretted it.

"Ah." The jorskal's smile faded. "You're here with your family?"

"Friends." A vision of blood and violence and sorcerous fire sprang to mind. "Well, clients really. Foreigners, I hardly know them, I'm guiding them to Glarosck Mountains."

"Ah." The line of the jorskal's jaw hardened. "I suppose we must tolerate them for the good of the economy. Come to afternoon prayers if you can. Our little temple is on the other side of town, by the river."

The very thought of sitting through hours of holy propaganda and sermonizing made him nauseous. "Alas, we are leaving this afternoon."

Upon hearing that he'd lost a prospective pew filler, the jorskal gave up on small talk. "Then I shall keep you no longer." He raised his hand. "Walk in glory...?"

"Jarz," said Ockzar feeling a secret glee in lying. Breed would be proud.

"Jarz." The holy man raised his hand and clenched his fist. "I will pray for you, my son."

I'm no son of yours, prattler. Ockzar lowered his head until the jorskal walked away. When he looked up, he saw a grizzled face peering at him through the shop window. He waved, and the face disappeared. A moment later, a key turned in the lock, and an old man stuck his head out and spat in the street.

"Come inside, where the air is less foul," the old fellow said and threw a filthy look in the direction of the jorskal before ducking inside. Happy to be out of the cold, Ockzar followed. The heat of a blazing stove in the corner made his cold cheeks burn. The shop smelled of wool, fur, and oiled skins. Coats, hats, and boots hung from the walls and rafters. Dozens of walking sticks and snowshoes were propped against the counter.

"Stay away from the jorskal. He's a wicked, wicked man." The old fellow's eyes momentarily blazed with hatred. "What can I get for you?"

Ockzar looked at his shoddy shoes. "Boots and socks, a set of walking poles, two oilskin sacks, and a pair of mittens. Why is he wicked?" Ockzar expected that he would say he was a drinker or fornicator, in which case, he wanted all the details.

"He likes to drown women."

"Oh." It was not the salacious gossip he was expecting. "That is indeed wicked. How is it that he has not been prosecuted for his crimes?

"He says they're evil witches, gets away with it like that."

"The Archonate doesn't believe in the existence of 'witches', evil or otherwise. This is the Age of Enlightenment."

"The light ain't reached here yet. Folk are either scared of him, or like what he does. What size mittens?"

The sudden change from serious to mundane threw him. It was likely that the old fellow had slipped into senility. Although the animosity was real as the jorskal didn't have anything nice to say about him either if he was Navyu Shevin. "Small and medium, please."

Ockzar was mindful not to encourage disparagement of the official because the Archonate had made sure that every village, town, and city had been well seeded with informers.

"Don't pay me no mind, lad." The old man grunted and turned his critical eye to Ockzar's poorly shod feet. "What happened to your shoes?"

Ockzar's heart began to race, even though he knew the history of his ill-fitting footwear could not be divined in a glance. The merchant couldn't possibly know that he'd taken them from a fellow prisoner who'd died in the infirmary. But Ockzar knew. He remembered waiting for the last breath before taking them from her still warm feet and marveling at his good fortune. "I was robbed on the road. I had to make do with what I could find."

The old man nodded as he unhooked a pair of mittens from the wall. "They'll spend money on banners and parades, but shit-all on patrolling the damn roads. You need to be careful around here."

"Yes, I know." Ockzar tried not to laugh when he considered that his traveling companions were probably the most dangerous beings he was likely to encounter.

Chapter Sixteen

I put my back to the door. "When you said, 'Shepherds of the Dead', you weren't being poetic, were you?"

Yalta turned around and cackled. "You've had three truths, young 'un. Now hush while we tend our flock." She winked. "They're not really a flock, I'm being poetic."

"To be clear, you mean the ghouls, don't you?" I felt a little queasy.

She chuckled. "'Shepherds of the Dead' not a big enough clue for you?"

"Now you mention it." While I considered my limited options with regards to getting the fuck away from here, the one called Kniza unhooked the pan from the fire. Her wet hands sizzled on the hot chain, or rather the water on her hands sizzled; her skin remained untouched, and she didn't so much as grimace from the searing contact. The ghouls began mewling and scratching at the door as the women ladled the brew into three pails. Kolna and Kniza each took one.

Yalta pointed to the third with her foot. "You take that, give these old bones a rest." She folded her hands in her lap.

"You mean me?" I knew who she meant; I was just hoping the incredulity in my tone might somehow cause her to change her mind.

"You see anyone else?"

So much for that. "They've already tried to eat me once."

Kolna tutted. "They didn't try to eat you. They don't eat people. Flesh cannot sustain them."

I pointed to my bloody shoulder. "I don't think they know that."

Kniza giggled but stopped when Kolna gave her the hard edge of her eye. "You'll be fine," the youngest witch gurgled. "They won't hurt you if you're with us."

Sensing this wasn't an argument I could win, I picked up the damn bucket. Although not unpleasant, the medicinal aroma of the herbal concoction was strong enough to make my eyes water. Kolna opened the door and spoke soothingly to the pack, clucking and shooing them as though they were chickens instead of murderous undead. To my surprise, they gave ground willingly. The last time I'd seen these fuckers, they'd been trying to kill, and I had presumed, eat me. Now when they snarled, it was at each other, as they jostled to get closer to the women and the buckets of slop.

"They're more beasts than human now, but we must not forget that they are victims." Yalta had come up behind me, as silent and as swift as a ghost. "It's what happens when ordinary mortals are sacrificed to the Moyazel. They become trapped between life and death, and it changes them."

"The Moyazel? Is that a local demon?"

She shook her head, spraying me with droplets of icy pond water. "No. it's a relic, something even more ancient than the Crow Mother who is as wise as she is old, and she is very wise." The crows perched on the snow-speckled roof of the cottage cawed as though in agreement. She smiled first at them and then at me, a curious light in her eye. "You don't seem perturbed by what I'm telling you, or by us."

"I've been around." One of the ghouls sniffed the bucket I was carrying. I shooed it with a wave. It snarled but backed away, its gaze fixed on the bucket and its contents.

Yalta nodded. "Perhaps our paths were meant to cross."

"Steady on, now. Let's not jump to outlandish conclusions."

"Don't people believe in Fate where you come from?"

"When it suits them. But those with half a brain don't believe every chance meeting is 'fated'. I count myself in that number."

"You only have half a brain? That would explain why you decided to camp on cursed ground." She laughed. "That aside, mortals don't meet us by chance. Ah. We're here. Hand me the pail."

As we'd talked, we'd walked along an animal track through the forest, which opened on to a clearing. In the middle of the clearing stood a bulbous, many trunked elm. Hundreds of spindly branches bristled from its low crown like the spines on a hedge pig's back.

"Wait here," said Kniza.

I was more than happy to oblige and watched the three of them approach the tree, followed by their terrifying flock. The ghouls hung back while the sisters began to walk a circular path that had been beaten into the ground around its wide base. As they walked, they started to sing in a language I did not understand and splash the branches with the magical brew. Upon contact with the tree, the concoction appeared to freeze. It set quickly and hung like iced cobwebs from the leafless boughs. A fine mist began to swirl around the tree, stirred by strange tides of magic that, even though I couldn't see, caused my hackles to rise. Swaying in time to the eerie song, the ghouls circled the tree, eyes shining like pale lamps in their contorted faces. Their mouths hung open; long tongues quested towards the branches laden with the ghostly brew.

When their buckets were empty, the women stopped singing and returned to the path. As soon as they were out of the way, the ghouls fell upon the tree and sucked the ethereal brew from the branches. As they gorged, they grew translucent and began to dissipate. At first, I thought it was a trick of the light, but as I watched, more and more of the pack began to drift apart like woodsmoke combed to fine threads by the spidery branches of the trees surrounding the clearing. Before long, only the four of us remained.

"That was interesting," I said, happy to break the oppressive silence that had fallen over the clearing.

"It will sate them for a while, but it's only temporary," said Kolna, her weary gaze following the dwindling shadows still drifting through the trees.

I took a step back. "Thanks for the insight, and for not burning me, or staking me, or cutting me into pieces, but I must find my friends before they get into any more trouble."

"You can't go," said Kniza. "We need your help." Kolna gave her a withering look, and Yalta cast her gaze to the heavens.

"I am not cut out to be a shepherd."

"That much is obvious," Yalta muttered and whacked at a shrub with her bucket like a petulant child.

"Then I can go?" I thumbed to the east. Took another hopeful step in that direction.

"We think you were sent. Don't we?" said Kolna. Kniza answered, "yes." Simultaneously, Yalta answered, "no." There then followed an exchange of awkward glances before they both said the opposite.

I folded my arms. "You should have rehearsed this."

"Aye, very possibly. It's because you're here," said Kolna. "And you're the only living being who has ever been able to see us."

"And you're the only one who has ever survived an attack." Kniza smiled.

"They think it's a sign." Yalta snorted. "In my day signs were things like two headed calves and the idols crying blood in the shrine to the Crow Mother. Real signs, not just 'someone turned up who can see us'. We had standards back then."

"I'm with thee, dame. It's not a sign, it's just a coincidence and anyway, I'm already sworn to a quest."

"But we need your help." It sounded like Kniza might have been crying, but it was hard to tell with all the water running down her face. "We can pacify the lost ones for a time, but the need for vengeance calls them back to the land of the living. They cannot find rest and everyone they kill becomes like them."

I didn't say anything, which I think they might have taken for consideration. In truth, I was just searching for a nice way to say I didn't care.

Kolna came over, put her clammy hand on my arm. "Please, help us. Kill the one who killed us and end the cycle."

"I would, but I can't fight a sorcerer, not even when I'm well, and your friends gave me a good going over." I hated that some of what I said wasn't a lie.

"He's no sorcerer, he's a devil." Kniza spat.

"I can't fight those either. I'm just a normal mortal, more or less."

"He isn't a sorcerer or a devil," said Kolna. "He's just a murderous bastard masquerading as a priest. He lied about us; said we were witches."

"We are witches," Yalta added, her red eyes shining with pride. "Good witches. By which I mean talented, not 'good, good', if you see what I mean?" She chuckled.

"I prefer wise women," said Kolna. "We are healers, soothsayers, midwives, and marriage counsellors amongst many other things. The Archonate might have outlawed the old ways, but we still protect our people, even from beyond the veil."

Again, I was failing to see how any of this was my problem. "I have troubles of my own."

"It won't take long," Kolna insisted. "Also, your friends went to our town. You can pick up their trail from Tartakoy."

"You have skills, why don't you go and kill this cove yourselves?" I enquired hopefully.

They looked as though a great weight had just dropped on their shoulders. Kniza wiped her gleaming cheeks. "We can't. It is the nature of the curse. We may wander the forest and the grave mounds, but we cannot cross the river and return to our home."

Yalta sighed. "Tartakoy is on the other side of the river. Even when it's as frozen as a dead dog's cock we can't cross it."

As we talked, we wandered back to the cottage. Along the way it stopped snowing, and the sky was clear and bright, lit as it was by a million stars.

"I don't have any weapons, or money, and look at the state of my clothes." I pointed out the bloodstains and rents. "I look like a vagrant. If your militia see me lurking around this cove's gaff, they'll either run me out of town, or throw me in the lockup."

"We can get you weapons and gold. You can buy some clothes," said Kolna. "Oh, and there's the map your friend left with you."

"He did? Out of interest, how much gold can you get?"

"He did, and enough," said Yalta.

"You can buy clothes in Tartakoy." Kniza smiled, perhaps sensing that locked deep within this bloody and battered exterior beat the heart of an avaricious thief. "Help us, please. I know the ghouls as you call them all look the same, but they were once children, old folk, young men and women, all innocents, all murdered and turned into those creatures that attacked you. You can free them, let them go on their way."

"All right, fuck's sake." They'd won me over at the promise of gold. "Call me soft, but I'll help."

"I still say that we should have made you swear a blood oath," said Yalta as we made our way to the river and the road that would take me to the delightful town of Tartakoy. Despite not being alive, it seemed that when

I was watching she moved with unnecessary slowness just to vex me.

"And I said, slot me now, for I am done making blood pacts. Take my word, or don't, but that's all you're getting."

Yalta narrowed her eyes. She was holding what looked like a sacrificial knife. "I wasn't going to cut your heart out; just bleed you a little, maybe take an eye, like the old days."

"No." I folded my arms. She looked like she wanted to shiv me. I dared her with a look.

"Stop it, both of you," said Kolna. "We're here." She gestured to a humpback bridge that straddled a sluggish river.

Yalta laughed. The knife vanished into the fold of her soggy skirt.

Kniza sighed. "It seems wrong that even though we died in water we cannot cross it."

"Tartakoy lies about a mile beyond the bridge," said Kolna. "Just follow the road until you come to a fork and take the left. It'll loop back down to the river, follow it into town, keep the river on your left."

I drew the blades I'd chosen from the selection they'd gathered from the burial mounds. They were old, but both held a reasonable edge and didn't shatter when I tested them against each other. Indeed, one of them, with a hilt cast in the likeness of a coiled serpent, had been well forged. Not only that, but the steel was clean despite being centuries old. Alas, they didn't bring any with diamond-encrusted hilts. Blades aside, it was nice to have a bag of coin nestled in my shirt. By the variety of noble faces stamped upon the pieces, I guessed they'd also come from the mounds. As all members of the Midnight Court and every wily farmer knew, old tombs were plunderful repositories of wealth. I sheathed the swords and turned to the women.

"What's the priest, er, jorskal's name?"

They remained tight-lipped. Something about them made my hackles rise. It was their eyes. Previously bright and alive, they now looked dead, devoid of warmth, or perhaps it was hope. I didn't ask which it was.

"You can't say what his name is?" They shook their heads. "Is there only one jorskal?" Nothing. "Come now, I don't want to slot some innocent cove." Kniza and Kolna exchanged a look that fell somewhere between uncertainty and concern. Yalta grinned and shrugged, making it clear that she gave no shits if I slotted every jorskal between here and Sevast.

"We haven't been home for a while. But if we're here, he is still alive." Kolna shuddered. "Tartakoy is too small to be served by more than one jorskal."

"I'll work it out. When I'm done, you and the ghouls will er, move on?"

Kolna furrowed her brow. "Yes. We'll 'move on' as you put it."

"I'm trying to be sensitive to your condition."

"Condition?" She laughed sharply. "We're dead, not pregnant." The first, pale sun's light was beginning to break across the teeth of the mountain peaks. "We've waited a long time for this. Don't fail us, Breed Blake."

That she knew my name was a fair trick, although she didn't need to convince me of her powers. I would do as I had promised. "You'll find out one way or the other soon enough, won't you?" I inclined my head before shouldering my small bag of grave robbed belongings. I could feel the weight of their expectation upon me as I headed to the bridge. It hammered into my back through the desperate strength of their dead-eyed gaze. It was so strong that I felt compelled to turn around and wasn't surprised to see that they had vanished.

The road to Tartakoy was reasonable given the harsh climate and its being in the middle of nowhere. The carcasses of dead urux, left where they had fallen by the roadside, were few and the broken carts rotting in ditches were hardly worthy of note. Some wagons passed, but the drivers and occupants paid me little heed as I was wrapped in a heavy, borrowed cloak of local manufacture. It smelled and felt like it had been made from the beard hair of old, dead humans, but it was the perfect shapeless garb to hide my features and my weapons, neither of which would endear a yellow-eyed stranger to the locals of anywhere.

As I'd suspected, Tartakoy was deeply unremarkable. People hurried about their business, encouraged no doubt to greater speed by the inclemency of the weather. A pair of shaggy dogs panted like dragons in the frigid air as they fought over a stiff rat carcass. I walked along the main street, which was lined with modest stores selling basic necessities. A sign hanging over the door of a three-story building on the far side of the square declared in rustic artistry that it was an inn called the *Star and Plough*. It was tempting to go in and ask after my associates, or if they were there, lambast them for abandoning me, but the sound of a solitary bell reminded me that I had killing to do. I followed the hollow ringing through the town to where the river widened into a glassy pond.

Just beyond the pond towered a forbidding structure that had to be a temple, for it had surely been designed with a mind to making people feel small and insignificant. The sturdy wooden walls had turned deep black with age, and its six pitched roofs looked like the hulls of ships stacked upside down, one upon the other. A solitary bell was hanging in the smallest dory at the top of the unwelcoming building. The gable end of every prow and stern were adorned with the symbol of the two suns. A stylized fist had obviously been recently added because the red paint was bright against the faded yellow of the suns.

A shadowed doorway stood between two massive support posts, each one made from a tree trunk as wide as an ogren. Something more than merely disagreeable aesthetics had got my hackles up, but I didn't have time to fathom what it was as a figure appeared in the doorway. It was a tall, lean human, garbed in grey save for the black, four-cornered hat he wore tipped low over his eyes. He didn't look like someone you'd want to share a drink with, neither did he look like a murderer, but then, those who killed for their own pleasure rather than for coin or king seldom advertised the fact. Indeed, this skinny cove didn't look capable of much, but as I knew very well, one should never underestimate a sorcerer.

Chapter Seventeen

Ockzar looked up and saw Nicodemus was standing atop the shattered keep. He wondered if he was posing deliberately or if it was just his perception of the fellow that made it seem so. His long hair rippled in the wind, his ridiculously square jaw was tilted to the sky, and his piercing eyes that shifted from deepest blue to scarlet in a flash narrowed as he stared into the teeth of the bitter wind. Definitely posing.

"I can't see a fucking thing," Nic shouted, both shattering the illusion and reassuring Ockzar that even though he was handsome, the Imperial had the mind and character of an ass. "Are you sure this is the right tower, Swann? Swann! Where is the prick? Swann!" he bellowed.

Swann crawled from the hole under the tower. Cobwebs clung to his hair and thick dust mantled his shoulders. "What?" he shouted, but the brazen wind whipped his words away.

"I said, is this the right place?" Nic bellowed.

"What?" shouted Swann. This time there was no answer. He turned to Ockzar. "I couldn't hear a word he said."

"You're not missing much." Ockzar dragged the packs into the lea of the only wall that didn't look like it was about to collapse. His feet were warm, but the new boots and the amount of walking had caused agonizing blisters to grow and burst on both heels and the balls of his feet. He had never been one for walking; his legs were disproportionately short compared to his body, and his middle, although much diminished during his time in prison, was designed by nature to be round. As activities went, a constitutional hike held less appeal for him than a dose of pox. "At least you're warm, Ockzar, there is that," he said in a bid to console himself. There were times he wished he was a simple peasant and could find solace in prayer and hopes of a happier afterlife. Alas, he had been burdened with an exceptional education and had no choice but to face reality. This was all there was and currently it was miserable.

In the privacy of his thoughts, he had to admit that the Archonate's plan to modernize the country had merit; it was just happening too damn slowly. Voskva was a wild land; whole armies had marched into the interior and had never been seen again. It was dangerous out here, untamed. It was not the place for a sophisticated man of words. "And yet here I am shackled to these foreign fools." He put his head in his hands. "They probably only brought me in case they run out of food. Everyone says Imperials are cannibals." At the mention of food, his treacherous stomach began to rumble. It summoned the bittersweet memory of home, of rising late and being summoned to the breakfast room by the smell of fresh bread and home-cured ham. The daydream was swept away with a sudden strong blast of freezing wind. Tears sprang unbidden. He scrubbed them away and convinced himself that the wind had caused them. Not that either of these two would care if they saw him crying. He was nothing to them, and yet they wouldn't let him go. "Not all prisons have bars, Ocky."

"Swing that fucking pendant, instead of grubbing around in the dirt, eh?" Nic growled as he bounded down the tower.

Swann huffed. "I'm not 'grubbing', jimma. I'm divining the magical vibrations of this place and your negative energy really isn't helping."

Nic laughed dismissively. "You haven't seen my negative energy yet. You know, my brother will be mightily displeased if we don't find it."

"I'm doing my best."

"You need to do better."

"I need a different job and better luck," Swann muttered as he patted the dust from his splendid coat. The *talismancer,* as he styled himself, took out the pendulum and paced before the ruins.

"Hoy, Pudding!" Nic shouted and toed a stone at Ockzar. "Earn your keep and get the kettle on. What's the holdup, Swann?"

"The magic isn't right here." Swann clenched his jaw and fixed his gaze upon the pendulum. "It's all messed up." As though to illustrate his point, the pendulum began to swing wildly before stopping dead.

"What?" Nic pulled a disgusted face, like he found knowledge offensive.

"Something must have happened here, something spectacularly awful." Swann shivered. He looked over his shoulder as though ghosts were crowding in.

Ockzar tried not to think of the ghouls. "During the Demon Wars, many battles raged in this part of Voskva," he blurted loudly just as the wind dropped to a whisper. "Entire cities were wiped off the map, their names lost to history, as you can see." He gestured to the ruins. "Because the people were superstitious, they believed the land to be cursed and the cities were never rebuilt. The east lost contact with the west, and warlords ruled neglected provinces like kings. They were lawless times." Like all children, he'd been taught about the Demon Wars and considered the tales to have been grossly exaggerated. What really interested him was the way Voskva had been divided and ruled by the greedy and brutal noble houses that thrived by keeping the people poor and ignorant. In his opinion, it was they who were the real monsters.

"If I wanted a history lesson, I'd..." Nic scratched his head as he briefly searched for the perfect retort before giving up. "I'd read a book or something."

Swann sniggered. Although it was amusing, Ockzar tried not to even breathe too loudly, let alone laugh. It didn't matter. Rather than pick a fight with the mage who could fight back, Nic vented his ire on Ockzar. "Come on, chubsie, move that lazy arse of yours and get a fucking fire going. I'm going to scout."

Ockzar went to gather kindling, mindful to stay within sight of the mage. After spending time in prison, he was confident that his precautions were not mere paranoia. Nicodemus was just the type to kill him quietly out of sight. It made his stomach churn, but in an odd way, the mix of fear and anticipation was exciting, like the day he and his friends had gone to see Jarz Vesla speaking in Polzatz Square...

"Go on Ocky, tell her." Misha still managed to look beautiful even though she was stumbling drunk.

The jorskal glowered at Ockzar as though he had spoken, when in truth he'd just been shoved forward by his rambunctiously sozzled friends. It was they who'd been heckling the heckler. Ockzar was too drunk to do much of anything except stand up. A thunderous round of applause drew all eyes to the podium where Vesla was delivering his fiery speech. He was a hero. "No! He's not a hero, he's a god, ha! How do you like that?" he slurred.

The jorskal narrowed her eyes and raised the holy symbol of the Glorious Suns as though it was a burning brand before thrusting it towards him. "Repent!" she intoned.

"Go on, Millmets." Misha giggled. Misha, with the dancing eyes, Misha for whom he would move the stars and the suns. "Be a good little *plijus* and bow to the hypocrite sigil."

While he tried to work out if she really wanted him to bow or not, another of his so-called friends threw a large plum at the jorskal. It hit her on the nose. Laughter was followed by the sound of running. Ockzar was rooted to the spot, transfixed by the sight of blood and plum pulp running down the jorskal's livid face and pristine vestments.

"Treason!" she shrieked and pointed at him. "Murder!"

"It was only a plum," Ockzar corrected, which did nothing to calm her. He looked around; his friends had gone. Misha had gone. "Misha?" He was going to tell her he loved her today.

"Treason! Guards! Guards!" the jorskal wailed, clutching her bloody, plum-splattered face. The crowd scattered; whistles blew. Booted feet came running, and despite his protestations, Ockzar was arrested...

As he relived the worst day of his life, he lit a fire and put a kettle of chai on to boil. It was maddening and exhausting. Even though he was free, his thoughts kept returning to the darkness, forcing him to remember the painful past repeatedly. *Not all prisons have bars, Ockzar. Not all prisons have bars.*

They drank the chai and ate black bread in grudging silence. What words were exchanged were few and terse, but at least Nic and Swann refrained from bickering while they ate. It likely had much to do with the drugs Swann was smoking and the last of the brandy that Nicodemus was throwing down his neck. An unfortunate side effect of them both being inebriated was that when they eventually set off to follow the route Swann had dowsed, they ended up walking in circles. For hours.

Ockzar had no practical outdoor skills. Indeed, his practical skills were limited to making false teeth and sewing, both of which he'd learned out of necessity. He was therefore, no help to them or himself as they followed the dubious trail to where a supposedly ancient relic lay just waiting to be discovered. The arrogance of the foreigners astounded him. That they thought they could just wander into Voskva and find their way with a few badly drawn maps was the height of hubris. The loyal Voskvan in him was pleased. Had it been summer, he would have been even more delighted by their ineptitude, but it was late autumn, and supplies would run out quickly if they continued to wander.

"Does it have a smell?" Nicodemus enquired.

Swann looked up. His nose was scarlet, his pupils huge, and frost clung to his straggly, smoke-stained beard. "Does what have a smell?"

Nic tipped his head and gave an obvious sideways glance at Ockzar. "You know, the 'thing'."

"Everything has a smell. As it is a relic of sorts it probably also smells of magic, but that is indescribable to a mundane."

Nicodemus bristled. "I don't mean magic, and I'm not mundane." He looked at Ockzar. "I'm not." He insisted upon reading entirely too much into Ockzar's expression. "Does the relic thing have a smell? Something I can track because you're getting us nowhere."

"If you'd done your research before setting off, we might have had more to go on than, 'it's in Voskva, somewhere to the east'." Swann was doing a good job of biting back his anger, but Ockzar could see it written in the hard line of his jaw and the flint in the look he gave Nic when his back was turned. "I'm good, but I can't work miracles. The metaphysical waters are very muddy here."

Something caught Ockzar's eye. He looked up, saw twin reeds of smoke rising above the trees. "What do you think that is?"

Swann squinted at the smoke. "Another village?"

Nic shook his head. "Not with just two chimneys."

"A woodcutter's hut then?" Swann sounded dismissive and continued to pace, waving the pendant.

All Ockzar knew was that woodsmoke meant a chimney, which meant a building, which might mean a warm meal and a bed for the night and a break from pointless wandering. He looked longingly towards the smoke.

"We might as well see what it is," said Nicodemus. "Locals may know where the fucking tower is. If there's nothing there, we'll camp up and begin searching again on the morrow."

A few pulls on his pipe and what resolve Swann had to continue drifted away. "Aye, sure, jimma, whatever you wish. It's your coin."

Nic snorted. "It's Leo's command, best you don't forget that."

The route Nic took to the source of the smoke was direct and did not take into consideration those with shorter legs or merely human strength and endurance. The shapeshifter bounded effortlessly through the dense vegetation, which seemed to consist entirely of nettles and brambles. Having been blessed with long, skinny legs, Swann also managed to pick his way through the vicious undergrowth. Ockzar bore the discomfort stoically. He had been to school; he knew what others perceived were his shortcomings and was content never to change them. Nic's constant admonishments of 'Hurry up, Pudding' and 'Pick up the pace, lard arse' had no effect on him. The foreigner didn't know those nerves had been burned out years ago by the cruel taunts of friends, family, and alumni.

A light snow began to fall as soft as goose feather down when they stumbled onto a paved road which they followed towards the smoke. After a short walk, the trees that flanked the road thinned, and they came upon a gated manor. Ockzar offered a silent thanks to good fortune. They might have been relics of a bygone age, but he was happy to see the gilded blue and scarlet domes of an old-fashioned mansion peeking through the treetops. His joy was short-lived, for as they approached the gate, he saw serfs sweeping snow from the path and scraping ice from a fountain in the courtyard.

"If it's a relic you seek this is the kind of place you'll find it," he said sniffily.

Sharp-eared when it suited him, Nicodemus pulled up. "What's that, Pud?"

"This is the Estate of a member of the Dvorishka." Blank looks sent him hunting for an explanation they would understand. "The old aristocracy. They were the rulers before the Enlightenment of the Archonate swept them from power. Do you see those poor people toiling? See how their faces are covered? They are serfs; owned by the lord of the manor. The Dvors make them cover their faces, lest they cause offence with their insolent gaze. It is an outrage that it has been allowed to continue here, but I suppose we are far from civilization." He gestured to the serfs, who did not acknowledge them as they followed the path to the manor house.

Nicodemus gave him a sour look. "Is that it? I thought for once you had something useful to say. Instead, we get another bleeding history lesson."

In an uncharacteristic gesture of solidarity, Swann patted Ockzar on the back. It was so unexpected that he flinched, making the mage giggle as he reached for the door. Before he had a chance to knock, it was flung open by an old fellow wearing a tassel cap and embroidered morning gown. Upon seeing them, he beamed delightedly.

"Visitors!" He clapped like an excited child. "I couldn't believe it when I saw you approaching. I thought my old eyes were playing tricks on me. I had to ask Moskin. I said, 'Moskin, are there people on the road?'. But Moskin has worse eyes than I do, so how would he know?" Despite his obvious age, the old man didn't stop for breath. 'Breathing through his eyelids,' as Ockzar's Aunt Galitza would say. A weary Ockzar wondered if it would be rude to sit down while he talked. His feet were burning sore.

"…But you're real! I so rarely have visitors these days. Come in, I will show you true, old-fashioned Voskvan hospitality. Not like those upstart beggars in the city." He spat before sweeping the tail of his magnificent coat behind him. "I, am the Dvorishnov Kashchei Askalyi Muynal Nyqvist." He clicked his heels. "And I bid you welcome to my home."

Although he hated to admit it, Ockzar could have kissed the Dvorishnov when he invited them in. True, he was a hideous relic and a terrible reminder of the ignorant and barbaric past, but it was wonderful to be warm.

Beneath the disapproving, painted gaze of dead-eyed Dvorishnovs and Dorishnovas, they were treated to traditional welcome drinks of strong, plum brandy. As was the custom, the Dvor first asked where they were from. When the next glass was poured, he enquired after their health and during the third, the health of their parents. While they drank and exchanged formalities, Ockzar noted with an uncomfortable mix of disgust and gratitude that the serfs were quietly making preparations for a meal. Finally, at the point he thought his stomach was going to digest itself, the Dvor led them into a garishly decorated banqueting hall where the table was set for fifty. Ockzar, Nicodemus, and

Swann were offered seats at one end of the table. Their host took his seat at the other, beneath a gold-trimmed canopy glittering with gems. Unsurprisingly and unopposed, Nicodemus took the seat at the head of their end. Ockzar didn't feel slighted; he was just grateful to sit down.

Ockzar was deliriously happy when the entrée of river eel arrived, accompanied by iced bottles of Voskvan fizz, which Ockzar saw was from Karlseran, the finest fizz producing region of Voskva. A rich, Pharrian ruby came with the next course of succulent roast stag beetle larvae. The food, like the wine, was exquisite. Indeed, after one mouthful of the baked gladyanna he almost wept. Peasant that he was, Nicodemus practically inhaled an entire suckling tusker without pausing to savor the honey glaze, and even the birdlike Swann polished off a large wedge of game pie and a stack of pickled, scarlet radishes. To add to his contentment, a roaring fire drenched the room in a soporific heat. Ockzar began to drowse and might have fallen into a satisfied sleep but for one small, niggling issue that marred the Dvorishnov's otherwise exemplary hospitality.

It was all the blasted serfs.

Masked and identically garbed, at least a dozen of the drudges silently waited on them and their master throughout the meal. If they weren't serving food or pouring wine, they were tending to the fire or trimming candle wicks. As much as the hungry, tired part of him wanted to just ignore it and enjoy the magical banquet, Ockzar's damn principles wouldn't let him. There was only one thing to do. He would get drunk.

"About this *quest* of yours." The Dvor smiled indulgently. Like the rest of them, his cheeks were ruddy from the warmth of the fire and the copious amounts of wine he'd put away. "Please, forgive me, I am old, and I forget things. Tell me again, what is it that you are looking for, the Vascell something?"

"Aye, something like that," said Swann. "This wine is really wonderful. It's like summer in a goblet, flowers in my mouth."

"Vascellum." Nicodemus let out a loud burp. "Stupid name if you ask me." Already drunk, every time he opened his mouth, he undermined Swann's attempt to obfuscate. It was most amusing.

Had Breed been alive, Ockzar might have been persuaded to help Swann out. As a native, he could have more easily fished for information and deflect awkward questions with regards the relic, but Breed was dead, and he wanted these fools to fail. A serf came over and refilled his goblet.

"Thank you," he said. They bowed but didn't speak. It was no good. No matter how much he drank, he couldn't ignore the injustice. Indeed, rather than subdue, the wine emboldened him. Ockzar dabbed the corners of his mouth with the perfectly crisp, linen napkin and cleared his throat. The Dvor looked at him as though seeing him for the first time.

"Yes, young man?"

"My dear, brother Voskvan," he said pointedly and felt a swell of pride rise in his chest at the directness of his address. "I cannot help but notice you have serfs."

Nic rolled his eyes and snatched a carafe of red from the table. "Here we go."

The old man nodded enthusiastically, not in the slightest bit embarrassed. It seemed that the Glorious Revolution had indeed passed him by. "I do. The same families have worked for me for generations. It is a great honor for them." He smiled and then, much to Ockzar's annoyance, turned to Swann. "So, what will you do with the heart should you find it?"

"I didn't say heart, did I?" Swann looked momentarily confused. "Oh wait." He clicked his fingers. "In translation Vascellum could mean, 'heart', couldn't it? I love languages." He chuckled, then forked a slab of roast tusker onto his plate. Had it been anyone else, Ockzar would have admired the skillful deflection. As it was Swann, it was more likely that he'd just forgotten the Dvor had asked him anything.

The Dvor however, had not forgotten. "Quite. Vascellum can be translated as, 'pump' but I feel that such bold adventurers as you are hunting something more esoteric, eh?"

Swann gave Nicodemus a questioning look. The beastman cast it back with a drunken shrug. Either they were consummate performers lulling him and the Dvor into a false sense of intellectual superiority, or they really were idiots who didn't have anything close to a plan to find the relic. From a patriotic point of view, it was a relief. On a more personal level, it was concerning that his fate rested in the hands of a pair of incompetents. To confirm his assumption, Swann sloppily backhanded his goblet off the table. There was a dull metallic thump, and the smell of Pharrian ruby burst upon the air. One of the masked serfs dropped stiffly to her knees and began swabbing the spill with a cloth.

Ockzar was suddenly moved to stand up for the aged peasant whose emaciated hands trembled as she sopped the splash of scarlet out of the rug. He swallowed another mincemeat dumpling before once again clearing his throat. The Dvor looked up. Far from being annoyed that his gold was rolling around the floor and his fine wine was soaking into the silk rugs, there was an amused glint in his eye. "Brother Kashchei." Ockzar began trying his best to adopt the same commanding tone as Jarz Vesla. "Are you aware that serfdom has been outlawed for years?" Nicodemus glared. Swann gave an almost imperceptible head shake and groaned quietly.

"We do things differently out here in the borderlands. Rules are for cities," said the Dvor.

Fortified by his great purpose and too much wine, Ockzar continued. "It is both illegal and immoral to treat people like faceless chattels."

The Dvor chuckled softly. "Why, my dear young friend. Do not exercise yourself on their behalf, it will ruin your digestion. I assure you; they don't mind a bit."

"I find that hard to believe." This was the kind of outrageous privilege he had only heard about. "Have you asked them what they want?" Ockzar thumped the table. "Have you asked them how they would like to be treated?" His hand hurt, but it didn't matter. He was fighting for the downtrodden, he was a revolutionary, and he was very drunk. "Well, have you asked them?"

The old man looked perplexed. "Why would I do that?"

"*Why would you do that*? Unbelievable!" Ockzar stood up and stumbled against the table. "How can you be so callous? These people are your fellow countrymen and women. They are your equals under the law."

The Dvor snorted. "They most certainly aren't."

Ockzar was stunned. The man was a monster. "How can you say that?"

The Dvor waved dismissively. "Why, because they're dead, dear boy. More wine?"

Chapter Eighteen

Country inns are the same not only the world over but *worlds* over, which is reassuring when you move around quite as much as I do.

Upon entering *The Star and Plough*, I was greeted by foul looks, witless gawking, and the coldest of shoulders. As I say, reassuring. And as with all baseless prejudice, the color of my coin was all that was required to temporarily blind the hosteler to the cut of my spiny jib, and I was made grudgingly welcome. While smoothing the way with rare metal, I perused the clientele to see if my erstwhile colleagues were amongst them. They were not, but I was sure their various scents lingered in the air.

After making sure I'd put enough fiscal easement on the bar to pay for room and board and make the presence of a foreign monster tolerable, I steered the conversation in the direction of the three cunts I was looking for. I say 'cunts' because, as I found out with subtle questioning, my comrades had not only stayed here but had eased the pain of my loss by getting pissed and tupping the serving wenches. It was with a love-drunk heart that the girl told me of the fine, foreign gentlemen who had stayed here yesterday. She waxed dreamily of how they had eaten, drunk, and fucked their way through a local fortune in food, drink, quim, and pel. It was touching to be so mourned.

I was torn between fulfilling my promise to the wet witches and catching up with my shoddy crew. Younger, more impetuous me would have hunted the relic alone and left Nic and Swann to answer to Leo as punishment for leaving me to be eaten by ghouls. Lucky for them, I was older and wiser and knew that Leo probably wouldn't care so long as he got the Vascellum.

Given that neither Ockzar nor Swann were prime examples of human athleticism, it was a safe bet that I'd catch up with them on the morrow, which left ample time to inhume the murderous jorskal and free the cursed spirits.

"How many nights are you staying?" the wench asked when she returned from the kitchen with a bowl of tusker stew and bread.

"Alas, mistress, pressing business takes me elsewhere. I'll be leaving on the morrow, after breaking my fast." *And killing your priest.*

She grunted, showing neither pleasure nor disappointment. "I'll show you the room. Laundry is extra."

"Is that a euphemism?"

"Eh?"

"Never mind."

After I'd eaten, I was shown to a gloomy room to the rear of the inn. It was above the privy with all the attendant olfactory delights that accompanied such a prime location. It was grossly overpriced but perfect for my needs. It afforded me a discrete means of ingress and egress and a view of the temple. Also, if I wanted a shit, I didn't have far to go. I lit the fire, put my feet up on the windowsill and watched the temple while sharpening my borrowed blades. Although the words were indistinct, the rhythm of the holy call and response carried on the chilly air. When the sermonizing was done and the off-key songs of praise had been sung, I watched the congregation file out. The last people to leave the temple were a young, human couple. The woman was carrying a bundle which I assumed was their child. The Jorskal had his arm around the young man's shoulders and seemed to be sharing a joke with them. He smiled warmly at the bundle and pulled a face, which I assume was supposed to entertain the infant.

It occurred to me that the witches could be lying, that they might very well be miscreants working to overthrow the powers of good in the area. There was a time I wouldn't have thought any more about it other than they had helped me, and I liked them. Now I at least entertained the thought that I might be doing the wrong thing. I don't know about you, but I called that progress.

There was only one way of knowing if the jorskal had retired for the night, and that was to go and see. If he had, I'd kill him before he knew he was dead, which was the best for both of us, given the situation was unavoidable. If he'd gone for a pint of ale or a late-night constitutional, then I'd lay in wait until he returned, which was dull and would result in a bit of a scare for the mark. Either way, I was confident the result would be the same. Thus resolved, I put a chair behind the door of my room and bound the key loop tight to the door handle so that it couldn't be forced from the lock. That done, I threw some left-over tusker fat on the fire to make oily smoke, with which I blackened my barrow blades.

When night fell, I banked the fire and climbed out of the window. The roof above the privy was covered in a treacherous layer of glassy ice, encouraging me to be careful as I crabbed my way across the shingles for fear of falling through the shithouse roof. In my youth, the cautionary tale of thieves who had drowned in cesspits because they'd been overcome by fumes put the fear of the gods into me and the other kinchin coves in the Guild. Of course, crashing through a privy roof probably wouldn't kill me, but the shame would be hard to bear.

Because Tartakoy was a small town, it lacked many things, including buildings, so skipping across rooftops to my destination was out of the question. Undaunted, I crept through all three streets while playing a one-sided game of hide-and-seek with a friendly dog and a drunk. I easily avoided the stumbling human, but the friendly hound got the crust of bread that I'd brought along for just such an encounter. Using stealth and patience, I worked my way behind the temple without being seen. A rustic cottage, which I assumed to be the priest's dwelling, had been tacked on to the back of the gloomy house of worship. Beside the cottage were a woodshed, an outhouse, and a vegetable garden.

There was no noise coming from the cottage, no lights or sounds of movement. Still, just in case the mark was sitting in quiet contemplation, I spent a couple of minutes listening at the door. An uncharacteristic shiver ran down my spine, accompanied by an unexpected sense of foreboding. I put it down to being out of practice and tried the door. I'd expected it to be locked and was not disappointed. Although it had been a while, it didn't take long to pick the simple lock with a piece of broken cloak pin I'd found in the common room of the inn and a nail I'd picked up in the street. I cracked the door, had a quick glance over my shoulder, and slipped inside. My eyes quickly adjusted to the lack of light, and I saw in a glance that the sparsely furnished room was unoccupied. A robe and four-cornered hat hung on the back of the inner door, which I presumed led to the temple. There was a single bed, a nightstand, and a closet. The flagstone floor was ice cold, the texture of the stone softened by a coating of luminescent green mold that also spotted the bedding, rug, and curtains.

It was so damp that I could taste the spores hanging in the air and wondered at the constitution of the human who could live here without succumbing to the black lung. The strong smell of water penetrated the stone floor, and I was sure I could hear a faint, hollow dripping beneath me. I came to the sudden and sobering realization that I was standing above a giant chasm, with nothing but a thin crust of earth and some flagstones between me and the underworld.

Mindful of the void below, I crept more cautiously over to the door. It opened onto a pokey kitchen-cum-parlor. A crock of gassy beer bubbled on the sideboard and hams and sausages were hanging from the rafters beside bunches of herbs. The worn cushion on the armchair was cold, but the embers still glowed in the ashes of the fire. I was halfway to the next door when the sound of echoing voices halted me. The tone was light, conversational. When I heard chairs scraping followed by footsteps, I backtracked to the bedroom and closed the door just as I heard the other open.

I could have retreated outside to be sure I wasn't discovered, but I was in a hurry, so I rolled under the bed. The conversation revolved around talk of livestock and how the preparations were going for the festival of Saint Sevard, whoever the fuck that was. Glasses clinked, and one of the speakers bid the other farewell. The door opened, and a pair of booted feet peeping coyly from beneath the hem of a grey robe shuffled into my field of vision. The jorskal closed the door with his back and exhaled heavily into what he thought was the privacy of his chamber. Unsurprisingly, he smelled of mold and something that I couldn't quite place, save that it was sweet in the manner of decay rather than confectionary.

While I pondered the smell, the robe was discarded, followed by the shoes. I was surprised to see that he wasn't wearing stockings, but when he turned, I saw the webbed skin between his toes and the omission made more sense. It appeared he was a tert, which was concerning as I'd been told he was a sorcerer and tert sorcerers were as rare as hens' cocks and a very dangerous breed indeed.

The disrobement continued and shirt followed breeches. A key turning in a lock was followed by the sound of an expensive set of tumblers falling before the door to a shoddy, old wardrobe creaked open. A faintly putredinous odor seeped into the room, and a sickly, green glow shone on the jorskal's pasty calves. Rather than take a garment from the wardrobe as I'd expected, he climbed inside. Bare feet slapped on wet stone, and the door began to close. Guessing that the lock of such an interesting item of furniture was more complicated than I could tackle with a broken pin, I scuttled from my hiding place and stole a quick peek to see if the mark was just indulging a peculiar fetish by climbing into the wardrobe. A flight of steps leading down saved both our embarrassment. I slipped inside before the door closed and with a heavy click, locked behind me. The clever cabinet with its elaborate lock told me that whatever his allegiance, the fellow was more than a simple country curate.

I pressed myself into the recess of the cupboard's carcass and waited until the distorted shadow of the jorskal danced lower down the wall. I dared a glance and was relieved to see that the stair curved away to the left, hiding me from the jorskal who had already rounded the corner. I followed, reasoning that if he came back up, I could kill him quicker than he could cast a spell. I based this assumption on nothing more than confidence in my skills and blissful ignorance of his.

The walls were decorated with carvings of stick figures dancing around something that looked like a pancake with eyes. I paused before the bottom and waited until a shadow crossed the floor, followed by the sound of stone grinding against stone. Like most villains whose lives depended on skulking, I'd learned to read errant creaks and groans and so could say with some degree of certainty that the jorskal had left the chamber and closed a heavy, stone door behind him.

When I was sure that he had gone, I slipped quietly into the room.

Three rows of three stone sarcophagi were lined up in a low-roofed chamber. The lids of the nine boxes had been stacked haphazardly against the wall where some had fallen and smashed, but the symbol of the interlocking suns was still visible on most of them. The newest lid bore the same symbol only with the addition of a fist marking the change in regime and dogma.

It seemed that the soon-to-be-slotted jorskal had made the place his own during his tenure. Scattered around the room, on the floor and the corners of sarcophagi were dozens of shallow, stone bowls that collected the drips of milky water leaking from the stalagmite-fanged roof. Coins of all values and metal jewelry glinted in the bowls of water. As they were clearly offerings, I helped myself to some of the choicer pieces. Either by accident or design, the bone boxes were also filled to the brim with water. The occupants had been weighted down with stones, the skeletal remains being the least rancid and therefore clearly visible. The newest guest, whose box was furthest from the door, was still quite soapy and hardly visible through the cloudy murk of fat water. "We've all been there," I mouthed. He didn't answer as I could see that his head had been removed and replaced with that of a fur-lipped river eel.

The thick, grey barbels that gave the beast its name swished slightly in no current at all. While being mindful not to get too close and risk dying a stupid death, I peered harder and saw the cause of the movement was grim but entirely mundane. River lice were crawling through the 'beard' as they chewed their way through the soft flesh of the eel's head. Something bright clasped in the corpse's human hands caught my avaricious eye, but given that along with his head, his genitals had been excised and replaced with the suggestive remains of the fur-lipped eel, I decided not to fish it out. It wasn't that I was squeamish; it was just that I wanted to prove Mother wrong and not die because I was *'a greedy, fucking idiot with less brains than the clart I wash away every month'*. Ah, Mother, she might be gone, but her words of wisdom would stay with me forever.

The other bodies had been similarly mutilated. The puzzle of what had happened to the heads and whatnots of the deceased was solved when I opened the door through which the twisted little fucker had departed. A row of heads in varying states of decay stared from a shelf that ran along the righthand side of a passageway lit by glowing green clusters of fungi. Beside the heads were other body parts. The grim trophies included fingers, ears, teeth, and eyes as well as the whatnots of men, women, and all manner of cove in between. Care had been taken to preserve them, and the vapors of vinegar solution made my eyes sting. With my hackles well and truly raised, I made my way past the grisly gallery and gave the stone door at the end a shove. Nothing happened. I shoved again, only harder this time. It didn't budge. I put my shoulder to it. A hidden hinge twitched, but that was all. I bit back a curse because it didn't behoove a professional to become fractious when things didn't go to plan. Angry thieves make mistakes, as I knew only too well. Before I had to expend too much effort thinking of a workaround, a key turned in a lock that was cunningly hidden in a fold in the stone. I must have been blind not to see it, but now was not the time to berate myself. Slow though the door would be to open and fast as I was, there was no way I could leg it to the end of the passage without being seen. So up it was. Hoping that I didn't lose the blades I'd tucked into my belt, I leaped up and wedged myself above the door with my back pressed into the angle where wall met roof. With nary a minute to spare, the door ground open, and the wet, naked jorskal passed beneath me.

A peach frill of iridescent fins ran down his bony spine, and the faint tracery of scales glittered green and silver on his narrow shoulders. The pink smile of what appeared to be gill slits were tucked discretely behind his ears. I counted it a blessing that we weren't in water as I leaped upon him, drove my knees into the middle of his back, wrapped my arms around his neck, and rode him to the floor.

I'd made allowance for him to be slippery and was also prepared for him to be strong. Much to my joy and delight, he was both, and I had a fight on my hands to keep my arm across his throat. I intended to snap his neck, but when I pressed myself against him and felt the thunder of his startled heart beating through his bones, another entirely unexpected desire overcame me.

I sank my teeth into his neck. My mouth flooded with blood. Light burst in my head, I tasted fire and was filled with an overwhelming, intoxicating sense of power.

I liked it. I liked it a lot.

I bit harder, sank my teeth deep into his throat, and gorged on his sweet claret. I drank him like a fine wine beneath the dead gaze of the gargoyles on the shelf and only stopped slurping when I felt his frantic heartbeat slow and finally stop. I released him and laughed as I leaped to my feet. I felt incredible. Like a serpent uncoiling, sorcery woke within me and lit a fire in my limbs.

"I have missed this," I heard myself say.

The body at my feet seemed to be made of rough clay, and I was...

"I'm a god!" I shouted; my voice thick with another's blood. This world was as nothing, made of mist and shadows, and only I was real. The door behind me creaked. Without thinking, I turned. The words of a spell blazed in my mind. White fire coalesced before me, and I smashed the door from its hinges. The stone shattered. The ground trembled. I strode into the vast chamber beyond, which was lit like the heavens by the light of a million, tiny bugs crawling like stars across the rocky firmament. The glittering lights were reflected in the mirror of an underground lake. Two massive, iron grills sealed with a sorcerer's sigil were set across the place where the water entered and where it left.

A rippling wake arrowed towards me from the far side of the lake. I waited. I had nothing to fear. Nothing could harm me. I was invincible.

When the Moyazel reared from the water like a cobra about to strike, I held my ground. She fixed me with her fierce, golden gaze and spread her finned arms. Her pearlescent scales sparkled like frost in moonlight.

"I am not—" I began, as she spat a fine mist at me. I coughed. "Afraid." The mist tasted bitter. My vision blurred; the bug lights seemed to descend from the walls and explode before my eyes in a dazzling, rainbow of colors so vibrant I could taste them. I fell towards the pool, and the starlit waters rushed up to meet me.

Chapter Nineteen

The deeper I sank, the colder I became. By some magic I could not comprehend, the water appeared as clear as the finest crystal. As I gently descended, I marveled at the tiny bubbles which had formed on my skin like delicate, silver beads. In a trance, I watched them twirl to the surface, which shone like the sky lit by a thousand, winking stars.

Am I dead? I wondered, dimly aware that I wasn't struggling to breathe.

"No." The unexpected reply intruded into my thoughts as though the voice was woven into the very substance of my mind, but it wasn't my voice. The crystal water rushed against my skin. I would have

drifted, but the pressure was even all around me, and I hung almost motionless in the calm eye of a scintillating whirlwind of fins and scales.

Underwater, the Moyazel was luminous— almost too bright to behold, pulsing with a rainbow of colors which shone through her translucent scales. Broad, white fins fluttered around her like silken pennants. She sculled the water with webbed hands as pale as alabaster. I estimated she was fifty feet long, but it was hard to tell as her sinuous body was in constant, graceful motion.

She smiled, and her face split vertically beneath her tiny snub nose to reveal a mouth filled with glass, dagger-sharp fangs. *'Come,'* she said in my mind.

'How can I hear you?' I thought.

'The water of life.' To illustrate, she belched a mouthful of milky vomit into the water.

Ask a stupid question, I suppose. As before, my skin tingled as the cloud engulfed me and numbed my limbs. I felt a rush of blood spike in my head, which felt remarkably like how it feels when one leaps off a cliff. It is terror and exhilaration combined. It rips through a body and explodes in the brain, instilling an incomparable feeling of euphoria. In short, it is quite a rush. High as a cloud, I sank to the bottom of the pool where the Moyazel was waiting.

"*Want,*" she said in my mind.

'What do you want?' I thought.

'Yes. Want.'

When I touched the bone-strewn, sandy bottom, I saw what I had failed to see from above. Made from slices of black glass no thicker than my arm were the stones of an angle gate.

And it was alive.

"*This cannot be,*" I said in my mind.

I felt the Moyazel's excitement and fear. Consequently, her thoughts were painfully confused and loud to the point of incoherence. She flitted anxiously around the monoliths, stirring up the sediment of grit and bones. So many bones.

"You sent. You send," she thought, her aching desire to be free bleeding from her into me.

I understood her pain. Now I knew what had got my hackles up when I'd first laid eyes on the temple. It wasn't the drab, parochial architecture; it was the gate. An old yearning rose within me, drew me to the stones. When feeling returned to my limbs, I swam over and touched the nearest shard. I say 'touched.' In truth, I embraced it like a long-lost friend and might have wept had I been the crying kind. Answering need with need, power woke within it and revealed the memories of the Moyazel, which were locked within it. She had been dragged here by a mage centuries ago and bled for her power. The reason why she had been chosen and the identity of the perpetrator were unknown to her; only sorrow remained. Trapped and alone, she had been used by coves like the jorskal for longer than she could remember. How she had remained sane was beyond me, for such a fate was cruel beyond measure, not only for her but gods' only knew how many sacrificial victims.

"Want!" the Moyazel shouted. Images of unfathomable places and strange beings filled my mind. It didn't take a genius to piece together meaning from the fragments of memory I was seeing. She wanted to go home.

Trapped as I was with the powerful otherworldly being, I had little choice but to help her escape, not that I had any objections. Despite having troubles of my own, I was sympathetic to her plight. There was also another reason why I wanted her gone. After being an unmitigated cunt, Fate had decided to throw me a bone. I would free the Moyazel and then use the gate to find Ludo and finish what I'd started. Perhaps the witches were right; perhaps this was meant.

While I hunted for the monolith that would unlock the gate, the Moyazel darted anxiously around the pool sending glittering streams of bubbles racing to the surface. Despite the distraction, it didn't take me long to find the keystone. Sparks lit within the smoky glass as I reached towards it. I put my hands on the surface and once again felt connected to the universe and the cold majesty of the Void. I turned the monolith, felt it grind on the narrow axis to which it had been fixed. The ground shuddered, the thunder of stalactites crashing into the water was followed by a rain of shards as I opened a door onto another world. There was no farewell, just a whip of her sinuous tail, and I was barged aside as she dived through the gate and swam into the inky darkness beyond.

I didn't lament her lack of gratitude or feel slighted at the absence of a fond farewell. She had her business to attend to, and I had mine. I wanted vengeance. I wanted to find Ludo and stomp the life from his misshapen body and burn the remains. I wanted to kill him, bring him back from the dead, and kill him again. So intense was my hatred that it trumped the bloodborne imperative of Duke Leo to find the accursed Vascellum. To hell with him and to hell with it.

Drunk on borrowed power, I fixed an image of Ludo in my mind and bent the magic of the gate to my will. For what felt like an age, nothing happened. I began to doubt myself, began to wonder if I did not merely imagine that I had the skill to do this. But then I reminded myself that there was no one more qualified. I was born in the Void, in that place between worlds where all paths crossed. The monoliths began to tremble as I sent my consciousness through them.

There! I saw the bastard. The bastard looked up and saw me.

"Hello, dear friend." He gave a lop-sided smile.

I cursed myself for being so clumsy, not that it mattered that he knew I had found him. Nothing in this world or any other would stop me wreaking my vengeance upon him. Using all the strength I possessed, I began to re-align the stones. I felt resistance as he tried to stop me, and we became locked in a magical tug-of-war.

Alas, power—particularly stolen power, is a finite resource as I discovered when, much to my chagrin, I began to drown. Furious, I foolishly continued to try to open a gate. I couldn't give up now that I was so close. Alas, the fight suddenly became very one-sided as Ludo wrenched control from my enfeebled hands. Cracks raced across the monoliths; the water became clouded with ivory silt. I was not ready to give up and continued to fight to open the gate even as Ludo fought to destroy it. In the end, my hungry lungs made the decision to drive me to the surface.

Gasping, I came up for air just as the stones exploded below me with a dull *whump*. I managed to suck a mouthful of air before I was engulfed by a wave that threw me towards the roof of the cave. Had I been wholly human, this would have been when I died. My clever body had the wit to turn my unruly descent into a dive, and I plunged cleanly into the turbulent pool. Smaller explosions reduced the angle gate to rubble but were not fierce enough to stop me from swimming to the shore. My ribs hurt like I'd been stomped by a herd of angry urux, but the pain was nothing compared to the hurt I felt because Ludo had escaped.

I stood up. My legs were shaking so much I almost fell back into the pool, which was once again a placid mirror reflecting the myriad lights of the bugs that lit the cavern, entirely unaware of what had just transpired. By some miracle, I still had gold tucked into my shirt; I had slotted the arsehole jorskal for the witches and freed the Moyazel from centuries of imprisonment. But I felt hollow inside. The only comfort I could take was that if I'd found one live gate, there must be others.

Lacking enthusiasm for the task, I packed the jorskal's bag. Sick though I still felt, I tried to put myself in his shoes and pack those things I imagined he would take with him if he decided to run away.

I packed some smalls, a comb, and a set of drab, secular garb. I left his tatty copy of the Archonate sanctioned Book of Prayer and the pitiful collection of temple silver. The locals would be less likely to look for him if he only took his own meager belongings. When I'd finished packing, I wrapped the corpse in a bedsheet. It was still full dark when I crept outside with my baggage and quiet save for the burble of water and night birds hunting in the woods. Before heading into the trees, I stuffed my feet in his shoes and laid an obvious trail from his door and down the path before climbing overhanging branches and working my way into the trees. I figured that when morning came, and the bells didn't ring, someone would come looking for the priest.

When they couldn't rouse him, that someone would fetch another someone, and they would discover he had done a moonlight flit. By then, everyone would know and rush to the cottage to find out what was wrong, obliterating most of the tracks. What the villagers did and how they did it concerned me not at all. As I had broken the wardrobe door and left it swinging, I was sure they'd be busy for a long time with what they discovered in the cavern.

Satisfied that I'd covered my tracks sufficiently, I made my way to the bridge. The witches were waiting on the other side. Drifting around them, camouflaged in the milky, predawn mist, were the shades of the dead.

"Present for you." With a dramatic flourish, I unrolled the sheet.

"You did it," said Kolna as the body rolled to a stop at her feet. I noted that she and her sisters were dry.

"'Twas never in doubt, madame." Although far from happy, I winked.

She scrubbed a tear from her cheek as she and her sisters embraced and stared at the body like it was the key to a door they could finally unlock. I just hoped the afterlife they craved was all they hoped it would be. When I had died, I'd experienced nothing, but perhaps we get the afterlife we deserve.

"It's strange, just thinking about this monster used to scare me to death," said Kniza.

Yalta rolled her eyes. "You were already dead, silly girl."

Kniza blushed. "Well, it used to scare me a lot. Anyway, I just wanted to say that he doesn't scare me now. Thank you, Breed Blake."

"A pleasure, Miss Kniza."

She giggled.

"What?"

"Well, we're all dry, and now you're all wet." Her voice was faint, and I could see the trees through her as though her image was painted on glass. "I think I'm going. Kolly?" She reached for her sister.

"It's all right, petal." The older woman smiled reassuringly. "You go on ahead, now. Don't be afraid. We won't be long."

Kniza tried to embrace her, but she was little more than a sketch of herself, drawn in light upon the air. She smiled at her sister before a breeze I did not feel gently carried her away.

Kolna sobbed in that way humans did when they were overwhelmed by a surfeit of emotions. When she saw that I was looking at her, she swatted at her face with a gossamer hand and gave an embarrassed laugh. "Look at me. You'd think I'd had enough of water." A wry smile on her lips, Kolna closed her eyes and drifted away.

"So, what happened to old fish face?" Yalta asked, her voice still strong and her form defiantly solid.

"He's there." I pointed to the body.

"The Moyazel, dolt."

"Dolt? That's charming. Shouldn't you be turning to smoke and fucking off with your sisters about now?"

"I will, presently. I'm just older than them, more strongly tied to the land."

"Like a barnacle, eh?"

She laughed. "More like a tick. So what happened to her?"

"Returned to her own world."

The old woman's hooded eyes widened slightly, and she nodded. "You did all right, stranger. The Crow Mother might remember. She might not, but such is the way of things." A strong wind blew through the trees, and the spirits flew apart like cobwebs. Yalta sat on the bridge and heaved a shuddering sigh. "I'll miss them. Don't get me wrong, they were bloody annoying most of the time, but you get used to things, like backache and piles, eh?" I nodded. The color was beginning to drain from the old woman. "Oh, I just remembered. He was in a cult. Can't remember what they called themselves, something to do with fish. Anyway, they might come looking for him. Just so you know." She kicked her feet and looked at her hands.

"Wait, what?"

"I thought I was the deaf one" She cleared her throat. "He was in a fish cult who might come after you, I mean him."

"And you're only telling me this now?"

"I was hoping I'd have gone over by now," she muttered more to herself than me.

"Did you know about this cult before you asked me to slot him?"

She rubbed her veiny hands as though trying to speed up her dissolution. "It didn't seem important at the time."

"To whom? I think it's important. What if they come after me? Do they have tattoos? Do they wear fish leather codpieces? Give me a clue what to look out for."

"I can't hear you; it's all very faint in the spirit realm," she whispered.

"Bollocks. I can still see you."

"What…who speaks…?" she said, pretending not to see me.

I sighed. "This is just stupid."

"I'm fading…"

I picked up a pebble and threw it at her. It passed through and plonked into the river.

"Finally!" She cackled triumphantly. And then she was gone.

"You old... Who are they? and what do I do with this?" The echo of my voice rang through the forest, drifted into silence. I kicked the body. Heavy wings fluttered in the canopy; pinion shadows crossed the ground. "Marvelous." With a mind to burying him in the woods, I went to pick up the jorskal when the ground beneath the corpse began to heave. As I wasn't enamored of gravedigging, I retreated to the bridge and watched with morbid interest as the earth began to chew up the body like it was meat in a grinder. Bones cracked, sinews and muscle snapped, and flesh was shredded and swallowed by the hungry earth. When it was over, there wasn't a spot of blood or sliver of bone to mark that he had ever existed.

My work done, I set off across country at a run. The sky was beginning to lighten, and I needed to get back to the inn before morning. Satisfying though it had been to free the witches and the Moyazel, I was still bitterly disappointed that I hadn't been able to open a gate onto Ludo. But at least I had learned that I could borrow power from a sorcerer if I drank their blood, much as Leo had drunk mine. I pulled up sharply and licked my lips. The sweet tang of copper danced on my tongue and made my stomach rumble. It occurred to me then that I had drunk the jorskal's blood without a second thought.

Indeed, I'd drunk his blood just like a...

A sudden, hideous realization struck me. I felt sick.

"Oh, bollocks."

Chapter Twenty

I ran my tongue over my fangs to make sure they weren't any sharper or longer than they should have been. They weren't, I was sure of it. I rolled over and closed my eyes.

Just in case I'd been mistaken the first hundred or so times I'd checked, I did it again. The result was the same, but I was in no mood to sleep. I lay in bed and listened to the sounds of the inn waking up. I listened to serving wenches shouting at grumpy cooks and grumpy cooks shouting at apparently lazy pot boys. I listened to dogs barking for scraps, doors slamming, and cobbles being sluiced. I acknowledged these things as I acknowledged that the mattress was less comfortable than a sack of stones and that I could see a sliver of grey sky through a crack in the crumbling plaster. But nothing could ease or distract me from the sickly feeling that I might be turning into a blood drinker. I hated blood drinkers, had fought dozens of the filthy, infernal parasites. The idea that I might become one filled me with dread.

"I don't want to be a parasite. Nobody wants to be a parasite," I said to the rafters. "People want to be dragons. Nobody wants to be a fucking infernal with bad breath." I examined my claws even though I wasn't sure what changes I was looking for. Finding nothing amiss, I got up and threw the last of the kindling on the fire. As I crouched by the hearth, I thought I'd try just one more thing to make absolutely sure that I wasn't turning. I tried to change shape. Yes, I know, you don't have to tell me how insane that was; just keep it to yourself, eh? I gave it my all but happily failed to transform myself into a monster.

The window rattled. I jumped, terrified that someone might have seen me grunting and straining by the hearth, which didn't look good from any angle. It was just the wind. While I'd been preoccupied with my mortality or lack thereof, morning had broken. I didn't know when the temple bell should call the faithful to prayers, but my guess was that it must be about now because all gods seemed to hate sleeping past cockcrow. I picked up my shirt from where I'd set it to dry by the fire. The bloodstains remained, but they didn't look fresh. Even so, I resolved to buy a replacement on my way out of town. As I couldn't easily explain carrying either object, I hammered the nail into a rafter and dropped the brooch pin between floorboards before taking apart the valuables I'd lifted from the jorskal's offering bowls. I stuffed the stones and the gold into a hunk of bread I'd kept aside for such a purpose. It wouldn't escape discovery if someone seriously searched my belongings, but I doubted that would happen after the locals saw what was under their temple.

After I dressed, I ventured down to the common room. I knew I had covered my tracks and that as far as anyone save a sad-looking urux, a dog, and a few rats knew, I had spent the night in my room. Just like a real bonafide guest, I even remembered to leave a few copper pennies for the chambermaid.

As it was early, I wasn't surprised that there were only two others in the common room. The table nearest the fire was occupied by a man and a boy. They were eating savory porridge with eggs and meat. Mugs of spiced chai steamed beside them. The food smelled good, so I ordered the same. The innkeeper shouted the order through to the kitchen and directed me to a table in the corner. I'd hardly had time to shit since my escape from the mine and resolved to buy not just a shirt but a whole set of clothes that were better suited to the climate before leaving town. Sitting there, waiting for breakfast while contemplating something as simple as buying a coat, I felt an unusual longing for an ordinary life, to be the cove I was pretending to be.

"Another day, two if it snows bad." The man ran a hunk of bread around his porridge bowl and shoveled the remains of his food into his mouth.

"What about Ladtkin?" the boy asked as he blew on his mug of chai.

"He'll meet us at Denepka Bridge." The driver reached over and ruffled his hair. "Don't worry, he'll be there."

A door slammed, and one of the serving wenches blew in like a galleon under full sail. "You won't be saying that if he's put a baby in your belly," she called over her shoulder. She was carrying a tray of food, which she deposited on my table. "Stupid bitch," she said under her breath. The aforesaid traipsed from the kitchen. Her eyes were red and she was sniffling.

"If you weren't such a—" The speed with which the blonde spoke lost me, but I thought she said something like, 'iron britches.' Whatever it was, it provoked a sudden and furious response from the bigger and meaner daughter of Voskva. She stormed over to the blonde and with perfect timing, slapped her across the face like she was trying to tenderize a steak. There followed an excellent brawl, which drew in another of the barmaids, a potboy, and a confused dog. I enjoyed the show while I ate my breakfast and basked in the sublime normality.

"You're just jealous that you got left with that fat, little bookworm," the recipient of the best slap I'd seen in years screamed as she hurled a breadbasket at her attacker.

"I wouldn't touch him or any of them because I have respect for myself, you fucking whore. But at least he was Voskvan. You slept with a foreigner."

"Ugly bitch! You're jealous!"

"Don't you call her…"

"…shut your face…"

"Let her go!"

And so it went. The battle was savage; the advantage went first one way, then the other. Many bread rolls were lost in the struggle, and a garlic sausage valiantly sacrificed itself to take the dog off the field. The decisive victory went to the innkeeper who came into the fray fresh from the kitchen. While the main combatants were locked in the slow death of hair pulling and kicking, he struck like a ruddy-faced python. With surprising dexterity for a man of his size, he got between the three women and dragged them apart. He even managed to cuff the smirking pot boy for good measure. As well as being thoroughly entertained by the scrap, I also learned the direction in which my comrades had headed, that the blonde had fallen in love with Nicodemus, and that her attacker was in love with her. It was a delicious, salacious slice of life, and for the first time in my many lives, I wished it was mine.

In good spirits, I flirted with the idea of taking off into the wilds of Voskva. I spoke the language well enough and was improving every day. I had portable skills, and I wasn't afraid of hard work. Someone like me would be a boon to any community. I could lead a peaceful, ordinary life, become a locksmith, or one of those other things honest coves did to fill their time between being born and dying. Alas, the road I walked was paved with bones, not good intentions. I had to steal for Duke Leo— a simple mission, but one already dripping in blood. After that, I had to kill what was left of Ludo and whoever stood between us. Mayhap once those deeds were done and my dead were at rest, perhaps then I might find some quiet place to abide. I pushed the plate away and drained my mug of chai. Aye, it was quite the fantasy, the lived reality of which would bore me to death within a week.

I bought clothes from a merchant who was also a practicing drunk with a maudlin disposition. After he'd performed the act of everyday clairvoyance by telling me that I wasn't from around here and that I looked like one o'them 'thosie-lizard things,' he raised a stone bottle of the local gut rot.

"To Jorskal Arngol. May the road he has taken lead him straight to a cold hell."

"I'm sorry?" Although my heart didn't skip a beat, the toast to my mark was jarring.

The old cove took a swig of the eye-blistering fumigatory and grimaced through the liquor's burn. "Our spiritual guide has abandoned his flock." He spat on the floor.

I gave a disinterested shrug. Alas, it prompted elaboration rather than cessation.

"The unholy father has fucked off, you see. Gone in the night like a thief."

"He was a thief?"

"I said, '*like* a thief'. He was a cockless, murdering *odbyt*. Good riddance, I say, good riddance." He sank down on his chair and began to cry and mutter, and then he laughed again before crying some more before falling into a tortured drunken stupor. Humans. If I lived another hundred years, I don't think I'll ever truly understand them.

I put on my new clothes, threw the old rags on the fire, and left the coins on the counter. I should have just left town after that, but curiosity got the better of me, and I decided to swing past the temple. I was not alone. Word had spread like the proverbial, and it looked like the whole town were rushing to see the evidence of the priest's atrocities for themselves. Aside from the excited, yet apprehensive chatter that ran through the crowd, I could also hear the unmistakable sound of fighting coming from up ahead. It wasn't the battlefield kind of melee. There was no clash of steel, no war horns, or battle cries. There was shouting and cursing and the strangled, inarticulate cries of those engaged in fisticuffs and those trying to stop them.

I eased my way around the pond to get an unobscured view of the temple. The doors were wide open. Standing in the doorway was a group of men and women armed with tree-felling axes, spiked clubs, and pitchforks. They faced a similar sized group of their fellow citizens, all tooled up with the finest weaponry you could find in a barn. Again, the speed, and in this case, the ferocity of their discourse thwarted my ability to understand the finer points of the argument, but any fool could catch the gist. Based on what they had found in the crypt, some of the locals wanted to burn the temple down and salt the earth, some of them didn't, and some just wanted to have a fight. It seemed that the disappearance of the jorskal had not only opened a gateway to another world but a lot of old wounds. The jorskal, or more, the authority vested in his office, had kept the peace in the town, and now that authority was gone. I wondered who amongst the brawlers were kin of Kniza, Kolna, and Yalta and whether their desire for vengeance was as strong as mine.

"Burn it! Burn it..." the mob facing the temple chanted.

"All of you, get back!" One of the defenders stepped from the doorway. He was a big cove with grey hair and eyes as pale as a winter sky. The buttons of his faded uniform jacket were tarnished and didn't have a chance in hell of fastening over his barrel belly. "As your *Komosor*," he bellowed. "I'm telling you all to go home. This will be dealt with by the proper authorities."

"The proper authorities sent him!"

"Fuck off, Blazkoy," one of the attackers shouted. Her scornful tone was echoed by the shouts of her supporters.

"The Archolya in Samsovar will deal with this, you have my word!" Blazkoy thundered, using the voice of authority common to all militiamen. Everyone shut up. For a minute, it looked like he might have backed them down, but then someone shouted and broke the spell.

"They sent both of you!" Someone shouted. The mob began jeering again.

"We can't trust them!"

"…Did you know?"

An uneven chorus of 'did you know?' was hurled at Blazkoy.

"No, of course I didn't!" he snapped. "Everyone, go home. Go home now! That's an order. He still spoke with the voice of command, but the look in his eye held less confidence.

"You don't fucking order us!"

A bottle arched from the attacking side and smashed against the door.

"Arngol will pay for his crimes, I swear. But this must be done the right way, under the law. Please, brothers and sisters, please go home."

The ire of the enraged townsfolk would not be salved by his promise, and the mob closed on the scared-looking defenders. Once more, I wondered if the spirits of the witches lingered, if they were watching their friends and enemies about to kick each other's heads in. While I pondered, someone threw a stone jug at the Komosor. His nose exploded, and he stumbled against the door, hands flying to his bloody face. The two factions closed. People screamed as the townsfolk began to pummel each other with varying degrees of skill and vehemence. When one of the attackers broke through and ran inside with a flaming torch, I deemed it time to leave.

I felt no guilt for exposing the jorskal's foul deeds and neither did I blame the witches for wanting to be free. The blame lay entirely with the twisted jorskal and his nasty, little cult. If he hadn't been a monster, there wouldn't have been anything for the brawling sons and daughters of Voskva to fight over. That's all it ever took; a single monster to give birth to the ouroboros of murder and violence. *A monster whose blood you drank*. As often happens, screams and the smell of burning followed me from the town.

Chapter Twenty-One

I set a fast pace as I crunched my way along the cinder road from Tartakoy. If the weather didn't turn, and I didn't get waylaid, I expected to catch up with my faithless companions within a day, thanks to Ockzar. He would be dragging like an anchor unless they'd dumped him, or worse, done away with him. That they had taken him with them after I was poisoned surprised me. It was possible that Nic had an attack of inspired thinking and had decided that the Voskvan might be useful after all.

About a mile from Tartakoy, the clatter of wheels alerted me to the carriage that came thundering down the road, taking a corner on two wheels in its haste. It was drawn by horses, which was rare enough in itself.

That they were huge, night-black beasts with wild, blue eyes even more worthy of note. The carriage they pulled echoed the onion domes so popular in Voskva, only it was made of steel and painted black. The door curtain was closed, but as it passed, a wide, webbed hand twitched the heavy velvet. The occupant was probably headed for a more genteel destination than Tartakoy, but I hadn't forgotten what the sodden witch had said about the jorskal being in a cult. When the carriage was out of sight, I set off at a run.

When the suns began to set like molten lead upon the iron edge of the world, I stopped running. Being banged up and shackled for a month had done me no favors, and I was sweating when I decided to look for somewhere to camp for the night. I decided against the forest and was scanning the hills when a flash of azure fire lit a snow-dusted ridge before me, followed by the unmistakable roar of a dragon. It had to be Swann and Nic. It was too much of a coincidence for another clutch of cunts to be out here, antagonizing dragons. "I hope it fucking eats you." My idle wishes would have no bearing on the matter, but I felt better for voicing them. Another roar shook the hills. Another flash lit the sky. I considered finding a sheltered nook and waiting for the fight to be over. Alas, if I left them to be slaughtered, Leo would not be happy.

I tucked my pack into a crevice before climbing up the rocky slope. An ice-eyed lynx watched me from the mouth of her den. Sensing I was no threat to her, she slunk back into the darkness as lightning arced overhead, filling the air with the pungent stink of burning magic. I flattened against the hillside as rocks tumbled around me. When they stopped falling, I crept forward, mindful that I could be turned to a lump of charcoal at any moment by an errant bolt of sorcerous shittery.

When I reached the top of the ridge, I stole a little looksie. Subsidence and erosion had formed a natural amphitheater behind the ridge. In the middle rose a dramatic island plateau of granite, which was of course crowned by ruins. A snaking staircase almost reached the plateau. The remains of a bridge lay beneath. Stood within the ruins was a pissed-off-looking dragon. It was an elderly beast; its muscles were wasted, its skin hung slack on its bony frame, and its scales were scarred and dull. What teeth it had were chipped, its horns had yellowed, and it was missing an eye. What surprised me more was that the bunch of cunts picking on the old bone bag weren't my cunts.

I had obviously arrived during the endgame of the battle. Trees were burned to blackened stumps. The plateau was wreathed in smoke, and the stairs were splattered with mortal and dragon blood.

A sorcerer was standing on the broadest sweep of the stair. Garbed in black, her raven hair and voluminous cloak billowed in an eldritch wind. The crystal in her ebony staff flared a brilliant azure as she screamed an incantation into the howling gale. The dragon answered with a roar that was more disgruntled than furious. Closer to the angry dragon than was perhaps wise, a warrior clad in black armor crouched behind a fallen column. He wasn't alone. Bellowing like a madman, a bull-headed cove leaped from a bluff above the plateau and rammed a barbed spear into the dragon's flank.

The beast let out an ear-piercing shriek as his attacker twisted the weapon. I felt for him and was pleased when he flicked his wing and swept Bullhead from the plateau. A black-feathered flight appeared in the dragon's neck. It was followed in quick succession by two more. They didn't penetrate deeply; indeed, one fell out as he swung his head around and breathed molten ice at the archer. She dropped behind the wall on which she'd been perched just before a wave of freezing spew splashed across it and sent fractures racing through the stone. While they were fighting, clouds gathered overhead and turned as dark as a bruise. Thunder growled and thorns of lightning pierced the sky above the plateau. There was more going on here than just hunting a dragon for sport or trophies.

The dragon opened his mouth and vomited icy destruction. Old memories surfaced, and I felt for the burn scar on my shoulder gained when I'd been on the receiving end of an ice dragon's fury. It wasn't there of course, that body had ceased to exist years ago, but the memory was painfully fresh. As though it sensed my antagonism, the dragon's crystalline gaze swept across the amphitheater, and our eyes met. Momentarily I was possessed by the old fear and excitement of staring death in the face. Before it had chance to earn the title, the sorcerer hammered her staff on the step. The dragon's head snapped around. I took the opportunity to duck behind some rocks and move, curiosity and possibly a death wish driving me closer to the action. Below me, near the mouth of the amphitheater, I spied a youth struggling to hold onto the reins of a pair of rightly terrified yuraxus hitched to a laden wagon.

The sorcerer began chanting another incantation. I didn't understand what she was saying, but there was no mistaking the smell of magic building before shimmering bands of energy ensnared the dragon's legs and bound it to the plateau. The warrior hiding behind the fallen column tore off his helm. He had a grey beard and a bloody nose and was breathing hard. He cast aside his shield and took a two-handed grip on the hilt of his sword. Emboldened now that the dragon was tethered, the archer ran around the ice-rimed wall and aimed upon the beast. Sigils on the shaft of her arrow glowed. As she nocked it to the string, the head burst into flames. Sensing its doom, the dragon roared its frustration and fought desperately to break free. The ground shook, the arrow flew wide, hit the wall of the amphitheater, and exploded, sending a massive slab of hillside crashing to the ground. The archer stumbled and fell. The frozen wall she had been hiding behind shattered. She screamed as a piece of stone remolded her shin. Meanwhile, Bullhead had gathered his wits and tried to re-join the fray. With another quick swipe of its wing, the dragon knocked him off the plateau again.

I admired its dexterity, although had it been me, I would have used my tail and turned the annoying fucker into a pancake. I guessed it was injured, or perhaps, being old, it lacked the flexibility and sacrificed that method of attack in favor of maintaining its balance, ensnared as it was in the sorcerous bonds. Call me sentimental, but even though it was knackered and outnumbered, I bet my imaginary coin on the dragon, more as a show of good faith rather than belief in its ability. Intent on thwarting my win even though she didn't know it, the sorcerer tightened her grip on the magical shackles. The dragon roared and beat its wings, but it could not break free. Such was the exertion of holding it, the sorcerer's nose began to bleed. While his comrades had taken a kicking, the old warrior had done nothing save look pained and clutch his chest. Finally, he martialed his resolve and faced the dragon down. Unsteady on his feet, his haggard face was the color of curdled milk. I couldn't see any obvious wounds, but then his left arm dropped to his side, and he stumbled. I was no physik, but it looked to me like his heart was failing in the middle of the fight.

"That's bad timing," I said, although I wasn't surprised. Humans being human— and he looked like a human— it wasn't uncommon for them to just drop dead from nothing much at all. Old ones were particularly susceptible to dying without warning, and this one looked old. While I put a few more imaginary coins on the dragon being victorious, lightning flashed overhead and painted the world in shades of silver and ebony. The old warrior gathered his strength and strode into the open, bearing his sword aloft. The dragon snarled. The mage yelled an incantation, and magical fire lanced from her staff and hit the dragon in the chest. The reek of blood and burning scales filled the air. It stumbled back as far as the sorcerous bonds would allow.

"You will die this day, Azdraburax!" the warrior shouted even though it was evident that the effort pained him. "Now is the time of reckoning when you will pay for all of your terrible deeds."

It wasn't an impressive speech, but I made allowances for someone in the middle of having a heart attack.

The dragon freed one of its legs and slapped the warrior across the amphitheater. "Barantz!" the sorcerer screamed as he hit the wall beneath where I was crouched and crashed to the ground. *Now* he really looked injured. Indeed, now he looked like a pile of scrap metal with a face.

"No!" the youth cried as he ran to the stricken warrior. It was a touching scene, but the glint of steel drew my attention away from the boy and the injured cove. His elegant sword had flown from his grasp and was wedged between rocks just a few feet from where I was hiding. The blade shimmered. Cloud shadows raced across its polished surface, and lightning danced upon its keen edge. Bellowing its anger, the dragon stirred up a whirlwind of dust and smoke as it beat its wings in a bid to break free of its remaining bonds. The sorcerer grounded her staff and leaned upon it. The dragon's eyes began to shine with an unearthly light.

"Master Barantz. Please. Don't die. Don't go." The boy sobbed as he cradled the warrior in his arms.

The old man's eyes flickered open. "I cannot stay, Thorfir. You must remember what I taught you. You must finish this."

"I can't, master. I'm not ready," the boy wailed. I was inclined to agree.

"Barantz!" the sorcerer shouted. "I can't hold him much longer," she cried as the sky above the plateau turned the color of blood. The dragon redoubled his efforts to free himself. "You must strike now, old man. Barantz? Barantz! Get up!"

The old warrior wasn't striking anything. I watched as he reached up with a mailed hand and gently brushed a tear from the boy's cheek. "Now is the time, boy. Don't be afraid. Trust your training, trust *Consequence*. Take the sword, Thorfir." The warrior coughed.

"We must do this now!" the sorcerer shouted, her voice drowned out by the roar of the dragon and the guttural growl of thunder.

"Where is it?" I heard the boy ask.

The warrior coughed. "What…?"

"The sword. I don't know where it is…"

"What?"

"It…it's not here…"

"Oh, shit..."

I didn't hear whatever else they said, save to note the panicked tone and desperate pitch of their voices. I was too busy retracing my steps back down the hillside with my prize. I stopped briefly to retrieve my pack and wrap the beautiful, glowing, hopefully incredibly valuable blade in my blanket before once more setting off at a run. Not being a novice, I made sure to hide my tracks and bounded from rock to rock. When I heard the dragon roar in triumph, I knew the chances of being pursued would be significantly reduced. I hit the dirt. Moments later, its massive shadow passed overhead, its laughter ringing through the storm-laden sky.

I probably shouldn't have taken the sword, but in my defense, the fight was unfair, and there are far more mortals in the world than dragons. All I was doing was evening the odds. Indeed, the more I thought about it, the more I realized I had done the world a favor by rescuing this fabulous, gem-encrusted weapon.

Just in case the dragon and the failed dragon killers didn't see things my way, I continued to flee at a run. Before I got too far from the scene of the rescue, a fierce and thunderous snowstorm blew up and forced me to find shelter. I squeezed myself within the fossilized roots of a long-dead tree. It wasn't warm, but it was out of the teeth of the wind that had no doubt been whipped into wildness by the sorcerer's and the dragon's magic. While I holed up and waited for the storm to subside, I took the opportunity to examine *Consequence*.

The blade had ceased to glow by the time I unwrapped it and was now a dull and unreflective grey. I licked the wave of the hamon. Other than the taste of blade oil, blood, and blanket fluff, there was something of the void about it, something cold and otherworldly locked within the metal. It was fashioned in the Shennish style. Rather than the more common shark or snakeskin, the hilt was bound in grey, dragon skin. As those familiar with dragons know, the only skin of a dragon malleable enough to wrap around the hilt of a sword was from its wotnots. The leather was bound with wire drawn from star steel— a luxurious if pointless touch, but as the benefactor, I wasn't complaining. A pair of dragons chased each other through clouds on the oval guard. The fierce beasts had sapphire chip scales and blue diamond eyes. Their frosty breath was carved from veneer slices of dragon scale, which shone with a cool iridescence. The contours of the clouds were inlaid with platinum, silver, and white gold. Unlike Volund's blade, it didn't change to conform to its wielder's hand. It was longer than I would have liked and a little blade heavy for my tastes, but there was no mistaking it was worth many times its weight in gold.

I turned the blade to catch what light was falling between the gaps in the ancient roots. Outside, the snow parted like a curtain, the movement of the flurries matching the movement of the sword as though orchestrated. I swung it as much as the space would allow and watched the snow dance in time to my movements.

When I stopped playing, I laid down and listened to the storm rage like a fractious child. Lulled by the furious gales, I fell asleep and woke refreshed the next morning. I ate some of the dried fish and butter I'd bought in Tartakoy along with a slug of the local, resin-distilled liquor, which I diluted with snowmelt. Thus fortified, I kicked my way out of the hollow through the drift of snow that had frozen in the tangle of roots. Outside, the light was clear, the air crisp and unsullied. I stretched and yawned and drew a breath of pure, storm-washed air before heading east with a spring in my step and a king's ransom strapped to my back.

Chapter Twenty-Two

I was still riding a wave of delight at the good fortune that had delivered the sword *Consequence* into my sticky fingers, when I was almost killed by a burning onion dome.

A high-pitched whistle drew my gaze to a bulbous comet arcing majestically over the trees. As I tried to fathom what I was looking at, a part of my brain noted its dangerous trajectory. Alarmed by what it saw, it informed another part of my noodle, which moved my arse in an away-wards direction. The dome fell from the sky and smashed into a tree near where I had been standing. It exploded, sending pieces of flaming turret and burning tree in all directions. I escaped unscathed, if confused. After poking around the remains, I concluded that it was exactly what it looked like; a tin-

skinned turret dome. Beneath the smell of hot metal
was the unmistakable aroma of sorcery. I looked to
the east, where an ominous pall of smoke was rising
above the treetops. Thick, black, and oily, it was
smoke brewed from wanton destruction, not hearth
fires or bread ovens. Surely this time, whatever
mischief it marked had to be down to my companions.
Curiosity and necessity compelled me to investigate.
I continued east, alert for more architectural
bombardment.

After following tendrils of smoke through the
forest, I came upon a gatehouse that had been lazily
repaired by magic at some time in the past. I knew this
because the spells that had held the stones together
were failing before my eyes. Cracks raced across the
walls. Ironwork melted into molten bubbles that
floated away. Walls shimmered and turned to sand,
and a window in the small bastion above the gate grew
a pair of arms, wrenched itself from the wall, and fell
screaming to its destruction on the cobbles below.

I had seen this kind of thing before. Rather than
pay mundane artisans, some tight-fisted sorcerers
'fixed' broken things themselves with ill-conceived
spells. Before I had the chance to venture further or
indeed walk away, I heard a familiar scream which
was accompanied by something that sounded like
wooden spindles clattering on the cobbles. I drew my
swords and stood to the side of the gate. Still
screaming, Ockzar ran past me. He was being chased
by a pair of chairs wielding cutlery in rudimentary
hands that seemed to have grown from the armrests. I

should have stepped in immediately, but as with the onion turret, it took a moment to comprehend what I was seeing. As evidenced by his scarlet mug, the chase had been hard and Ockzar was exhausted. He ran around a water trough, I guessed in the hope he might fox his lumbering attackers. But the furniture was not so easily deterred. One chair went right; the other left around the trough, trapping him.

"Oi!" I shouted. The chairs turned to 'face' me.

"Gasvoy's Ghost! *Breed!*" Ockzar exclaimed.

"Ockzar."

The chairs rushed me.

"Are you a ghost?" he sobbed.

The foremost chair bounded towards me. "Not yet," I said as I sidestepped the stiff-limbed attack.

He yelped as the other chair sneakily edged around the trough, forcing him to move. "I can't believe it's really you."

"Trust me, I'm definitely me."

"I'm being attacked by furniture. I don't know anything anymore. You might be a ghost."

"You don't believe in ghosts, remember? You said, 'only ignorant peasants believed in the supernatural'." I kicked the chair and cracked a leg. It tottered awkwardly and threw a fork at me.

"You were bloody dead."

I swatted the fork away with *Consequence*. "You're not the first person to make that mistake."

He hauled a bucket from the trough and threw it at his upholstered pursuer. "What do you mean 'mistake'?"

"It was the ghouls' fault."

"What was? Oh, fuck." He yelped as the chair slashed at him with an ornate steak knife.

"I was paralyzed by the ghouls' saliva when one of them bit me." My chair leaped at me again, but due to losing a leg, its timing was woeful. I grabbed it by the arm wielding the knife, picked it up, and smashed it against the trough. Upon 'seeing' its partner reduced to matchwood, the other chair sprinted for the trees. "You don't see that every day."

Ockzar slumped against the trough. "I don't understand."

"It didn't want to get turned into kindling."

He rolled his eyes. "Not the chair. *You.* I don't understand how you are alive."

"I'm sorry that my continued existence confounds you, Ockzar. How dreadfully remiss of me not to just be dead."

"Nothing in nature can cause such complete paralysis that the victim appears as dead as you did."

I shrugged. "It's a kind of magic."

I could almost see the cogs turning as he regarded me thoughtfully. Eventually, he climbed to his feet and rushed over with outstretched arms. I didn't know what he was planning but assumed that he wasn't going to tackle me to the ground or punch me. I was right. It was much worse than that. He hugged me. I squirmed from his clammy embrace. "It's good to see you too, but don't do that again. Displays of affection make me uncomfortable."

Blushing, he backed away. "I understand. I've had an awful time of it. I used to think the mines were bad but, oh, your comrades. They're awful, possibly insane." He glanced nervously over his shoulder as a flock of napkins swooped from a window in the manor house and flapped into the forest.

"They're in there, aren't they?" I asked, although I was sure I knew the answer. Ockzar was staring at the napkins and didn't reply. "Ockzar?" I clicked my fingers.

Obviously shaken, he dragged his gaze from the trees and back to me. "Sorry. What did you say?" Sweat beaded his face. "Did you see that? You saw that, didn't you?"

Oh, but it was tempting to lie. "Yes, I saw that," I conceded to save his sanity. "Where are Nic and Swann?"

"They're in there. I think." He pointed to the house. "That is, they were."

"What happened?"

"We found a tower, but it wasn't the right tower, apparently." He rolled his eyes. "Then we saw smoke and came here seeking directions, and I confess, I was keen to rest my sore feet and find somewhere warm to spend the night. Now, I know he's a nobleman, but in the circumstances, I was willing to give the Dvor the benefit of the doubt. He seemed anachronistic, but not a bad sort, just senile, so I could forgive him much, you understand?"

I could feel myself aging. "Just, go on."

"It was the servants! You wouldn't have believed it, or perhaps you would." He laughed nervously, eyed me with suspicion. "Anyway. We were eating." He snorted. "I say 'eating'. As you can imagine, those two were drinking to excess and behaving like rabid zashonishas. I know it's probably a cultural difference, but it behooves people to learn good manners and…"

I took a few deep breaths and thought happy thoughts while he rambled on. "…Which is obviously the wrong way to eat it, but as I say, I put that down to him being foreign. Anyway, I made mention of serfdom because as you know, I cannot stand oppression. Then the Dvor said his servants were dead."

"Are Nic and Swann dead?" I asked, hoping to cut to the meat of the matter.

"What? No." He looked at me like *I* was the blathering fool. "At least they weren't when I last saw them. "The servants were dead, which caused Nic to fly into a rage.

"So, this Dvor killed his servants, and then invited you to dinner. Got it."

He wiped his brow on his sleeve. "Yes, but you see, we didn't know that they were dead."

"Were the bodies hidden?"

"No. They were wearing masks and I assume they had some magical glamour cast upon them to hide the smell of decay."

"You've lost me."

He splashed water on his sweaty face. "It's simple enough. I made a comment about serfdom being outlawed, and that's when the Dvor revealed that his servants were dead.

"Ah. I'm with you again. The servants were animated."

"Yes."

"So, this Dvor is a necromancer?"

"Is he?"

"I don't...Yes, probably. Never mind. So, when you found out the servants were dead, he attacked you?"

Ockzar looked at his feet. "Not exactly."

"No?"

He smiled nervously. "Nicodemus attacked the Dvor. But in his defense, he was in his cups by this point."

"What did Swann do?"

"He was also very drunk."

I pinched the skin between my eyes. "Go on."

"He also attacked the Dvor. It was awful. I tried to stop them. When everything started to change, when the furniture began to attack us, I ran for my life."

The tale was so full of shit you could spread it on a field. "Just take me to where you last saw the others."

"No. Absolutely not. No, no, no." He shook his head so vigorously I feared it might unscrew. "Can't you hear it? It's like a war in there. I saw a wall melt like candlewax. I'm not going back." He folded his arms. I think it was supposed to be a gesture of defiance, but it looked more like he was hugging himself.

"Stay here then." I thrust my pack into his arms. "And keep out of sight. I don't want any more chairs coming after you or gods forbid, a couch."

"What are you going to do?"

"Find the idiot twins I suppose." I have often found that the solution to most problems is to stab them until they cease to be. I admit, it is not a solution to everyone's taste, but it works for me. Unfortunately, not in this case. Once again, I had cause to curse my obligation to Leo.

From what I could see of the house, it had been a typically characterful Voskvan manor. Alas, the magic that had obviously sustained it for decades, if not centuries, was unraveling. As I approached the main entrance, a woman on fire stumbled outside. She wasn't screaming despite burning as brightly as a tallow candle. Due in part to her lack of distress and knowing that fresh meat smells different to old meat when it was cooking, I guessed she was one of the animated dead Ockzar had told me about. Living or dead, she was beyond all help. I stepped aside. She stumbled past me and fell into a topiary hedge. The flames roared while she remained silent, paper skin flying as she withered. Half of another wizened corpse crashed through an upstairs window and landed beside her. I made my way inside. The first living cove I saw was an elderly human lying slumped at the bottom of the staircase. He reached out towards me with a frail, bloodstained hand. "Help me," he called. "Please. Help me."

I tucked *Consequence* into my belt and approached. His embroidered robe was rent and blood-soaked, his skin deathly pale.

"You the Dvor?" I asked out of politeness.

He nodded. "Who are you?" Blood trickled from his lips and spidered down the creases in his parchment skin. His breath smelled of sorcery and death.

"No one. I was just passing, and I saw the smoke."

He coughed again. The smell of blood was overpowering. I resisted the urge to lick my lips. "I was hoping father had returned. He would take them to task. Do you know they attacked me? In my own home." He grabbed my arm and drew me close. "They want that which is mine. But they shall not have it." His breath bubbled in his chest. "They want my heart. They want my power."

I reluctantly tore my gaze from the big vein beating in his throat. "Sorry, did you say heart?"

He nodded. "Where is it?" I asked.

"The Forgasty Vash." He pointed to the door. "Tower Hill', you would call it."

"It's a hill? Of course, it is." I laughed.

"Father told me to keep it safe, so I put it in the cave. 'Find a good hiding place', he said. And I did, Father." He smiled at me. "You would be so proud of me." The smile faded and was replaced by a look of disappointment. "You're not father." He laughed. "When I was younger, I wanted to live forever. I've done quite well at that. I should have worked harder at keeping my faculties, eh?"

"I know what you mean." And I did. If not for Mother, I'd be just as addled as this old fool. "Where did the men go who attacked you?"

He laughed, and his eyes shone with mirth. "My house has them. It is my last..." He coughed, misted the air with blood. "My last trick." The rattle in his heaving chest suddenly stopped, and his eyes glazed as the spark of life died.

I searched his pockets and lifted a bunch of keys, a healthy coin purse, and a fire opal ring. I left the piece of knotted string and an old boiled sweet. Upon his demise, the magic he had wielded began to die with him, and the animated dead became the more usual kind of corpse. Most fell like discarded dolls; others slowed like cunning automata whose springs were uncoiling. I followed the trail of the Dvor's blood up the stairs, past body parts and smashed furniture. At the end of the balcony, a door had been ripped off its hinges, and the walls were scorched and splattered with claret. I could hear noise coming from inside and approached cautiously.

Crouching just inside was another live serf. The old cove was sobbing quietly and cradling one of the now-true-dead undead servants. Her mask lay on the floor beside her, revealing the face of a well preserved, if somewhat waxen young woman. Braided, flaxen hair framed her dollish face. The old man lifted her hand to his lips and kissed it. I gave them a respectfully wide berth. If theirs was the tragedy, then comedy lay upon the other side of the devastated chamber. The huge bed lay overturned, and the mattress had been pinned to the wall by fire pokers. Hanging from the curtains, bound hand and foot by the animated, velvet drapery was Swann.

Gagged by an embroidered swag of fabric, his eyes grew wide when he saw me. I waved. "Yes, it's me. No, I'm not dead. The ghouls paralyzed me with their spit. Yes, you have made an arse of things. Where's the other prick?"

His gaze shifted to a heavy armoire lying on the floor. The doors were splayed open and flapping weakly on squeaking hinges.

"He's under there?"

Swann nodded. The curtains tightened their grip, and his eyes rolled back in his head, which was when I realized he couldn't breathe. I drew *Consequence* and rested the flat of the blade on my shoulder.

"Why do you tempt me so, Fate?" My conscience got the better of me, and I cut him down before he stopped twitching. I stabbed the drapes a few times leaving him to grapple with the squirming fabric while I kicked in the back of the wardrobe. A hand thrust through a pile of moth-eaten fur coats, which instantly knotted around the thick wrist and tried to drag it back into the smothering darkness. Less carefully than I probably should have been, I cut through the coats until I reached Nic and hauled him out.

"Breed?" He gasped. "Damn your eyes, it is you. Where's that mad, old cunt?"

"Dead. You killed him."

"Never mind him. You were dead, jimma," said Swann as he untangled himself from the remains of the curtains.

"I told you. I was paralyzed by the ghouls' spit."

"Mad, old fucker," said Nic.

"I'm sorry?"

"The Dvor," Nic tapped his skull. "He wasn't all there. Went berserk, I think. It's all a bit hazy." He laughed. "You know how it is. You should have seen Swann. He was fucking useless, weren't you, Swann? He got his arse proper kicked by that old geezer." He clapped his hands. "But I got him." He stood up, spat blood.

"Yes, you got him good," I said.

Nic beamed.

"And you left me again. With ghouls this time."

"You looked dead." He shrugged. "Anyway, you're here now. And we're close to the Vascellum." He breezed past me, slowing only to slap me on the back.

Swann limped over rubbing his neck. "I should have guessed there would be wards, but murderous furniture? That's a new one on me. It all happened so fast."

"Murdering your host?" I think I did a reasonable job of keeping the contempt I felt from my voice.

"What? Did you have to squeeze it in before dessert got cold?"

Swann looked hurt. "He was a necromancer."

"And?"

That seemed to stump him. "It's er, like really bad, you know?"

I looked at the old cove sobbing over the corpse by the door. "You're a real hero, Swann."

"Hardly. Nic did most of the damage." He didn't see the track of my gaze because he was too busy searching his pockets. Eventually, he found his pipe and relief lit on his face. He looked at me and smiled. "But nevermind me. It's good to see you again, Chas."

"I could say the same." But as it would have been a lie, I didn't.

Chapter Twenty-Three

"Just don't," I said and tried to warn Swann away with a snarl, but he kept pace with me as we marched north to Tower Hill. A light snowfall dampened the smell of burning mansion, but its ghost trailed us; an olfactory accusation of guilt that none of my fuckwitted companions seemed to notice.

"I thought you were dead, jimma," he whined. His words fell on deaf ears. Not least because no one softens towards those who whine, least of all me. My anger at being left by the pair of gilt-edged cunts had not abated, and the needless destruction they had wrought only served to harden my animosity towards them. Their wanton abuse of power irked me. Even Mother, a blood-thirsty psychopath, only killed when she had a reason.

Granted, it might not be *much* of a reason, but it was always more than, 'we were drunk'.

"Must we run?" Ockzar called. In a desire to reach the Forgasty Vash before the servants could report the murder of their lord, I had set a fast pace, and he was struggling to keep up.

"Shut the fuck up, Tusky," Nic growled, to the benefit of no one.

"Why don't you shut up?" said Ockzar, in what I could only assume was a desire to get himself killed. Nic stopped walking and slowly turned to face him.

"And my name isn't 'Tusky', 'tubby', 'blubber gut', 'fatty' or 'pig boy'. It's Ockzar. Or Millmets if you prefer formality." His ruddy cheeks turned a deeper shade of red as he drew himself up to his full height, puffed out his chest, and sucked in his gut. Nicodemus advanced towards him with hands clawed and fangs bared. I sidled up behind Nic as Ockzar suddenly came to his senses and began to back away. Swann clamped his hands around his head as though in preparation to shut out the screams and walked off, muttering to himself.

"Who the fuck do you think you're talking to, you fat, little shit?" Nic didn't shout. He was coldly furious, and if I read him right, surprised that his victim had stood up to him.

Ockzar snorted. "Am I fat or little?" He clearly wanted to die.

"You're fat *and* little."

"I'm heavy, I'll grant, but to use Imperial measurements, I am five feet eight inches tall, hardly diminutive by human standards. You are just overly tall. You sir, are lanky." He grinned like he'd scored a point, as though deft wordplay mattered to a walking shithouse like Nicodemus.

"I'm what now?" Nic loomed over him.

In a bid to warn the Voskvan to shut his pie hole, I pulled a pained expression and shook my head. He looked quizzical, but then it appeared to dawn on him that he might have made a terrible mistake mouthing off to the enforcer. I could have told him what would happen. The poor cull had thought he'd been engaging in a civilized dispute which could be settled by reason or won with wit. Too late, he realized that he'd actually been poking a nest of angry scorpions with his cock.

He swallowed hard. "What I mean is, you're a little on the tall side. It can, er, skew your perception."

Nic grabbed Ockzar by his collars and dragged him onto his toes. "My perception is skewed? Do you perceive how fucking annoying you are?"

Ockzar couldn't answer because he was being throttled. I waited for Nic to decide that the lesson not to pick a fight with a gang enforcer had been learned.

When Ockzar began to dance like a gibbet poppet, it occurred to me that the lesson might be more of a death sentence.

"All right, that's enough," I said lightly, trying to downplay the situation. Nic ignored me. I tapped him on the shoulder.

He shrugged me off. "He's dead weight."

"Put him down." I wasn't surprised that he was ignoring me. I'd have been more surprised had he listened. Given who he was and the world he lived in, Nic had a point to prove, standards to maintain. The dull throb of a hangover headache began to pound in my skull as the desire to slot him warred with the blood bound obligation I had to Duke Leo. Nevertheless, I am a stubborn fucker, and pain has never been my master. On the contrary, it is often a spur. I drew *Consequence*. The sword's dull blade brightened and reflected the snow-laden sky like a mirror. It felt alive in my hand and keen to spill blood.

"He's not worth it, Breed," Nic growled.

"That's a matter of opinion. Now let him go, *Nic*."

"I'll let him go when I'm ready, *Breed*."

A nervous Swann sucked at his pipe like a babe on the tit. "Sparring with names!" He spluttered as the harsh smoke burned his lungs. "How very mature."

I tightened my grip on the sword hilt. "I said, let him go." My nose began to bleed as something in my blood demanded that I walk away. I lowered the blade. Ockzar stopped struggling.

Did I mention I'm a stubborn fucker?

I kicked Nicodemus in the back of the knee. In his human form he was as much subject to the laws of bone and sinew as the next cove and he went down, releasing Ockzar as he fought to regain his balance. Gasping, the Voskvan stumbled away clutching his throat. I sheathed the sword and raised my hands in a gesture of peace.

In an instant, Nic was up, red eyes blazing. "You cunt, you'll—"

Peace is so overrated. I punched him in the face. To my great relief, he did not turn into a slavering rat man but fell into a knuckle-induced swoon.

"What are you doing?" Swann raged.

"Stopping him killing Ockzar."

"He wasn't killing him!" Swann yelled.

"He wasn't giving him a fucking neck rub."

Not even the sieve-brained narcomancer could defend the blatantly indefensible. He slumped, gave me the beaten puppy face. "We're friends. We shouldn't be fighting each other."

"*We* weren't fighting. *He* was murdering *him*." I pointed to the aforementioned. "And we are not friends. We're a bad hand thrown together by Fate." He looked confused, so I felt I ought to elucidate. "Friends don't ensorcell each other. Friends don't leave friends to rot in prison. Friends don't betray friends to blood drinking cunts who send them off on pointless fucking quests to the other side of the shitting world. We have been friend*ly* briefly, but that rotting pig bladder of a balloon has well and truly burst."

"I'd just like to say that I haven't done any of those things," Ockzar rasped.

"Shut up, Ockzar," Swann and I snapped.

Nic came round and climbed to his feet, murder in his gaze. I waited, hoping he would make my day and attack me. He licked blood from his lips. "You're lucky my brother told me not to hurt you."

"Aren't I, though? I keep pinching myself to make sure I'm not dreaming."

"I want to reach the hill afore it gets dark so get your catamite moving." Pleased with himself, Nic gave a lopsided grin and walked off.

"I prefer 'prison bitch'," Ockzar wheezed.

An amalgam of hard and soft stone mashed together during some ancient, world-shaping upheaval; Tower Hill was well named. A millennium of ice, snow, sun, and rain had worked the rock into a fair approximation of the onion-domed towers so beloved of Voskvan architects. I wondered if after another thousand years of erosion it would be called 'Nob Hill' or perhaps the architectural style would change to match what nature created.

"That waterfall has a lot of iron in it." Ockzar pointed to the rust-colored stream running from the lip of the cave mouth high above us. "Unusual for this area, but not unheard of," he informed me in his capacity as official, Fount of All Voskvan Knowledge.

The reek coming from the stream told me that it wasn't merely iron rich water running down the hillside.

"You should stay here, Ockzar and guard the bags," I said, a familiar discontent beginning to roil in my gut.

"Why?" He cupped his hands.

"I wouldn't drink that if I was you," I said as I watched him reach towards the ruddy fall splashing down the hillside.

"Why not?"

Nic sniffed. "It's dragon piss."

Ockzar froze. I patted him on the back.

"Do you think it's in there?" he whispered while casting his fearful gaze towards the summit.

I rolled my shoulders. "Only one way to find out."

"I'll stay here and guard the bags," said Ockzar.

I nodded. "I'll sneak in and find the Vascellum."

Nic looked suspicious, Swann uncertain. "What do you mean?" Swann asked.

"I mean, I'll sneak in." I made sneak fingers and walked them through the air. "And if it's there, I'll steal the Vascellum."

Swann slowly shook his head. "We can't let you go alone. We'll come with you, jimma."

Nic said nothing.

"No. you won't. You can go instead of me if you wish. But if there is a dragon in there, and we go in together, there will be a big fucking fight and we will all die."

"You don't know that. I can weave charms to hide our presence." A burning flake of pel landed on his coat and began to smolder. He didn't notice, and I didn't tell him.

"It's really not a good idea."

"Why?" he said. A thin curl of smoke from his sleeve drifted into his tangled hair.

"Because one cove sneaking in stands a better chance of getting the Vascellum. Trust me, I've done this before."

"You've stolen from a dragon's lair?" Nic folded his arms; a know nothing grin on his face.

"Yes," I answered.

His idiot smile widened. "While the dragon was at home?"

"Yes."

His smile faded. "How the fuck did you get away with that?"

Naturally, I didn't tell him that, but for a stroke of luck, I would have been smeared across a mountain by the dragon. "Because I'm good at what I do. That's why your brother sent me."

He eyeballed me long and hard like he could stare a truth from me that he wanted to believe. I wished him well for he'd had as much of that as I was willing to give. He admitted defeat with a disgruntled shrug. "Whatever. I can't be arsed to argue. Go do what you do best, thief and try not to get eaten."

I sketched an elaborate, 'fuck you' bow.

They retreated to the cover of the trees, and I climbed the hill. It was easier than I'd expected on account of there being a rough flight of steps cut into the rock. As I made the ascent, the ground rumbled, and pieces of jagged, inch-thick ice fractured, broke off, and slid down the hill. Some of the deadly slivers came close to taking my head off, but I was more concerned that it sounded like the dragon was home. I couldn't hear it, but the closer I got to the cave, the more I felt sure that I could feel its living presence. I confess, as much as I was apprehensive, the old, larcenous part of me was excited at the prospect of cracking another dragon's crib. I paused beneath the lip of the cave and listened as though my life depended on it. A long, snoring breath sent a lightning thrill through me. The dragon was home, and as far as I could fathom, it was asleep.

I gripped the lip and took a gander. To my dismay, I saw the booted feet of someone standing about two feet from my face. So much for keen hearing. I tracked my gaze from the toes of the grey boots to velvet breaches embroidered with black and scarlet flowers. I craned to see past a similarly embroidered fur-trimmed coat and up above the wide, three-buckled belt. Then, with a feeling of mounting dread, I leaned back and looked beyond long, grey whiskers and into the steel-grey eyes that I had but recently seen in the face of a dragon.

"I saved your life," I exclaimed.

He raised a bushy, frost-tipped brow. "How do you figure that, thief?"

Bearing in mind I talk quickly, he grabbed me by the back of my coat and effortlessly tossed me into the cave before I could answer. As I smashed through stalactites, I considered that I should have been grateful that he hadn't thrown me from the hill.

"You think you know me, cur?" he said as he dramatically swept his coattails behind him, almost daring me to speak. I glanced over my shoulder and saw an opening in the back of the cave but thought better of making a run for it.

"You're the dragon. You were fighting those mortals in the ruins. I stole the magic sword they were going to slot you with, and you escaped," I sputtered, aware that my life depended on putting my case before he decided to kill me.

He canted his head. I think he smiled behind his whiskers, but it was hard to tell. "Why do you call me dragon?"

"Because you are. I know this because I was once like you, in another life."

"Liar!" He roared. The cave shook, and more ice broke off and skidded down the hill. This wasn't going well. "If you had been a drakoi, you would not have insulted me by trying to sneak into my lair."

"I wasn't trying to sneak in."

"You did not announce yourself."

"You didn't give me chance."

"You were sneaking."

"I was climbing."

"You look sneaky."

"Oh, come on. I can't help how I look."

He sniffed. "You are no dragon. You are a mortal. I shall eat you, and then I shall eat your pig-skin friends skulking in the trees."

"I said, I *was* a dragon. I was cursed, and now I'm just a mortal." I drew the blade quicker than I had ever drawn a sword in my life. "A mortal with a blade that can kill you." Thunder rumbled overhead, and the blade gleamed like polished silver. We stared at each other for what felt like a very long time until, praise be to all the denizens of heaven and hell, he burst out laughing.

"Not quite the reaction I was expecting." To give him his due, he had quite the infectious giggle, and very soon I found myself sniggering. I lowered *Consequence*. "Seriously though, I did save your life, and you do owe me."

"Saved my life?" He snorted. "I was playing with them. But if nothing else, you have made me laugh. But why have you come here? I have no gold to reward you with, no magical swords." He gestured to *Consequence*. "I certainly don't have anyone chained up in need of rescuing. Speaking of which, did you see that little shit, the one with the Raven Knight?"

"The old cove?"

"Aye, Barantz. Did you see his 'apprentice'?"

"I, maybe. Thorval or something?"

"Thorfir, that's the one. Useless wretch typical of the youth of today. He Should never have been made an apprentice if you ask me." He leaned his elbows upon the flattened head of an ancient stalagmite, the grey roots of which must have been planted when the world was young. "I remember when Barantz was apprenticed to old Komita. Now she was a fine Raven, a worthy adversary, and Barantz had promise. But then…" He made a drinking motion. "He had issues, poor fellow. Possibly my fault. I did destroy Unkindness Keep and eat Komita, but it was a good fight and a worthy death…" He laughed as old coves do when they cast their minds upon the seas of reverie and drift into the deep waters of the past. As I felt we were getting along, I let him go on a bit before clearing my throat. His unnerving grey gaze focused on me. I saw the shadow of the dragon in his human features and wished with all my heart I could see it in my own. "What did you say you wanted? If it's gold I don't have any."

Sensing they were kindred spirits in age and character I thought I'd try a blag. "I came for the Dvor's heart. He sent me to fetch it."

He frowned. "The what?"

"The sorcerer who lives down the road? He said his heart was here."

It took a moment but then enlightenment dawned. "Oh, him. He plays with the dead, you know. I don't judge; I've known some very amicable undead, and to be honest, when it comes to mortals those that are living are, for the most part, a sack of arseholes."

"I can't argue with that."

He nodded his approval. "Maybe there is something of the scale about you. I'll tell you what. I'll take your word that you helped thwart the Ravens' unjust attempt at wreaking vengeance upon me. Give me the sword, and I'll give you the heart, and we'll call it even."

I reached for the barrow sword. He snorted and shrugged his shoulders which sounded like leathery wings creaking ready to unfurl. With some reluctance, I offered him *Consequence*, hilt first. Even though we were in a cave, snow clouds raced across the shining, grey blade. He smiled as he took it.

"It's been a long time, old friend..." he said and ran a grey claw along the edge, drawing sparks from the metal. He once again lost himself so completely in the stacks of memory that I felt I was alone. After some minutes he stretched, as though waking from a deep sleep. The shadow of wings patterned the cave wall.

Although a man stood before me, the majestic presence of a dragon filled the cavern. I took a step back for fear of being trampled in the moment of transformation that I felt was about to occur. But he didn't change. The presence diminished, the light of remembered triumphs faded from his eyes and was replaced by the ashen gaze of weighted years.

"They're all gone now, you know. Enemies… Friends. All of them. All that mattered anyway." His cold gaze drifted from me to the wintery sky. "Time for me to be going too. Somewhere high, I think. Somewhere nice and cold to sleep the winter through." He shot me a wicked grin. "High enough that thieves cannot reach it." He stood at the mouth of the cave, the blade in his hand a suggestion of light painted with racing shadows.

"What about the heart?" I said, pushing my luck as far as I dared.

He gestured dismissively to the rear of the cavern and the fissure through which a dirge wind droned. And then he leaped. The mortal guise fell away, and the dragon took to the wing. Two powerful beats and he soared into the cloud-crowned heights. His ragged wings wove snow flurries like ribbons, and his ice-honed roar summoned lightning from the sky.

I was so jealous. Mother had saved my life, but I'd lost so much. Memories crashed upon me like a landslide; Malin, Delgaro, the White Palace…home. I missed them all. I missed being a dragon. So much better to have never known such power than to have it taken away. Morose and ill-humored, I approached the fissure. The reek of dragon shit was so pungent that it made my eyes water.

A short, angled passage led down from the cavern. Although well-greased by decades of excreta, I wasn't surprised to see that it was mostly clear. For you see, much like rabbits, dragons shit neat, round pellets. Alas for me, dragon pellets are as big as an ogren's head.

But I digress.

Feeling a mixture of reluctance and anticipation, I made my way to the end of the passage. It opened onto another cavern. The roof was toothed with gleaming stalactites, between which beetles swarmed, and bats huddled. In the center of the cavern rose an island that looked like a massive, broken stalagmite. A black stone column stood upon the island. Bolted to it was a clawed, iron hand. Clutched within it was what I guessed was the Dvor's 'heart'. It might have been glass, or perhaps a huge chunk of ruby, for it shone with a deep, bloody luster. Whatever it was, it was mine for the taking just as soon as I worked out how to cross the lake of steaming dragon shit that surrounded it.

Chapter Twenty-Four

I thrust my barrow sword through the hard crust of dragon crap. The tip did not reach the bottom before I ran out of blade.

Cursing, I withdrew it and flicked the ordure from the steel and wiped it on my coat before the acidic shit began to eat through the metal. Fresh or rotted, dragon crap isn't good for steel, skin, or scales.

The island was roughly thirty-five feet from the mouth of the passage, not an impossible leap with a good tailwind. I could fetch Swann and get him to apport me, but if I did that, I'd have to talk to him and Nic and I didn't want to do that until I'd exhausted every other option to reach the prize. Also, I wanted to get a good look at the sparkle before they did.

I cast my gaze to the cave ceiling, which was alive with all manner of critters going about their business oblivious to my presence. It was the perfect roost for the colony of bats hanging above the fetid brew.

Like the rooftops of Appleton, the ceiling would be my road. I plotted the path I would take as I secured those things about my person that I might lose before beginning the climb. It was only a short distance, but I tested every hold. One slip would plunge me into, if not a world of shit, a good-sized bath of the stuff.

"Chas?" Ockzar's trembling voice echoed down the passage. "Breed, are you here?"

"In here," I shouted, startling a flock of beetles to noisy flight.

"Where? I can see a tunnel. Are you down there? I'm coming down." The beetles I'd disturbed swarmed down the passage, chased by a cloud of bats. The echo of chitinous and coriaceous wings was accompanied by the sound of Ockzar yelling. I kept climbing. After the flapping and the screaming stopped, Ockzar's fear-frozen face peered from the passage.

"That smell. It's horrible. Is that?"

"Yes." I continued to climb towards the heart. "Don't pull a face, I know you've smelled worse."

"I was trying to put that behind me. What are you doing?"

"Have a guess. Where are the others?"

"Hiding in the trees. When they saw the dragon, they sent me up to see if you were, you know." He shoved his glasses up his nose.

"And they sent you rather than come themselves?"

"Swann and I drew straws." His gaze tracked to the heart in the claw. "Is that it?"

"I fucking hope so, or this is an unpleasant waste of time and a good sword."

"Do be careful."

"Oh, all right then." I know he was only trying to be helpful in that irritating, state-the-obvious way humans did when they had nothing useful to say, but I was being hissed at by beetles the size of my head while bats were pissing on me. The last thing I needed was Ockzar offering advice and gasping every time I moved. Lightheaded from the smell, I swung onto the filth-besmeared plinth.

"Careful!" Ockzar yelled and gestured protectively.

I cut him from my attention and focused on the heart and the claw. Up close, I could see that it wasn't a ruby. What I'd taken for translucency was hollowness. The color came from the contents of the heart-shaped vessel,

which I'd bet my wily old arse was the Dvor's claret.
After all, in the necromantic arts, blood was power.

'Now all you have to do is take it...' The wind
blowing through the cave seemed to whisper.

"All I have to do is take it."

"What?" Ockzar called.

"Nothing. Just talking to the ghosts."

"There are ghosts?"

"Hush, or they'll hear you. You don't want that."

I only had half an eye on him, but I swear I saw him
cover his mouth to stop himself nervously chattering as
he was wont to do. The blessed silence which followed
allowed me to return my full attention to the Vascellum.
It was just sitting there, lightly gripped in the clawed
fingers, waiting to be lifted. Care would be required.
The anatomically correct heart pipes weren't stoppered,
so tipping the vessel might spill whatever the fuck was
in it. Dragon guardian aside, the claw had to be for more
than decorative purposes. Lacking magical skills, I
would have to work with more mundane means to
determine how it had been protected. I'd bet my
wotnots that it was warded out the arse and defended by
a raft of fiendish traps. I looked for any marks in the
dust which lay thickly upon it (there were none). I
scrutinized the claw, the plinth, and the roof from every
angle. To my dismay, I did not find any mechanisms or
sigils warning me of what lay in wait for a careless thief.

But then, perhaps there weren't any? They say the suns shine on every dog's arse at least once in its lifetime. Could this be my day?

As I reached towards the claw, Ockzar sneezed.

I rounded upon him. "Why not just throw a fucking rock at me and have done?"

"Sorry," he stage whispered. "It's the dust."

When I regained my composure, I carefully slipped my hands between the steel talons and took hold of the vessel. I was prepared for something to happen, so I didn't start when I felt a pulse quicken as I touched the glass. I didn't move, didn't fucking breathe. Like a rock, I kept a hold of my prize and waited for gears to turn and whatever traps I had triggered to spring.

Nothing happened.

I waited a little longer. When nothing continued to happen, I dared a glance towards Ockzar. He shrugged. Gently, *ever so* gently, I began to maneuver the heart from the claws, no mean feat given it was now as lively as a jar of angry bees. Glass scraped against iron. I turned the heart and eased it from the claw.

I don't suffer from sweaty palms, and after a lifetime practicing all manner of sly prestidigitation, I have become quite the dexterous cove. But I'm not the hero of a novel; perfect when they need to be. Like you, I'm fallible at the most inopportune moments, like right then. Today's touch of ill-fortune was catching my sleeve on the tip of a claw as I withdrew the heart from its clutches. The tiny snag was enough to jar my arm, and the already trembling Vascellum leaped from my grasp. Time slowed as I chased it to the ground. I caught it; the contents slopped up the pipes and splashed over my hands. It was most definitely blood but not your ordinary, run-of-the-mill claret, oh no. The splash ran across my hands and then appeared to sink through skin and scale.

A pit opened in my gut. "That can't be good." The world spun so quickly I felt like I'd been slammed headfirst into a charging urux. I passed out. When I opened my eyes, I saw mountains rise through ashen seas, touch a fire-scarred sky, erupt, collapse, and drown beneath molten waves...

"Breed!" I blinked. The hellscape was gone. Ockzar was in the passage. He was shouting and flailing his arms in a panic.

I was still holding the Vascellum. I could hear it beating, the sound growing louder. No, it wasn't the heart. It was the beating of wings. Hundreds of them. "Get down, Ockzar!"

He hit the ground as a cloud of shrieking beetles and bats swooped into the cavern and arrowed towards me. I crouched by the plinth, curled around the Vascellum, and tried to brace. Teeth like razors and claws like knives shredded my clothes and tore into my flesh.

Blood ran like rain. With a grim sense of acceptance, I realized this was a storm I could not weather.

And then they were gone, and Swann was beside me.

"Can you hear me?" he asked.

I was in the dragon cave. The bats hadn't gone; I had. Swann, Nic and Ockzar were peering down at me. "I don't feel very good." I heard myself say as the world began to darken at the edges.

I dreamed of bats, beetles, dragons, and *blood*. Lakes of blood, blood-red mountains beneath burning clouds lit by crimson lightning. It was not the worst dream I'd ever had or of a world I had ever visited so far as I knew, but something within me longed for it, like a child longs for its mother's breast.

The dream drifted into nonsense, and awareness of the waking world returned in pieces; the feel of a blanket, the smell of woodsmoke, the prickle of pine needles sharp against my tender back. My coat had been thrown over me, and my pack was my pillow. I tasted snow, but I didn't feel the cold because my lacerated skin burned with the heat of infection. Nearby, someone was stirring a pot of chai. The spoon thunked loudly against the metal pot. *Tunk, tunk, tunk.* Wood crackled and spit.

"Pine is the worst firewood," Ockzar muttered.

"Shut up, gundiguts," said Nic, without vehemence.

"Enough, please. I have a headache," said Swann. The snap of a locket clasp followed his words. I reluctantly opened my eyes. Nic was sitting by the fire, cradling the heart like it was a babe, a contented smile on his face. Ockzar was making chai, and Swann was staring moodily into flames that he had fashioned to resemble the face of his lover. When he saw that I was looking at him, the talismancer touched an amber bead on his wrist, and the face in the flames vanished.

He smiled wearily. "You spend more time unconscious than awake."

I sat up. "It's not my fault." Someone had kindly wrapped me up and put a pair of gloves on my savaged hands, but I could feel the dozens of tiny cuts when I flexed my fingers. The clothes I'd been dressed in were too big for me and smelled of dog rat. Nic's spare clothes then. "The fucking bats went insane."

Ockzar poured a mug of chai and passed it to me across the fire. He looked relieved, or perhaps I saw what I wanted to see in his expression.

"You did it. I have to admit, after everything; getting banged up, taken down by ghouls, and that dragon." Nic gave a wry smile as he wrapped the heart. "I had my doubts about you, but I should have known Leo knew what he was doing."

I think he was trying to compliment me, but as I felt like I'd been skinned and dipped in salt, I wasn't feeling the love. I raised the mug in salute. *Fuck Leo and fuck you too.*

"We'll head back at first light. According to the map, there's a village south of here." Nic jabbed the map. "We'll stock up on supplies there and continue south before cutting up towards the coast."

"Back to Sevast?" I didn't want to go back to the place where I'd been conscripted. Although now I wasn't under the power of Swann's shitty geas, the outcome would be very different if they tried to pinch me again.

"You would be better heading for Crakanov," said Ockzar. "It's about twenty miles from Sevast. It's where the fishing fleet overwinters but they'll still be making runs to the Empire now, before the ice comes in."

"No," said Nic. "I have contacts in Sevast."

"So do I." I took another swig of chai. "They arrested me and threw me in prison."

"Breed's right. It is a dangerous place for fugitives," Ockzar added. I sensed his desire to avoid the port was more to do with his safety than ours.

"You're coming with us?" I asked. The chai was warm, spiced with rum. He looked pained. I imagined it was because he didn't have the slightest idea where he was going or what he was going to do.

"He ain't coming with us," Nic growled. "No way."

I stood up. Even the soles of my feet hurt. "If you want to come with us, Ockzar, you can."

"Don't I get a say?" Swann asked.

"No," Nic and I answered.

Ockzar sat up, cleared his throat, and affected an air of nonchalance even though I could see the big vein in his neck beating like a marching drum. "I feel it is my duty to accompany you to Crakanov if that is where you choose to go. I cannot go with you to Sevast because I am known there."

Nic snorted as he finished wrapping the heart before putting it in the map box. I noticed now that the lid was marked with the letter 'L'. He turned the key in the lock; four tumblers rolled. Like an amateur, he let everyone see him put the key in his coat pocket. I tugged off one of my gloves. The flesh was livid around the many tiny wounds. There was no sign of pus and no heat beyond the sear of fresh wounds but being savaged by rabid bats in a cave full of dragon shit was never a good thing. I drained the mug of chai which did nothing to quench my thirst.

"You two can do what you want. I'm going to find passage in Crakanov," I said and saw Ockzar's shoulders immediately relax. Still feeling like hammered shit, I lay back and began to drowse. *'Night is a beast made all of darkness, with teeth of ice and cold stars for eyes'*, a voice whispered in my mind. I yawned, tasted death in the wind.

Chapter Twenty-Five

By the time we reached the road to Crakanov, I was looking forward to spending the night in a building with walls and a roof and other such luxuries. I could survive well enough out in the wilderness, but I preferred the wildness of cities. I missed the sounds; the warm bodies pressed close, the smell of... *Blood. I miss the smell of hot, sweet blood.* A sibilant voice whispered in my mind. And it was true. The desire to sup claret had been upon me since Duke Leo saved me from the Paradox of Power, and it had only grown more insistent after finding the Vascellum.

I did not feel myself, or rather I did not feel alone in my own skin. Something, some blood-borne parasite, had infected me. I was sure that I could hear it whispering to me, telling me of its hunger, of the dreadful thirst that only blood could slake.

"Breed!" Ockzar yelled.

I looked up. A pair of yuraxus were bearing down on me, steaming the air with their hot, snotty breath. I stepped aside and ducked beneath the lazy sweep of their untrimmed horns.

"Watch where you're going, you fucking dolt!" the wagon driver bellowed as she drove the beasts past, whip raised in threat. *Tear her head off*, the voice whispered in my mind. *Tear her head off, drink her like wine*.

"Fuck off." I hissed through gritted teeth.

"What were you thinking?" It was Ockzar. He looked concerned.

"Not much, why?"

"You were almost crushed to death."

I laughed. "No, I wasn't."

"You seem distracted."

"What do you expect? You never shut up."

"That's both untrue and unfair. You've not been yourself since the cave. You should have rested longer."

"I'm fine, see?" I raised my hands to show how well the bites had healed. I could see he wanted to challenge the claim, but perhaps sensing he was onto a loser, he held his tongue.

As we walked, my gaze ranged over the long procession of wagons drifting towards the city. A coffin on the back of one of them caught my eye. Two riders on yuraxus flanked the wagon. A huge cove with horns and a boy trailed behind on foot.

"Breed?" Ockzar enquired.

I'd stopped again, this time as I tried to fathom what it was about the funeral party that had caught my eye. With a start, I realized that I knew them. In as much as I'd stolen a sword from them. "That isn't good."

"What isn't?" Ockzar's gaze followed mine. "The coffin?"

"No."

He didn't look convinced. "It's not unusual to see coffins being brought into the city for funeral blessings. I admit, it is superstitious, but not unusual."

"It's not the coffin." It was the people with the coffin that concerned me, although I couldn't tell him that.

His smile widened. "It's the contents, eh? I understand. After everything we've seen, I've been jumping at my own shadow." He shuddered. "I content myself with knowing what we have experienced is uncommon."

"You're right there."

"I have my moments." He forced a weak smile before his face fell. "I'm going to miss you."

"Come with us, then. See the world." I don't know why I said it, but in truth, a part of me would miss him too. Like a pulled muscle, I'd got used to the Voskvan's presence.

"I cannot. My people need me here. As much as I would like to see the world, I cannot abandon them or the cause."

"Which cause is that again?" I teased.

"Reform of the Archonate," he whispered after first glancing over his shoulder.

I could have hugged the little twerp. He really believed he could change the world by writing a few pamphlets. That he believed the written word could sway hearts, change minds, and inspire great deeds made me smile. Such foolishness, such naivety! As all who bartered morals for power knew, it was steel and gold, not ink and parchment that commanded mortal minds. I put my arm around his shoulders. "Come on, lets catch up with the others."

Annoyed that he'd been outvoted and eager to get out of Voskva with the prize, Nic had plowed ahead through the slower traffic. Being a spider-limbed stick insect of a human, Swann wasn't far behind him, leaving Ockzar and me to bring up the rear. I didn't want to lose sight of the White Rat and the Vascellum, so I coaxed an extra measure of speed from the Voskvan, and we managed to catch up. As we were in public, my ill-matched crew kept conversation strictly to mundane matters. Alas, Ockzar took the lengthy silences as an invitation to regale me with facts about the port city, its inhabitants, and their customs.

Cultural distractions aside, I was on my uppers, not least because of the proximity of the crew I'd just robbed, but I was always wary when visiting strange cities. Because of the unusually open-minded and athletic predilections of my parents, I was a red and scaly minority in a world peopled mainly by soft skins that came in various, dull shades of beige through to earthen. Even the shapeshifter fit in better than I did, for although Nic was on the large side, his human bulk was not exceptional here. As for Swann, he could very well have been a Voskvan. Like the majority, he was sun-starved and currently sported a straggly, blonde beard as was the fashion hereabouts. I pulled my hood down, and my scarf up as the queue for the gate slowed and waited for my turn to enter.

Due to the cold and inclement weather, the guards at the gate were waving everyone through without paying much attention to anyone. With Nic forging a path like an icebreaker, we pushed our way through the crowd and towards food vendors and tavern booths whose wares enticed the hungry and, more importantly, thirsty travelers. For no reason in particular, we cut right instead of left, or perhaps it was Fate's choice because it was bored and in need of entertainment. Whichever it was, we burst from the crowded square into a street of blacksmiths, wheelwrights, and cheap tavern tents. To my great joy and delight, the carriage bearing the body of poor old Barantz was hitched outside the nearest wheelwright.

The injured archer and the sorceress were inside, huddled by the firepit. The wheelwright was outside, tutting and chin-stroking by the back axle of the wagon with the bull-headed cove. The only sign he'd been battered was that one of his horns was broken – not bad considering he'd gone toe to claw with a dragon. Young Thorfir was tethering the yuraxus. The boy was garbed in ill-fitting armor, and an ordinary-looking sword was strapped to his oversized belt. When he turned, I saw his eyes were red-rimmed. I wasn't surprised, *Consequence* was a fine sword, and he must have been gutted to lose it. Of the whole crew, he was the one who might have seen me when I lifted the blade. It seemed unlikely as they hadn't chased me down, but a niggling doubt always lingered in situations like this.

"Any idea who this bunch might be?"

Desperate to have an answer for everything, Ockzar smiled and raised a crooked finger which he used to indicate the commencement of a lesson. "I would say they're members of a Mendicant Cult. See the banner?"

He pointed to what I'd taken to be a blanket draped over the coffin. "It says, 'Raven Order', or something. I can't quite make it out from here." He leaned in and whispered. "Not all of the Mendicants are Voskvan, but the Archonate tolerates them for some reason."

"What are they, sellswords?"

"You mean mercenaries?"

"Aye."

"No." He shook his head disapprovingly and huffed. "They are much worse. The mendicant orders think themselves to be, how would you say it? 'knights' or perhaps 'monks' is a better word?" He gave me a questioning look.

"I have no idea."

"In my opinion." He lowered his voice. "They are quasi-mystical fanatics and cultists, trading in ignorance and superstition."

"They do what now?"

"They kill monsters."

I snorted. "Not always."

"What was that?"

"Nothing."

Much to my annoyance, Nic allowed himself to be collared by a wench at one of the tavern tents who suggestively invited him to sample her wares. Their ribald laughter did not go down well with the big mercenary by the wagon who shot them a filthy look. They didn't notice or didn't care and continued to flirt loudly. I sensed the seed of a bad situation was being sown, but before I had the chance to go over and tell Nic to shut his pie hole Ockzar put his hand on my arm.

"You know," he began, choosing the worst time to strike up a meaningful conversation. "I want you to know that no matter what happens, I value your friendship. You're the only person in a long time who has not only shown me respect, but you have also shown me—"

"Just shut the fuck up a minute," I snapped.

"—kindness." His face fell like the pieces of a broken mirror.

It has been said that I can be a proper cunt at times but being mean to the Voskvan felt like I was punching a baby in the throat. "I'm sorry, Ockzar. It's just that…" Bullhead was still glaring murderously at Nic, who was loitering by the tent and joking with the wench. "We might have a problem."

"My lord lies dead before you. Have some respect!" Bullhead shouted at Nic and stomped into the middle of the muddy alley. Not that I like to characterize people by what they looked like, but he didn't strike me as the kind of cove who could deal with feelings of loss and grief without killing someone.

Not bothering to look up from the wench's dumplings, Nic waved him away with all the sensitivity of a punch in the jewels. Similarly lacking in diplomatic aplomb, the Bull snorted, lowered his head, and unslung his very big spear. I could see where this was going, as could the sorceress and the archer, whose attention had suddenly turned to the street and was now fixed on their angry comrade. The locals were also wise enough to know trouble when they saw it and melted away like snow on a pyre.

"Oh, this doesn't look good," said Ockzar.

"No, it doesn't. Who's your money on?"

"Someone needs to do something," he said. To my surprise, he took a step forward and cleared his throat. "Sir," he said to Bullhead. "Might I have a word?"

"What the fuck do you want?" Bull snarled at Ockzar.

"My employer is foreign and means no offence, sir."

The bull said something in Voskvan that I didn't catch. Nic raised the small cup of spirit he'd just been handed.

Hands clasped like a supplicant, Ockzar nodded at Bull. It was impressive how quickly he assumed the same groveling demeanor I'd seen him adopt when we were in the mines. It was a peculiar magic that he had mastered, to appear so weak, so entirely beneath contempt, that thugs couldn't even be bothered to give him a kicking. "I assure you sir, he would be mortified if he understood our customs, but he's from the Empire and you know what they're like."

"Tell him to stop guffawing and shut his mouth or I'll shut it for him."

Hero that he was, Swann ducked into the beer tent like he didn't know us. Rather than follow him in and put an end to it, Nic continued to loiter in the doorway, a wicked gleam in his eyes. He wasn't just being dense. He was deliberately baiting the wouldbe dragon slayer.

"Absolutely, sir. So very sorry." Ockzar bobbed his head submissively and slowly edged around the mendicant. Seeing the situation was about to be resolved, I relaxed, which was when I realized I'd been tense. Alas, my relief was short-lived. Out of nowhere, the big bastard's temper reignited, and he shoved Ockzar in the back as he passed.

"Go on, you little *zyavoch!*" Bullhead snapped. "Tell that grinning fool to change his face before I run him through." It was just a tap but hard enough to throw Ockzar off balance. He stumbled, slipped, and sprawled full length in the mud. Nic roared with laughter, as did the tavern wench, further angering the bull-headed cove.

At this point several things happened at once.

The bull raised his spear and drew back his arm. Ockzar screamed. The sorceress shouted something, and blue fire wreathed her staff. The archer strung her bow. The wheelwright dived under the wagon. Thorfir was knocked off his feet by a rearing yuraxus. Swann stuck his head out of the tent flap, and Nic shoved him back inside.

Without thinking, I grabbed Bull by the scruff and hurled him towards the cart. I had intended to spoil his aim, but I was much stronger than I realized, which surprised me more than anyone. Instead of joining Ockzar in the icy mud, the bull hit the coffin and knocked it off the cart. There was a loud thump followed by the squeak of nails and a collective gasp as the lid tore loose, and the body was pitched from the bone box.

"Oh, bollocks," I said. '*Kill them all,*' hissed the voice in my head. I stood a moment, shocked by my prodigious strength, irritated by the annoying voice taunting me from inside my skull, and concerned that I had just made a lot of enemies. "It really isn't my fault," I said as an arrow spun towards me. It appeared to be flying unnaturally slowly which allowed me ample time to sidestep. It was followed by a finger of crackling, blue fire which burned the air where but a moment before I had been standing. I shielded my eyes and watched the coruscating thorns of magical energy crawl past me and burn a hole in the side of the tavern tent. By now, Ockzar was trying to get up, but like the arrow, he was moving very slowly. I saw that he was shouting at me, but his words were unintelligible, drawn-out to the point that they sounded more like the drone of a bee than words. Bullhead came to his senses and climbed unsteadily to his feet. '*Kill them, drink their blood*' the voice demanded. "This isn't right." I said, and then time speeded up.

"Breed!" Ockzar yelled.

"Ockzar?" I reached out, helped him back on his feet. "Something isn't right."

"You think?" Quite rightly, he sounded angry.

"I don't feel right. We should get away from here now, before the…" Bullhead was behind him. He raised his weapon; steel gleamed grey upon the spearhead, the shaft flexed as it flew. Ockzar was between it and me. I shoved him aside and caught it in the gut. For all of two heartbeats, it felt no worse than a good hard punch. Then the pain hit. The thing in my head recoiled. I could see Swann straining to get past Nic, a look of horror on his face. The look on Nic's was a study of cold indifference. My prodigious strength deserted me. I sank to my knees thinking that this was such a stupid, pointless way to die and that my knees were cold and muddy.

Ockzar sank beside me, his hands hovering, unsure. He reached for the spear. I shoved his hands away. "Leave it, I'm screwed." I managed to say through the blistering pain. Bullhead stomped over with the sorceress. The archer with the splinted leg stayed where she was with an arrow loosely nocked to her bowstring.

I tried to push Ockzar away, tried to tell him to fuck off, but my mouth was full of blood, not words. Fucking Nic. As soon as the opportunity presented itself, he'd got rid of me in such a way that it wouldn't look like it was anything to do with him. It wasn't that I hadn't seen it coming. I'd noticed the change in him as soon as we'd got the Vascellum, but I'd been too preoccupied with the fucking voices in my head to do anything about it. I watched in grim anticipation of more pain as Bullhead reached for the spear. Pull or push? I wondered idly.

He pushed, drove me back into the ground. The sorceress shouted at him, grabbed his arm. He shrugged her off, gave it a twist, and then withdrew. The pain vanished. I focused on Ockzar. The daft fucker was crying, peering down at me like a beetroot with a face.

'*You should bite him, drink his blood,*' the serpent whispered.

"Oh, do fuck off," I replied.

I had strange dreams, which meant that I wasn't dead. I dreamed that I was looking down at myself. I was lying in the sleety, muddy road between the tavern tent and the wheelwright. The battered and bloated corpse of Barantz was face down beside the wagon. A pack of optimistic dogs lurked nearby, sniffing the blood flowing from my carcass and the juices that were leaking out of Barantz. A Militiaman was arguing with the sorceress. Bullhead was angrily pacing, and the archer was comforting the boy. The wheelwright was with the tavern wench, trying to look inconspicuous, and my comrades were nowhere to be seen.

I wasn't angry with Ockzar, but there was a cold corner of hell waiting for those faithless shitstains Nicodemus and Swann.

"…I was angry," said Bullhead.

"…irresponsible…" the sorceress snapped.

"Stop it, please, just stop…" A child sobbed.

"You must come…"

"Just fuck off…"

"Why don't you make me?"

Magic warmed the air.

I don't know what happened next. I was nothing more than a supernumerary in this particular drama. Having played my part, I was unceremoniously loaded onto a cart like a sack of turnips and driven off stage.

In my strange dream of life-during-death, I noted that I did not go alone to the paupers' pit. I traveled in the company of a cove who had carelessly managed to lose their legs and a shriveled old bone bag that had frozen as solid as a rock. Being the last one in the cart was not exactly a privilege but being the first one out meant that I avoided being doused in quicklime after being deposited in the current grave of the unwanted. And that was a good thing because quicklime burns, and I wasn't dead. Not entirely.

I was mostly dead and entirely furious with myself. If only I hadn't tried to protect that idiot Ockzar. What was it they said? 'No good deed goes unpunished'. Dirt rained down upon me. Below me, corpse gas hissed as decomposing bodies split. The mass began to shift as rats and maggots got busy with the feast. I hadn't been eaten by rats before and wondered if it was like being torn apart by demons. While I mused upon the subject, time passed. Frost, that quiet assassin, crept over the pit and mercifully killed the stench of corruption. Snow fell and blanketed the unsightly tangle of limbs in a pristine shroud. It was all rather peaceful until voices and a searching light intruded on my deathless not slumber.

"Here," called a gruff voice.

"Well, start digging." It was Ockzar.

"You didn't pay for digging."

"I most certainly did. Hey, wait! Come back, you dogs."

"What was that? What did you say?"

"Nothing," he said, and gave a hopeless sigh.

Silence and snow fell.

"Gasvoy's Ghost." Cursing, Ockzar slid into the pit. The mound shifted; stiff limbs creaked. Trembling, sweating hands grabbed my arms and tried to untangle me from the frozen knot of bodies. He failed. Snowflakes and tears fell on my cheeks. Sobbing was followed by more cursing, which was followed by more sobbing, and then…

The tune changed. I heard a sharp wince of pain just before sweet, hot blood dripped onto my lips. My drifting mind focused.

"Oh, Ocky, you are so clumsy." His mother laughs, and it is the most joyful sound he has ever heard. I am with him, tied to him by the thread of his life's essence that is dripping into my mouth. I am with him for first steps, first love, first loss. For a brief, dizzying moment, I am him.

"Bite him." *The thing in my mind has woken, and it is hungry.* "Drain him dry," *the Vascellum demands. I surge from the grave, grip his bloody wrist, and bite down.*

"Breed, no! Stop! Please, gods. Stop…" *The hot coppery warmth spreads like fire through my cold body. Strength returns to frozen limbs, and the slow beat of my heart quickens.* "Breed…please…" Ockzar begs.

Ah, Ockzar, poor Ockzar.

What is it they say about good deeds?

Chapter Twenty-Six

Something hard and flat hit me on the head. I ignored the first strike because I was happily supping Ockzar's claret, but then it happened again. And again. I looked up and got a shoe in the chops.

"Ow!" The blood trance lifted. "Ockzar?" The Voskvan was kneeling over me, shoe in hand. "You just hit me with a fucking shoe." I rubbed my stinging cheek.

"You were drinking my blood, you, you *odbyt*!" He waved the shoe threateningly while clutching his injured hand to his chest.

"What?" Sense returned. "Oh. Yes. I suppose that was a bit rude." I sheepishly wiped the deliciousness from my lips.

"A bit rude?" I thought he was going to hit me again. He snorted. "Be thankful I only hit you with a shoe and not a sword or a rock or something equally deadly." Still nursing his injured wrist, he stumbled from the pit. I tried to steady him, but he shrugged me off and struggled out alone.

"I'm really sorry, Ocky." The warmth of a summer's day in his family dacha lingered in my mind. I could still hear the laughter and feel the soft breeze blowing through the window redolent with the scent of roses...

"Don't you 'Ocky' me," he hissed as he brushed himself down. "I wish I'd never come here."

I crawled after him. My claws felt a little sharper, my senses keener, but I was weak. "Wait, Ockzar. Please. I'm sorry. Please, wait." I lay in the snow, my heart pounding with stolen blood, my head aching with a surfeit of memories and burdened by an alien presence. The thing was still there, poised like a serpent ready to strike. *'Drink, yes. Drink little Ocky'.* Its laughter taunted me. "I'm sorry, Ockzar. Please, come back."

He paced between grave pits, unsure, hurt, and unusually for him, still angry. "What? So, you can bite me again?"

'Yes, bite him,' the serpent hissed. "Fuck off."

"What did you say?"

"Not you. I need your help, Ockzar."

He stopped, hovered nervously beyond my reach. "What are you, Breed?"

"I don't know." It's funny how refreshing the truth always tastes, like a rare and exotic fruit.

"You almost threw that oaf over a wagon."

"That was not my plan and anyway, he was asking for it."

"I agree, he was, but that's not the point. I know you are a strong being, but you're not that strong. How did you do it? How is it we are speaking when you were dead and buried?"

"I don't know, but like you, I can guess. That's why you're here, right? That's why you fed me your blood." I looked at the hole in my gut. It was sore, but it was healing.

"I had an inkling." He reached into his pocket and took something that he turned thoughtfully in his trembling hands before throwing it on the ground. It was a sharpened, wooden stake. I picked it up. It had been whittled from thorn wood and was stamped with the fist and sun of the Archonate.

"You know it doesn't work if you just throw it on the ground."

"I know what to do with it, thank you very much."

"Why didn't you use it then?"

"I don't know. I had every intention of doing so." He smiled sadly and shrugged. "I just couldn't."

"Is that an official stamp?"

"Yes. I bought it from a jorskal. It's been officially blessed. It, er, should burn the flesh of infernals and purge evil from the soul. If you believe in that kind of thing."

I picked it up and was quietly relieved when my flesh did not ignite. "Either you've been done, or I'm the wrong kind of infernal." A terrible, gut-clenching hunger pang seized me. "So, what happened after that cunt stabbed me?"

He groaned. "It was chaos, horrible, you wouldn't believe it. A crowd gathered, everyone started shouting. Then the militia and an archolya turned up. There was a fight. I don't know what about or who started it. Oh, and a dog bit me, and then I hid behind the beer tent."

"Very wise." Too tired to move, I lay where I was and watched the snow flurries dance. "What about Nic and Swann, what happened to them?"

"They sneaked out of the tent through the back. To be fair, Swann didn't want to leave, but I heard Nic say that they had to get to the docks."

"You hid from them?" I asked as dog rats regrouped and began fighting over the fresher meat.

"Based on their conversation, I felt it the best course."

"Give me the abridged version."

"Nic said that they should leave with the Vascellum and that if he saw me, he'd wring my neck."

"That was it?"

"You said abridged."

"Not that abridged. Didn't they say anything about me?"

He drew an exasperated breath. "Nic said, you had served your purpose. He was very dismissive of you and your abilities, disparaging even."

"Cunt."

"Quite. Then Swann said something on the lines of what would Leo say about leaving you and indeed, letting you die. Nic said he knew his own brother and so long as he got the Vascellum it didn't matter what happened to the thief. He said you were a useless scaly—"

"Yes, all right. What else?"

"Swann said, he didn't know how you did what you did to the mercenary. Nic said something like it was a gift from Leo. It was all very cryptic. And then Nic called you a no- mark and Swann said, speaking of no-marks, what happened to Ockzar? Which coming from him is a joke." He gave a hard, fake laugh. "Nic said, if he knows what's good for him, by which he meant me, he's dug a hole and climbed in, and that's when he said if he saw me again, he'd wring my neck. And then the swine made some very derogatory comments about my mother. After that I presume that they headed to the docks. I stayed to find out what the militia were going to do with you, but they were busy trying to arrest the brute who stabbed you. There was some talk of selling your body to an anatomist, but the wheelwright said to send you to the communal grave pits, which, I might add, are free to all including non-citizens."

"Very generous."

"Isn't it? Having seen how you've been since the dragon's lair I was concerned you might you know, turn." He looked at his feet. "Anyway, that's when I decided to purchase the stake. I also hired a couple of watchmen to help me, the thieving liars."

"Help you what?"

"Find your body and you know, make sure you were…at rest. Anyway, here we are."

"Haven't you been a busy fellow."

"I am exhausted, a matter not helped by being bled by a six-foot mosquito."

"Do not liken me to a mosquito. I've had a bad do with that pernicious breed."

"Is there any breed you haven't had a bad do with?"

"You make a fair point. Nic's wrong about his brother, by the way. Leo wants me to return, or he wouldn't have…" Put a geas on me. "Made me promise to return." Now that I thought about it, the imperative to do so was as strong as ever.

"They are despicable, both of them."

"Aren't they though?" I wasn't surprised that they'd left me again. It was only ever a marriage of inconvenience as far as all were concerned. In Swann's case, I knew his leaving me wasn't personal. He was powerful in his own, Paradox and pel addled way, but he feared what Leo might do to his beloved Effie. The shapeshifting prick was another matter. "I'd like to have a little chat with Nic."

"Ah. That's a euphemism for wanting to slot him, isn't it?" Ockzar smiled. He was learning. "I shan't hold you back. He is a prime example of the corruption of privilege."

"He's a gang boss's enforcer."

"He is a noble of the Midnight Court, is he not? All those who maintain the titles and trappings of 'nobles' are cut from the same cloth, no matter to whom they hold allegiance. They are all members of inherently corrupt systems.

"Well, thank you for that lesson, Brother Ockzar."

"You're welcome."

"Sweet Salvation, I'm hungry," I said. Ockzar backed away. "Fear not, 'firebrand philosopher' is off the menu."

He smiled and stood a little taller. "You think I'm a firebrand?"

"I think you might want to look away." Before being forced to tell him I was being ironic, I rolled into the pit and did for the three nearest dog rats. I know I was upsetting the natural order of things, but even in nature, shit happens, and today that shit was me happening to the rats.

As I am not a monster, I killed them quickly and drained them dry before the blood had a chance to cool in their ratty veins. They were a poor vintage but enough to ease my cramping guts and lend strength to tired limbs. The memories carried in their blood were a tumble of fleeting images. They were gone as quickly as they came, making only the slightest impression on my over-burdened mind and rousing little interest from the thing lodging within me. It occurred to me that the voice in my head might be of my own making, that I could be as mad as a box of frogs. Either way, I was glad of the silence.

Refreshed, I climbed out of the pit and wondered if the slavering infernals I'd fought in the past had gone mad when they became blood drinkers. Was sanity the price they paid for immortality?

"Do you think infernals can walk abroad in daylight?" I asked Ockzar. He looked horrified. "What's wrong?" In a panic, I looked at my hands and felt my jaw. Aside from a spot of rat claret, everything seemed in order.

He swallowed. "You said 'look away', but I didn't. I regret that now."

"Oh, is that all? I was worried that I looked like a monstrous infernal."

"No." He shook his head vigorously. "No, you look fine. I mean, you're covered in blood, and the filth of the grave, but otherwise you look just peachy. As to your other question, I don't know if infernals can walk abroad in daylight, but we're about to find out." His gaze tracked to where the first rays of the first sun were biting into the dark rind of the horizon. Feeling a mix of dread and anticipation, I watched the light cut through the vestiges of night shadows and crawl towards me.

"What are you doing?" Ockzar asked.

"Waiting to see if I burst into flames."

"Ah, well, you might melt instead. I've heard that most types of infernals melt. Some explode, some implode, but both are apparently rare. Are you sure you want to take the chance that you might combust?" He snorted. "I can't believe we're even discussing this."

"I'm not discussing it, you are. I'm just the poor fucker who's worried they might burst into flames. Now I'm worried that I might also melt, explode or possibly implode."

"It's rare."

"It's shit."

"I'll just be over here." He backed away. "Just in case, you understand?"

"Aye. Thanks."

I dug my claws into my palms and faced the light. It wasn't warm, tempered as it was by the gelid air, but there is no light as sharp as that which shines in the morning. I braced and waited. When it hit me, I was relieved to discover that I didn't explode, burn, or fucking implode.

"How do you feel?" Ockzar called from where he was hiding behind a broken wagon.

"Cold. What happened to my coat?"

"I imagine the gravediggers must have taken it. They don't get paid much."

"I suppose I should be grateful that they didn't take my teeth."

"I'm not sure I share the sentiment," he said sniffily. "Wait, you bit me. Does that mean I'll acquire a taste for blood? Oh, do you think I'll be able to pick someone up with my bare hands?" He grinned.

"I don't know. I'm not an expert on this kind of thing. I don't even know what I am or what Leo did to me or…" Something stopped me from mentioning the Vascellum. "All I know is I have to get back home and possibly kill Nic. '*Yessss, kill them,*' the serpent hissed. "Shut up."

"I didn't say anything."

"Not you."

"No? Of course not. Why would I think you were talking to me?" He sounded disgruntled.

"Trust me, you don't want to know."

"Have it your way." He rubbed his eyes. "But why go back at all?"

"I thought you said you weren't going to ask?"

"About whom you were talking to if not me. I am absolutely dying to know why you are going back to the Empire."

 "I have to."

"Voskva is a big, beautiful country. You could lose a whole city in Turkaniv Forest alone. There's plenty of space for a thoasa, even a bright red one with a big mouth."

"Not when you make enemies like mine, Ockzar. Sometimes the whole world isn't big enough." I couldn't tell him that I had no choice, that Leo's power over me was literally flowing through my veins. *'I can help you,'* the voice in my head whispered. *'Just kill them, kill them all, and feed me, and I will make you strong.'*

Whatever it was, be it a conjuration of my insanity, or a bloodborne parasite that I'd picked up in the dragon's cave, it was growing louder, more insistent, and though I didn't want to admit it, stronger. I could feel it shaping the contours of my mind, fighting Leo's enchantment for possession of my soul.

As I looked like someone who had just crawled from their grave, I stayed out of sight while Ockzar paid for a room in a fleapit near the dock. I didn't question why he was helping me, and he didn't offer to explain, which suited us both. He had his reasons, and I had more important things to think about than fathoming them, like tracking Nic and Swann, killing the shapeshifting rat bastard, and taking the Vascellum. I also resolved that, if I had to, I'd do both of them. Swann had chosen his side, and even though he had the best of reasons, they meant nothing to me. That I couldn't trust him was all that mattered.

Ockzar went to the rag market, leaving me to clean myself up. The room was several notches below shabby, but there was a fire in the hearth, a table, a bed, and most importantly, a kettle. The window, which had glass in every pane, overlooked a fish market. Beyond the market, I could see the thin pewter line of the turgid ocean crosshatched with the black masts of ships. Before throwing the filthy water from the window, I peered at my reflection in the tin bowl. I looked like me. What scars I'd gained in recent times were healing well. I wondered what would happen when, *if* Leo released me from the spell of his blood magic. A gentle tap on the door provided a welcome distraction from troubling thoughts. "It's me," Ockzar whispered. "Ockzar."

I let him in. "Gasvoy's Ghost!" he exclaimed. "You could have warned me." He thrust a bundle of clothes into my arms before rushing inside gaze averted.

"Warned you what?" I closed and latched the door.

"That you were naked." He turned his back and went over to the hearth, blinkering his face with mittened hands.

"Fuck's sake. You didn't make this much of a fuss when you saw me in a grave pit."

"You were dressed in the pit."

"Well, I must say, your attitude is quite the kick in the vanities. I'll have you know I've been bedded *without paying for it* on more than one occasion, and it's clearly not because of my charming personality."

"I'm sure you have a perfectly fine physique. It is just that civilized people do not strut around naked in front of strangers."

"We've robbed corpses together, Ockzar, you're hardly a stranger."

I had a rummage through the clothes. They stank of flea powder and mold, but they were better than those I had taken off.

"What am I then?" he asked.

"You choose the strangest times to get all metaphysical."

He sighed. "To you. If I am not a stranger, what am I to you?"

That was a tough one. I was torn between 'supercilious faux intellectual' and 'millstone around my neck that is occasionally useful'. "I suppose you're a friend. But don't flatter yourself. Indeed, be worried. Few who have attained that rarest of titles have lived long or peaceful lives."

A stupid grin spread across his face until he noticed that I was still naked, whereupon he turned scarlet and swiftly returned his gaze to the fire. "Oh, I almost forgot. While I was out, I took a detour to the dockmaster's office."

"Aye?"

"For a small donation I was able to check passenger lists from every vessel that has left for the Empire since the er, *unfortunate incident* where you were rendered—."

"All right, all right. Labor the point anymore and we'll have to slap its arse and give it a name. Did they leave?"

"Thomas Swann and Chas Amberley sailed on the passenger ship *Spirit of the New Dawn* this morning."

Nic had stolen the prize *and* my name. I laughed. "Cheeky bastard." It was a nice touch.

"What's so funny?"

I pulled on a pair of oversized grey slops and a heavy old rubakha with a faded band of red embroidery around the collar. "Not much. We need to book passage."

"We?"

"Well, do you want to come?" I said although I was sure which way he was leaning.

"I have much to do here. The revolution won't—"

"Just, yes or no, Ocky."

"I suppose I should see the corruption of your decadent Empire for myself if I am to help my people avoid making the same foolish mistakes. And, you know." He shrugged.

"What?"

"Everyone needs a friend."

"Stop it, I may cry."

"Really?"

I laughed. "No."

Chapter Twenty-Seven

"**D**o you want the bad news or the good news?" Ockzar asked on returning from his second sojourn of the day.

"Good news, always," I said.

He stamped snow from his boots and took off his coat before stoking the fire. "I've secured passage for us on a cargo vessel which leaves this very night, so we'd better start packing." He chuckled. "Not that there's much to pack."

"Cargo ship?"

"Yes. The not so good news is that it's working passage." He shrugged. "It's all we could afford and only then because their physiker has gone down with the pox."

"I'm not a...Ah, I see. You're the replacement physiker. What am I, your assistant?"

He took off his spectacles and cleared the fog from the lenses. "General crew, I'm afraid, but she's apparently a fast ship even fully laden." He put on his spectacles and peered at me like I was something in a jar. "Are you all right?"

"Yes, why?"

"You look, never mind. Do you want some toast? I have butter."

My stomach revolted at the thought. "No thanks, I'm not hungry." '*Bread and blood, bread and blood...*' whispered the serpent as it glided idly through my mind. I ignored it as best I could and occupied myself by watching my meticulous, if not downright fussy companion cut thick slices of bread and then skewer them on a prison shank he'd acquired from somewhere before holding them to the flames.

"Always seems like a lot of effort just to burn bread," I observed.

"I don't intend to burn it. I prefer a light, golden charring. Mother and I would often make toast this way in the drawing room." He smiled at the fire as though her face danced in the flames. When he deemed them dark enough, which was more 'charcoaled' than 'golden', he rubbed each chunk with a stick of butter before scoffing them where he crouched beside the hearth. An unwholesome hunger gnawed at my guts. Thanks to an unfortunately curious rat that had strayed too close when it thought I was asleep, the hunger was in check, although I didn't know how long that would last.

"Aside of scriptomancy, you're also versed in the dark art of mathematics are you not, Ockzar?"

He swelled with pride. "I have a reasonable grasp, aye, but my specialties at university were philosophy, economics, and politics, as is right and proper for any man or woman who wishes to—"

"Bore someone to death? Do you know numbers or not?"

He huffed. "I do, and better to be boring than rude."

"Debatable. Now, puzzle me this; how many rats do you think live in the holds of a Voskvan cargo vessel?"

Having an ego that shrank and grew like a blacksmith's bellows, his face broadened into a wry smile. "What a peculiar question. Why in the world do you want to know that?" And then it dawned on him, and the smile faded.

Driven by a combination of an ironclad prow and a fur-clad sorcerer upon the bowsprit, exhorting the elements to bend to his will, a wide-bellied icebreaker powered from the port. The ship left behind a crackled path of broken floes that *The Dimitra*, the vessel on which we had gainful employment, would follow.

"You've got to be fucking kidding, Ockzar?"

"What do you mean?" He squinted up at the patched hull of the ship as a dock crane that was straining under the weight swung a bag of sand into the hold. All hands were on deck, securing the cargo and setting the rigging ready for sailing. A few gave us the side-eye while the captain and helmsman ignored us in favor of sharing a jug of something while they leaned on the wheel.

"The ship. Look at it."

"It's not pretty, I'll grant you, but it does the trip to Valen at least three times a year." Another cargo net bulging with boxes was lowered into the hold.

"All aboard who's coming aboard!" a crew member with a braided black beard shouted. Ockzar picked up his backpack and marched up the gangplank. The shouting cove stopped him with a finger in the chest. "You the sawbones?"

"Yes, Ockzar Millmets at your service."

The fellow nodded dismissively. "Grona will show you the infirmary. Grona!" he shouted. "Where is that lazy shit?"

"Keep your hair on, I'm coming." Grona climbed from the deck hatch. He was a gangly, stoop-shouldered fellow with a sad face and a woolen hat pulled down over his bean-shaped head.

"Take him to the infirmary," said the sailor with the black beard.

"He the new 'bones?" Grona sniffed and wiped his nose with the back of his hand. "Only, I got this rash." He began fumbling with the buttons of his breeches.

Ockzar's eyes widened in alarm. "Not here, my man. Come and see me when we're underway."

"I'm First Mate Yorgan," said black beard. "You the new hand?" He looked me up and down.

"Aye, aye," I said, trying to sound like this wasn't my first time as ship's crew.

He snorted. "Captain says that yer a lubber working your passage, eh?"

I shrugged. "Fell on hard times, you know how it is."

"Dissolution!" a fellow called from the end of the quay. He was wearing a long grey overcoat and grey fur hat. "It is the curse of the Empire."

"Look lively, landie," said Yorgan. "Or the archolya will preach you to death afore the anchor's upped."

"I heard that, Brother Yorgan. You're already on a warning. One more and your wages will be garnished."

"Fuck you, sneak," Yorgan muttered as he turned away.

"What was that? Yorgan what did you say?" The archolya thrust his kit bag into my arms and swept past me. "Take it to my quarters. Captain!" He called to the captain, who pretended he hadn't heard him. "A word if you would, Captain."

"His quarters are next to the infirmary," said Yorgan. "Don't underestimate the prick. He can have you flogged, or worse if you don't follow the Archonate's 'Path of Righteousness'."

"I'll bear that in mind, keep my head down." *Or suck his blood and throw him overboard,* depending on how much he annoyed me. I was no expert on matters maritime unless you count what it is like to sail inside a kraken, but in my limited experience, the ship was as much of a dump as I'd first thought. The decks had been repaired in dozens of places, and buckets were strategically located under damp, watermarked deck boards. The ladders between decks were missing rungs, and the ceilings were black and greasy with lantern smoke which hung heavily in the air, along with the usual smells one would associate with a dozen crew crammed into a small space for weeks at a time.

After asking for directions to the infirmary, I dumped the archolya's bag in his quarters. It was cramped, but like the officers, he had the luxury of not sharing with anyone. Ockzar had better accommodation in that the infirmary had a bunk cabin and a sick bay with beautiful views of the ocean. So long as no one got ill, he had it all to himself.

"You have no need to worry about rats," said Ockzar, who was inspecting the infirmary with a kerchief over his nose.

"Why's that?" I asked. A foul smell lingered in the air.

"I just found the ship's cat. Not sure what it died of, but it's been dead a while."

"Ah. That would explain the smell." The grim discovery set the tone for the voyage, but I'm getting ahead of myself.

In the sparsely furnished crew quarters, bunks hung like dead kresps from the deck beams marked by the stains of many voyages. There was space under the sagging hammocks for a footlocker, a piss bucket was strapped into the corner, and there was a communal table bolted to the floor at the far end of the low-roofed cabin. It was smoky, and it stank of human. I decided I would spend as little time in there as possible, a task which First Mate Yorgan already had well in hand.

As soon as I'd stowed my few belongings, he had me grafting along with the regulars as we left the port and headed beyond the skirt of coastal ice and out into the Great Ocean. As was only to be expected, the crew didn't speak to the new hand beyond the necessary.

After a hard twelve-hour shift, I was given a hot bowl of decent stew and bread, which I tossed overboard when no one was looking before taking to my bunk. I lay there, happily ignored, and listened to them share anecdotes and gossip. They talked about their spouses, their children, parents, friends, and enemies. Any mention of the Archonate was done in whispers and most often cut short when knowing looks turned to the hatch as though to remind all that there was a member of the Archonate onboard. I know you're thinking that I was bored or possibly amused by their small lives, but I wasn't. If anything, I was envious. I wondered again what it might be like to live a simple life, to have friends who weren't merely hostages of Fate and mundane enemies who weren't bent on destroying the world or having dominion over it.

If by some miracle Leo discharged me from his service, I considered that I might take up with Cobb and company again, teach Sakura what she needed to learn to survive and prosper. Being something of a dramatist, Ockzar would enjoy meeting the theatricals. If that was untenable, I'd go elsewhere, keep my head down, and try to live an ordinary life.

'I hunger,' said the serpent needling my mind and killing the fantasy. I wondered how long it would be satisfied with rat blood as I made my way on deck. Although it was colder than an ice dragon's wotnots, I leaned upon the rail, listened to the slap of waves against the hull, and waited for the suns to rise. I hated that my mind had been meddled with by Leo, Swann, and whatever the fuck I'd picked up in the cave to the point I didn't know my own thoughts. Being destroyed by the Paradox would have been better than being a puppet in the games of others. I gripped the rail. I should just fucking jump overboard. That would show all of them. "How'd you like that, eh?" I said to the serpent in my mind.

"Are ye going t'be sick?" It was Captain Petrov. The smell of cheap rum preceded him along the deck. "If you're going to be sick, do it over the larboard side or the sea'll throw it right back at you and all over my deck."

"Aye, Captain."

He gave a small, satisfied grunt and tugged a pipe from his pocket, which he jammed between his teeth before continuing on his way to the poop deck. I stood awhile; my gaze drawn towards the rising suns by the gulls gliding lazily across the rolling acres of the ocean.

"You called, sir?" As a lowly deckhand I was mindful to knock on the physiker's door before entering.

Ockzar's luxurious privacy had been invaded three days out by a couple of sailors who had come down with an ague. Rechler had died in the early hours of the morning two days ago. The second, Mimana, was barely hanging on the last time I'd seen her.

"I need help putting her in the canvas." Ockzar gestured to Mimana's body, which lay on the sickbed. He pushed his spectacles up on his head and then leaned his dimpled knuckles on the edge of the table.

"Ah. She didn't make it?"

"No." he looked despairingly at the corpse.

"What's up? It's not like you could have done anything."

"No." Not only was he being terse, but he wouldn't look at me.

I kicked the door closed. "What's wrong with you?"

Without looking at me, he threw back the sheet. Mimana was pale and drawn, and her hair clung to her sweat-soaked brow. He turned her head, revealing two infected looking puncture wounds on her neck. "Know anything about these?" he asked before throwing the sheet back over her. He stood up, folded his arms. "Well?"

"Well, what?" I was being obtuse because I was angry, and although I had no right to be, hurt that he should think I'd killed her when I hadn't. Indeed, I'd stubbornly ignored the urge to drink blood for the week we'd been at sea. Like an ordinary crew member, I'd worked hard, choked down normal food, and wiled away the hours off shift laying in my hammock, listening to the crew talking about their lives. I was polite but kept my own counsel, and I had quickly found my place as, believe it or not, *the quiet thoasa.* Me. Yes, I know.

"Did you do this?" he hissed.

I wanted to slap the stupid out of him. "No, I didn't fucking eat my crewmate. Not so much as a rat has passed my lips since we've been aboard. Trust me, Ockzar, if I was going to be stupid enough to slot the people who make the ship work, I'd dump the bodies overboard." *'Kill clean, yes, but kill.'* I sighed. Now he'd done it. All the talk of murder had woken up my bloodhungry lodger. Judging by Ockzar's expression, he remained unconvinced by my denial. "It wasn't me."

"Well, who then? Who killed them?"

"I don't fucking know. I've told you, I'm not an expert on infernals—if that's what killed them. It could be anything. A rabid seagull, I don't know."

"A rabid seagull that draws blood from puncture wounds in the neck? Look at her gums, they're whiter than my arse."

"I'll take your word for it."

"She has severe anemia."

"Well, it's not going to fucking hurt her now, is it?"

Footsteps put a halt to the argument before it could get any more heated. The door opened, and the captain entered. He ignored Ockzar and me and went straight to the body.

"Yorgan said she'd passed." With only the slightest hesitation, he lifted the sheet. He was about to cover her when he stopped and, like Ockzar, turned her head and once more exposed the bite marks. I leaned in and pretended I hadn't seen them before, and most importantly, I kept my mouth shut. "What d'you make of these?" he asked Ockzar.

"A bite of some sort."

"Y'think it has anything to do with what killed her?"

"I cannot say. She sickened and died much as Rechler. Chances are they picked something up in Crakanov."

The captain grunted. Over the course of the week, I'd got used to what the various grunts meant. This one was 'unconvinced'. "Like what?"

For a moment, I thought Ockzar was going to stumble and choke, but he remained calm and stayed in role as the arrogant physiker. "I shall not trouble you with medical terms. In short, an ague. It's not the sweats, nor the puce tremble, but it could be any number of other similar, weakening fevers."

"Could it be a blood drinker?"

My heart sank. Even though I knew I hadn't killed the crew, I felt guilty. Worse, I felt exposed.

Ockzar's eyes widened. For a second, I thought I was sunk and that he was going to panic and drop me in the shit.

"Captain Petrov, I am a man of science." He straightened and tucked his thumbs into the straps of his apron. "Disease is not caused by 'evil'. People do not die because they are cursed, hexed, or ensorcelled. Not in the modern world. Now, I do not doubt that monsters still exist, I have seen more than my fair share of strange things in the wilds." His gaze flicked briefly to me. "But thanks to the might of the Archonate, they do not hang around the docks of Crakanov waiting to prey on sailors."

"You mind your tone, physiker. I'm captain of this vessel."

"And I am the physician, not a wise woman wielding charms and selling folk cures in the market."

It was a masterful performance. I felt like clapping as more footsteps approached the cabin.

"Shall I come back later?" I said, too close to the limelight for my liking.

"Stay where you are," Petrov ordered.

It rankled, but I stayed where I was and tried to look inconspicuous and, above all, innocent.

"How do you two know each other?" The captain gestured to me but spoke to Ockzar.

"Chas works for my family. As I explained, I am attending the University of Merfrere for further studies. Although Pharria is civilized to a point, I need a servant from the home country."

"A servant?" The archolya entered without knocking.

"While I am studying the intricacies of surgery, I need someone to take care of my needs, or would you rather I starve and go ragged while learning skills that I shall bring home to Voskva for the benefit of all?"

The state-sponsored prelate-cum-spy tilted his chin and stared at Ockzar down the bridge of his nose. "I am baffled as to why you think you could learn anything, or why you would even want to go to the most decadent corner of the Empire when we have the greatest universities and the finest teachers at home in our glorious Motherland."

Ockzar looked up at him and gave a slow, insolent blink. "With all due respect, you are a man of the cloth, not of science. Science doesn't recognize or respect borders."

I was surprised by his uncharacteristic bravery although, I suppose the captain and the archolya were considerably less intimidating than Nic or prison guards who threatened daily to fuck him and or eat him when he was a prisoner in the mines.

Having lost the debate, the archolya gave Ockzar a venomous look but held his tongue. The captain sighed deeply and rubbed his grizzled chin.

"Archolya Yashinev?" he said.

Playing his part to the hilt, Ockzar rolled his eyes and shook his head.

The holy man straightened and smiled in triumph. "We should stand vigil over our sister this night. I will offer prayers on her behalf and be ready should whatever devil murdered her come to claim her soul."

"She can't stay here," said Ockzar. "I am sure your quarters will be more than adequate."

"What?" The archolya's superior smile vanished.

"The latest practice in the Glorious Dawn of the Nation Sanitorium: Number One, is called, 'sanitation'. All deceased are removed from treatment rooms. It is un-sanitary to leave her here."

"My quarters are too small."

"The physik is right," said Petrov. "She shouldn't be in here." He turned to me. "Put her in the canvas. Sew it good and tight and do a neat job for our sister."

"Aye, Captain."

"Captain Petrov, I must object," the archolya whined.

"No, you mustn't," said Petrov with the finality of the grave before turning to me. "See it done."

Chapter Twenty-Eight

It was the end of the evening meal. The candles had burned low, the plates had been licked clean, and the crew were nursing the last dregs of the watch's rum ration.

"What say you, Yorgan?" Borgust, the midshipman asked. The other sailors at the table turned to Yorgan, who was cleaning an ancient handcannon.

"About what?" he said, gnarled fingers working an oily rag into the trigger mechanism.

"This vigil, what they're saying about Mim being killed by a devil and her soul being claimed tonight."

"That's not what he said," I clarified, as I was the one from whom the gossip-mangled scuttlebutt had originated. "He said *if* she'd been murdered by a devil. The physik said she and Rechler had mostly likely died of an ague."

Borgust swabbed his bowl with a piece of black bread which he waved around like a priest bestowing a benediction. "Aye, but the archolya said it was a devil, and he's the expert on devils. Ain't that right, Yorgan?"

Yorgan sighted down the barrel. "Don't know. I just do as I'm told. Chas, Borgust, Romor, finish up and then check the hold. Weather's on the turn and I want t'make sure the cargo's secure. Fennic, you're with me on Dog Watch. We'll do a quick patrol then relieve Shulskov and Mazurka."

Fennic gulped. "Outside the archolya's cabin?"

"Aye." He loaded the barker and got up from the table. "And I don't want to hear any more talk of devils. The only devil you need contend with is the ocean. You leave the other kind to Yashinev. You hear me?"

"We hears you, Yorg," ship's cook Elke declared, her wooden leg hammering a slow rhythm on the deck as she cleared away the dishes. "But you listen to me, young 'un. This is an ill-starred voyage. That cat dying was a bad omen. I said it then, and I says it now."

"Don't start," said Yorgan as he tucked the handcannon into his belt and threw on his oilskin coat. "And that goes for the rest of you."

Borgust tossed me a belaying pin. He kept the cutlass for himself. Romor, a tall, dark-haired cove with a persistent cough and runny nose, had a boat hook. We each had a lantern. "I don't suppose you've got anything smaller, do you?" I said as I waved the stick, which was used to secure ropes and good for little else.

"If you've got anything better, lubber, you're welcome to use it." Borgust gave a treacle brown smile and spat another wad of chewed maca leaf over the side.

"I'll just pull a couple of swords out my arse, shall I?" They both laughed, which cracked the shell of fear that had been closing around the crew like pack ice since Mim's death. It was in my best interest to keep it friendly; as the newcomer—one with fangs and scales, I was sure to be caught if the net of suspicion was cast any wider than devil or ague.

"You go first, lubber," said Borgust.

I gave him a stern look.

"They say *tasklisk* have sharp senses is all, so it makes sense you go first," he said and offered a weak, apologetic smile.

"Do they? What do they say about cowardly humans?"

He grinned. "That they die of old age."

Romor wiped his nose on his shiny sleeve and unlocked the cargo hatch. I shuttered my lantern and climbed inside. Welcomed by the darkness, the smell of sand seemed out of place in the middle of the ocean. Halfway down the ladder, I caught the slightest taste of something even more out of place, but not entirely unexpected given the current circumstances. I wasn't sure if I should be relieved or disappointed.

"What is it? What's wrong? Borgust asked, his pale face peering down, his brow leaded with concern.

"Nothing." I'd caught a whiff of something unpleasant. Not quite death, not quite blood. It was a mix of both, with just a hint of hell. I cautiously made my way into the belly of the ship, where I again tasted the air. The smell was gone, and I wondered if I had imagined the infernal odor. The others hesitantly followed, stiff limbed and tense. In a bid to chase away every shadow, Borgust nervously waved his lantern around, half blinding me in the process. Romor caught the boat hook on the ladder and stumbled the last few feet. The usual, eye-watering stink of rat piss was surprisingly absent, and I wasn't the only one to notice.

"Ain't seen any rats," said Romor.

Borgust nodded. The blade trembled in his hand. Light danced on the steel, signalling his fear. "Maybe Elke was right. She's always had a sense for such things." As the words left his mouth, the ship lurched, and the hatch slammed shut, almost snuffing the lanterns and ruffling the shadows.

I laughed. "That was timing, eh?" They didn't laugh with me. I cleared my throat and continued in a more sober vein. "We'd best check the cargo."

"Aye. Pick up that damn hook, Romi. Chas, check the ropes aft."

"I've cut my finger." Romor held up his hand. Bright blood ran from a shallow gash. My treacherous stomach began to rumble loudly, and I headed aft before anyone else heard it.

"What are we hauling again?" I asked.

"Silver sand and some furniture," Borgust replied with a shrug, "I think. Just relieved it isn't salt fish. I got so fat the last time we hauled fish my wife didn't recognize me when I got home. Wife, wives." He chuckled.

"How many do you have?" I asked for want of something to talk about other than devils and curses while I checked ropes and knots.

"Just the three. Don't tell Yashinev for fuck's sake. I've had enough sermonizing this week. I damn well hate that the Archies send 'spiritual advisors' with us.

They didn't used to. First it was a random ship would be 'blessed' with one. Now they go on all vessels heading to the Ring Kingdoms."

"It's like they don't trust you."

"Aye, that's it exactly. Still, it's a small price to pay. I mean, no one can argue that life is better under the Archonate than under the Dvors. Were you in Voskva when they were in charge?"

"No."

"Let me tell you, it was proper shit back then— unless you were a Dvor or one of their arse-kissers."

As we talked, we worked our way around the cargo hold, tightening straps and testing knots while the repetitive timpani of wind-orchestrated rain lashed the decks. Thunder cracked overhead, and the sea battered the rolling hull.

"Did you hear that?" Romor called from the far side of the hold.

"Just rats in the ballast," answered Borgust before turning to me. "Sounded like rats, didn't it?"

"It sounded like claws, aye."

"But not rats?"

"Er…Oh, look at that." I pointed out one of the lids on the furniture crates that had lifted, revealing a row of nails standing proud. Borgust approached it like there was a snake inside and hammered his fist on the loose lid until the nails bit. We both watched it until we were sure it wasn't going to spring open while half expecting it would. When it didn't, Borgust's shoulders relaxed. I cannot say I was as tense as the humans, but I felt their trepidation.

"You go aft," said Borgust. "I'll do forward with Ro…Ro?" A purposeful skittering was the only answer. "Romor?"

"What?" Romor suddenly appeared from around a sack of sand.

"You fucker, you did that on purpose," said the midshipman.

Romor wiped his nose on his sleeve and grinned. "Didn't mean to scare you, old timer. I was just tightening a loose strap."

"Didn't mean to, my arse. You're lucky I'm a way down here, or I'd have stuck you like a pig shark."

Romor chuckled. "Course you would." He made his way over to another of the sacks, which was straining against the ropes as the ship began to buck in the rising swell. One of the ropes holding a crate snapped and whipped back. The box slewed sideways and slammed into the hull. I managed to stay upright, Borgust grabbed hold of one of the ropes holding the sacks of sand, but Romor fell and slid across the deck on his arse as the ship listed. Water poured through the now flapping hatch, and the ballast rocks in the bowels of the boat growled as they ground against each other.

"Is this normal?" I shouted above the raging storm.

"Aye. It's the time of year for squalls. This'll probably be our last run 'till spring." The midshipman steadied himself and made his way over to the free crate. "Gimme a hand with this."

"What do you want me to do?"

"When we're running level, shove it back towards that mooring ring. If you feel us start to haul over, get from behind it or it'll crush ya. Romor! Get over here now." Ro didn't answer. "Seaman Dalyakin, stop fucking around!"

Rather than being slick, the deck planks near the crate felt gritty underfoot. At first, I thought it must be spilled sand, but then I saw dirt leaking from the box. "I thought you said this was furniture?" I said as I toed the muddy slurry, which was beginning to drip between the deck planks.

"That's what it says in the manifest. Now just take hold of—"

I tasted blood in the air and looked up. Hot, sweet nectar was spraying in a fine mist from a slit in Borgust's hairy throat. Slightly more surprised than me, the midshipman blinked as his head fell to the right and his body to the left. "Oh fuck. Romor!" I yelled and

back-pedaled, acutely aware that I was unarmed, save
for a small stick.

"Well, this is awkward," said a voice from above me.
I backed against the hull. The fiend made no move
towards me but hung by his long fingers and toes from
the deck beams. His head was twisted at an unnatural
angle; his luminous gaze darted like that of a raptor on
the lookout for a tasty morsel. "To whom do you
belong?" he said. His long, black tongue unrolled like a
scroll and flickered as he tasted the air. Lank, silver hair
clung to his pale skull. His traditional, Voskvan shirt
was richly embroidered but frayed and spotted with
blood old and new. His coat was trimmed with fur, but
the fur was balding. It looked like he hadn't bothered to
change the outfit in a hundred years, which was just lazy
if you asked me.

Once again, Romor appeared from around a crate
and with more courage than I might have shown in his
position, charged the murderous infernal with the boat
hook. As much as I didn't want to watch, I couldn't look
away as the monster scuttled across the roof like a giant
bug and pounced on the sailor, batting the hook aside
like it was a toy. Growling, the fiend dislocated his jaw
and bit the unfortunate cove's face off, much like a dog
worrying a bone. It was a grim sight, and due to a lack
of face parts, poor Romor died choking on his blood,
unable even to scream. When the fiend was done
sucking and slurping and chewing, it licked its face with
its long tongue and turned to me, regaining as it did a
semblance of humanity. "That was very rude of me but

needs must. You understand." He burped and gestured to the twitching corpse. "Care for seconds?"

"I've already eaten, thanks." I wondered if the sailor's memories were swimming through his wicked mind as he spoke. Or perhaps a venerable bloodsucker like him was able to kill without taking the consciousness of their victims into themselves. I also wondered if it was a trick I might learn and then quickly chastised myself for harboring such mercenary thoughts while my comrades of the keel bled out before me.

"I am Vashtun Terpelz, also called the Black Dvor, Lord Protector of the Principality of Kalinzagori and loyal servant of the throne." The infernal flourished a bow, spattering the nearby crates with claret. "Who is your master?"

"Duke Leopold of Valen, Prince of the Midnight Court," I said with a lack of hesitation that caught me by surprise. "I also don't mean to be rude," I said as I sidestepped the river of blood flowing towards me as the prow of the ship reared. "But did you just compel me?"

"Absolutely not. It would be bad form to tamper with another *vordalki's* minion."

"I am not a minion," I said, sounding whinier than I'd intended. "Also, please don't kill any more of the crew. We're in the middle of the Great Ocean and you need them to sail the boat."

"I take what I wish, although you might have a point. I'll think on it while I digest."

The hatch was thrown open, and one of the crew shouted down. "Ahoy down there. Everything all right, Borgust?"

"Help!" I shouted impulsively. The infernal hissed and bared his fangs as he floated back into the shadows and vanished. Someone dropped into the hold brandishing a handcannon and a lantern. It was Yorgan. "Over here!" I yelled, unsure if by doing so I'd condemned myself or the sailor. Knowing my luck, it was probably both. The light swung towards me, followed by the barrel of a handcannon. I got the spine-tingling feeling you get when a loaded barker is pointed at your face and promptly raised my hands. "Don't shoot, it's me, Chas."

He took a step, shone the lantern on Romor, and recoiled like he'd been bitten. "Shul's blood! Who...Romor? Fuck. What happened? What fucking happened?" Yorgan growled and waved the handcannon at me, at the bodies, at the shadows. The other sailors on the dog watch dropped down behind him, saw the bodies, and began shouting and cursing and, in one case, puking. Meanwhile, I was convinced Terpelz would appear from whatever shadows the monstrous fuck was hiding in and chew their faces off. But there was no point trying to warn them as they were in the middle of a shouting panic.

Yorgan waved the barker at Romor, then pointed it at me. "I said, what fucking happened?"

It seemed obvious to me, but then I remembered these coves were merely sailors and unused to such things. "A monster chewed his face off."

His terrified gaze darted around the hold, to the loose crate, to Romor, to Borgust, back to me. "Don't you fucking move." He turned to Fennic, who was cowering by the ladder. "Fetch the irons."

"Did you hear me?" I said, although I knew where this was going. "There's a monster on the ship, in here, with you."

"*With you*?" He narrowed his eyes.

Fuck! "With *us*."

'*You could just kill them*,' the voice of whatever was slithering around in my head suggested casually. "Fuck off!" I shouted. Alas, I used my outside voice rather than the one in my head.

Yorgan cocked the barker.

Chapter Twenty-Nine

"And that's how I ended up in chains," I said, and waggled my hands, which were shackled above my head.

Ockzar sighed. "Where's this 'monster' now?"

"You said that like you don't believe me."

"It's been a long day. Where did it go?"

"It vanished into the shadows." Borgust and Romor had been taken away by shaken sailors who, for the most part, avoided making eye contact with me. The deck was immediately swabbed and strewn with sawdust to soak up the gory residue, but the stink of death and violence was burned into the air. I'd repeated almost all of what happened to anyone who asked until I was hoarse, but when a search of the crates and the sandbags revealed no sign of the infernal, I was shackled to the wall. I could have stopped them, but to do so would have confirmed my guilt in their minds, and I would have been forced to kill the entire crew. As they hadn't got as far as knotting a hempen necklace, I held my water, for now. I didn't want to go to war with the sailors because I liked them and, as I had pointed out to my new, toothsome friend, Terpelz, you need a crew to sail a ship.

Ockzar sighed again and rested his elbow on one of the crates before squeezing the bridge of his nose and making his spectacles dance. "I want to believe you, *Chas*. I really do." He leaned in close because we were not alone. "But you lie as you breathe."

"Oh, that's rich coming from you. That's just…" I shook my head. "Just make sure you don't go anywhere on your own. Stay up on deck, stay in the light."

"Because infernals fear the light, eh?" he said, his voice dripping with sarcasm.

"Most, yes. I think."

His lips thinned to a hard line. "Gasvoy's Ghost, Breed. This doesn't look good. You were found with their still warm, still bleeding bodies."

"And if Yorgan hadn't come when he did, I would be one of them."

"Oh, really?"

"Yes, really." That was a lie, but one told for the best of reasons. I had to be at liberty if I was going to hunt down the real monster or, failing that, protect Ockzar from him when he next got peckish.

"The captain's going to question you as soon as we're through the storm."

"He can question me all he likes. A better use of time would be to tear this ship apart and find the fucking infernal that's eating his crew." The ship lurched drunkenly. I dug my claws into the tarred wooden deck to stop myself swinging around.

"Why did you let them chain you?"

"Because I like it, why do you think?"

"I think trouble follows you like a shadow."

"This is not my fault! I'll grant, the way things have been going I can see why you might think so, but I assure you; I'm doing my very best to be reasonable about this, I really am. However, my forbearance will not extend to letting them hang me from the yard arm, so be warned. It is in your best interest to advocate on my behalf."

"What do you think I've been doing? Looking at my arsehole with a mirror?"

"Well, to be honest, Ockzar—"

"—Just don't." He wagged his finger at me like it was a shiv. "Just. Don't. This is no time for levity."

"One has to laugh in the face of adversity. Trust me, this is the perfect time."

"The archolya wants to 'question' you too. He's ex-Ministerium. You know what that means?"

"No, but don't tell me, let me guess. He's one of those twisted pig pizzles who enjoys torturing people for the glory of Voskva, and because it's the only way he can burp his syphilitic maggot?"

"I cannot vouch for the last, but yes, in essence. He wants to make a name for himself, I know the type. And keep your voice down. The walls have ears."

An image of the infernal came to mind. "Aye, they probably do."

"We're locking up, Physik," one of the sailors called to Ockzar.

"I have to go." He smiled in a vain attempt to appear reassuring. "I'll speak to the captain again, although I have little currency now that we know it wasn't an ague that killed the others."

"Do your best. I'll just hang around here, for now. Or, you know, be murdered by a monster."

Evidently disapproving of the gallows humor, he shook his head and hurried over to the ladder. No one had seen fit to leave a lantern, so I was plunged into near-complete blackness when the hatch was dropped and bolted. I waited patiently for Terpelz to show his ugly mug. The longer I was in darkness, the sharper my senses became. It turned out there were still a few wily rats alive, and they came out briefly, their inquisitive little noses twitching, luminous green eyes tiny points of interest in the otherwise dull pitch.

The first sign that Terpelz was about to make an appearance was when a mist began to ooze up from between the deck planks. Sensing the unmistakable presence of preternatural evil, the rats scampered into their bolt holes. The mist coalesced before me, and the fiend materialized. Like the rats, his pale eyes shone in the darkness. He folded his triple-jointed fingers over his narrow chest and sniffed me.

"Ah, the plump one was here. I think I will save him for dessert." The long, dark tongue protruded from between his bloodless lips, and he licked my cheek, which was as disgusting as you might imagine. To my surprise, it was he who recoiled, bony hands clutching at his coat as though I'd slapped him. He loomed above me, which I'm sure would have been an eerie sight to anyone who didn't have one foot in the blood drinker's world. I, however, was unimpressed. "Why are you doing this?"

He gave me a quizzical look. "Doing what?"

"Travelling in the hold of a ship while killing the fucking crew. Why aren't you haunting some gloomy ruin, eating local goatherders and unwary travelers?"

"Nobody herds goats in Kalinzagori. It's cattle country. Also, I'm…" He looked away, I would have said sheepishly, but there was nothing of the sheep about this old wolf.

"You're what, bored?"

"Yesss!" His eyes lit up, and he smiled a smile that was too wide and devoid of warmth. "It is exactly that. I am bored. The world has changed without me. I see glimpses; towering chimneys rising in the distance, the taste of industry blowing in the wind. The local farms were abandoned, the young flocked to the cities. Cities teeming with life like well stocked fishponds. I wish to see it, to taste the wonders of this new world, a world that has forgotten creatures like me. Also, I hate the cold. I would like to dwell somewhere warmer."

"Makes sense, I suppose, so long as you stay out of the sun. But would you be so kind, sir to lay off eating the crew as you embark on your journey of discovery?"

"Oh, no. That is quite impossible. I do not know about your master—"

"—He's more my employer."

"—Your *master*. But I am ancient and possessed of a powerful hunger. Unless the wind carries us more swiftly to our destination, they will all die."

"That's a relief. Thank you."

He canted his head. "For what, child?"

"Confirming you're a prick. I'd hate to slot an addled old scrote who didn't know what he was doing. I mean, I'd have done it, but I would have felt bad about it." I tensed, strained against the chains. The bolt groaned; the links began to stretch.

He raised his hand, which was as translucent as smoke. "Do you think you can kill me before I kill your little pet?" I stopped trying to break the chains. He smiled. "The smell of the physiker is all over you. I heard you talking; like squabbling siblings, which was charming in its way. Now think on this; while you are breaking those irons, I will pass through the floor and tear out his heart." Damn him. Upon seeing comprehension on my face, he nodded. "Good. You know I speak the truth."

"So?" I shrugged, tried to bluff while I worked out what I could do to stop him from killing Ockzar. "You're going to kill him anyway."

"I was, but I see you have an attachment; therefore, I am amenable to making a bargain that will be mutually beneficial." He reached towards me, his hand a ghostly shadow. Even so, he refrained from touching me.

Rather than shout or curse, I laughed. Not long or joyfully, but because as I'd said to Ockzar, in moments like this, one must. Much like an animal trying to fathom human speech, the fiendish Dvor tilted his head from side to side and smiled hesitantly, uncomprehending.

"Well?" He fanned his bony fingers.

"What do you want in exchange for his life?"

"Feign ignorance of my presence."

"And let them hang me?"

He shrugged. "I have no issue with you convincing the meat that you are not the hunter, just omit all mention of me. In return, I will not gut your pet and suck the life blood from his still-beating heart."

"So, you're asking me to sacrifice my life for his. How do I know you'll keep your word, given that you're an infernal monster and all?"

"Because my word is my bond!" A malevolent glow lit in his eyes. "I am the Black Dvor. I have commanded legions, conquered the lands of my enemies from the Sea of Smarna to the Edrugai Mountains."

"My word is also my bond," I lied smoothly. "If you touch my friend, I will do you."

He canted his head. "Do me?"

"Slot you."

He shrugged. "Your Voskvan is appalling."

"I will end you. Is that plain enough?"

Recognition lit in his eyes. "Why didn't you just say so?"

"I did."

"You didn't. You talked about slots and 'doing' me, doing what to me? The young talk nonsense." He huffed. "You must speak plainly and clearly. Don't they teach anything these days?"

"I was trying to be dramatic, to emphasise my threat."

"Well, it didn't come across."

"Hurt him and I'll kill you. There. Is that clear enough?"

The smug fuck gave a condescending smile. "I'll be...*around*." He melted into the shadows, and the mist dissipated. I listened to the creaking deck, the snap of canvas, and the wind-scaled shouts of the crew for half of an hour before testing the chains again.

As soon as I took the strain, a pair of pale eyes appeared in the darkness. "I wouldn't do that if I was you." His voice echoed in the hold.

"Oh, come on! Haven't you got anything better to do?"

"I didn't bring any books, and thanks to Romor and Borgust I am not in need of sustenance currently, so, no."

"You know their names?" I said, and slyly tried to stretch the cuffs so I might slip my hands free.

"I know all their names. And I can still see you, so don't try anything, for the sake of your pet piglet."

I stopped attempting to break the chains. The shriveled, old fuck had the advantage of me for as long as I valued Ockzar's life above my own. Acknowledging such a weakness vexed me. It was almost as annoying as knowing that the value I placed on his life was a fragile thing and, should push come to shove, I might discount it altogether and let him die.

I've said it before, but most often the hardest thing to do is to do nothing. If I can't talk my way out of trouble, I usually run from it or kill it. Today, I was just hanging around, swaying with the ship as it sailed through the dregs of the storm, waiting for Terpelz or Petrov's next move.

It was night when the hatch was thrown open, and Grona slid down the ladder. He was carrying what looked and sounded like a bag of tools. Archolya Yashinev followed him. Being a man who understood the importance of appearance, Yashinev took his time descending the ladder. He was carrying a black, leather bag and looked like he was about to deliver a sermon in his best, grey robes and black stole. Although he appeared sober and severe, I could smell his excitement from ten feet away. Even though I'd been tortured by the best, my heart began to beat a little faster when Grona dropped the sack of tools and rolled up his sleeves. While I watched the sailor limber up, the archolya watched me. I pretended to look scared.

Grona rolled his shoulders and cracked his meaty knuckles. His expression seemed fixed in one of boredom, as though he was preparing to swab the deck instead of give me a paneling.

"I told the captain all I know. I swear," I stammered, playing up the part of innocent. "I had nothing to do with it."

Yashinev nodded. "I know, I know. But I must be sure. The spiritual wellbeing, the essential purity of everyone aboard this ship, including you, is in my hands." He laughed softly, cupped his hands. "I do not expect an ignorant heathen like you to understand, but spiritual purity is a precious thing, like a baby bird."

"I was in here with Borgust and Ro and then...there was so much blood, and those eyes..." I shuddered for effect.

Yashinev was also playing a role and sighed heavily, a pained expression on his face, like he didn't want to hurt me but had no choice in the matter. "I want to believe you, truly I do, but there is a darkness aboard this ship. A malevolent, murderous presence is killing our brothers and sisters. It might be hiding in any one of us, including you."

"I swear, there isn't any room for anyone else but me in me, honest." Cold laughter rang in my mind, mocking the lie.

"Then show me!" Yashinev implored. "Show me that it isn't in you, and I will rejoice."

"How can I show you something that doesn't exist?"

The archolya nodded absently as he opened his bag and took out a silver aspergillum which he began to wave. While mumbling prayers, he liberally sprinkled what I took to be holy water around the hold. In the midst of sprinkling, he tipped the nod to Grona, who squared up before me.

"I haven't done anything!" I pleaded, taking the opportunity to breathe out in preparation for the gut punch I felt was coming.

Grona shrugged, his expression hardly changing from that of bored neutrality as he drew back his arm and punched me in the gut. It didn't wind me, but it didn't exactly tickle. I moaned appropriately and noted that the color rose in the holy man's cheeks as he pretended not to watch Grona work me over. Minutes later, with sweat stippling his forehead, the sailor stopped whaling on me. I hung on the chains, head down. It felt like I'd been beaten by a sickly child, but I had studied Cobb's company and was confident I looked like someone who had sustained a sound thrashing.

While Grona quenched his thirst with a belt of something Yashinev offered him from a silver flask, the archolya splashed me vigorously with the aspergillum. "Confess!" he bellowed while attempting to drown me in holy water.

"I...didn't...do...anything,"   I   groaned. "Please...you have to believe me," I sobbed breathlessly. Cobb would have been proud.

The archolya grabbed me by my sodden shirt and shook me. "Confess, demon!" He slapped me across the face. "Show yourself, show your true face. I command thee! Reveal thy foul visage!" He gripped my chin with one hand and drew a silver knife from his robes with the other. He held it too close to my face for me to focus on it before stabbing me in the fat of my shoulder. It was only a small thing, little bigger than a fruit knife, but it hurt. The howl of pain he elicited was not feigned.

His eyes lit up. "Aha! Do you see, Grona? Demons hate silver."

"You just fucking stabbed me!" I wailed loud enough for the crew up top to hear my suffering because I was in fact, suffering.

Yashinev withdrew the knife, shoved me against the hull, and stabbed me again in the same place. The blade bit deeper this time, scraped bone, and sent a blinding pain up my arm. I was very tempted to bite his fucking face off, but I wasn't going to give him the satisfaction.

I screamed instead and then lolled as though I'd fallen into a swoon.

He released me. "Fetch the brazier," he said.

Grona belched loudly. "Can't."

"And…Sorry, what did you say?"

"Can't. Captain says no fires in the hold."

My tormentor raised his hand. "That won't do." He approached Grona and lowered his voice to a hiss. "What do you mean no fires in the hold?"

"Just that. No fires," said Grona lacking any such discretion. "Captain says it's too dangerous."

"We're dealing with demonic forces!"

"You'll have to deal with 'em without fire."

"But I need to heat the irons to draw the demon out."

The sailor clicked his tongue thoughtfully; feet shuffled on the gritty deck. "I could heat 'em in the galley. They should stay warm until I get back."

"Warm?"

"Aye."

"I can't draw a demon out with a *warm* poker."

"I could just hit 'em with the irons. Give my hands a rest. Tasklisk have got proper tough hides. Look at my knuckles, they're red raw."

Yashinev sighed. "Never mind your fucking knuckles. What about a bucket of coals? Can I have a bucket of coals down here?"

"Don't know. Do you want me to ask the captain?"

"Do you know I was in the Ministerium for three years? Three years of unblemished service to the Archonate. I met Archon Dunnatev twice, *twice*. He even spoke to me on one of those occasions. And then just one tiny incident, one minor indiscretion and I get sent to Crakanov to be spiritual advisor on fucking cargo ships. Cargo ships going to the accursed Empire no less."

"So, shall I go speak to the captain now or…?"

"Yes, go. Go, damn it, and tell him I need it."

That I had a different demon inside of me was an irony I couldn't ignore. Particularly since it did not take kindly to me bleeding. It woke in me a furious hunger that I had to fight to control. Sweat poured down my face as it gnawed at my guts and tried to provoke me to rip the chains off the wall and attack. I licked my busted lip to get a taste of claret, even if it was my own.

Yashinev paced up and down the aisle between the bags of silver sand until his patience ran out. "Grona!" he called, loud enough to startle me. "Where is the dolt? Grona!" He huffed then angrily climbed the ladder. It wasn't long before I heard a voice whispering from the shadows.

"I sense your thirst," said Terpelz. "I can help you." A pale hand appeared before me like a magician's trick, a bloody slash in the slender wrist. "Take sustenance from me."

I ached to drink his blood, to slake the terrible thirst that had me in its grip, and I wasn't alone. The serpent raged, screamed in my skull, so loud I could hardly hear myself think. I'd never felt a craving so powerful, never wanted something so much. The serpent amplified my desire. The wrist came closer. The potent aroma of blood welled from the slash. As my resolve began to crumble, the hatch was thrown open, and a gust of wind blew into the darkness. The hand vanished like smoke as Yashinev descended the ladder. I was too exhausted to think, but I knew that my tormentor had saved me from something much worse than a beating. The archolya's cheeks were flushed. Rain beaded his face and spotted his otherwise immaculate robes. He stomped over.

"No fire," he said, fuming. He was looking at me, but I don't think he was talking to me. He drew the knife again. "I'll just have to do my best to save your soul from evil without a purifying flame." He cut my shirt open and ran his hands down my bruised ribs like a butcher deciding which cut to take first. "Confess and repent your sins."

It was my turn to sigh.

"That's enough!" Ockzar's pink face appeared through the hatch. He was so close, but I didn't have the strength to call to him, to tell him to stay away because I didn't want to bite him again. "Yorgan!" he called to the midshipman who slid down the ladder and into the hold.

"All right, that's enough," said Yorgan tiredly. "No more stabbing, Captain's orders." He put his hand on Yashinev's shoulder.

The archolya spun. "Unhand me!" As he turned, he sliced the side of Yorgan's hand. Blood flew. I felt a growl roll in my throat. Shouting for help, Ockzar climbed down the ladder. Cursing, Yorgan grabbed Yashinev's hand and tried to wrestle the knife from him. A thick mist boiled through the blood-splattered deck. I tried to call Ockzar, but I couldn't form the words. It didn't matter. He was already moving, ducking around Yorgan and Yashinev.

"Where did this bloody mist come from?" said Ockzar, as more sailors dropped into the hold and piled on the archolya, but it was too late. Something else was in there with us; something altogether more dangerous was snarling in the mist. Ockzar unlocked the cuffs, and I fell into his arms. "We need to get out of here," he said as the Black Dvor loomed out of the mist behind him.

Chapter Thirty

I dropped to the deck, let my weight drag Ockzar down with me as the Dvor pounced on the nearest warm body and bit into his head like it was a ripe apple. Shulskov was the unlucky sailor and screamed as the Dvor spat out a piece of skull and began feasting on his noodle.

Understandably horrified, Ockzar was rigid with fear, but I managed to get him crawling between the sacks of sand and away from the vicious brawl, the focus of which had shifted from Yashinev to Terpelz.

"Get into the light, everyone on deck, now!" It was the ever-resourceful Yorgan. Despite being stuck by the archolya, the midshipman had the wherewithal to martial the crew. Yashinev was the first up the ladder.

"Come on, Ockzar," I said, as I hauled him towards the ladder. Leaden limbed, he had only climbed a few rungs when the hatch began to close. I put my shoulder under his backside and pushed him through the opening before those above could close it. As I reached for the last rung, a bony hand wrapped around my ankle and tried to pull me down. I slipped, Ockzar grabbed my wrist. I hung a moment like a rag between two dogs. In truth, I didn't know where I belonged: down in the darkness with the monster, or in the light with Ockzar. The crew decided for me. Yorgan grabbed the back of my shirt and someone I couldn't see grabbed my arm. I kicked at the Dvor's hand. Claws like knives dug into my ankle and began pulling me down. More hands grabbed me. There was a sharp pain in my calf as the claws tore through the tendon. Well, two could play at that game. I kicked with my free foot and slashed him with my talons. The Dvor's blood-slicked grip finally slipped, and I shot from the hold and landed on deck like the catch of the day. Someone slammed the hatch and locked it behind me. Someone else shouted for a hammer and nails. The call went up for Shulskov. I was content to just lie there a while, safe under the wan suns' light. I looked down at my ankle, saw the flesh was beginning to blacken.

"Can you sit up?" Ockzar's face loomed large and worried above me.

I sat up. "So it seems." The air smelled of blood and salt. Pain washed over me. "Or maybe not." I lay down again and dug my claws into the deck as fire crawled up my leg.

"Help me get Chas to the infirmary," Ockzar ordered.

Although I was proud of him, his suggestion was a death sentence. I rolled over and grabbed his arm. "Not inside. It can move through walls."

"Gasvoy's Ghost, really?" He ran his hand through his hair. "We can't go below!" he shouted. "It can move through the walls. Everyone, it can move through the walls. Don't go below!" It took a while, but with his help, I managed to stand. My vision swam. Nausea gripped me. Ockzar helped me over to the stairs leading to the poop deck, out of the way of the terrified sailors who were frantically battening down the hatches.

"We must get to the lifeboats," said Yashinev. "Grona, go to my cabin and bring my things. Grona! Grona?"

"Grona isn't going anywhere but to the sheets," said Captain Petrov calmly, but there was steel in his gaze when he glanced at the archolya. As the initial excitement began to die, there came a terrible scream from the crew deck. Everyone looked at the hatch, but nobody moved towards it. The scream died abruptly. "Who's missing?"

"Shulskov," said Yorgan.

"And Fennic," said Grona.

"I'm here, you blind prick," said Fennic. "It's Mazurka."

"Damn it," said Petrov. "Yorg, physik, archolya and…" He turned saw me. "And Chas, up to the helm. The rest of you, arm yourselves and guard the hatches."

"We need to take to the lifeboats and burn this ship and the monster with it," said an increasingly panicking Yashinev. I hoped his comments would be enough to get the bastard tossed overboard, but Petrov proved himself to be a better cove than I and did not give the order.

The captain folded his arms. "I ain't going to burn my ship."

"You will do as you are told, Captain Petrov," said Yashinev. Despite his actions revealing him to be a fucking idiot, he still wielded power over the crew by dint of his position.

"I'm captain of this ship," said Petrov with quiet resolve.

"Fuck you and fuck your shitty ship. There is a demon in the hold, man!" Spit flew from Yashinev's lips. "Demons are my jurisdiction. This is a matter for the Ministerium." The crew milling on the main deck looked up, their faces drawn, their eyes wide with fear.

NO GOOD DEED   413

"There ain't room for everyone and supplies on the boat, Cap'n," said Yorgan. "We should draw straws."

Petrov nodded. "Send a boarding party below to get supplies. Pick your team, Yorg."

"Aye, Captain." Yorgan picked a handful of the meanest looking crew members. Grim faced, they tooled up.

The self-satisfied smile that had settled on Yashinev's face vanished. He snorted. "I will not be drawing a straw."

"I would expect nothing less of an archolya of the Ministerium," said Petrov. "As you say, the demon is your responsibility."

It took a moment for the captain's words to sink in. When it did, Yashinev grew pale. "Jurisdiction." He laughed nervously. "I said, it is within my jurisdiction. I cannot stay here." Petrov remained unmoved. "Captain! I can't stay. I must return to Voskva, I must make my report to the Ministerium."

"I have quill and ink; you can write it down," said Petrov, a touch of acid in his tone.

Yashinev made a sound like he was choking on bile. "Be careful, Petrov. You are walking on thin ice. I have powerful friends."

The hard line of a bitter smile crossed Petrov's face. "*Had*. You're all at sea now, Archolya." He looked beyond Yashinev to Fennic. "Lash this bastard to the wheel."

Without a moment's pause, Fennic grabbed Yashinev.

"Unhand me!" The archolya struggled, but a swift knee in the jewels took the wind from his sails.

Petrov watched, his jaw set in a grimace. "You torture one of my crew, cut another, talk to me like shit *on my own ship* and then think you can just take a seat on my fucking lifeboat?"

It took a moment for me to realize that the tortured crew member he was talking about was me. I was touched, and sadly I had also been poisoned by the Dvor and was already so sick that I couldn't see straight, but I was touched. A few of the crew cast wary glances towards the wheel where Fennic was in the process of binding the cursing and crying Yashinev. I clutched the blanket Ockzar had given me to my shivering body and watched a knot of three malcontents nominate Grona to be their spokesperson. He climbed the steps to the helm. "Captain Petrov?"

"Grona."

"Me and some of the lads don't think you should be treating a man of the faith like that." As he spoke, the suns hid behind a bank of dark clouds. The ocean turned black; the breakers grew iron-edged fangs that snarled at the vessel like wolves ready to pounce. Then suddenly, the clouds parted, and the light broke cleanly on glittering, crystal waves. Gulls wheeled, screamed for their supper. The captain nodded slowly. "Aye. I know you don't."

"Come on, Breed, time to get up," said Ockzar.

"Is it? I was just watching Grona making the captain's job of choosing who's staying and who's leaving easy. You know that cock snot Grona gave me a proper kicking. Sorry, Ocky, I'm rambling." A terrible thirst had awoken in me. It was like a thing alive, like a serpent writhing in my veins. And here was Ockzar, and he smelled so damn good, I could just eat him up.

"We need to be ready when they draw straws," he whispered. "I've seen this done before. It is better to draw earlier rather than later. I'm not sure if first is best, but definitely earlier."

"Ockzar..." I said. Once again, I was torn between his kindness and my thirst, between kissing him or killing him. I already knew he tasted delicious, and if I went for him this time, I doubt he would be able to fight me off with a shoe.

Oblivious to my potentially deadly dilemma, he smiled at me. "It's all right, you go before me; you've earned the right. I'm only sorry I couldn't persuade

Captain Petrov to let us rescue you sooner." He pulled the blanket around me.

"Ockzar." I tried again to get a word in.

He ignored me. "Just save your strength. You'll need—"

I grabbed his shirt and pulled him close. He smelled so very sweet. "I'm not drawing a straw."

"Don't say such foolish things. That's just the fever talking." He smiled unconvincingly and tried to pull away.

I tightened my grip. "Listen. If I go, everyone on that boat will die, do you understand?"

'*Yesss…*' the serpent in me hissed.

"Not you. Fuck's sake, stop interrupting!"

Ockzar's face crumpled, tears welled in his eyes. "You're sick, Breed. I'm not going to leave you."

"You must. Don't worry, Yashinev and Grona will keep me company." Hunger and pain were conspiring to make me a monster. I resisted the urge to bite his chubby, little face and reluctantly released him. Drinking blood would heal me, but it would also destroy me.

'*It's not your fault, Breed,*' the serpent whispered seductively. '*You didn't cause this. You're just a victim, like me. Drink and be healed.*'

"Just go, Ockzar," I said and drew the blanket around me as tight as a winding sheet.

"I said, I'm not going to leave you."

"Just fuck off, Tusky. You're useless to me." I was aiming to hurt, to drive him away. His cheeks flushed. I felt no triumph seeing the pain I caused writ upon his face. Stung by my rejection, he left without a word and busied himself amongst the crew. Like me, he'd found a measure of acceptance on board, and like shit on roses, it had made him grow. If nothing else good came out of this ill-starred journey, seeing him gain the respect he had always craved counted for something. A sudden cramp tried to fold me like parchment. I played it down. Although it was plain to any that had eyes, I was not in a good way. What none of them could guess was that I was a monster before the Dvor got his claws in me. He'd just helped me along the dark path. As I sat by the wheel feeling sorry for myself, the lifeboat was lowered and made ready. At the same time, Yorgan led his heavily armed team of five below for supplies.

Time passed, and as the suns dived for the roiling edge of the world, four of them returned. They were bloody, but they had supplies. No one wasted time mourning the lost crew member, not now at least. Indeed, there was a palpable sense of guilty relief that, if my calculations were correct, straws no longer needed to be drawn for a seat in the boat. With me, Grona, and Yashinev staying behind, everyone else had a place.

Grona appeared to accept that he'd talked himself into being left behind with his usual bovine lack of concern. Yashinev was less of a thick-pated stoic and ran through threats, promises, begging, and back again before someone had the good sense to gag him. Ockzar stayed away from me and milled on the lower deck as the crew waited for their turn to get in the boat. I didn't blame him for avoiding me, indeed, I was grateful as I didn't like mopey farewells. Petrov was another matter. I noticed as he climbed the steps to the helm that his gnarled hand lingered on the polished rail like he was saying a silent goodbye. He shook his head as he passed Yashinev and came over to me, whereupon he dropped a bottle of rum in my lap. The dark liquid sloshed against the thick green glass. He took a step back.

Even my fingers hurt, but it would have been rude not to have a drink. I picked up the bottle, pulled the cork with my teeth, and took a swig. It wasn't bad as rum went and burned pleasantly on the way down, momentarily balancing the sting of the Dvor's poison. "Appreciated, Captain."

"I don't like what that little *odbyt* did." He cast a withering glance towards the archolya. "And I don't like that I believed him when he said you had a demon in you."

"I'd like to say no harm done." Because I'm a martyr to my cause, I laughed through the pain.

Taciturn as ever, Petrov nodded. "Aye, so would I. Good luck to you, Chas. If it's any consolation to you, you fit right in and would have been welcome to stay."

"You not going down with your ship, Captain?" I had another swig of rum; it was really rather good.

As he headed down to the main deck, he called over his shoulder. "Not if I can help it."

I turned to Yashinev. "This is bloody good rum."

He glared and mumbled something through the gag that I had no interest in deciphering. Molten gold spread across the horizon, and the fire of the dying sunslight spun gold on the shrouds.

I watched Petrov cast a last, nostalgic glance across the almost empty deck before climbing into the lifeboat. I wasn't surprised to see Ockzar had stayed on board. The pale blade of the lifeboat sail unfurled and snapped taut as it caught the wind. As the suns dipped below the horizon, the boat was already tacking northwest. The pale faces of the lucky survivors turned towards the ship as they sped away from certain death and towards the uncertainty of the cruel sea.

An unhappy Ockzar plodded up the stairs and sat heavily beside me. I handed him the bottle. He took a gulp and shuddered. The glow of his rosy cheeks deepened. "I know you were only being mean to make me leave."

"Didn't fucking work, did it?"

He laughed. I watched him watch the lifeboat skim across the darkening waves. I could see the longing in his eyes, but it was anchored by the resolute set of his whisp whiskered jaw. If I'd had a hat, I would have taken it off to him. It's easy to be brave when you're strong, easy to stand your ground when you're a warrior or sorcerer, when you're a powerful being. Ockzar was none of those things, and yet here he was. It was a stupid decision by any measure, but it would be a dull and joyless world if we always did the sensible thing. Very selfishly, I was glad of the company, although his presence complicated the vague plan I'd come up with while waiting for the others to fuck off. Gulls settled on the mast spars and bowsprit and shouted incessantly, no doubt demanding that we hurry up and die so that they could feast.

"I've always wondered where they go," said Ockzar.

"Where who go?" I said, distracted by Grona, who was swinging a fishing gaff on the lower deck, and Yashinev, who was trying to get his attention. Given the ropes had been tied by professional sailors, I doubted his chances of breaking free, but he might convince the moronic sailor to free him.

"The gulls," Ockzar continued thoughtfully. "I've always wondered." He laughed, walked to the rail, and turned his face to the horizon. "Upon occasion that is. I don't think about gulls constantly, or indeed often."

"I didn't think you did." Using the rail, I levered myself off the deck. I felt sick, and my foot was turning an unpleasant shade of purple. If I didn't do something about it, I would either die a painful death or become one of the restless dead in thrall to the vordalki waiting for darkness so he could come up top and eat us.

"I remember when I was a child," Ockzar continued. "I would sit on the beach while the others swam, and I would watch the gulls wheeling overhead."

"No swimming, Ockzar? You do surprise me." I limped over to the wheel. Ockzar had his back to me.

He chuckled. "I never saw the appeal of full immersion in cold saltwater teeming with predatory, aquatic creatures. I am fond of a bath of warm water with lots of soap, perhaps a glass of fizz, or two to encourage sweating." Deep in the grip of sweet remembrance, he didn't notice the mist seeping through the deck as the last fingers of sunslight painted the tips of spars a tarnished gold.

"So do you think gulls hunt ships to sleep on?" I asked. Yashinev looked beyond me to the lower deck. His eyes filled with fear, his struggles grew more frantic. I cast a glance over my shoulder, saw the shadow beginning to form behind Grona. "That's the least of your worries, cunt," I hissed.

Yashinev began to sob. Caught in a sudden gust, the sheets snapped, masking the sound of me breaking the archolya's neck. I put my finger to his lips. "Shhhh…"

I'm not going to pretend that this was righteous vengeance; that I believed Yashinev deserved to die because he was a wicked man. I was not the cove to sit in judgment of these things. He could have been the benefactor of an orphanage for all I knew or cared. He'd hurt me, and now, because I needed what he had, I was going to return the favor. I sank my teeth into the fat, throbbing vein in his neck. The gulls took flight, a net of silver against the fading scarlet blush of the clouds.

Ockzar turned towards me. "Breed, it's here," he hissed.

I turned away and wiped my mouth. On the lower deck, Terpelz had his fangs fastened on Grona's face. The fiend looked up, pale eyes shining malevolently. "Get behind me, Ockzar."

Grinning, Terpelz dropped Grona's twitching corpse, which was swallowed by the supernatural fog that blanketed the deck and oozed over the sides of the ship. He didn't bother to wipe his face, which was glazed and glistening with the sailor's blood as he glided towards us.

"You disappointed me, minion. Nevertheless, here we are. Shall we share dessert?"

Neystaya crept into the chapel, her arms white as the snow that was falling. But unlike the snow, she was warm, ... Yashinev's memories ran through my mind as his blood coursed through my veins. *Pyres burned, prayers were said, the smell of incense mixed with the scent of perfume clinging to Nestaya's hair… 'Never leave me,' she said. 'Never,' I replied.* No, not me, him, Yashinev.

"Well?" said Terpelz folding his bloody hands over his chest.

"Oh, you were being serious?"

"Yes."

"No."

"No?"

"No, I won't share."

"Share what?" Ockzar hissed. "What's going on?"

"Shh, Ockzar, the monsters are talking." I cleared my throat. "I'm not going to share, but I do have a proposition for you." My chest burned, the flesh hissed, and I think I saw a thin wisp of silvery smoke escape the cut as the knife wounds Yashinev had inflicted healed.

Like the beast he was, Terpelz canted his head. The sky darkened quickly as leaden clouds gathered overhead. "Speak," he said at last.

My mind raced as I tried to stall long enough for the poison to be purged from my body. "Well, I was thinking that you should leave the ship."

He laughed. "Why would I do that?"

"Because this boat isn't big enough for both of us."

"Er, three of us, actually," Ockzar whispered. I gently elbowed him in the chest.

Thunder rumbled. Terpelz narrowed his eyes. "Do you mock me?"

"Heaven forfend." I smiled as strength returned to my aching limbs. "I suggest you take to a barrel and use your weather witchery to sail to dry land, much like a bottle cast upon the waves. Or perhaps you can turn into a crow, or a bat, or somesuch, and fly to your destination."

"All this to save the meat." He shook his head and glided a little closer.

"Ockzar isn't merely meat," I said and backed up.

"Merely?" said Ockzar.

"Shh," I side-mouthed while keeping the best part of my attention on the infernal. "And if you must make a food analogy, he's more of a stuffed dumpling."

"Oh, thank you very much." Ockzar huffed.

"Shut up, I'm defending you."

"It sounds like it. Just don't let him eat me."

Terpelz glided to the bottom of the steps.

"Stay here," I said to Ockzar and went to the top of the steps. "That's close enough."

"I was old when Voskva was young. You and your-master-over-the-water are as nothing to me."

It began to rain. "No lightning?" I asked.

"Lightning starts fires. We wouldn't want the ship to burn, Captain Petrov would be most annoyed. Now, where was I? Ah, yes." He cleared his throat. "I was old before the Mage Lords fashioned your ancestors out of shit and wishes. You cannot prevail against me, maggot."

I shrugged and thought about all the others who'd said similar. I'd proven many of them wrong. There were probably an equal number who'd kicked the living shit out of me, but I didn't want to think about them now because it was bad for morale. "How about me and him take to a barrel then?"

"You should have left with the others. Or perhaps made less of a fuss when you were being questioned by *him*." His gaze drifted to Yashinev, who was hanging over the wheel like a sloppy drunk. I let my gaze be led to the archolya, and the next thing I felt was a sudden displacement of air as something preternaturally fast rushed towards me. I dived aside, heard claws score the deck where I had been standing. Ockzar yelped. I looked up. Terpelz was looming above him. Without thinking, I leaped onto the infernal's back. His mortified flesh was as hard as stone. Trying to dislodge me, he spun away from Ockzar. I did the first thing that came to mind and bit Terpelz in the neck.

On reflection, I realize it was not the wisest thing to do, but I'll forgive myself because at the time I was up against it. I'm sure that his blood wasn't actually as hot as lava, it just felt like it. I screamed in pain as the hot claret scoured my throat. The Dvor howled, reached a bony claw behind him, tore me from his back, and hurled me onto the lower deck. I tucked and rolled when I hit, but momentum carried me into the capstan. Winded, I watched the light of a thousand stars burst before my eyes. I didn't have time to contemplate the stunning beauty as another blast of rushing air told me Terpelz was closing. I crouched, ready to spring.

"You cannot stand against me, maggot," he hissed. Dark smoke billowed around him. "I have destroyed empires!"

I licked his blood from my lips. "So have I." I leaped, claws raking, fangs bared. He vanished. I landed, hunted for him in the fog. He found me first. A cold hand grabbed my neck, and once again, he threw me across the deck. I managed to turn and hit the steps to the poop deck with my shoulder instead of my face, but before I could get up, he was on me and planted a foot on my chest. My bones creaked.

Terpelz leered at me. "What did I tell you?"

I grabbed his ankle and tried to throw him off. He exerted more pressure. My ribs cracked. I tried to dig my claws into his leg, but it was like trying to scratch marble. By now, I was fighting to draw breath as his crushing weight bore down. I didn't even have the breath to shout to Ockzar to tell him to jump overboard, that to drown was better than having his face chewed off.

As it turns out, that was just as well.

With his attention on me, the real hero of this tale had time to fashion a crude firepot. I wish I could say I'd been privy to his plan, but the first I knew about it was when the bottle of rum with a flaming wick hit Terpelz in the head. The bottle smashed, the rum spilled and caught fire, wreathing the monster's noggin in flames. Screaming, he clutched his head and stumbled blindly away, releasing the pressure on my chest.

"Get him in the water!" Ockzar bellowed.

"But you've just set him on fire," I gasped, confused.

"Fire won't kill him. Running water!" He jabbed at the sea.

"All right, fuck's sake." I grabbed Grona's boathook and rammed it into the infernal's guts. Again, his flesh was so hard it felt like I was hitting stone. I shoved and drove him back to the rail as the fire began to burn itself out. His face was charred, but his fierce eyes still shone with a pale intensity. I flipped the boathook, snagged his ankle, and yanked him off his feet. As he began to fall, I put my head down and charged. Lightning flashed. He flailed as he fell into the sea. The waves boiled around him. Thrashing wildly and screaming like all the demons of hell met in one voice, he clawed at the air, but it was to no avail. I watched as the sea stripped the flesh from his ancient bones. The howling stopped. In minutes, centuries of the bloody parasite's tyranny came to an end. My borrowed strength deserted me, and I sank to the deck, exhausted. The fog dissipated, the clouds parted, the sea calmed. I dared a look over the rail. Not so much as an oil slick marked the Dvor's demise.

Ockzar came over. "Not bad for a dumpling," he said, polishing his spectacles on his torn shirt. Despite his nonchalance, I noted that his hands were shaking.

"How did you…?"

"Know that Vordalki were destroyed by running water?"

"Aye."

He smirked. "I read it in a book. You should try it sometime."

"How did you light the rum, smart arse?"

"The watch lantern has a striker." He pointed to where the lantern was hanging at the bow. "I poured the lantern oil into the rum, to improve adhesion and ensure it burned rather than merely extinguishing itself upon impact. I then used my shirt as a wick and, well, you saw the result."

I climbed to my feet. "Aye, that's what I would have done."

His smile widened. "Of course you would."

Chapter Thirty-One

The dreamy caress of a mermaid stroking my cheek turned into the sad reality of Ockzar slapping my face. It was day, and the suns were hiding behind a benign if dreary wall of grey cloud. I'd fallen into a dream-filled sleep whilst laying on the deck. In these dreams, I'd commanded armies and fucked in a chapel. And by 'I', I mean, Yashinev and Terpelz, whose memories had tangled into an unholy mess in my unconscious mind.

"You're alive," Ockzar smiled before taking a sip of what smelled like chai. "Would you like a sip? Only, I'm afraid we're all out of rats."

I sat up. He'd covered me with a blanket. For a change, everything ached. "Do fuck off, Tobias, there's a good chap."

He regarded me quizzically. "What did you call me?"

"Ockzar. And yes, I'd like a drink. Did you find any more of Petrov's rum?"

"I did. And yes, I also disposed of Grona. You're welcome." He pointedly sipped his chai.

"Did you take his teeth?" I grinned, and after a moment's hesitation, the philosopher's resolve broke, and he smiled back.

"I didn't dare, for fear he might rise from the dead and want them back." He shuddered. "I cannot believe what happened. It almost doesn't seem real in the cold light of day."

I looked to the wheel where a blanket had been thrown over Yashinev. "Why didn't you dispose of that cunt too?"

"I really couldn't face it. I tried, but his eyes are open. I began to cut through the knots, but he was…it was like he was watching me. I just couldn't. It's strange, and you know me, I'm not squeamish. It just made my flesh crawl."

"Don't worry about it." I huddled under the blanket while he poured me a measure of rum from a sadly small flask. Another rumpled bedroll lay near mine, surrounded by the remains of a meal of salt beef and black bread. "Is this all there is?" I said when he handed me the miserly tot.

"That I have found. I can't say I've conducted an extensive search. Even without a vordalki stalking the hold it's still quite unpleasant below decks, what with all the bodies." He shuddered again and fastened the top button on his coat. "Lack of rum is the least of our worries, wouldn't you say?"

I thought about it for a moment as I savored the delicious spirit. "No, but do tell me your thoughts on the matter."

"Well look." He gestured to the ship.

"What?"

"How do we sail it?"

"Not with a corpse tied to the wheel would be my first guess. Aside of that, I haven't a clue." It seemed odd that in all my lives I'd never had call to sail a ship. I necked the rum, put my hands behind my head, and stretched out on the deck.

"Do you have any idea where we are?" His gaze turned to the grey-blue sea.

"Somewhere in the Great Ocean?"

"Well, yes. But we need to know what latitude and longitude and distance to the nearest coast. We need to know all manner of things, I shouldn't wonder. Only I am ignorant as to what they might be."

I could see that I wasn't going to get any peace. I sat up. "Go find a book that explains it. There are bound to be some in Petrov's cabin."

"There aren't, I checked when I went hunting for rum. If a storm blows up the ship could be destroyed. And then there's a matter of supplies, food and drink for me and whatever sustenance you require these days."

I knew what he was driving at. "Fuck's sake." I got up and made my way to the stern.

"Where are you going?" said Ockzar following me, his mug of chai slopping as the deck rocked beneath us gentle as a crib.

"I'm going to take a dump, all right?"

"Oh." He pulled up. "You could use the privy."

"You could mind your own." I arranged my breeches, grabbed a rope, and braced my feet on the rail. "The salt spray really freshens up the nethers. You should try it." I laughed, delighting in his embarrassment. "Don't know about you, but I think more clearly after a good—"

"—Yes, I know, you've said, many times."

"What can I say? I was raised in a sewer."

"Is the Empire really that bad?"

I finished and jumped down off the rail and sorted myself out. "It's just like Voskva, only warmer."

He snorted, shook his head. "It's ruled by a so-called, 'God King'."

"I think Durstan's given up any such pretentions."

"Indeed?"

"So I hear. He's not been the same since a ziggurat fell on his head."

"I don't understand. Is that a saying where you come from?"

"Possibly."

Ockzar rubbed his face and yawned. "I'm so tired."

"Go for a kip. Take the captain's bed."

"I'd rather sleep up here, thank you." He cast a dark look towards the hold. "After the mines I swore I'd never go underground again unless I had to. Below decks feels like being underground, especially now with that fresh corpse stink."

I shrugged. "Suit yourself. I headed to the hatch. My ribs were sore, and I was still limping, but I wasn't badly off considering.

"Where are you going?"

"To bring up the bodies and have a look around for charts."

"Good luck. The only thing Petrov left was a stocking with a hole in it and a blotter on his desk with, 'Here Be Krakens' scrawled upon it. I think. It was hard to decipher his terrible handwriting. I despair of the state of education in the old days. Although, there is yet much to be desired even now in the provinces. If I was in charge, all children would have at least one year of free education."

"That's nice." Fascinating though it was to hear Ockzar's manifesto for a better Voskva, I headed down to the captain's cabin. The stink of death was strong, and silence only added to the grim atmosphere. Petrov was a practical cove, and aside from a few bad paintings of ships, a nightshirt, and a chamber pot, there wasn't much in the way of creature comforts in his cabin. I ran my hand over the blotting pad. I didn't read Voskvan at all on account of their letters being wrong, but something Ockzar said gave me an idea.

It might have been because I was not quite myself, it might also have been that I was delusional. After all, I was hearing voices. Or it might have been the booze had addled my mind, but I had an idea which, had anyone suggested it to me, I would have laughed at. I went back on deck where Ockzar was hacking at a loaf of bread.

"Lend me your knife."

A look of suspicion clouded his face. "What are you going to do with it?"

"Cut your throat and sacrifice you to ancient gods, what do you think?"

"You say that like it isn't a possibility."

"I just have an idea is all which probably won't work but it's worth trying."

"What is it?"

"I don't want to tell you because it sounds stupid even to me. Just hand it over."

He wiped it on his breeches before grudgingly giving it to me. I took it to the bowsprit and clambered out along the spar.

"What are you doing?" Ockzar asked as he brushed crumbs from his coat.

"Possibly the most stupid thing I've done all day."

He squinted at the sky. "And the suns not yet over the yard arm, how exciting."

I drew the blade across the palm of my left hand, mindful not to cut too deep and damage my finger strings, but enough to get blood welling. It stung, and I thought I felt the serpent recoil within me. Or perhaps I was growing squeamish in my old age. Either way, I chummed the water with my blood and watched the inky trail of red drip into the deeps.

"I call the kraken," I whispered and tried to will my wish down the thread of my claret.

"Breed?" Ockzar had dared his dislike of Yashinev's scarecrow corpse and come to the fo'c'sle. "In all seriousness, are you feeling well?" he asked, like someone who thought I'd lost my mind.

I squeezed the last drops of blood from the shallow wound. "I, Deep Water, call the brachuri." I felt particularly stupid, but as Ockzar was the only witness and would die with me should we fail to reach land, it was an embarrassment I could live with.

He sniggered. "I think you've had too much sun."

The ship sat low in the still water, which was as smooth as glass and had been so for two, long, dull days. I had not entirely given up hope of rescue, but I had also taken to considering other options while I waited for another gull to take the bait.

"I'm going to do it," said Ockzar, who was pacing on the main deck, a borrowed hat perched on his surprisingly large noggin.

"Fucking leave him," I said as the gulls hovered over Yashinev's increasingly fragrant bone bag. "I thought you enjoyed fresh meat?"

"Not seagull meat. I'm fine with the hard tack and weevil biscuits, thanks all the same. That—" He pointed imperiously to the corpse lashed to the wheel. "Must be removed."

"No."

"We need to use the fucking wheel!" He stamped his foot.

"For what? Look around there's no wind, no waves. The ship is pointing in vaguely the right direction, I think. I promise, as soon as the wind picks up, I'll chuck him overboard, but until then, he stays."

"You're disgusting."

I folded my arms sat back against the rail. "Because I drink the blood of seagulls?"

"That and the way you catch them."

"I thought it was quite ingenious. The Archolya Yashinev always wanted to serve the people, and now he is." Over the course of two days, I'd become a good shot with the old harpoon I'd found in the stores. It made a mess of the birds, but it did the trick, and I'd only hit the body once.

"Why don't you just spear fish?"

I shook my head. "That wouldn't be a good idea."

He laughed bitterly. "Oh, yes, I forgot. You're friends with the fish— sorry, with a *kraken*."

"I forgive you your ill temper and condescension. It's probably the sunslight frying your thick, Voskvan brain box."

"Frying *my* brain? At least I don't stand on the edge of a ship, bleeding and asking a kraken to come and help me."

When he put it like that, it did sound stupid. "Fuck it. I'll swim then. The Empire is roughly that way." I pointed south. "It can't be too far; we've been at sea for days."

"Go on, then. Swim for it. See how far you get before realizing what a terrible mistake you've made. Then swim back if you can, that is, unless a kraken eats you." He leaned against the opposite rail and folded his arms like my more stupid, shorter, fatter, paler twin. I narrowed my eyes. He narrowed his. He was mocking me, nay, he was goading me.

"You're acting like this is my fault," I railed.

"You won't let me untie that corpse from the wheel. It's repugnant."

"He had me beaten, and he stabbed me, twice."

"So that's the excuse, is it? He behaves like a savage, so you do?"

"It's not that." I didn't tell him that a nasty little voice was almost constantly whispering in my mind. I didn't tell him that it said I should rip out his heart and eat it like a ripe peach. Neither did I mention the only respite I got from its incessant goading was when I was drinking fucking seagull blood, which tasted vaguely of fish.

Evil, whispering voices aside, I had an almost physical need to get back to Valen and Leo, as though the Prince of the Midnight Court was calling to me. "And anyway, he can't feel anything."

"Instead of waiting for sea horses to pull us to Valen, we need to try and sail the ship."

"Just be patient."

"We're going to die!" he raged.

"Eventually, aye."

"You're insane."

"Quite possibly." He couldn't see that about a hundred feet behind him, the sea was beginning to heave and swell. When the ship started to gently roll to starboard, he followed the track of my gaze.

"Gasvoy's…" His words were drowned as the skin of the ocean split, and the head of the kraken broke the surface. Some fifty feet from the ship, its gigantic tentacles thrashed the waves before they uncoiled, gripped the rail of the boat, and drew us closer. Standing just behind the gigantic, bulbous head, ankle-deep in water was someone I recognized.

"Grey Hide!" I shouted and gave a cheery wave to the old brachuri. Dozens more of the crustaceous warriors swarmed over the partially submerged back of the beast, pincers snapping, armored tails swinging. Given their particularly crabby physiognomy, it was hard to tell if they were pleased to see us or if they were going to kill us.

"You really do know a kraken." said Ockzar. He clung to the rail as water poured over the gunwales.

"I did say."

"Please tell me you are firmest friends with these sea demons."

"Possibly wouldn't call them that." It struck me that I didn't know this *exact* crew, that they merely resembled those I had met but once in less than pleasant circumstances in another world. "They're more, friends of friends."

Grey Hide leaned on his harpoon staff. All four of his eyestalks were directed toward me and all four eyes narrowed in steely contemplation. What felt like a long time passed with us eyeballing each other before he gave a deep-throated whistle. One of the smaller tentacles whipped over the side and came towards me. There was nothing much I could have done to avoid it, so I stood still and let it enfold me. It plucked me from the deck with surprising gentleness and deposited me on its head beside Grey Hide. The brachuri leaned towards me.

"Who youm, skin bag?"

"Actually, sirrah, the last time we met you called me, Deep Water." He showed no recognition, and why would he? "You also thanked me and called me 'savior' for saving the lives of some fry." It was with mounting concern that I noted there wasn't a flicker of recognition in his eyes. But they had come, hadn't they? They had answered my summons. I pressed on. "You broke my hammer—but I don't bear a grudge." I added hastily. "You told me the waters of your fief run wild and deep." A shudder ran through the kraken's back.

Grey Hide couldn't frown as such, but the tailless elder canted his head questioningly. "That sounds like me. I think Youm met weem in Strange Waters."

I clicked my fingers. "Exactly! That's what you said, and then you said, I should call upon you any time I needed assistance, like now."

He shook his head. The many piercings in his wide, skull shell jangled. "That doesn't sound like weem."

"'Tis the abridged version, but that was the essence of our discourse. Oh, there was something else. You said to remember that 'You wanted to live'." The kraken trembled, almost throwing me off my feet. The brachuri warriors closed in. Out of the corner of my eye, I could see Ockzar's pale face peering nervously from behind the mast.

"What do youm want?"

"A tow, to the Empire, the er, what did you call it? 'The land of ash and death'? The one to the south."

The gathered brachuri chirped and clacked their pincers. I still didn't know if they were keen to help or were about to cut me to pieces. Grey Hide sat back on the stump of his severed tail. A shiver ran down my spine. He looked the same in every detail that I could recall, yet it wasn't the Grey Hide I'd met all those years ago. I felt a terrible pang of homesickness, a sudden yearning for the simple life of a guild enforcer. A more powerful compulsion swept aside my pathetic desire. I had to return to Valen and Duke Leo with all haste.

"Yes. Weem want to live," said Grey Hide. His eyestalks twitched thoughtfully. "When the blood tide comes, youm remember, eh?"

I didn't know what he meant the first time we'd met, and I didn't know now. "Absolutely." I smiled warmly. "You have my word. Can we go now?"

"No."

"*No?*"

Grey Hide warbled and clicked, and one of the warty scabs on the kraken's back peeled back. A Shushun, one of the lamprey creatures that served the brachuri, slithered out clutching something dripping in slime. "Weem got something for youm," said the brachuri elder. "Weem been waiting for youm."

I didn't like the sound of that. "You don't have to give me anything save a tow to the Empire." At the behest of the old brachuri, the shushun servant turned to me, its toothsome mouth dripping with foul-smelling spit. Crouching and servile, it timidly approached and held out a slimy stick of gods-only-knew what. I took it and smiled as my finger sank into thick mucus and closed around a hard shaft. "Thank you," I said and politely inclined my head.

Grey Hide grunted. "Never thought weem would see the day." He tapped his staff on the kraken's back. The water around the hulking leviathan began to boil as its huge gills churned. Another tentacle wrapped around me and dumped me back on the ship. Grey Hide and the rest of the brachuri stood behind the kraken's head as the leviathan slowly sank below the waves, causing the ship to rock.

"If I hadn't seen it with my own eyes," said Ockzar, an expression of puzzlement crossed with fear writ upon his sunburned face. "Who are you, Breed?"

I shrugged. I felt rather than saw the kraken approach the stern of the ship. The timbers creaked and groaned as it grabbed hold of the hull below the waterline.

"Is it really going to push us?"

"Aye, I think it is."

"This is sorcery unlike any I have ever heard of." Obviously astonished, he laughed. "Or I'm dreaming. What did they give you?" His voice trembled with excitement. His gaze darted, unable to settle as he searched the seething water for sight of the kraken. "Did they give you something valuable, a token perhaps?"

I'd almost forgotten the slimy stick due to the numbing shushun spit which coated the thing. I scraped the thick mucus off against the rail.

Ockzar came over. "What is it?"

I was speechless.

"Breed?"

"It's er, it's." I rubbed my eyes and instantly regretted it.

"It looks like the shaft of something, an axe perhaps."

"A hammer." The sea boiled around us; the ship lurched forward. "It's the shaft of a hammer."

Chapter Thirty-Two

The *Dimitra* did not survive the crossing intact. Ockzar and I tried ineptly to take in the sheets, but the kraken moved quicker than us and some were ripped from the masts before we could save them. In the grip of a creature more used to smashing than pushing, the hull was damaged and began to let in water due to the strain of being forced through the waves.

When it finally released us, the vessel slewed sideways. Water sloshed around in the hold, throwing cargo around like toys. Helpless, we drifted towards the coast, broadside on, until a friendly current spun us like a bottle. By pure chance, we ended up aimed prow first as we bobbed towards land.

Ockzar crawled from under the shrouds, over which shreds of torn canvas hung like the banners of a losing army. "I think that was the worst experience of my life. It is not meant for mortals to move at such ferocious speed. My humors have been displaced. Oh shit, is the ship going to sink? It's going to sink, isn't it?"

"No. Well, not for hours. Probably not for hours." I grinned. I was elated, overjoyed to see the coast of the Empire and to have the shaft of the hammer, of the Hammer of the North— *my father's* hammer, in my possession once more.

"We could make a raft," Ockzar suggested, whilst ineffectively tugging at a piece of fallen canvas.

"Or we could drift a bit closer to the shore and swim for it," I countered. I was not in the mood to build anything.

He looked around forlorn, despairing. "Why did they just dump us here, miles from land?"

"Because kraken are too big to get close to shore, which is a good thing, or no harbor would be safe." The ship creaked ominously.

"Will you help me make a raft?" Ockzar implored.

"No." I laughed. "You can see the fucking houses, never mind the shore. We're close enough to swim, not to mention, do you want to explain all this to the law when you sail into the nearest harbor?" I gestured to the wrecked ship and Yashinev's battered corpse still tethered to the wheel. "If we swim, we can fetch up unseen and put a bit of distance between us and all this."

"I don't swim." He folded his arms.

"Don't?"

He blushed. "I understand the principle, but never quite managed to master the coordinated physical effort required to propel myself, or indeed, stay afloat."

"Because I'm a kind and generous soul, I'll give you a piggyback."

He peered into the water. "Are you sure they're gone?"

"No. But if it makes you feel better, we'll drift a bit closer before disembarking. And I don't think they'd do for us after towing us across the Great Ocean." I came up behind him and looked into the depths. "Look at that, we could be twins," I said as our reflections swam side by side upon the milky jade water.

"It's the cheekbones." His smile turned to a frown. "Stop making me laugh. I'm still angry with you."

"Why?"

He looked at Yashinev. "Well, there's him for a start, and you never mentioned you had powers over the denizens of the ocean. When we met, I had no idea— couldn't begin to imagine how strange and dangerous..." He sighed. "You have shown me another world, one I am not sure I am entirely comfortable with." He drew a long breath and exhaled heavily, evidently relieved to have said his piece.

I slapped him on the shoulder. "Sorry, jimma. When we met, I was under a geas, and I wasn't myself. I didn't deceive you on purpose. Truth be told, when Swann flooded the mine, I didn't have time to explain myself. If I had a year, I couldn't begin to tell you all there is to know about me."

He looked me squarely in the eyes. "I believe you. Gods help me for being a fool, but I believe you."

"I know. Scary, ain't it?"

"Just a bit."

The sound of gurgling coming from below preceded the ship determinedly listing to port. "Get your gear and wrap it in an oilskin. It's time to go."

"When I said, 'get your gear' I didn't mean bring everything that isn't nailed down," I said to Ockzar as I swam between black fangs of rock thick with barnacles and bearded by clumps of seaweed. Ockzar didn't answer. He just clung to my neck and shivered. "How is it you're cold? You're from Voskva. And coated in a reasonable layer of blubber."

"H…human. N…not wars…spawn."

"Any excuse. Hold on." I let a breaker carry me in and concentrated on steering myself between the rocks instead of smashing my face upon them. A gallery of barnacles scraped the skin from my forearm, but I managed to navigate the rising tide and slap of surf to take us into the shallows. When our shadow passed, crabs and other critters scuttled for shelter amongst the glistening black rock. "You can let go now," I said and tapped Ockzar's clammy arm. He let go and scrambled stiff-limbed up the beach. I dug my claws into the sand and enjoyed the feel of water slamming against my legs. I turned and sighted the sea through the gaps in the rocks. "Thanks," I said, sure that the kraken was out there somewhere.

I would have liked to press on, but as Ockzar had turned a rather unflattering shade of blue I figured I should do something to try and stop him dying. I dragged him to some nearby dunes and sat him down while I gathered driftwood. He had been wise enough to pack a flint and striker, which with a few feathers and dry grass kindled a decent fire. It roared to life thanks to the strong breeze blowing off the ocean. "I used to be able to click my fingers and create fire." I snorted. "I used to be able to breathe fire, come to that."

"Not now, Breed," said Ockzar, as he shuffled close enough to the flames to start steaming. It was a cold, blustery day, but we were protected from the worst of the wind in a dell between the grass-crested dunes. "Where are we?"

"Oh, let me just pull the map out of my arse and I'll tell you."

"This is your homeland." He looked genuinely surprised at my lack of geographical knowledge. "I could draw the contours of Voskva in the sand before I could walk."

"Do you know how to pick a pocket?"

He laughed. "Obviously not, and I see where you're going with that question, but you are not a youth anymore. You could learn all manner of subjects, including geography, if you'd a mind to."

"Just as soon as I am released from Duke Leo's service, then I promise, I'll immerse myself in study and self-improvement."

"A pursuit in which I would be more than happy to participate."

"That's settled then; we shall become students of the Empire, travelling the land in our carriage and attending lectures in the finest universities."

"Such as they are." He smiled playfully.

Joking aside, the idea of spending a few years just learning from scrolls, books, and venerable scholars was appealing. Alas, I had places to be and people to kill.

"Are you all right?" asked Ockzar. "You look thoughtful."

I stoked the fire. "Don't be fooled, it's just the cast of my face."

He smiled; his face lit up in the glow of the flames. "I'm familiar with your countenance in repose. I believe I have seen most of your moods from coldly murderous to sardonic—a particular favorite of yours. Then there is that rarest of beasts; 'thoughtful' or as in this case, dare I say, melancholic."

"Depends if you like your teeth." I smiled.

"It's not an insult."

"I know. I just don't do 'melancholy'."

"No, of course you don't."

Neither of us spoke for a while which suited me. I was content to listen to the whisper of surf dancing lightly over shingles, the roar of breakers, and the mournful cries of seabirds.

"I'm worried for you, Breed," said Ockzar, breaking the sweet silence. "I am worried for your *condition*."

I poked the fire, added another twisted piece of driftwood, and watched something bound from a crack before the flames could devour it. I empathized. "By, 'condition', you mean that I drink blood as well as dine on more common vittles?"

"You died, my friend."

I chuckled. "It isn't as rare as you might imagine."

He heaved a heavy sigh. "Again, I no longer doubt you when you say such things. But surely it is not a state of being that you find desirable?"

"Oh, I don't know. I mean, I can walk abroad during the day; I don't have a compulsion to rip out your throat and drink your blood. Or the blood of any other sentient, come to that." *'Liar,'* the serpent hissed. "I have everything under control," I said, and stabbed the fire.

***

Despite what Ockzar thought, I did not get lost searching for the road to Valen. I merely considered the best way to approach the city to avoid unnecessary encounters with greenshanks or clanks.

"I admit, it looks impressive, but I think I can smell it from here," said Ockzar as we cut across country on a road that would, I hoped, take us around the city to Leo's dilapidated mansion.

"This is nothing. Wait until the wind's blowing in the right direction, or even better, the height of summer."

He shook his head. "The first thing the Archonate did after the Glorious Revolution was build sewerage systems in every major city in Voskva."

"With slave labor?"

"Educational work parties were used, yes, but for the good of all."

"Uh-huh. This way." I pointed out a partially submerged road of marble slabs. Mist roiled lazily at ankle height, and the air was damp and tasted of earthy rot and decay.

"Are you sure?" He eyed the road suspiciously. "Only, the suns will be going down soon, and that fog is bound to thicken. We might get lost…again."

"We won't get lost at all." To the west lay Valen, the sparkle of streetlamps already picking holes in the lilac gloam. "I tell you what. It won't take but a few minutes to conclude my business with the duke. There's an inn near the Swan Theatre in town called, *The Merry Widows.*

"Swan Theatre?" He looked worried.

"Nothing to do with the talismancer. It's a highly reputable establishment and extremely popular. I'll meet you there in about an hour, three at most."

He looked askance. "Are you trying to dump me?"

"Don't be silly. There's just no point you getting soaked. The tide sweeps into the lowlands and drowns these roads. You'll hate it and I don't much fancy listening to you moan about it for the duration."

He didn't look convinced.

"I'll be there before you know it, I promise."

He did the worst thing he could do and looked hurt. Damn the man, why did he have to play the wounded puppy now when I had to dump him? I tried to convince myself it wouldn't be for long, but as I knew I was a lying cunt, that didn't wash. "Here," I said, and on a whim, perhaps to prove my honesty to myself as much as him, I handed him the shaft of the Hammer's hammer. A look of incredulity lit upon his face as he took it from me. "Don't lose it, or I swear, I'll skin you alive."

"Of course not, that is, I won't lose it." He beamed like a child.

"Just take the road back that way and head for the lights. It's safe enough, just don't mouth off at the greenshanks."

"I do not 'mouth off', as you say. I am here to observe and look down upon your civilization, not 'mouth off'." He stuffed the broken artifact into his bundle. I wasn't worried that he might lose it; it had found its way back to me across time and from another world. Relieved, I watched him plod towards the city with his pack slung over his shoulder.

"Keep to the main roads," I called. "And don't talk to strangers!" He turned and waved. I watched him until he took the road to Valen, and then I headed to Leo's, driven by a nagging sense of urgency.

A bank of fog rolled up the estuary obscuring the road, but I fancied that way off in the distance, I could see the cold lights of Leo's demesne burning through the fog. As much as I wanted to believe that in a couple of hours, I'd be sitting in the rather charming inn, enjoying a bottle of wine with Ockzar, listening to him tell me how bad it was compared to Voskvan fizz, I didn't think it was going to happen. Not only had I failed Leo, but why would he release me from his service? If I were him— a prince of a court in flux, I'd hang on to all those who were handy with a blade; better yet, those who were disposable.

Up ahead, a flock of crows burst from their roost in a willow thicket, shouting angrily at whatever had disturbed them. I was still some way off, so it couldn't have been me. Beyond the trees stood the remains of a gatehouse. One side of the relic had slid into the mire and the teeth of old stone stood out against the dancing glow of firelight coming from within the derelict building. I continued, outwardly nonchalant, inwardly alert, tasting the air for whoever or whatever were warming their cockles in the ruin. A gently undulating bridge lay between me and the gatehouse. Scarred by age and covered in pillows of moss and clumps of lurid fungus, it had the look of somewhere a fairy tale troll might have chosen to take up residence. When I was halfway across, the wind shifted and carried with it a familiar smell. I looked beyond the gatehouse to the manor. So close. As I had become aware of him, he had become aware of me, and shadows danced within the ruins.

A hulking silhouette appeared in the archway of the gate. "Breed," said Nic.

"Well, if it isn't proof that shit can step in itself."

He chuckled. "That's funny. You know, I'd almost given up on you." He had a bottle in his hand and leaned against the wall, presumably to steady himself as the reek of booze was almost as strong as that of wet rat. He took a swig of whatever he was drinking. "Come closer. Don't worry, I'm all alone."

"Alone, sure," I said to myself as dozens of beady, emerald rat eyes winked in the fog. "Listen, I'd love to stay and chat about old times, but I'm here to see your brother."

"No need. I gave him the Vascellum."

"Did you tell him you left me to die?"

"I told him you were dead. Close enough, eh?" He stepped from the shadows. He looked like he'd been in an argument with a brick wall and had lost. Half his face was a bloody pulp. One eye was either closed or missing.

"What they fuck happened to you?"

"Nothing, I'm fine."

"I don't give a shit if you're fine or not. I'm just curious to know who used your face as an anvil. I'd like to buy them a drink."

"How are you still alive? I have seen you die twice now. What's your secret?"

I smiled. "Ask your brother."

"Ah, well. He isn't talking to me. He wasn't best pleased that I left you truth be told. There was me, thinking I'd done him a favor, but no." He laughed, spat blood. "He knew. Somehow Leo knew you weren't dead. When I told him that I'd seen you die in the mud, he just laughed at me."

"That's because you're a clown."

"You know, when I kill you, I'm going to tear you limb-from-limb, burn the pieces, and salt the ashes, just to be sure."

"Tsk, tsk, what would Leo say?"

"Fuck Leo," he snarled. "He's convinced you'll turn up. Do you believe that?"

"Evidently."

"He's in there right now." He stabbed a clawed finger towards the house. His eyes grew wider, and the irises shifted from brown to scarlet. "He's waiting for you. *You.*" He gave a hard laugh and thumped himself in the chest. "It was me gave him his precious, fucking Vascellum and he looked at it, *at me,* like I'd handed him a steaming turd." He downed the contents of the bottle before smashing it against the wall. "What makes you so special, tert?"

I shrugged. "Charm, wit, good looks, an encyclopedic knowledge of curse words. So many things, you festering cunt pock." As he was also a lying pustule, I scanned the gatehouse for any accomplices, half expecting to see the tell-tale wisps of Swann's pel pipe, but I neither saw nor smelled anyone else. "What are you doing out here? Did the guard dog die? Did you do a mess on the carpet?"

"He threw me out! He did this." Nic pointed to his bloody face. "He told me to go." His morose gaze turned inward. "I have served him all my life. Decades of loyalty. He's supposed to be my brother. And yet the one time I use my initiative—"

"—You end up in the dog rat house. My heart bleeds for you."

He dropped to all fours, dug his claws into the muddy road. "It will."

The sound of breaking bones heralded the change in form. Because I'm not an idiot or a believer in fair fights, I didn't wait for him to finish turning from a mouthy prick into a ravening monster. I charged. He looked up just in time to see me taking a swing at him. My claws were long and sharp. I caught him under the chin and tore his face off. To make sure the job was done and to slake my terrible thirst, I leaped upon his back and rode him into the ground. His faceless head lolled. Like my claws, my teeth were long and sharp…

In death, the thing that was not quite human, and not quite a rat, twisted and writhed. I jumped clear as unguided by a living mind; whatever rancid magic wrought the transformation ran amok through his dying body. Bones burst from his back, extra limbs sprouted from those he already possessed, fur grew and was shed, grew again, claws tore at the ground. As his memories ran through my mind, his bone bag tore itself apart. Finally, with a last, quivering spasm, the thing that had been Nicodemus grew still.

And that was when the rats swarmed across the marsh and flowed towards the gatehouse like a dark wave.

Chapter Thirty-Three

Having little time to gather my wits and divest myself of Nic's memories, I clambered onto the gatehouse. There I stayed, the grimmest of gargoyles, and watched the sleek horde of rats devour the deconstructed bone bag.

Tearing him to pieces seemed an odd way to treat their master, but the rodents set about the enforcer with savage enthusiasm. Even though the desire to discharge my duty to Leo was strong, part of me yearned to be on my way to *the Merry Widows*. *Soon,* I promised myself, as the rats melted into the swamp leaving naught but a bloody stain and the stink of offal behind them.

Like the last time I'd visited, the mansion was wreathed in mist which engendered an air of sinister mystery, as I am sure was the intention. The copper doors were swinging open, spots of blood were slowly fading to pink in the waterlogged entrance hall. I didn't bother to knock, but I tasted the air when I entered. It smelled of mold, wet fur, blood, and death. Bespeaking the tale of his violent and disgraced departure from his brother's house, claret mottled the marble staircase. With a feeling of dread weighing heavily upon me, I made my way to the duke's chamber.

Leo was standing by the window, his hands behind his back. He smiled when I entered. To give credence to my growing sense of foreboding, an incongruous stone sarcophagus stood in the middle of the floor. The smashed remains of the Vascellum glittered upon the lid.

"Not sure I like the new table," I said as I splashed through the inch of scummy bog water that skinned the floor. It was hard to imagine this foppish, little gent had given Nic a kicking but worth remembering because he had.

Leo's black eyes were unreadable. "I knew you wouldn't let me down." There was an unmistakable note of triumph in his tone.

"I didn't have much choice in the matter, did I?" I glanced over my shoulder, saw that Wulf's ax was still hanging above the door.

"Much like freedom, choice is overrated." Leo gave a wry smile. "I have come to learn that most creatures are happier when someone else tells them what to do. Come in, Breed. Come closer, let me look at you."

I did as he bid. Although the compulsion was not explicit, it lay under his words like veins beneath the skin. A sudden chill invaded my bones as I drew near the sarcophagus. "You have the Vascellum, release me." I knew that wasn't going to happen before the words left my mouth, but I do like the sound of my own voice.

"No preamble?" He stroked his hairless chin, a youth with ancient eyes. "I was looking forward to hearing all about your adventures in Voskva."

"I thought your beloved brother would have told you all there was to know."

His smile didn't falter. "As we both know, Nicodemus is not the most erudite fellow. I want to hear what you have to say."

I suddenly felt exhausted. "Stop fucking with me. You've got what you want, now let me go—"

Bright as a meteor burning in the firmament, something exploded in the city. Shortly thereafter, a fire-driven wind roared across the marsh. The blast was so powerful that the lanterns guttered and swung wildly on their chains. "What the fuck was that?"

Leo didn't flinch. Neither did he seem in the least surprised as flames reached into the sky above Valen. "It was inevitable, tragic, and on the scale of things, irrelevant. But let's talk about you. More importantly, that which you have brought me." His tail flicked lazily from side to side. "I have waited patiently for the pieces to fall into place. There were times when I doubted, times when I thought all was lost. Do you know what it is like to live half a life, Breed? To dwell only in the shadows."

"Yes, and?" I didn't know where this was leading, but I knew it wasn't anywhere I wanted to go.

"I believe you. Like me, you are a singular creature. Extraordinary, without peers, in your own way."

"It's what I keep telling people. But I fear if you flatter me any more my head will swell and burst. What do you want, Duke?"

"That which will resurrect my love, my friend."

"Then we're done. You have it." I pointed to the shards on the sarcophagus. "That's all we found."

His tail flicked angrily. "As you would say, don't fuck with me. I know what you took. This?" He gestured to the Vascellum with a bloody claw. "Is a tease, a hint at best, at worst a distraction that would only fool idiots like my brother."

I laughed as we circled the bone box, me going one way and he the other. "As my mother would say, you shouldn't speak ill of the dead." There was a momentary flash of anger in his otherwise implacable expression. "You know, I used to be a sorcerer."

"I know."

"And a dragon." We continued to circle the box. "I was very good at both."

"Yes. I know. I saw it all when I tasted your blood. I had an inkling of your potential when I sampled the tantalizing drop you left on the book. It was enough to convince me that you were sent by Fate to aid me. So, I waited, and I watched for the opportunity to present itself for me to, *know you better*. That opportunity came when I saved you from the Paradox. You do remember that I saved your life?" He leaned on the sarcophagus and lovingly stroked the lid. "I saw it all then. Your mind was like an open book to me."

"As you were to me."

He chuckled mirthlessly. "No, I wasn't. I have used blood magic too long to make such a mistake."

I was right. This wasn't headed anywhere good. "Who's in the box?"

He smiled. "Can't you guess?"

I could, I just didn't want to. "No."

He laughed. "The rats bring me things of value, things that have been lost or discarded." He glanced at Wulf's ax, then back at the box. "The untimely sacrificed. This is Fate." He stroked the lid. "This was meant to be."

"It really wasn't."

"Not in your tale, perhaps. But this is my story. I'm afraid your role is small, but the part you play is vital."

"Don't get me wrong, I like a theatrical metaphor as much as the next cove, but I've got places to be. Keep your word, Duke, and release me." I refrained from saying, 'please' just in case it was my last word. I wasn't going to give this, ogren's dildo the satisfaction of hearing me beg.

He drew a knife from the sleeve of his velvet coat. "And I thought you'd be pleased."

This was the point where I should have come up with a clever way to extricate myself from the situation. Alas, nothing came to mind, leaving me with but one chance to get out of this stinking pot of arsepickle. "How do you work that—" I said and made to leap upon him as I had his brother, and similarly remove his smug, little face, for as Mother often said; *when wit fails, blades prevail'.* Or, in this case, claws.

I want to say that my beautifully simple plan worked. But that would be a lie, and I hardly ever lie to you. Instead of ripping his gizzard out, I walked calmly around the sarcophagus until I stood before him. Not for the first time in my life I was a passenger in my traitorous body. "As I was saying, how do you work that out? Take your time. I'm sure it's a fascinating explanation."

He tutted. "Inappropriate humor is a habit of yours. It is irritating and no doubt a defensive reaction to adversity. Understandable, given the circumstances, but you needn't be afraid." He shoved the lid off the box. The noise reverberated around the chamber, set bats to flight, and caused the rats to scatter. "I promise, it won't hurt. Hold out your arm."

"No."

'Yesss...' The serpent, the Vascellum, hissed in my mind. "Wait!" I begged.

"Oh, but I have. I have waited for centuries. And now I will see a new dawn break, and it will be glorious."

"So, you're not retiring?" I asked, desperate to buy myself more time.

"I was planning on leaving Valen, but then I tasted your blood, and I had a revelation."

"You're welcome. Now, let me go and I'll call us even."

"I will. Soon." The knife flashed as it caught the light. "Hold out your arm."

"No," I said as I held my arm over the box like a fucking idiot. I glanced down, saw a shrouded body within. "Don't do this." It was so unfair. Even though I strained with every fiber of my being to be free, all I could do was watch as Leo opened my arm from elbow to wrist. Being a master of blood magic, he knew exactly what to do and, with the precision of a surgeon, severed the main artery that ran between the bones of my forearm. Blood sheeted the body, soaked the linen shroud, and outlined a face I knew better than my own. My heart sank as the Vascellum fled the prison of my flesh.

"You are released," said Leo breathlessly.

"And you are a cunt," I said as I stumbled back, my claret spraying everywhere. The world began to darken at the edges. I gripped my arm above the elbow in a bid to stem the bleeding. It was all too little too late, but I am not immune to panic. Leo dropped to his knees and bowed his head. A pale hand gripped the edge of the sarcophagus. Bloody fingers dug into the stone.

"Behold," Leo said, blood tears coursing down his cheeks. "Halda, the Red Witch has risen." Robed in scarlet, pale skin glistening with my blood, Mother rose from the coffin. But it wasn't her, not really. It wore her form, but this wasn't her. It *couldn't* be. My mother smelled of wine and sorcery. The thing standing before me smelled of blood and fury.

"It isn't her," I said, even as I saw the silver scar on her neck that marked where Ludo had cut off her head.

"Only the Vascellum; the Heart of Darkness could restore her. Who better than her own offspring to carry it? Do you see now that this was meant to be?"

I sank to the floor, unable to reconcile what I saw with what I knew. Mother was dead. Her dreadful, red-eyed gaze fell upon me. She climbed from the bone box and reached towards me. I looked into her red eyes. Red eyes with slit pupils—the eyes of a serpent looking out of my mother's face. "You are not Halda the Red Witch." *Although I wish to all the gods and with all my heart that you were.* "You're a snake." The face I knew better than my own twisted in fury. She grabbed me by the shirt and dragged me to my feet.

"Kiss me, child, and I will forgive you. Kiss your mother and be healed," it hissed.

A clever cove might play along, and I am a clever cove, but I am also headstrong and stubborn and possessed of a terrible temper. Before Leo thought to put the 'fluence on me, I spat in her eye.

In return, she hurled me through the window.

She threw me with such force that I hit the mud and then bounced across the mire like a skimmed stone. I fetched up against a tree stump and tumbled gracelessly into a pool of black water. Winded and choking on mud, I clawed at the bank with my one good arm. Sensing the sudden arrival of dinner, things slithered through the reeds.

If I didn't move, I'd die. "Come on, Breed, move your arse." In pain but determined, I began to drag myself out of the muddy water, my sights set on reaching the gatehouse still faintly outlined by the light of Nic's dying fire. I was making slow progress when a gristly tentacle coiled around my ankle and began to pull me back into the mire. I grabbed the branch of the dead tree and kicked at whatever held me. It tightened its grip, pulled harder. The branch broke.

"For fuck's—"

I went under and swallowed a mouthful of marsh water. I am warspawn, I am strong, but that last, inopportune breath undid me. I began to drown. Sensing a feast, those rats not sated eating Nic slid from the bank and joined my attacker. I wondered if I would drown before I was disemboweled and which of those deaths would be least painful. Without warning, the tentacle uncoiled. I didn't question the stroke of luck, but with what little strength remained, I lurched for the surface as the rats began to nip at me. Spent, all I could do was flail like a drunk. But then I realized they weren't trying to bite me. They were biting my clothes, trying to drag me. I stopped fighting.

When I next opened my eyes, I found that I was lying on solid, if sodden ground. Someone was standing over me, another ghost from my past come to visit. She shooed her furry helpers away and crouched to get a better look. She was wearing a fur mantle fringed with beaded rat tails, but her face was the same as I remembered, mischievous dark eyes, a long nose, straggly hair, and huge, front teeth.

"Clary?" I gasped. "It's good to see you."

She wrinkled her rattish nose. "No one's called me that in a long time." Her dark eyes shone in the moonlight. "I, am the Rat Queen."

"Rat Queen?"

She nodded.

It seemed that Fate had chosen to throw me a bone after all. I forced myself to sit up and sketched an unsteady bow. "Your servant, Majesty."

The End.

Free Books

If you haven't already read them; head over to my website to get two free *Chronicles of Breed* prequel stories!

I love telling the stories of Breed's exploits; *The Best Laid Plans* and *A Fistful Of Rubies* are available for free if you type the link below into your web browser and join my mailing list.

https://kdavies.net/nltac

Author's Note

I would like to ask that you consider leaving me a review, they really help. Obviously, it would be awesome if you tell everyone how much you liked this book, but even if you didn't its always great to get feedback from my readers.

Typing this link into your internet browser will take

you to Amazon's review page.

https://kdavies.net/rngd

Thanks again.

K.T.

About the Author

When I'm not writing books, I work the day job, wrangle my kids and three dogs. I play computer games, ride horses, practice medieval martial arts, throw axes, and read, not at the same time, that could get messy.

I have a website here https://kdavies.net

And a Facebook page at https://www.facebook.com/KTScribbles where we can hang out, have a couple of brewskis, and talk about the good old days.

I am also on Instagram at https://www.instagram.com/kt.davies/

Once again, thank you so much for going on a ride with me and Breed. I hope I see you again soon.

All the best,

K.T.

Printed in Great Britain
by Amazon